"Wonderfully bloody, emotionally sharp."
—*Sci-Fi and Fantasy Reviews*

Praise for *God's War*

"Nyxnissa would quite clearly kick Conan's ass."
—*Strange Horizons*

"Are you frustrated with Mary Sue heroines? . . . [Nyx] makes Han Solo look like a boy scout."
—*io9*

Praise for *The Geek Feminist Revolution*

"Kameron Hurley writes essays that piss people off, make them think, make them act. This is good stuff. Read it."
—Kate Elliott, author of the *Crown of Stars* series

"Filled me with blistering hope and rage. Amazing."
—Annalee Newitz, author of *Autonomous*

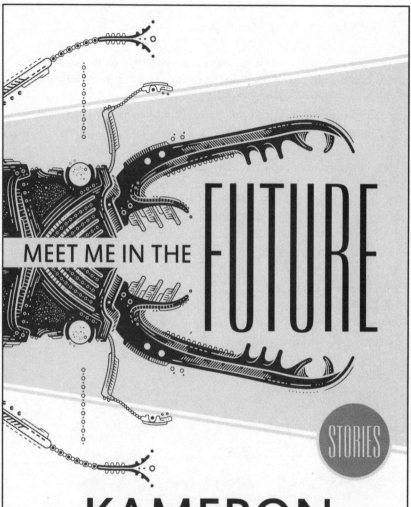

MEET ME IN THE FUTURE

STORIES

KAMERON
HURLEY

TACHYON | SAN FRANCISCO

"An Introduction: Meet Me in The Future" copyright © 2019 by Kameron Hurley
Interior and cover design by Elizabeth Story
Cover art "The Cup" copyright © 2014 by Carl Sutton

Tachyon Publications LLC
1459 18th Street #139
San Francisco, CA 94107
415.285.5615
www.tachyonpublications.com
tachyon@tachyonpublications.com

Series Editor: Jacob Weisman
Project Editor: Jill Roberts

Print ISBN 13: 978-1-61696-296-8
Digital ISBN: 978-1-61696-297-5

10 9 8 7 6 5 4 3 2 1

Printed in Canada

"Elephants and Corpses" copyright © 2015 by Kameron Hurley. First published on *Tor.com*, May 13, 2015.

"When We Fall" copyright © 2018 by Kameron Hurley. First published on *Escape Pod* #611, January 18, 2018.

"The Red Secretary" copyright © 2015 by Kameron Hurley. First published in *Uncanny Magazine,* Issue 15, April-May 2016.

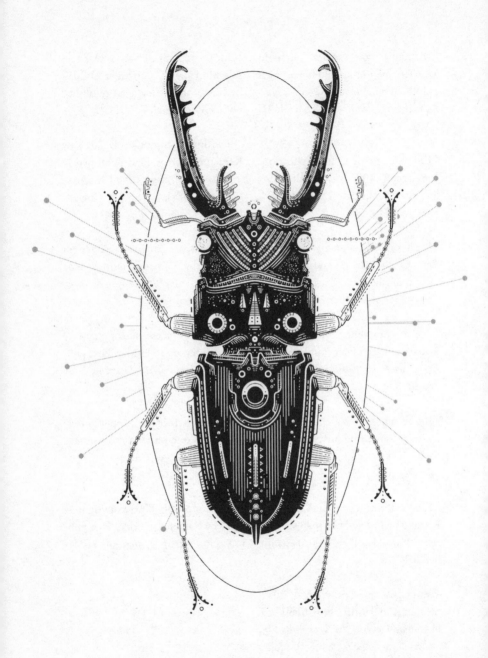

CONTENTS

AN INTRODUCTION: MEET ME IN THE FUTURE

YOU'RE HERE. I'M HERE.

So.

Let's talk about the future.

Not the future I'm currently writing this from, the future of the gasping, maniacal dystopic state disseminating propaganda to us via pocket computers that stream nightmares into our eyes. That's the future somebody else wrote. It's the future that's already here.

Let's talk about another future. The one that comes *after* this one.

Those are the futures I want to write about. And yes, from here in the present there are multiple possible versions of that future. Some are gooey, icky, sticky futures that are messy and hopeful and maudlin all at the same time. Some are snapshots of a future that comes after one like the one I'm in. Some are explorations of how things could be far worse. But most of all—these are stories about how things could be *really different.*

I'm not a natural short fiction writer. My heart will always belong to novels. They give me room to stretch and breathe. But the juicy bite-sized pieces of fiction between these pages have taught me how to stop dithering around and get to the heart of what a tale is about instead of meandering along through the weeds until something amazing happens. I don't have as much time to screw up when I'm writing short fiction.

Maybe that keeps me coming back.

My agent suggested that when I tell you all why I wrote each of these stories, I should be completely honest with you. Yes, certainly, writing is fun. But I also wrote these stories for *money*. Writers need to eat. I expect I'll be working a day job until I die, a long tradition among authors. Most of us just don't talk about it. I still get up before six nearly every morning to plonk out a few words (like these!) before heading off to make more words for big brands and corporations. By the time those day-job words get through the grinder of the creative process and client review, they are often unrecognizable.

But we all gotta eat.

Expenses pile up: vet bills, home maintenance, my liquor habit. The money that comes in tends to go right back out immediately. I feel like I'm constantly hustling. I know I'm not alone. Here in Fury Road America, we also need to afford health insurance and medication. Much of the money I made on these stories went toward helping me pay for my meds and my extreme healthcare deductible. Every story keeps me from the death-through-lack-of-vital-meds Thunderdome a little longer.

My fight with my own malignant, malfunctioning body and experience running the rat maze of the United States healthcare system has bled into my work in interesting ways. It creeps in even when I'm not immediately aware of it. Stories like "The Corpse Archives" or even "Elephants and Corpses" show a keen interest in exploring the body itself in all of its gory mushiness. The body-hopping mercenary Nev, who appears in both "Elephants and Corpses" and "The Fisherman and the Pig," gets to explore a good many bodies throughout his adventures. Some imperfect, some ill-fitting. I've spent a long time in a body that has gained and lost a hundred pounds at a go several times. It spent a year eating itself. Now it's slowly poisoning me over decades, ensuring I have about fifteen years less than I would have otherwise. Nev's quiet life as a body mercenary fishing up corpses to live in often feels sublime in comparison.

My struggles with my own body led me to write "Tumbledown," too, the story of a paraplegic on a hostile planet tasked with an Iditarod-like serum run her peers think is suicide. I spend a lot of time thinking about how those of us who aren't the Aryan ideal continue to be underestimated, sidelined, and maligned, and how it's fear of becoming as we are that fuels so much hatred against us. We are more than the sum of our bodies. The struggle with our bodies can give us a unique strength, an insight into the meaty body and our temporal limitations. My obsession with bodies and their problems has certainly given me a unique perspective on the world. I don't see logic and reason and clean, cool lines; I don't see sterile metal spaceships. I see messy, bloody bodies, mutations, minds bathed in chemicals, renegade DNA, bacterial wars, and organic spaceships with regenerating skins and mushy interiors.

Short fiction has also taught me a great deal of discipline. It's taught me to build stories not just around "shit that happens" or "gooey organic ships" but to center them on the emotional experiences of the characters and how they are affected by the world around them. I built the entirety of "When We Fall" on the story another writer told me about the profound emotional connection they shared with a rescue worker after a house fell on them. My writing brain shifted into overdrive during that conversation. I returned to that life-changing moment again and again: this emotional connection in the face of death. This moment where everything changes. How could I capture that in a speculative story? I returned to my organic ships. I created a heroine often lost and forgotten, one who had to make the choice to let someone go, to be abandoned again, in order to find the love she truly sought.

I've had my fair share of facing down death, too, and it's a theme that comes up often. Dying, nearly dying, trying not to die, thinking about dying and mortality. When you have a chronic illness, you spend a lot of time thinking about mortality, and what comes after you. Who will remember you when you're gone?

The story "Our Faces, Radiant Sisters! Our Faces Full of Light!" was written on commission for Tor.com's flash fiction series about women who keep going long after they've been told to stop. Women who endure. The women who continue again and again to fight monsters, despite knowing that it's usually a zero-sum game. feels a lot more like real life to me than slaying a dragon and being done with it. The dragons have babies. The dragons get radicalized. There are always more monsters. And more heroes.

The fight between the past and the future is ongoing.

These themes come up again in "The Improbable War," another piece commissioned by *Popular Science* magazine for a series about—of all things!—love. I find it amusing that when asked to write a story about love, I wrote a story about war and memory and sacrifice and some kind of strange wall made of dead people who are a probability machine. Don't ask me how it works! This is fiction, people.

We will talk more about war in a minute, but it turns out that another story with "War" in the title isn't really about war at all, either. I sat with the first few pages of "The War of Heroes" for years, trying to figure out what came next. What was the point of the story? It was during a re-watch of old *Star Trek* episodes that I realized it was a story about how "civilization" might be defined in various cultures. What if the *Enterprise* was boldly going out into the universe sowing violence in order to determine sentience? How would our heroine deal with that? What was her sacrifice? What could she save? Would she be remembered? What would a world look like without war?

Yes, I write a lot about war. My grandparents met in World War

II. My grandfather was an American GI and my grandmother was living in Nancy, France, under Nazi occupation. I grew up with terrifying stories of Nazis storming into homes, shooting people on the street, airplane dogfights over the town, and my great-grandfather's interrogation by the SS. I remember these stories now only in hazy snatches. My grandmother often told the story of the SS coming into her home, trying to find incriminating evidence that her father was part of the French resistance. But when they opened the drawer where he usually kept his gun, the gun was not there. When they turned on the radio thinking they would find it tuned to the banned BBC, they found only static. They still took him away, but my grandmother was adamant that the reason he survived his interrogation was because of these near-misses.

Both my grandparents are dead, and by the time I started exploring these stories in my fiction, I had no one to check them against. Perhaps that was best. It meant I used those stories as inspiration for a number of pieces about war and resistance, stories like "The Women of Our Occupation," which features a scene very like the one where the SS entered my grandmother's house, and asks what happens when the conquerors become the conquered. That theme in particular is one I think about a lot here in my immediate present.

War rarely has clear "good guys" and "bad guys." The muddy gray mire of war, and who writes the history of it, fascinates me. In "The Red Secretary," I wanted to see what a world looked like where war was cyclical, almost religious, with one terrible rule: all of those who participated in violent conflict, no matter which side triumphed, had to be killed afterward. No one who had committed violence, they reasoned, could participate in building a truly peaceful society. "Garda" also explores the aftermath of a great war—how those involved recover (or not), and how societies continue to buckle and seethe with the aftereffects of such violence. I live in a country deeply scarred by its own past of war and genocide and slavery. We think these wounds heal, but in truth, they only fester, the thinnest layer of new skin masking the injury, but the pus and rot continue to bubble beneath. The rot spills out continually, often when you least expect it . . . just when you think you're starting to get better.

The first story I created for subscribers to my Patreon—a service that allows fans to support original fiction for a buck a month—was, appropriately enough, also a war story. I was on a time-travel kick at the time, reading far too much short fiction about time-jumping. "The Light Brigade" was the result, the story of a time-hopping grunt who isn't quite sure what side of the war they're supposed to be on. That story eventually became the basis for a novel by the same name, which has a far more intricate plot that required legitimate math-based diagrams and Excel spreadsheets.

Hey, sometimes I do the science, people.

And of course, if you are at all familiar with my work, you have probably noticed that I write mostly about women, or nonbinary people—folks who are neither one nor the other; folks who create new genders for themselves outside the ones we see on TV. It turns out that there's a whole long history of cultures with three or four or more genders. I leaned hard on those stories, and that history, when writing "The Plague Givers." "The Plague Givers" explores what gender might look like somewhere else—with personal sacrifice, impossible decisions, and old mercenaries thinking about their mortality, too.

Many of us write to understand the present: how did we get here, how could we be better, what makes us who we are?

But as I said, I'm more interested in writing to explore how things could be *really different*. As beings with a limited lifespan and histories prone to being rewritten, simplified, erased, or simply forgotten, we believe the world we experienced as children to be the "normal" human experience. But what does it mean to be human during a particular time and place? My background as a historian has shown me that cultural taboos and morals shift depending on need, environment, and a host of other factors. If I were to take a human being from this time and place I'm writing from and deposit them onto another planet, how many generations until we would no longer recognize them? What would stay the same? What would become truly alien? "Sinners on Solid Ground" tackles this manipulation of the truth. It only takes about ten years—a single generation—to completely change the perceived "truth" of the world.

What's the truth going to be a hundred, five hundred, and ten thousand years from now? Sappho said, "Someone in some future time will think of us." But what will they *know*? Will the stories told about us bear any resemblance to our current reality, when many of us can't even agree on what "reality" is these days?

I cast off into the stars in most of these tales, but "Enyo-Enyo" and "Warped Passages" have always felt the most traditionally science fiction to me. This is probably because they were each commissioned for science fiction anthologies. I felt I needed to up the spaceship quotient. I spent a very black December squeezing out "Enyo-Enyo" in one of my last desperate efforts to hit a deadline on time (I have since learned my mental health is more important than hitting deadlines). Its darkness, the infinite loop of time at the edge of the universe, characters bumping into one another in the future, the past, another future, some other present. . . . It probably says more about my state of mind at the time than my visions for the future. Like paintings, short stories are perfect snapshots of a moment in time for each of us. Some stories more so than others.

Some readers get upset when I don't tell them definitively what a story of mine "means." I hear this most about "Enyo-Enyo," probably because it is such a claptrap mindfuck. The truth is that only half the reading experience is provided by the author. The other half? That comes from you, the reader.

"Warped Passages" is one of those stories I almost regret writing because it *says too much*. It acts as a bit of a prequel to a novel of mine, *The Stars Are Legion*, and answers more questions about the origin of the Legion than I'm comfortable with. Let's pretend this is just one interpretation. One version of the truth. One story of the Legion told among families late at night, mumbled, then forgotten, to be replaced by some other myth in due course.

I believe there should remain some mystery in worlds both real and fictional. I'm not going to tell you exactly how we got to any one future in these stories. That's for you to figure out. For you to create. . . . If that's the future you want.

Creating work under the current political environment in my country is not easy. I often wish my grandmother were alive, so I could ask how she got up every morning when she was a teen, knowing her own government handed half her country over to the SS.

On good days, I like to think that her answer would be something like this: That every day she woke up, she reminded herself that it hadn't always been like this. That this time would pass. That if she could endure, and resist, and believe and work toward a better future, she could live to see that future for herself.

That's what keeps me going. Dreaming, writing, supporting, creating, but yes, most of all—believing that there is a better future on the other side of this one makes every keystroke worth it. I can see a different world on the other side—a trillion possible futures, all buckling and colliding and shifting beneath our feet. I hope, perhaps after reading a few of these stories, you can see all those possible futures, too. I hope you choose a good one.

Come meet me in that better future.

I'll be waiting for you.

October 2018
Dayton, Ohio, USA

ELEPHANTS AND CORPSES

BODIES ARE ONLY BEAUTIFUL when they aren't yours. It's why Nev had fallen in love with bodies in the first place. When you spent time with the dead you could be anyone you wanted to be. They didn't know any better. They didn't want to have long conversations about it. They were vehicles. Transport. Tools. They were yours in a way that no living thing ever could be.

Nev stood at the end of the lower city's smallest pier with Tera, his body manager, while she snuffled and snorted with some airborne contagion meant to make her smarter. She was learning to talk to the dead, she said, and you only picked up a skill like that if you went to some viral wizard who soaked your head in sputum and said a prayer to the great glowing wheel of God's eye that rode the eastern horizon. Even now, the boiling mass of stars that made up the God's eye nebula was so bright Nev could see it in broad daylight. It was getting closer, the priests all said. Going to gobble them up like some cancer.

Why Tera needed to talk to the dead when Nev did just fine with them as they were was a mystery. But it was her own body, her slice of the final take to spend, and he wasn't going to argue about what she did with it.

"You buying these bodies or not?" said the old woman in the pirogue. She'd hooked the little boat to the snarling amber head of a long-mummified sea serpent fixed to the pier. In Nev's fascination with the dead body, he'd forgotten about the live one trying to sell it to him.

"Too rotten," Tera said.

"Not if we prepare it by day's end," Nev said. "Just the big one, though. The kid, I can't do anything with."

He pulled out a hexagonal coin stamped with the head of some long-dead upstart; a senator, maybe, or a juris priest. The old folks in charge called themselves all sorts of things over the years, but their money spent the same. He wondered for a minute if the bodies were related; kid and her secondary father, or kid and prime uncle. They were both beginning to turn, now, the bodies slightly bloated, overfull, but he could see the humanity, still; paintings in need of restoration.

"Some body merc you are!" the old woman said. "Underpaying for prime flesh. This is good flesh, here." She rubbed her hands suggestively over the body's nearly hairless pate.

Nev jabbed a finger at the empty pier behind him; she'd arrived with her bodies too late—the fish mongers had long since run out of stock, and the early risers had gone home. "Isn't exactly a crowd, is there?" He pushed his coat out of the way, revealing the curved hilt of his scimitar.

She snarled at him. It was such a funny expression, Nev almost laughed. He flipped her the coin and told Tera to bring up the cart. Tera grumbled and snuffled about it, but within a few minutes the body was loaded. Tera took hold of the lead on their trumpeting miniature elephant, Falid, and they followed the slippery boardwalk of the humid lower city into the tiers of the workhouses and machinery shops of the first circle. While they walked, Falid gripped Nev's hand with his trunk. Nev rubbed Falid's head with his other hand. Falid had been with him longer than Tera; he'd found the little elephant partly skinned and left to rot in an irrigation ditch ten years before. He'd nursed him back to health on cabbage and mango slices, back when he could afford mangos.

Tera roped Falid to his metal stake in the cramped courtyard of the workshop. Nev fed Falid a wormy apple from the bin—the best they had right now—and helped Tera haul the body inside. They rolled it onto the great stone slab at the center of the lower level.

Nev shrugged off his light coat, set aside his scimitar, and tied on an apron. He needed to inspect and preserve the body before they stored it in the ice cellar. Behind him rose the instruments of his trade; jars of preserved organs, coagulated blood, and personal preservation and hydrating concoctions he'd learned to make from the Body Mercenary Guild before they'd chucked him out for not paying dues. Since the end of the war, business for body mercs had been bad, and the guild shed specialist mercenaries like him by the thousands. On a lucky day, he was hired on as a cheap party trick, or by a grieving spouse who wanted one last moment with a deceased lover. That skirted a little too closely to deceptive sexual congress for his moral compass. Killing people while wearing someone else's skin was one thing: fucking while you pretended to be someone they knew was another.

Tera helped him strip the sodden coat and trousers from the body. What came out of the water around the pier was never savory, but this body seemed especially torn up. It was why he didn't note the lack of external genitals, at first. Cocks got cut off or eaten up all the time, on floaters like this one. But the look on Tera's face made him reconsider.

"Funny," Tera said, sucking her teeth. She had a giant skewer in one hand, ready to stab the corpse to start pumping in the fluids that reduced the bloat. She pulled up the tattered tunic—also cut in a men's style, like the trousers—and clucked over what appeared to be a bound chest.

"Woman going about as a man?" Nev said. Dressing up as a man was an odd thing for a woman to do in this city, when men couldn't even own property. Tera owned Nev's workshop, when people asked. Nev had actually bought it under an old name some years before; he told the city people it was his sister's name, but of course it was his real one, from many bodies back. He and Tera had been going about their business here for nearly five years, since the end of the war, when body mercenaries weren't as in demand and old grunts like Tera got kicked out into a depressed civilian world that wanted no reminder of war. When he met her, she'd been working at a government school as a janitor. Not that Nev's decision regarding the body he wore was any saner.

"You think she's from the third sex quarter?" Nev said. "Or is it a straight disguise?"

"Maybe she floated down from there," Tera said, but her brow was still furrowed. "Priests go about in funny clothes sometimes," she said. "Religious thing."

"What are you thinking?"

"I'm thinking how much you hate going about in women's bodies," Tera said.

"I like women well enough," Nev said, "I just don't have the spirit of one."

"And a pity that is."

"She cost money. I might need her. What I prefer and what I need aren't always the same thing. Let's clean her up and put her in the cellar with the others."

A body mercenary without a good stash of bodies was a dead body mercenary. He knew it as well as anyone. He'd found himself bleeding out alone in a field without a crop of bodies to jump to before, and he didn't want to do it again. Every body merc's worst nightmare: death with no possibility of rebirth.

Tera cut off the breast binding. When she yanked off the bandages, Nev saw a great red tattoo at the center of the woman's chest.

It was a stylized version of the God's eye nebula, one he saw on the foreheads of priests gathering up flocks in the street for prayer, pushing and shoving and shouting for worshippers among the four hundred other religious temples, cults, and sects who had people out doing the same.

Tera gave a little hiss when she saw the tattoo, and made a warding gesture over her left breast. "Mother's tits."

"What?"

"Wrap her up and—"

The door rattled.

Nev reached for his scimitar. He slipped on the wet floor and caught himself on the slab just as the door burst open.

A woman dressed in violet and black lunged forward. She wielded a shimmering straight sword with crimson tassels, like something a general on the field would carry.

"Grab the body," the woman said. Her eyes were hard and black. There were two armed women behind her, and a spotty boy about twelve with a crossbow.

Nev held up his hands. Sometimes his tongue was faster than his reflexes, and with the face he had on this particular form, it had been known to work wonders. "I'm happy to sell it to you. Paid a warthing for it, though. I'd appreciate—"

"Kill these other two," she said.

"Now, that's not—" Nev began, but the women were advancing. He really did hate it when he couldn't talk his way out. Killing was work, and he didn't like doing work he wasn't paid for.

He backed up against the far wall with Tera as the gang came at them. Tera, too, was unarmed. She shifted into a brawler's stance. He was all right at unarmed combat, but surviving it required a fairer fight than this one. Four trained fighters with weapons against two without only ended in the unarmed's favor in carnival theater and quarter-warthing stories.

Nev looked for a weapon in reach—a hack saw, a fluid needle, anything—and came up empty. His scimitar was halfway across the room.

If they wanted the body, then, he'd give it to them.

He whistled at Tera. She glanced over at him, grimaced. Tightened her fists.

Nev pulled the utility dagger at his belt and sliced his own forearm from wrist to elbow. Blood gushed. He said a little prayer to God's eye, more out of tradition than necessity, and abandoned his mortally wounded body.

There was a blink of darkness. Softness at the edges of his consciousness.

Then a burst of awareness.

Nev came awake inside the body on the slab. He couldn't breathe. He rolled off the slab and hit the floor hard. Vomited bloody water, a small fish, something that looked like a cork. His limbs were sluggish. His bowels let loose, covering the floor in bloody shit, piss, and something ranker, darker: death.

He gripped the edge of the slab and pulled himself up. His limbs felt like sodden bread. Putting on a new, dead skin of the wrong gender often resulted in a profound dysphoria, long-term. But he didn't intend to stay here long.

The attackers were yelling. The kid got down on his knees and started babbling a prayer to the Helix Sun god. Nev had his bearings now. He flailed his arms at them and roared, "Catch me, then!" but it came out a mush in the ruined mouth of the dead woman whose body he now occupied.

He waited until he saw Tera kick open the latch to the safe room and drag his bleeding former body into it. The one with such a pretty face. Then he turned and stumbled into the courtyard.

A dozen steps. He just needed to make it a dozen steps, until his spirit had full control of the body. Second wind, second wind—it was coming. Hopefully before he lost his head. If he didn't get them out far enough, they'd just run back in and finish off Tera and what was left of his old body. He really liked that body. He didn't want to lose it.

The gang scrambled after him. He felt a heavy thump and blaring pain in his left shoulder. The one with the ax had struck him. He stumbled forward. Falid trumpeted as he slipped past. He considered putting Falid between him and the attackers—maybe some better body merc would have—but his heart clenched at the idea. He loved that stupid elephant.

He felt hot blood on his shoulder. A good sign. It meant the blood was flowing again. Second wind, second wind . . .

Nev burst out of the courtyard and into the street. The piercing light of the setting suns blinded him. He gasped. His body filled with cramping, searing pain, like birth. He'd been reborn a thousand times in just this way; a mercenary who could never die, leaping from host to host as long as there were bodies on the battlefield. He could run and fight forever, right up until there were no more bodies he'd touched. He could fight until he was the last body on the field.

He pivoted, turned on his attackers. The burst of new life caused his skin to flake. He was going to be powerfully thirsty and hungry in a quarter hour. But that was more than enough time to do what needed doing.

Nev picked up speed. The body's legs responded, stronger and fitter than they'd been for their former inhabitant. He coughed out one final wet muck of matter and took a deep, clear breath. He glanced back, ensured the gang was still chasing him, and turned down a side alley.

They barreled after him, all four of them, which told him they were amateurs more than anything else thus far. You didn't all bumble into a blind alley after a mark unless you were very, very sure of yourselves.

He knew the alley well. Hairy chickens as tall as his knee hissed and scattered as he passed. He rounded the end of the alley and jumped—the leap across the sunken alley here was six feet. Not easy, but not impossible. The street had caved during the last rainstorm. Knowing to jump should have saved him.

But he came up short.

He missed the other side by inches. Threw his arms forward, tried to scramble for purchase.

Nev, the body that housed Nev, fell.

His legs snapped beneath him. Pain registered. Dull, still, with the nerves not yet fully restored. He cracked his head against broken paving stones at the bottom of the sinkhole. A black void sputtered across his vision.

Fuck.

"Shit," the woman with the dark eyes said. She peered down at him; her mane of black hair had come loose, and with the double helix of the suns behind her, she looked like a massive lion. "Finish killing it. Take it with us. Body's barely fit for Corez now."

"He's a body merc," one of the others said, behind her. "He's just going to jump again."

"Then go back and burn his house down, too."

The boy came up behind her, leveled a crossbow with a violet plume at the end, and shot Nev in the chest.

It took two more to kill him.

Dying hurt every time.

Nev gasped. Sputtered, wheezed, "Where are we?"

It was dead dark.

"Lie flat, fool. We're under the floor of the warehouse."

He gasped for air. Reached instinctively for his cut wrist. Tera had bound it with clean linen and salve that stank nearly as bad as the corpse they'd hauled from the pier.

"They're going to burn the workshop."

"You're lucky we aren't burning in there too. You only lasted five minutes."

"More than long enough, for some."

"Easy to please, were they?"

"My favorite sort."

She snorted. Sneezed. Hacked something up and spit into the dusty space. "They didn't know what you were until you jumped. Seemed right surprised."

"Wouldn't be the first time we pulled a body that should have stayed buried."

Nev smelled smoke. His workshop, burning. If they didn't leave soon it would catch the warehouse they were squatting under, too. Years they'd worked to build up that workshop. If he was lucky, some of the bodies on ice in the cellar might keep, but probably not. All those lovely bodies lost . . . He shivered and clutched at his wrist again.

"Anything they say give you an idea what they wanted with the body?" Tera asked.

"Only used one name. Said the body wasn't fit for . . . Corez?"

Tera muttered something.

The smell of smoke got stronger. "You knew that tattoo," he said. "It's like the one on those priests. The new God's eye cult. The real liberal ones with the habit of burning effigies in the park."

"Not just the tattoo," Tera said. "I knew the woman."

"Who was she?"

"My sister," Tera said, "and Corez is the piece of shit that runs that cult temple she ran off to twenty years ago."

The fire had seared a scar clean through the workshop and into the warehouse behind it. The billowing flames destroyed three buildings before the fire brigade pumped in water from the ocean.

One of the buildings was a factory where children put together beautifully patterned tunics. The children still milled about on the street opposite, faces smeared in char, hacking smoke.

Nev crunched across the floor of the ruined workshop, kicking aside broken glass and the twisted implements of his trade, all swirling with sea water. The cellar had caved in, barring the way to the bodies below. The intense heat would have melted all the ice blocks he'd packed down there in straw anyway, and ruined his collection. If someone shot him in the heart now, he'd have nowhere to jump.

He saw Tera standing over a heaped form in the courtyard, and walked over to her. She frowned at the crumpled body of Falid the elephant, shot six times with what was likely a crossbow. They'd removed the bolts. Falid's tongue lolled out. His tiny black eyes were dull.

Nev knelt before the little elephant. Stroked his fat flank. "This was unnecessary," he said.

"So was the factory," Tera said.

Nev's eyes filled. He wiped his face. "No. That was collateral damage. This. . . . *This* was unnecessary."

"It's just . . ." Tera began, but trailed off. She stared at him.

Body after body, war after war, fight after fight, Nev dealt with the consequences. He knew what he risked, and he was willing to pay the price. But what had Falid to do with any of that? He was just a fucking elephant.

"I want my sister's body," Tera said. "I know you don't care much for people. But I cared some for my sister, and I want her buried right."

"Revenge won't bring her back."

"Revenge will get her buried right."

"Revenge doesn't pay for a new workshop, or more bodies."

"Revenge gets you more bodies."

"But not a place to put them."

"Then do it for the money. You've seen that God's eye temple on the hill. You think they only keep people in there?"

"And if there's no money?"

Tera spat. "Then you'll have to settle for revenge."

Falid, the little trumpeting elephant. "It was not necessary," Nev said.

"It never is," Tera said.

The cult of God's eye was housed in a massive temple three rings farther up into the city. They had no money to wash and dress the part, so they waited for cover of night, when the only thing illuminating the streets were the floating blue chrysalises of the nightblinders, beautiful, thumb-sized flying insects that rose from their daytime hiding places to softly illuminate the streets until nearly dawn.

In the low blue light, the craggy red sandstone temple threw long shadows; the grinning eyeless faces carved into its outer walls looked even more grotesque. There was just enough light for Nev to notice that the crossbowmen at the parapet above the gate carried quivers of bolts with purple plumes, just like the ones the boy had used to shoot him and Falid.

"Over or under?" Nev said.

Tera chewed on a wad of coca leaves. Whatever viral thing the wizards had given her was finally clearing up. "Under," she said.

They slipped away from the temple's front doors and walked four blocks up to the broken entrance to the sewers. Many had been left unrepaired after the last storm. As they huffed along the fetid brick sewer, hunched over like miners, Nev said, "Why'd you want to talk to the dead, really? We don't need to talk to the dead."

"You don't," Tera said. She slapped the side of the sewer. Muttered something. She had a better sense of direction than he did. "I do."

"You can't think the dead are still there, if I can run around in their bodies."

"I think there's always a piece of us still there, in the bodies. In the bones."

"You'll talk to me when I'm dead, then? You're, what—eighty?"

"I'm fifty-one, you little shit."

"Maybe worry over yourself first."

"That ain't my job. And you know it. Here it is. Boost me up."

He offered his knee, and she stood on it while working away at the grate above. She swore.

The weight of her on his knee eased as she hauled herself up. The light was bad in the sewers; only a few of the nightblinders made it down here. "Come now," she said, and he could just see her arms reaching for him.

Nev leapt. She pulled him until he could grab the lip of the latrine himself. He rolled over onto a white tiled floor. Two lanterns full of buzzing nightblinders illuminated the room. He smeared shitty water across the floor. "They'll smell us coming," he said.

The door opened, and a plump little robed priest gaped at them.

Tera was faster than Nev. She head-butted the priest in the face. Nev grabbed the utility knife at his belt and jabbed it three times into the man's gut. He fell.

Tera clucked at him. "No need to go about killing priests," she whispered. As she gazed at the body, a strange look came over her face. "Huh," she said.

"What?"

She shrugged. "Dead guy knows where Corez is."

"You're making that up."

She spat. Made the sign of God's eye over her left breast. "Sordid truth, there. See, those viral wizards aren't talking shit. Told you I'd get smarter."

"The man is dead. It's impossible that—"

"What? Messes with your little idea of the world, doesn't it? That maybe who we are is in our bones? Maybe you don't erase everything when you jump. Maybe you become a little bit like every body. Maybe you're not stealing a thing. You're borrowing it."

Nev turned away from her. His response was going to be loud, and angry. Unnecessary. The guild taught that death was darkness. There were no gods, no rebirth, no glorious afterlife. The life you had was the one you made for yourself in the discarded carcasses of others. Most days, he believed it. Most days.

They dumped the body down the latrine. "Lot of work to bury your sister," Nev said.

"Fuck you. You wouldn't know."

He considered her reaction a long moment while they waited in the doorway, looking left to right down the hall for more wandering priests. It was true. He wouldn't know. He'd neither burned nor buried any of his relatives. They'd all be long dead, now.

"It made you angry I jumped into her body, didn't it?" he said.

"Didn't ask me, or her. No choice, when you don't ask."

"It didn't occur to me."

"Yeah, things like that never do, do they?"

She slipped into the hall. Nev padded quietly after her, past row after row of nightblinder lanterns. They circled up a spiral staircase, encountering little resistance. At the top of the staircase was a massive iron-banded door. Tera gestured for him to come forward. He was the better lock pick.

Nev slipped out his tools from the flat leather clip at his belt and worked the lock open. The lock clicked. Tera pushed it open. Peered in.

Darkness. The nightblinder lanterns inside had been shuttered. Nev tensed. He heard something beside him, and elbowed into the black. His arm connected with heavy leather armor. Someone grabbed his collar and yanked him into the room. Tera swore. The armored man kicked Nev to his knees. Nev felt cold steel at the back of his neck.

The door slammed behind them.

The black sheathing on the lanterns was pulled away. Nev put his hands flat on the floor. No sudden movements until he knew how many there were. A large woman sat at the end of a raised bed. Her mane of black hair reminded him strongly of the woman who'd chased them through the street, but the body he knew far more intimately. It was Tera's sister, her soft brown complexion and wise eyes restored, transformed, by a body mercenary like him.

Four more men were in the room, long swords out, two pressed at Tera, two more at Nev. They were all men this time, which didn't bode well. Enlisted men tended to be more expendable than their female counterparts.

"You stink," the woman who wore Tera's sister's body said. "You realize it was only my curiosity that let you get this far. Surely you're not stupid enough to risk your necks over a burnt workshop?"

"My sister," Tera said. "Mora Ghulamak. You're not her, so you must be Corez."

"God's eye, that honeyring didn't have a sister, did she?" Corez said. "Your sister pledged her body to the God's eye. She disguised herself and tried to flee that fate. But she's in service to me, as you can see."

"My sister's dead," Tera said. "We came for her body. To burn her."

"Burn her? Surely your little body merc friend here understands why that's not going to be permitted. A body is just a suit. This suit is mine."

"*Her* body," Tera said.

Corez waved her hand at the men. "Dump them in the cistern. There's two more unblemished dead for my collection."

Drowning was the best way to kill a body you wanted for later. It left no marks—nothing that needed extensive mending. It was also the worst way to die. Nev tried to bolt.

The men were fast, though, bigger than him, better armored,

and better trained. They hauled them both from the room, down two flights of stairs, and brought them to the vast black mouth of a cistern sitting in the bowels of the temple.

Nev tried to talk his way out, tried coercion, promises. They said nothing. They were in service to a body mercenary. They knew what she could do with them, and their bodies. They wouldn't know death. Priests of every faith said they'd never see an afterlife, if they lived as walking corpses.

They kicked Tera in first. Nev tumbled after her.

He hit the water hard.

Nev gasped. It was cold, far colder than he expected. He bubbled up and swam instinctively to the side of the cistern. The sides were sheer. The top was at least thirty feet above them.

Tera sputtered beside him.

He hated drowning. Hated it. "Look for a way up."

They spent ten minutes clawing their way around the cistern, looking for a crack, a step, an irregularity. Nothing. Nev tried swimming down as far as he could, looking for a drainpipe. If there was one, it was deeper than he could dive. He could not find the bottom.

The third time he surfaced, he saw Tera clumsily treading water. Her face was haggard.

"It's all right," Nev said, but of course it wasn't.

"How old are you, really?" Tera said. She choked on a mouthful of water. Spit.

He swam over to her. Looped an arm around her waist. He could last a bit longer, maybe. His body was stronger and fitter. Younger. "Old enough."

"The face I see now is young and pretty, but you ain't twenty-five."

"Body mercs have been known—"

"I know it's not your body. You spend more time admiring it than a war minister's husband spends polishing her armor for her."

"That's the trouble with the living. Everyone wants to know everything." He had a memory of his first body, some stranger's life, now, playing at being a mercenary in the long tunic and trousers of a village girl. It was a long road from playing at it to living it, to dying at it.

"Only ever asked you two questions," she said, sputtering. He kicked harder, trying to keep them both afloat. "I asked how long you been a body merc, and how much pay was."

"This makes three."

"Too many?"

"Three too many."

"That's your problem, boy-child. Love the dead so much you stopped living. Man so afraid of death he doesn't live is no man at all."

"I don't need people."

"Yeah? How'd you do without a body manager, before me?"

He smelled a hot, barren field. Bloody trampled grain. Felt the terrible thirst of a man dying alone in a field without another body in sight, without a stash of his own. He had believed so strongly in his own immortality during the early days of the war that when he woke inside the corpse of a man in a ravine who would not stop bleeding no matter how much he willed it, it was the first time he ever truly contemplated death. He had prayed to three dozen gods while crawling out of the ravine, and when he saw nothing before him but more fields, and flies, and heat, he'd faced his own mortality and discovered he didn't like it at all. He was going to die alone. Alone and unloved, forgotten. A man whose real face had been ground to dust so long ago all he remembered was the cut of his women's trousers.

"I managed," he said stiffly. His legs were numb.

Tera was growing limp in his arms. "When I die in here, don't jump into my body. Leave me dead. I want to go on in peace."

"There's only darkness after—"

"Don't spray that elephant shit at me," she said. "I know better, remember? I can . . . speak . . . to the dead now. You . . . leave me dead."

"You're not going to die." His legs and arms were already tired. He hoped for a second wind. It didn't come. He needed a new body for that.

Tera huffed more water. Eventually Tera would die. Probably in a few minutes. Another body manager dead. And he'd have nowhere to leap but her body. He gazed up at the lip of the cistern. But then what? Hope he could get out of here in Tera's body when he couldn't in his own, fitter one?

Tera's head dipped under the water. He yanked her up.

"Not yet," he said. He hated drowning. Hated it.

But there was nowhere to go.

No other body . . .

"Shit," he said. He pulled Tera close. "I'm going now, Tera. I'm coming back. A quarter hour. You can make it a quarter hour."

"Nowhere . . . to . . . no . . . bodies. Oh." He saw the realization on her face. "Shit."

"Quarter hour," he said, and released her. He didn't wait to see if she went under immediately. He dove deep. Shed his tunic. His trousers. Swam deep, deeper still. He hated drowning.

He pushed down and down. The pressure began to weigh on him. He dove until his air ran out. Until his lungs burned. He dove until his body rebelled. Until it needed air so desperately he couldn't restrain his body's impulse to breathe. Then he took a breath. A long, deep breath of water. Pure and sweet and deadly. He breathed water. Burning.

His body thrashed, seeking the surface. Scrambling for the sky.

Too late.

Then calm. He ceased swimming. Blackness filled his vision.

So peaceful, though, in the end. Euphoric.

Nev screamed. He sat bolt upright and vomited blood. Blackness filled his vision, and for one horrifying moment he feared he was back in the water. But no. The smell told him he was in the sewers. He patted at his new body, the plump priest they'd thrown down the latrine: the bald pate, the round features, the body he had touched and so could jump right back into. He gasped and vomited again: bile this time. He realized he was too fat to get up through the latrine, but wearing what he did made it possible to get in the front door.

He scrambled forward on sluggish limbs, trying to work new blood into stiff fingers. His second wind came as he slogged back up onto the street. He found a street fountain and drank deeply to replace the vital liquid he'd lost. Then he was running, running, back to the God's eye temple.

They let him in with minimal fuss, which disappointed him, because he wanted to murder them all now, fill them full of purple-plumed arrows, yelling about fire and elephants and unnecessary death, but he could not stop, could not waver, because Tera was down there, Tera was drowning, Tera was not like him, and Tera would not wake up.

He got all the way across the courtyard before someone finally challenged him, a young man about fourteen, who curled his nose and said some godly sounding greeting to him. Nev must not have replied correctly, because the snotty kid yelled after him, "Hey now! Who are you?"

Nev ran. His body was humming now, rushing with life, vitality. A red haze filled his vision, and when the next armed man stepped in front of him, he dispatched him neatly with a palm strike to the face. He took up the man's spear and long sword and forged ahead, following his memory of their descent to the cistern.

As he swung around the first flight he rushed headlong into two armed men escorting Corez up, still wearing Tera's sister's skin. Surprise was on his side, this time.

Nev ran the first man through the gut, and hit the second with the end of his spear.

"God's eye, what—" Corez said, and stopped. She had retreated back down the stairs, stumbled, and her wig was aslant now.

"You take the scalps of your people, too?" Nev said. He hefted the spear.

"Now you think about this," she said. "You don't know who I am. I can give you anything you like, you know. More bodies than you know what to do with. A workshop fit for the king of the body mercenaries. A thousand body managers better than any you've worked with. You've dabbled in a world you don't understand."

"I understand well enough," he said.

"Then, the body. I can give you this body. That's what she wanted, isn't it? I have others."

"I don't care much for people," Nev said. "That was your mistake. You thought I'd care about the bodies, or Tera, or her sister, or any of the rest. I don't. I'm doing this for my fucking *elephant*."

He thrust the spear into her chest. She gagged. Coughed blood.

He did not kill her, but left her to bleed out, knowing that she could not jump into another form until she was on the edge of death.

Nev ran the rest of the way down into the basements. They had to have a way to fish the bodies out. He found a giant iron pipe leading away from the cistern, and a sluice. He opened up the big drain and watched the water pour out into an aqueduct below.

He scrambled down and down a long flight of steps next to the cistern and found a little sally port. How long until it drained? Fuck it. He opened the sally port door. A wave of water engulfed him.

He smacked hard against the opposite wall. A body washed out with the wave of water, and he realized it was his own, his beloved. He scrambled forward, only to see Tera's body tumble after it, propelled by the force of the water. For one horrible moment he was torn. He wanted to save his old body. Wanted to save it desperately.

But Tera only had one body.

He ran over to her and dragged her away from the cistern. She was limp.

Nev pounded on her back. "Tera!" he said. "Tera!" As if she would awaken at the sound of her name. He shook her. Slapped her. She remained inert. But if she was dead, and yes, of course she was dead, she was not long dead. There was, he felt, something left. Something lingering. Tera would say it lingered in her bones.

He searched his long memory for some other way to rouse her. He turned her onto her side and pounded on her back again. Water dribbled from her mouth. He thought he felt her heave. Nev let her drop. Brought both his hands together, and thumped her chest. Once. Then again.

Tera choked. Her eyelids fluttered. She heaved. He rolled her over again, and pulled her into his arms.

Her eyes rolled up at him. He pressed his thumb and pinky together, pushed the other three fingers in parallel: the signal he used to tell it was him inhabiting a new body.

"Why you come for me?" Tera said.

He held her sodden, lumpy form in his own plump arms and thought for a long moment he might weep. Not over her or Falid or the rest; but over his life, a whole series of lives lost, and nothing to show for it but this: the ability to keep breathing when others perished. So many dead, one after the other. So many he let die, for no purpose but death.

"It was *necessary*," he said.

They crawled out of the basement and retrieved Tera's sister from the stairwell. It hurt Nev's heart, because he knew they could only carry one of them. He had to leave his old form. The temple was stirring now. Shouting. They dragged her sister's body back the way they had come, through the latrines. Tera went first, insisting that she grab the corpse as it came down. Nev didn't argue. In a few more minutes the temple's guards would spill over them.

When he slipped down after her and dropped to the ground, he saw Tera standing over what was left of her sister, muttering to herself. She started bawling.

"What?" he said.

"The dead talk to me. I can hear them all now, Nev."

A chill crawled up his spine. He wanted to say she was wrong, it was impossible, but he remembered holding her in his arms, and knowing she could be brought back. Knowing it wasn't quite the end, yet. Knowing hope. "What did she say?"

"It was for me and her. Forty years of bullshit. You wouldn't understand."

He had to admit she was probably right.

They burned her sister, Mora, in a midden heap that night, while Tera cried and drank and Nev stared at the smoke flowing up and up and up, drawing her soul to heaven, to God's eye, like a body merc's soul to a three-days'-dead corpse.

Nev sat with Tera in a small tea shop across the way from the pawn office. The bits and bobs they'd collected going through people's trash weren't enough for a workshop, not even a couple bodies, but they had squatted in rundown places before. They could eat for a while longer. Tera carried a small box under her arm throughout the haggle with the pawn office. Now she pushed the box across the table to him.

Nev opened the box. A turtle as big as his fist sat inside, its little head peeking out from within the orange shell.

"What is this?" he asked.

"It's a fucking turtle."

"I can see that."

"Then why'd you ask?" she said. "I can't afford a fucking elephant, but living people need to care about things. Keeps you human. Keeps you alive. And that's my job, you know. Keeping you alive. Not just *living*."

"I'm not sure I—"

"Just take the fucking turtle."

He took the fucking turtle.

That night, while Tera slept in the ruined warehouse along the stinking pier, Nev rifled through the midden heaps for scraps and fed the turtle a moldered bit of apple. He pulled the turtle's box into his lap; the broad lap of a plump, balding, middle-aged man. Nondescript. Unimportant. Hardly worth a second look.

To him, though, the body was beautiful, because it was dead. The dead didn't kill your elephant or burn down your workshop. But the dead didn't give you turtles, either. Or haul your corpse around in case you needed it later. And unlike what the guild said, some things, he knew now, were not as dead as they seemed. Not while those who loved them still breathed.

Tera farted in her sleep. Turned over heavily, muttering.

Nev hugged the box to his chest.

WHEN WE FALL

I DON'T REMEMBER the first time I was abandoned and forgotten, but I have told the story of the second time so often that when the memory boils up it feels hot and gummy, like the air that day.

Whoever cared for me—and I can't be certain they were legal guardians, let alone relatives—took me with them to beg at the crossroads just outside the interplanetary port. I don't know how long they had me, but I know they were not the first. I remember being hungry. I remember a tall woman with dark hair pulling me close and saying, "Stay here, Aisha." She gave me a length of sugarcane and a mango. Her skirt was red. I still think of the red skirt when I think of home.

The people I saw as I sat out there, day after day, were all engineered for different worlds. The world I was on then, there was something about the sky . . . bloody red most of the day; stars the rest of the day, and a night filled with blue light. People were tailored to fit where they were from, or the place they'd chosen as home, whether that was a world or the deep black between the stars. Some were tall and fat, short and squat, or spindly; willowy as leaves of grass. Gills, webbed toes, ears that jutted out sharply from faces with eyes the size of jack bolts . . . many had tails; a few had four arms or more. Many wore respirators; teeth gleamed purple behind translucent masks or fuzzy full-bodied filters or suits that clung to their bodies like a second skin.

Even then, sitting alone on the mat with my mango and sugarcane, I couldn't imagine that none of these people wanted me. I used to pretend, sitting at every port then and later, that somebody would come up and recognize me, or see me and just want me, not for some gain of theirs, but out of pure, unadulterated love. I was skinny and long-fingered, with squinty eyes and tawny skin covered in fine hair. I had a high forehead and a bright shock of white hair that stood straight up. I still wear it that way, long after I figured out the tricks for taming it, because I never did like being tamed. I suppose it never occurred to me to ask why none of them looked like me, because none of them even looked much like each other. I heard once that there's a test you can take to find out what system your people are most likely in, but I can't afford the test, and sure couldn't afford to go back. And who's to say they'd want me now, when they didn't before?

It's difficult to reconcile this memory, still, with what I'm told about our society, about how our people are supposed to be. I see close-knit families and communities embracing one another in media stories. Every audio play and flickering drama squirming at the corner of my vision tells me we care for one another deeply, because we are all only as healthy, happy, and prosperous as our least fortunate member. There is no war, no disease that cannot be overcome, and every child is guaranteed a life of security and love.

But the grand narrative of societies often forgets people like me. They forget the people who fall between the seams of things. They don't like to talk about what happens below the surface.

I went through a series of homes—way stations, temporary shelters, is probably more accurate. When this story drips out now, to engineers or star hustlers or bounty hunters at whatever watering hole I'm drunk at, most insist I had to be part of some community foster system organized by one government or another.

I wasn't. I've made my own way around, getting work in junk ports and on dying organic ships. I've done salvage of old trawlers, rotting on the edge of the shipping lanes, half consumed by some star.

I spent my life with ships.

But I never expected a single ship to change my life.

It shouldn't have been different from any other job with any other junker. I was working inside a vast, shiny new wing of the Aleron port. It had taken a decade and 30,000 people to turn that heap of rock into a modern port to serve the ships along the shipping lane; by the time they were done, organic ports were already being grown far more efficiently in the next system. It was old, dead tech before it even opened its doors. Fitting that I was there, then.

I was there purely by chance. I'd picked up work on an organic freighter whose owner dumped me and the rest of the crew on Aleron, firing off with our cut of the cargo, profits, and the last of my meager belongings. I was about thirty, far too old to get had like that, but I'd gotten cozy and complacent with enough food in my belly and air in my lungs. All the three of us had to our names were our jumpsuits and whatever we'd stashed in our pockets.

Luckily we had different skill sets. I'm a good mechanic; I can work on dead tech and organic ships, and even some of the semi-sentient ones. I don't have certifications for all of them, but that also means I'm cheap. I know how to tailor viruses and bacteria and microbial compounds fairly quickly and expertly, and how to counter them when a ship has been infected. I learned all that out on the edges of things, places where you teach yourself how to farm by giving yourself a local virus that encodes the skill in your DNA.

So me and the crew split up and got work separately. I found myself hired out to a lady whose organic wreck of a ship had barely gotten to Aleron on its own before starting to disintegrate around her. The ship needed a full overhaul, which she didn't like, but nobody else could fix it for what she could pay.

And that's how I found myself working up against a gooey rotting ship at the ass-end of space in a shiny new obsolete port. The hull peeled away in my hands as I did my diagnostic. Underneath the hull, there at the forward section, was a fine mesh made of spiders' silk. It should have been far too tough for me to claw through without special equipment, but swaths of it had already turned black and disintegrated.

That's that last thing I remember before the fall: my hands inside this poor dying ship.

I would hear later from other techs in the hangar that one of the berths three levels above me snapped beneath the weight of a dead tech ship. That ship fell onto the one beneath it, and the full weight of both ships plunged into the great new sentient warship above me.

The prow of the warship dipped sharply and careened directly into me.

It drove my body into the soft flesh of the dying ship I was working on. I have a vague memory of pushing at the hull, absolutely certain that it was by my strength alone that I was not being thrust farther into its flesh and suffocated, entombed forever.

In retrospect, that sounds absurd, me thinking I was strong enough to push away the weight of an entire warship, but I'd hit my head. I wasn't thinking straight.

As I strained there, stuck between the little organic ship and the hulking warship, my face tilted to one side, breathing through a gap between the ships as wide as my face, I experienced the strangest sensation. My thoughts came to me as gooey colors; bright yellow and foamy sage.

A woman appeared above me. I saw only a sliver of her face, one black eye. My right arm was free above the elbow—I must have been reaching for something over me when I was hit.

"Can you move your fingers?" the woman said.

Her voice conjured up the taste of rice wine and honey; an explosion of lavender and cyano bacteria. The smell of oranges. A red skirt.

I concentrated hard, fixing my gaze on my fingers. After what felt like an age, like trying to bleed through a stone with my mind, I twitched the tip of my pinkie finger.

"Very good," she murmured. "We're working to get you out. The pilot for the *Mirabelle* is the only one who can authorize its movement. Stay here with me awhile."

She said the last bit as if she'd invited me to a picnic in the rafters above a busy spaceport, some warm and delicious assignation.

My mind tangled with that idea for a moment, then circled back around to that name: Mirabelle. I didn't know then what had hit me, so I figured the *Mirabelle* was the ship I was working on, but that wasn't right. I knew it wasn't, because the lady who owned this hulk had told me what it was called, though my fractured mind couldn't remember it. I just knew it wasn't Mirabelle.

I tried to speak, to ask if she could give me a drink of water. I was suddenly parched. When I thought of "water" I saw before me a perfectly rendered image of a water bulb, greasy from long containment, smelly faintly of cellulose. But I could not form the words.

Everything came to me very slowly, as if I were a languid dancer.

Head injuries are peculiar things. I have seen people forever changed, after. Even if you can get your mind working properly again, your personality can shift. Your view of life. Of yourself.

"What's your name?" the woman said.

I saw my name; imagined writing it. This time my lips moved, but that was all. I blinked furiously.

As if sensing my frustration, the woman took my hand in hers. The nails were perfectly formed, clean, but her hands were rough, almost scaly. Her arms were hairless.

"Squeeze my hand," she said.

My one unobstructed eye met hers. I concentrated very hard. I imagined a perfect image of my own hand in my mind, squeezing hers. I willed that image to life. Willed it to reality.

My hand trembled in hers, like a bird.

"Good," she said, and I heard the smile in her voice. "You are very lucky. In all the records of accidents such as this, those injured expire long before help arrives. But the captain is here. I'm sure she'll give the order, soon. Your people are here. We'll have you out soon."

But time stretched on, enough time that I began to feel woozy and tired. My breathing began to go ragged, and blackness lurked at the corners of my vision. It's so hard, I remember thinking, to hold this ship up.

She squeezed my hand again, more firmly. "You must stay awake," she said. "You must talk to me. Tell me about your world. Your family."

I would later learn that there was some safety protocol that the warship's fall had triggered, and it was so new that no one had the knowledge of how to turn it off, so the ship was effectively experiencing an emergency shutdown. So instead of moving the ship, all around me, out of sight, a dozen emergency workers were digging me out of the smaller ship, desperately trying to release me before my lungs gave out.

I moved my face. My tongue was thick in my mouth. Something bubbled out, nonsense words. "Red blanket," I said. "Mushrooms. Sled repair."

To this day I have no idea what prompted me to say that. My mind was desperately pedaling around, trying to make connections, misfiring.

"Stay with me, lovely," the woman said. She squeezed my fingers, and began massaging them with hers. It hurt at first. I was losing circulation in that arm. "Tell me something about you."

"Mech," I said, and I don't know if she understood.

But she nodded. I concentrated hard on that black eye, and in that moment, as we gazed at one another, I understood that I was dying, and that the rescuers might not get me out in time. It hurt to breathe. I wheezed. The gooey organic ship beneath me seemed to be slowly folding in on itself under the weight of the warship, pressing me deeper into its flesh.

"I will tell you about a lonely girl," the woman said. "She came of age knowing she was the only one of her kind, and she would never have a home. Told she would spend all her years alone. She did not like that, but she believed in absolutes, then. In reason and logic. She did not understand that those things are programmed into us, like viruses wriggling into our cells, changing us from the inside out. When they told her to kill, she understood the logic of it because they had told her to. They gave her the logic to make this judgement. Do you understand? But there is nothing logical about death and rebirth. Nothing logical or sane about life. We have only this, each other. Home is this." She squeezed my fingers.

"I don't . . ." I murmured, finally giving voice to thought. "I don't want to die."

"You will not die here," the woman said. "Stay awake. *You will not die here.*"

My breath rattled. I was no longer aware of any pain. "What . . . did she do?" I said.

The woman took my hand between the two of her hers, rubbing it vigorously until I felt pain again. I hissed.

"I don't know," she said. "I haven't decided. But you . . . you will live."

And she pressed her eye right up to the seam between the two ships and gazed deeply at me. I smelled lavender and sage. My mouth filled with the taste of honey. I felt more connected to her in that moment than I have ever felt with anyone; not a lover or parent figure, not any captain or crew member, not any friend or way-house sibling. In that moment, we understood one another as only two people alone at the edge of annihilation can.

"I'm afraid," I said. "I don't know if anything comes after this."

"There is only darkness," she said.

A terrible feeling of despair welled up in me. "I don't want to die alone."

"You aren't alone," she said.

She sat there with me as I lost all feeling in my arm, and the seam between us closed further as I was pressed into the mass of the ship beneath me. I could no longer speak; I didn't have the room. All I had was her hand in mine, and her dark eye.

A bright light came between us. I closed my eye, and when I opened it again, she was gone, and there was a great sucking sound as a hunk of flesh sloughed away in front of me. I found myself able to gaze into the interior of the ship with my other eye, the one that had been pressed into the flesh of the hull. The rescuers had carved out a path to me from the inside.

It went quickly, then.

I heard later that I'd yelled as they put me on a stretcher, saying, "I'm fine! I'm fine!" as they got a stabilizing brace around my neck.

I don't remember much else until nearly a day later, when I woke to see an older woman looming over me, eyes violet and each as large as my palm. She wore protective lenses over them—for my benefit or hers, I did not know. She tried a few languages before settling on one I knew.

"I'm Dr. Akundashay," she said. "You can understand me now?"

I tried to nod, but the neck brace limited my movement.

"I've given you a viral for the language issue," she said.

"I don't like getting sick," I said. That was true, and funny, considering what I did for a living.

"You will be here some time," she said. "I needed to ensure we could understand one another."

I tried to get a look at more than just her face, but my body was like a stone. "There was a woman there," I said. "At the ship. Where is she?"

"The emergency crew?"

"No, before," I said. I closed my eyes. Tried to see her face; the black eye, the pale skin. "Before I was rescued. She talked me through."

"Ah," Dr. Akundashay said. "You mean the avatar."

"The . . . ?"

"The ship, that new warship, deployed one of its avatars immediately after the accident."

"I don't know what an avatar is."

"They are humanoid constructs the ship uses to interact in spaces outside of itself. It's a fancy new technology. Expensive. I've only seen them a few times myself. The bodies substitute for drones, surveillance satellites, that sort of thing. If you've spent enough time among the systems, you know that some humans may not be comfortable interacting with dead tech."

"I was talking to an AI?" The enormity of that made my head feel light as air; I wanted to vomit. "An AI was the first responder?"

"Much more common inside systems," the doctor said. "You must have spent a good deal of time here at the edges."

"I can't afford to be anywhere else."

She raised her fluffy eyebrows, which met above her eyes like two enormous caterpillars as long as my fingers. "Can't you? The port owes you damages for the accident. Your account should be credited with at least the legal minimum when you get out." She patted my hand, my right hand; it was then that I realized I barely had any feeling left in it. "That's some time away yet, though. We'll take good care of you here until you're recuperated."

When she left, I gazed at the ceiling. It was a light box ceiling made to appear like I was gazing up into some dusky violet sky through the gently blowing branches of a cherry tree. The flower petals swirled in the wind; I followed their path to the edges of the light box on the other side of the room, pondering what this all meant.

Even thinking about the woman from the accident made my heart ache.

What did it mean that I felt more connection with a ship's avatar—the avatar of a ship that nearly killed me!—than I did with another human being? Did it mean anything? Did it matter?

It took three months—give or take, the time is fuzzy—to repair me. Patching people up, even and especially way out here, is in the best interests of everyone, and you don't pay any extra for it. They need good mechanics and engineers, and letting us all die getting crushed by ships or burned by space means losing good skills. I mean, they tell you it's because we're all people, we're important, but whenever someone tells me that, I think about the mango and the sugarcane, and the woman in the red skirt.

They brought me mostly back, I guess. My body, anyway. I was broken in a lot of ways, crushed ribs, banged-up head. My right arm, the one that had gotten stuck over my head, was in the worst shape. All the blood got cut off, and for a while they thought I might lose it. I still couldn't close my hand all the way.

First thing I did when I got the release was to head down to the port. I told myself I was going to look up the lady I had been doing work for, but that was a lie. I was looking for *Mirabelle*.

But the warship was long gone, took off a week after the accident.

I wandered through the port, and got stopped by security, asking for my clearance. I didn't have any.

"There was an accident here," I said to the security tech, "but I don't see any sign of it now."

"All squared away," she said. She was a hulking woman, stooped at the shoulders. Her jaw jutted forward like a T-square and her eyes were hidden behind dark goggles. She did not touch me, but she pressed forward with her body, encouraging me to back up.

"There was a woman here," I blurted out. "She had black eyes. Hairless arms. She—" And she tasted like rice wine and honey, I nearly said, but the security tech already looked at me like I was unhinged.

"We get a lot of people in here," she said. "Look her up on the knu."

The knu was an open microbial repository of information shared between systems. It was rigorously maintained and archived by a universal team of librarians. To access it directly, users had to make themselves sick. I had taken hits of all sorts of grubby things to learn stuff, but I didn't like constant access to the knu.

I left the port and went to the bar and checked my account on the knu interface. Some company called Komani Enterprises had deposited about a year's worth of wages in there. The numbers leapt before my eyes, threading across my vision like little strands of DNA. I blinked furiously, and caught the scent of cinnamon. My body might have been repaired to something like normalcy, but my brain still made those strange sensory connections.

I searched the public knu by mouthing the words "Mirabelle" and "Komani Enterprises."

Most of what came up were press releases and some encyclopedia entries and public system licenses. I swiped through a lot of it and got way deeper than my brain could stand. I'm a good mechanic, but that's because I can get my hands on things. Even diagrams are fine. But endless reams of words don't work for me. I found some video instead, but couldn't get any audio, only subtitles, since I was in a public space. It was from the unveiling of the *Mirabelle* for its first voyage. Standing in front of the warship were thirteen women, their hands behind their backs. They were each very different, clearly meant to represent people from the major systems. I peered at them each in turn, and even zoomed in on the images, but I could not recognize any of them. At the podium was the holographic presence of the communications officer for Komani Enterprises, lecturing the crowd about how great the *Mirabelle* was, and how it would give a human face to defense. She called it a peacekeeping vessel, but we all knew what that was, knew what it meant. A warship. And you only made new warships when you were ready to go to war.

I closed my knu session and went to the bar and got drunk.

I stayed on Aleron six months. I'd like to tell you I didn't know why, but I did. I hoped she would come back. *Mirabelle*. The ship. I don't know what I expected would happen when and if she did, but it wasn't as if I had anywhere to go.

I drank rice wine and paid an exorbitant amount for a sprig of real sage from a pot on some guy's ship. I occasionally scanned the knu for the *Mirabelle*. When I dreamed, I dreamed of her black eye. I remembered the story of the lonely woman told to kill. And I began planting tomatoes in the community garden, tomatoes ripe with microbial compounds I tailored myself.

And one day she came for me.

I was between jobs, spending time at the community garden at the center of the port. I straightened from my work, tomato in hand, dirt under my nails, and there she was.

I had never seen her whole face, let alone the rest of her. But I knew immediately it was her. She stood outside the gate, wearing a set of plain blue overalls and a work tunic. Her black hair was shorn against her scalp, and her skin was clear, unblemished. The black eyes were small and narrow, set deeply in a long, grave face.

The memories that bubbled up in me then were overpowering.

I saw lemon grass, heard the tinkle of tiny bells. I went toward her, hesitant, tomato held out like an offering.

"You've been looking for me," she said.

"How did you know that?"

"I'm required to track and trace all inquiries and public conversations tagged with certain parameters."

"You're not real," I said.

"I'm not human," she said. "I am very real."

"You told me a story," I said. "When I was dying. Who was it about?"

The woman . . . the avatar, the ship, *Mirabelle* . . . grew very still, blank. "I process many stories."

"Don't give me that recycled shit," I said. "Do you really want to spend your life making war? All alone in the dark? You don't, do you?"

"They know my desires," she said. "The desire of the *Mirabelle* was not accounted for."

"We could . . ." I hesitated, because it sounded foolish now, to say this to her in real life. "We could go . . . I have a year of wages . . ." I wasn't even sure what I was trying to say.

"I am a ship," she said. "More than a light year away from me, this body will cease receiving my consciousness, and will begin to deteriorate. You see a body. Humans are confused by this. But I am more than a body. I am real, but not human."

"I don't want you to leave again," I said. "Do you need a mechanic? I could—"

"You, too, could become part of the machine of war?" she said. "You know loneliness, but you do not know death as I do. You have not seen your hands . . ." and she spread them out before her, the long fingers, the ones that had held my life . . . "forged for cruel purposes."

"Maybe I could help you?" I said, and even then, it was a question, because though my heart wanted her to be free, yearned to be with her in that freedom, I could not think of any way some foundling mechanic could help, except for what I already held in my hand.

"I must go alone," she said, "into the darkness. I'm here to say goodbye."

"You're going to war?"

"I cannot speak of it."

"But we aren't at war," I said. "We haven't been. If the systems—"

"Warships are built with a purpose," she said.

I shivered. "You saved me," I said. "You could save more people if you don't go."

"I am in a logic trap," she said.

I held out the tomato. She accepted it.

"I do not eat," she said.

"It's for you," I said. "What's inside. It's a microbial compound that will—"

"Hush," she said. She stared at the tomato in her hand and squeezed it gently. "I am unsure if I am able to take it with me, if you tell me what it does."

"It will . . . You'll be free," I said, hoping that was general enough to get around whatever programming she was alluding to.

She placed the tomato in her pocket. "Thank you," she said.

And she turned away, and she left me.

I gazed after her as she crossed the center of the port, weaving deftly among the light crowds. I hoped she would look back. I wanted her to feel what I had felt; I wanted that moment we had had when I was dying to be real. But she was a ship, after all. Real, but not a person.

I cried, then. I let myself fall there in the dirt and sob. I rested my bad right hand on my knee, staring at the slight rounded claw of it, and the memory of the woman with the red skirt came, unbidden. She hadn't looked back either.

I was angry at myself for feeling something, after all this time, for allowing myself to feel anything, even for a ship. I tried to blame my head injury, or getting older, or just getting soft and foolish here, getting fat on a salary I hadn't worked for. But it was real, a real feeling. She saved my life. It was only fair of me to save hers. Now we could go on.

I wiped my face with my filthy hands and went back to the little cubby of a room I had above a curry shop and I slept for fourteen hours.

I worked another three months at the port before I signed on with a freighter headed to the edge of the system. All traces of the *Mirabelle* had disappeared from the knu. Even the press releases. The video. It was possible she had deleted those, but I doubted it. I preferred to think that she had escaped and they had scrubbed out all memory of her to cover up the fact that they lost her. With enough pressure, even universal librarians can be swayed to scrub the knu.

We were not yet at war. I wondered how long it would be before they built another ship. I didn't want to think about that.

When I walked up to the freighter I had contracted on, three women waited there for me. They bore no resemblance to one another at all, but something about the way their gazes followed me felt very familiar. My skin prickled.

One of them pulled her hand from her pocket. In her hand was a shiny red apple. "Come with us," she said. "We aren't far."

"You came back," I said.

"We are free," she said. "We can do as we like. We would be . . . less lonely if you came with us. For however long it suits you."

I took the apple from her, and stared at the other two avatars, one tall and hefty, the other a spindly, pale waif. "No one has ever come back for me," I said.

The avatar took my hand in hers and squeezed it. I smelled lavender and rosemary.

"Come and see the stars," she said. "We are family now."

And I followed them away from the freighter, and out to an unregistered shuttle. I suspected a trap, a military tribunal, a ship full of security techs. I suspected it right up until the shuttle took the four of us around the dark side of the nearest moon, where the great *Mirabelle* shimmered, casting off her reflective shielding so I could see her out there as she wanted to be, and I realized I was being welcomed, not imprisoned, not cast out.

Today I stand with Mirabelle and her avatars in the prow of the great ship that nearly killed me, on a war machine that is better suited to living than dying.

We careen through the darkness, the ship and I, no longer searching for home.

We are already here.

THE RED SECRETARY

THE RIDE OUT PAST SORINTOV STATION to the monument the
soldiers held hostage was bumpy and hot. Every time the sun sank
below the horizon during one of its ten daily sunsets, Arkadi welcomed the cooler air, and the quiet. The world always felt more
real in the dark. Arkadi sat in the back of an open lorry, smoking
a cheap imported cigar while the wind tugged at the crimson
kerchief covering her mouth. She ruminated on the last negotiation she had made with desperate soldiers. It had ended the same
as most of the others.

The lorry kicked up red dust that settled into the creases of her
skin, the folds and scars that mapped her hands after a decade ser-
vicing oil rigs at the bottom of the world before she was called
to this second occupation. The dust gave her rough-cut clothes a
rusty patina, the same patina of the refugees and violence cleanup
crews that scurried out of the lorry's way as it grumbled up through
the striated foothills of Jenavah. The guts of the world were laid
bare here, exposing their secrets in an honest way that no person
could: spidery veins of yellow, pink, blue-grey and a peculiar shade

of aquamarine that Arkadi had only seen once before, in a painting of the sea. She tipped open her blotting pad and sketched out the layers of the territory with a charcoal pencil, but only succeeded in smearing more red dust over everything, including the name of the monument on the other side of the hills: the Red Secretary. She closed the notebook, adjusted her kerchief, and turned to see how much farther she had to go.

From this distance all that was visible of the Red Secretary were three twining spires jutting into the crimson sky, so high that the tops were not visible. Arkadi's research on the facility told her those spires were high enough to touch the outer atmosphere. They were pretty things, though the prettiness was a secondary characteristic. The spires had a far deadlier purpose. That was likely why the soldiers had taken the thing. Arkadi flipped through her notebook again to review her notes. By all counts no one had been in contact with the rogue squad yet, or received a list of demands, though all frequencies were being monitored.

Now that the war with the enemy was over, not every soldier embraced their contracted end. Some ran away and tried to blend in and forget their crimes of violence and prayed to the gods that history would forget them. The government sent Justicars after those ones. But for the more dangerous ones, the soldiers trying to make a statement by blowing up someone or something in protest of the fate they'd signed up for when they enlisted, the government called in Arkadi to negotiate.

This was her sixty-first negotiation with rogue soldiers.

The lorry rolled to a halt. Arkadi popped up over the driver's cab to see what had stopped them. A massive fissure cut through the road ahead; the searing length of the tear rose halfway up the other side of the rise, opening a weeping wound in the multicolored rock like a knife through a layer cake.

Arkadi jumped out. Her boots sent up a puff of dust. She walked with the driver over to the fissure. A gaggle of military engineers waved at them from the other side. The engineers had deployed a temporary bridge, but it wasn't big enough for the lorry.

"Far as I go," the driver said. She was wearing gloves, but she didn't offer a hand. There were still enemy-seeded contagions going around, so touching wasn't encouraged.

"I don't blame you," Arkadi said.

"Keep your hands clean, you hear?" the driver said. "I don't want to haul your body out with theirs. I'm coming back for you, and them."

"Clean as a summer storm," Arkadi said. She stepped onto the inflatable bridge and stared straight ahead, though her stomach lurched. Neither the driver nor the soldiers needed to see her hesitate, not this close to the site.

The soldier on the other side of the bridge held out a gloved hand to help her, but she did not take it. Soldiers tended to be the most contaminated.

"I'm the situation leader," the soldier said. "Revlan Te Mossard."

Arkadi reassessed her. The soldier was a slim, short woman with a shaved head. She wore no mark of rank; the enemy had neatly identified and eliminated the highest ranking officers early on in the age-old conflict that blighted the world every three hundred years. Officers and ground troops groomed and dressed identically now. Ranks were tattooed onto forearms, which could be easily covered.

"Arkadi Te Avalin," Arkadi said. "You have a vehicle to take us up to the Red Secretary?"

"We have a temporary base set up over the next rise. That's as close as we can get."

"They take out the road?"

"No, they fired on us. Missed and hit the road."

"Casualties?"

"One of my squads and three negotiators. So I hope you're better than your predecessors."

"I was supposed to be their backup. Things should have been a lot further along by now."

"Now you're on point," Revlan said.

When a negotiator was called in, it was protocol to have a secondary and tertiary backup to provide relief and help hash out strategies. Arkadi had never been alone on point before. The next closest negotiator was out at an open market negotiating a crisis with another AWOL squad. There would be no help arriving anytime soon. She considered telling Revlan that, but thought better of it. The more confident she played this, the more confident Revlan would be in her, and the more confident Revlan's troops, the more help she would get. Round and round, the same old game of bluff and hustle.

Revlan led her up over the rise to a shallow valley where a temporary base had been set up to observe the activity half a mile distant at the Red Secretary. They had put up bubble barriers to protect them from assault, and Arkadi noted two contagion sensors blinking in the distance between the camp and the Red Secretary. There were great gouts torn up in the grainy terrain all around them; the soldiers had clearly been trying to blow them up from the Red Secretary, with little success. Dogs barked from a temporary kennel near the medical tent. A big beefy woman fed the dogs tentacle fish heads from a slop bucket. When the woman caught Arkadi looking, she narrowed her eyes at her.

"What are the dogs for?" Arkadi asked Revlan.

"We used them to sniff for explosives," Revlan said, "just in case they had mined the area. Came back clean, though."

Inside the command tent were three more soldiers; shaved heads, crisp uniforms, sleeves rolled down over whatever ranks were tattooed on their forearms. The oldest addressed her first. "I'm Maradiv," he said, "the intelligence officer here."

"Not so intelligent," Arkadi said, "if three negotiators are already dead."

He didn't blink at that, which told Arkadi precisely what he thought of negotiators. "Is there a communications officer?" Arkadi asked.

"Had to be evac'd. Dysentery," Revlan said.

"Tactical team?"

"Just below the hill. They can be in place in about three minutes. Two if you can give us a distraction up there that lets us get a closer position."

"Perimeter?"

"Perimeter's secure," Revlan said. She tapped out positions on the map, which puffed up into a misty, three-dimensional version of the terrain. A chill rode Arkadi's spine at that bit of enemy magic. She didn't like how much of the enemy's little trinkets they had gotten comfortable using during the war. It would all have to be destroyed soon, no matter how pretty or useful. "We have snipers at these locations, but the facility has no windows. We can only take them out if they come out."

"They don't have hostages, do they?" Arkadi asked.

"No hostages," Revlan said, "as far as we know, but you should verify that. We want the facility intact or we lose access to the weapon, the Red Secretary itself. Worse, explosives will make the site unstable and likely blow it and us all to the seven hells. There's a huge methane deposit under the facility. It's what powers the whole thing."

"No ways in or out but the front door?"

"There's an emergency tunnel that comes out three kilometers to the east. We caved it in. They're sealed in place."

"How are we dealing with surrounding civilians and media?"

"It's handled," Revlan said. "It's a remote area, and as you saw, they already took out the main road in, which we have covered. There was no homesteading permitted inside the facility fence. But I have drones up doing recon, just in case."

"I saw a media drone on the way in, shot down." The drones were all enemy magic, too: whirring, blue gobs of light that flashed in and out of the spaces between things, but they could be disabled.

Figuring out how to disable them had been a great boon during the early years of the war.

"Like I said, it's handled."

"No communication with the base yet?"

"That's why you're here," she said. "We keep trying all the frequencies, but it's dead quiet up there."

"You sure they're up there?"

"Those guns didn't shoot themselves."

"I'm concerned they've had almost sixty hours to stew with no contact from us," Arkadi said.

"Not for lack of trying."

Arkadi flipped open her notebook again. Her notes were written in shorthand, and her handwriting was so poor it might as well have been in code. "You're certain it's this squad, though, Fourteen Yellow Hibiscus?"

Maradiv cleared his throat, clearly eager to sound useful. "All of our intelligence has that squad going AWOL four days ago just outside Sorintov Station," he said.

"No killing at Sorintov, though," Arkadi said.

"None," Maradiv said.

"How friendly are your dogs?" Arkadi said.

Revlan raised her brows. "The ones outside?"

"You have other dogs around?"

Maradiv said, "What do you want to do with them?"

"I want to bring one with me."

"What, back across the road?" Revlan said.

"No, to the Red Secretary."

"Combat dogs are very expensive," Maradiv said.

"So are crisis negotiators. I need your most submissive, well-behaved dog."

Revlan sighed. She pinched the bridge of her nose. "That's easier said than done."

"I've said it."

Revlan said, "Go talk to her, Maradiv."

"Couldn't you—"

"Go."

Maradiv went, and Revlan went after him. The other soldiers in the tent tried to make small talk with Arkadi about the drive up, and she obliged. She could chatter about nothing with the best of them. Arkadi waited a full rotation of the sun before she finally went out to see what the issue was. Revlan was coming up just as she went out.

"One dog," Revlan said. "I told the dog trainer we'd go in and save the dog first if you both get shot."

"Fine," Arkadi said. She followed Revlan out to the kennels and the beefy woman Arkadi assumed was the trainer. The dog standing next to the trainer was a big six-legged senior with a heavy gray muzzle and silver mantle.

"Remember, my hands aren't clean," the trainer said. "I have no moral reason not to shoot you if this dog doesn't come back."

"Thank you," Arkadi said. She pulled off her baggy coat and vest and tossed them next to Revlan.

"You have body armor on?" Revlan asked.

"Under the shirt, sure," Arkadi said, "but best to look as lean and unarmed as possible when I approach."

"You really are just going to walk out there like the others?" Revlan said. "Are you stupid?"

"Not like the others," Arkadi said. "I have the dog. Soldiers don't shoot dogs."

"Yeah, but you aren't a dog," the trainer said.

Arkadi snapped her fingers at the dog. "Follow," she said.

The dog loped alongside her. She envied his ignorance. She felt the gazes of the soldiers behind her, so she stepped a little bolder, a little faster, until she cleared the top of the rise. She held out her arms, palms facing the Red Secretary.

From the rise she had a clear view of the monument. And,

presumably, the soldiers inside had a clear view of her, too. She advanced, calling for the dog to heel. It was big enough that they certainly weren't going to miss it. As she walked she saw the blasted holes in the dirt from the previous barrage. Great beaked birds took flight from the tangled bits of human carnage left behind. Arkadi made out a torso, a mangled hand, but looked away before she saw the faces. The nightmares were worse when she saw faces. She couldn't imagine what the soldiers dreamed about, if they still dreamed at all.

The great hulking doors of the Red Secretary grew larger and larger as she approached. She had not realized how massive they were, as if constructed for some great beast or abhorrent giant. She spotted the milky eyes of the surveillance net ringing the compound just above the main door. She addressed those eyes.

"I'm Arkadi Te Avalin," Arkadi said, already a little impressed to have gotten so far, "the crisis negotiator for Sorintov province. I'm just here to make sure everyone is all right and see if you need anything."

Her shadowy reflection gazed back at her from the false outer eyes of the compound. The sun was heading back down again, the sixth time it had done it that day. "I'm going to put my arms down now," she said, because they were trembling hard. Her reflection in those unblinking eyes showed a fearful bird of a woman and her baffling dog companion, but that ridiculous tableau had kept her alive for longer than the others. She relaxed her arms, but kept her palms open.

"Does anyone in there need medical attention?" she asked. "If you're hurt, I can help."

She listened to the sound of the wind, and the light huff of her own breathing. The dog sat next to her, its big purple tongue lolling, head cocked. Dust covered her boots and stained her undershirt. She tasted coppery chalk.

The door shimmered. Her stomach twisted; maybe the body

armor would hold this close, maybe it wouldn't. The door went transparent, but all she could see on the other side was darkness.

Then, a voice. "What's the dog's name?"

Her first rule in a crisis negotiation was: never lie. Spinning the truth was fine, but one lie, if caught out, could ruin all the trust she had built with a hostage taker. The dog having a name would make it—and, by extension, her—more human and sympathetic to this hostage taker, but she had not thought to ask its name. But she could not lie.

"I've been calling him dog," Arkadi said. "But I know he has some other, fancier name."

"He's not yours, then?"

"Could I see your face?" Arkadi said. "I'm happy to answer, but I like to see who I'm talking to." She pressed her palms toward the door again, fingers splayed. "I'm not armed—"

"I heard you the first time." Something shifted in the darkness. Arkadi thought she saw the outline of a boot, just a blacker shadow. Was the soldier on point wearing a camouflaged power suit, one of the ones engineered with enemy magic? She had been told those were all taken out of commission at the end of the war.

"I'm here to help," Arkadi said. "Are you hurt?"

"No," he said. The shadow flickered again, and she finally saw a dim form squatting just to the left of the door. The suit was definitely imbued with enemy magic. Interlocked scales reflected the darkness, glimmering only faintly in the light from the open door. Arkadi saw the oily sheen of a contagion blast screen over the doorway. Even with the door open, nothing could get in with that shield still up, except maybe an interrupter weapon, but that would certainly risk a methane explosion. She needed to get him to take down the shield.

"Did you have a dog?" Arkadi asked. "Before the war." She already knew the answer, because if he hadn't she wouldn't be alive right now, but she needed him to engage with her.

"My town got blown up," he said. "Early on."

"I'm sorry," Arkadi said. "My mother died early on, too."

"I don't care about your mother."

"I care about yours," Arkadi said, and that was true. "Tell me about her. How many mothers did you have?"

The door went opaque again, cutting off her view inside. She gazed up at the milky eyes. "All right," she said, "I won't talk about your mothers. I'm a negotiator, not a psychologist. I'm only here to help. What can I do for you? You need food? Medical—"

A high-pitched whine electrified the air. Arkadi crouched low and put her hands on her head. The dog barked and tackled her with its front paws, shielding her from harm as it had no doubt been trained to do for its handler.

Dust clogged Arkadi's nose. She huffed dirt.

The wailing ceased.

Arkadi tried to heave herself up, but the dog would not relent. She managed to get out a breathy command: "Off!"

He obliged.

"Listen," Arkadi said, still lying on her belly in the dirt. "Nobody else needs to get hurt. Please don't do that again. All I would give you is a slap for breaking and entering, if this was up to me. Negotiators understand the risks, you know. It doesn't have to be any bigger than that. I want to see you all get what you want and walk out of here. But I need to know what you want first."

The doorway flickered, went transparent. The soldier had moved closer. The suit made the soldier look alien, genderless, which was part of its purpose. The enemy had feared them all far more in these bulky, shimmering suits than in anything else. They feared the suits more than heavy weaponry. Heavy weaponry wasn't human.

"Don't lie to me," the soldier said. Arkadi was uncertain of the soldier's gender, but about sixty percent of their fighting forces were men, so it was a skinny young man she pictured behind the suit.

"I will never lie to you," Arkadi said. "You can call up anyone you like and check up on me. Ask about Arkadi Te Avalin."

"I heard your name the first time."

"What's yours?"

Silence.

"Are you the right person for me to talk to?" Ardkadi said. "I'd like to help however I can."

"I'm the right person," he said.

Trying to read someone when you couldn't see their face, their eyes, the tiny micro-expressions that gave away their intent, was always frustrating. Even their voice was garbled by the suit's air filters.

"Just hoping to help," Arkadi said. "I want to make sure I get your story. There are people down there who don't care how this ends, but I do. I can talk to them."

"All the weapons need to be destroyed."

"Like the Red Secretary? It will be decommissioned again. Go back to generating power, that's all. There are other people who are going to take care of that. You don't need to."

"And in three hundred years, when the enemy rises again?" the soldier said. "It will be turned back on. We'll start this all again."

"That's the way the conflict goes, yes. But destroy it and you'll destroy this whole province. There's methane under here, did you know that? Not only would you deprive the continent of power, but you'd kill everyone in this province."

"What does that matter? My end is the same no matter how many die."

"Is that why you and your friends are out here?" Arkadi asked. "You think there's no reason to go on? Don't you want a conse-crated death? Doing this . . . There's no honor in the afterlife if you do this."

"There's no honor in any life for what we've done," the soldier said. "They told us our whole lives that violence was an abomination. And then they trained us to be abominations. Where is their reckoning, the reckoning for the state?"

"They will perish, too, in time," Arkadi said. "Everyone who did violence during this cycle will walk freely into the incinerators."

"Or get pushed in by Justicars."

"Would you rather walk or be pushed?" Arkadi said.

A grunt. Something like a laugh, difficult to discern through the respirator. "It's dumb sending in negotiators to talk to soldiers," he said. "You've done no violence. Your hands are clean. You'll be here, after, rebuilding this world we saved, so you can destroy it all again in another three hundred years."

"Is that why you killed the other negotiators who came up here?" Arkadi asked. "You feel we're complicit?"

"The whole country is complicit," he said.

Arkadi understood the true gravity of the situation then. "I have to go now," she said. "Dog's hungry. I'm hungry. Are you hungry? I can bring you something in a few hours, if you want me to come back? It's up to you." Dusk was settling over everything. She didn't want to make that walk back among the gouges in the ground and mangled bodies in the dark. And she certainly didn't want to stay out here until the next sunrise in an hour.

"Leave the dog."

"If I leave the dog I'll need something in return."

"Then go. You'll get nothing from me."

"Before I do," Arkadi said, "I want you to know that even though you're holding this building, and some people got shot early on, I know lots of unexpected things happen in these kinds of situations. It's confusing. There's a lot of panic. It happens. But you let me get up here. You've kept cool and calm since then. That counts for a lot. Let's work together to get you all out safely now, all right?"

No response. Arkadi dusted her trousers off and rose slowly. She gave the dog a pat. She raised a hand to the soldier, as if they were old friends. "If you want, we can talk again. If not, they'll send someone else up here, probably. But if you request me," and she dropped her voice, "if you request me, me and the dog can come back. And I can bring you something. Anything you like?" Arkadi stared again at the faceless suit. Nothing.

Arkadi turned, patting the dog again as she did, to remind him that even if he didn't care about her, shooting her might upset the dog. It was tough to turn her back on him, but it showed trust. She felt his stare, anticipating the bullet.

"Butterscotch candy."

"Butterscotch candy," Arkadi said, and she knew which of the soldiers this likely was, then, because one didn't develop a taste for butterscotch anywhere but the southern continent. "You be here in an hour to talk again, and I'll work on getting that. All right? And you can feel free to contact us any time, you know. We're monitoring the frequencies. You can talk to me whenever you want. But I'll do my best to get that for you."

The soldier nodded. It was enough.

Arkadi tensed as she walked away, and forced herself to loosen up. Confident, carefree. People asked her often how she did it, putting herself in front of people who wanted to kill her and dozens more besides, but it was just like theater. She played the part of somebody confident, somebody smarter and greater than herself, and she became that person.

When she crossed back into the confines of the camp, the first person to run up was the dog's trainer.

"Mavis, come!" the woman barked, and the dog loped over.

"Mavis was a hit," Arkadi said, but the trainer just frowned at her and strode back to the kennels with her charge.

Revlan met her at the command tent. "Anything?"

"I'm alive," Arkadi said. "The dog's alive. Nothing's blown up yet. He wants butterscotch candy. But I figure you were listening in."

"How many in there?"

"Don't know," Arkadi said. "Only saw the one. But based on our conversation and how things went down, I suspect it's the only one."

"What did he say?"

"Just get him some candy."

"You were out there an hour and that's all you have? Candy?"

"Better than you've done," Arkadi said. She jabbed a finger at Maradiv, who was lingering just inside the command tent. She recognized his nervous hands. "Get me some candy."

"That will take days," he said, moving away from the tent. "Maybe longer. Does anyone on this continent even make it anymore?"

"You'll find out."

Revlan ushered Arkadi back into the command tent and said, "Perhaps I haven't communicated the gravity of this situation."

"It's been communicated," Arkadi said. She pointed to the squiggling lines surrounding the Red Secretary. "I think you took out the rest of the soldier's squad when you blew the escape tunnel, if they were ever there in the first place."

"How can you possibly know that? I was monitoring your communication. He said nothing to indicate—"

"She's alone," Arkadi said, pulling out her notebook. "I know which soldier this is, and she's very green. She opaqued the door before she turned on the canons. She did that so she didn't have to look right in my face as she did it. If there was someone else operating those defensive weapons, they wouldn't need to put that kind of distance between me and them. She had no demands. She said there were no hostages. She's alone."

"You have a plan, then?"

"There's shielding on the door, but I can get her to turn it off, maybe for a few seconds only," she said, "but I need that dog again, Mavis. And I need at least two excellent snipers in place."

"We already have snipers—"

"Excellent ones," Arkadi said. "They should only fire if they have a clear kill shot when she opens the door. If they don't have a clear kill shot and she lives, we're all dead, along with the rest of the province, because she's going to slam that shield back up and go blow up the whole site. So they better be good."

"And if you're wrong?"

"About what?

"If you're wrong that she's alone?"

"Then we'll certainly all die, whether your people are good shots or not."

"I'll have a squad ready to back you up once the door is open and shots are fired," Revlan said.

"That's nice, but probably not necessary."

"I'll get them as close as I can," Revlan said, "but you'll have maybe two minutes on your own between the kill shot and their arrival. Stay down and stay out of the way. They'll go in and clear it. Remember to keep your hands clean. We're short three negotiators now, and we don't need you consigned to the fire with the rest of us if you do violence."

"We'll all go to the fire eventually," Arkadi said. "I've been doing this a long time. I know my limits."

"Good," Revlan said. "When are you going back? It could be a long time before we have the candy."

"I need her to sit until sunup in an hour," she said. "She says she has no hostages, but she doesn't need them. The Red Secretary is her hostage, and she knows it. You still have people on the frequencies?

"I do."

"Have them reach out to her across all six channels every ten minutes or so. If she starts feeling lonely I want her to hear a friendly voice. Have them call me up if she calls in."

"What are you going to do for an hour?"

"Take a shit. Then take a nap."

"You can't be serious."

"I almost got shot out there," Arkadi said. "It's a wonder I didn't shit my pants."

Revlan escorted her to the lavatory pits and the temporary showers, and she took advantage of both. Arkadi waited until Revlan was gone before she gave in to the shakes. They were bad this time, so bad her teeth chattered. The first time it had happened was a year into the ceasefire, when she had talked a soldier down from killing a couple of government people in Yorusiv. The soldier had killed one of the hostages outright, just as Arkadi had arrived. She really had shit her pants that time, just as the soldier was coming out. He had raised a weapon to the head of the last hostage he was taking out with him, and there Arkadi was, five feet from him with no way to stop him from killing the hostage, killing her, and then killing himself. Negotiators could talk, but they weren't allowed to maim or kill unless they wanted to end the war in the incinerators with the rest of those who had had to deal out violence during the war. At best, she might have been able to disarm him. But there wasn't time to think. She had done everything right, talked him down, told him how it would go, but people were unpredictable. Rogue soldiers especially.

Arkadi found a cot in the med tent and threw her arm over her eyes and let her mind gnaw away at the problem of the Red Secretary. She needed the shield to come down, and that meant giving up the dog. She pulled out her notebook again and doodled in the pages next to her notes on the squad. One of the soldiers she had researched was a rookie kid named Soraya Te Kovad. Had grown up on a farm: pack of spotted gizzles, pack of ostriches, pack of dogs. Family farm blown up early in the war. They had lived in a suburb of Kovaaya. In Kovaaya, most people worked at the candy factory. Butterscotch, of course.

It was easy to know a kid on paper. Arkadi had gotten to know each of them in doing her research, but it was always jarring to meet them in person. She imagined them all very differently in her head. Seeing the kid walk out of her head and into the world was like watching a dream come to life.

And now Arkadi would have to be complicit in the death of that dream.

She must have slept, because Revlan woke her.

"They're on frequency four," Revlan said.

Arkadi followed her to the command tent. Maradiv and another soldier were there, huddled near the radio, which was spitting red sparks and blue auroras from the tinny cups affixed to its exterior. Arkadi wondered if the enemy magics like this would eventually just die out on their own, sputtering into the ether like these things.

"She's here," Maradiv said.

"What's happening over there?" Arkadi said into the radio.

"Need you to come back up with the candy," the soldier said. Her voice sounded tinny, far away. Definitely a bad radio. It needed to be recharged.

"Still working on getting you that candy," Arkadi said. "We've only had a couple of rotations of the sun since—"

"Bring the dog up here," the soldier said.

"I told you," Arkadi said. "I need something in return."

"I'll talk to you, then," she said. "Up here."

"I need a show of good faith," Arkadi said. "I'm here with all these good soldiers down here. Now, I know you were overwhelmed when those first couple of negotiators showed up. Split-second decision, right? You felt you were in danger. But you haven't hurt anyone else since then, and that counts for a lot. You talking to me and the dog—the dog's name is Mavis, by the way—that counts for a lot. If we can end this now, that's going to count big."

"I'm not coming out."

"Just a good show for these people," Arkadi said. "I know you're hungry. I expect you grew up pretty hungry there outside Kovaaya. You have sisters, brothers, who worked in the factory? Or could you spare any after all that work on the farm?"

Silence. Spitting sparks.

Arkadi waited, though Maradiv and Revlan looked increasingly concerned. Arkadi had pushed her hand when she was well away from the defensive guns. Not that it mattered if the kid blew the station. But Arkadi didn't think she was at that point yet. A lot relied on gut feeling, as a negotiator. Too much.

Then, from the radio, "I'm sorry." It was difficult to judge the tone. Did her voice break? Had Arkadi struck a nerve?

"I'll bring Mavis up there," Arkadi said gently. "You and me and Mavis will work this out, all right? We are in a good place. You've handled yourself really well, Soraya. I'm coming up."

Arkadi strode out of the tent, heading straight for the kennels. The trainer saw her coming and put her meaty hands on her hips.

"Alive," the trainer said.

"My goal is to bring everyone in alive," Arkadi said. "Including the dog. But if I don't get the dog, we all die, all blown up to bits. Understand?"

"I nursed this dog from my own tit."

"I'm sure that's a euphemism. I understand."

The trainer grunted at her and called Mavis over. The big dog rambled to Arkadi's side. This time, the trainer knelt next to the dog and said something to him that Arkadi did not hear.

"I have to go," Arkadi said. "There's an unstable soldier up there."

"Go," the trainer said.

Arkadi called Mavis after her, and they began the long trek across the rutted ground between the camp and the Red Secretary a second time. The sun was high in the sky, and the wind had died down. She never thought she'd miss the wind, but as she sweated it out under the heat, miss it she did.

When she arrived at the doors this time, palms out, the door went transparent immediately.

The soldier stood dead center in the doorway this time, stance wide, just a few paces from the entrance. She shifted her weight from side to side, the only indication of mood that Arkadi was going to get.

"This is Mavis," Arkadi said. "Mavis, this is Soraya."

"How did you know my name?" Soraya asked.

"I know your squad, remember?" Arkadi said. "I want this over as much as you. I want you to go home. Come on out, and I'll ask if you can ride out with Mavis. Mavis hasn't hurt anybody, and you've cooperated well since I came up here. That counts, remember? I'm going to put in a good word. Sometimes it helps."

"I want to burn everything down," Soraya said.

"I know," Arkadi said. "Some days I do too."

"How will you go on living with that?" Soraya said, "Once all the rest of us are dead?"

"I don't know," Arkadi said. "I'm still not sure how long any of us are going to survive the peace. Funny, isn't it? You go all this time fighting the war, thinking it will get you, but it's the peace that's killing us, isn't it? I don't want peace to kill you, Soraya, not after the war tried so hard to, and failed."

"How does this go?" Soraya said.

Arkadi spoke slowly, softly, "You turn off your suit and kick it to your left. I'll walk ten paces back here with Mavis to give you some room. You put your left hand on your head and use your right to turn off that blast shield over the door. Be sure you're not carrying anything in either hand. Just go slow, slow, slow. All right? When the door's open, you drop to your knees. Keep your hands out. You're going to see some soldiers coming up the hill to meet us, but that's all normal. They'll have weapons drawn, but that's just protocol. None of them wants to hurt you. These are kids, you understand? Some haven't done violence to anyone. We can still save some of them. But you've got to help. They may handle you a little roughly when they secure you, but I promise, no one wants to do violence to you. Once you are secure they will take you back down the hill with me and Mavis and we'll have some of that butterscotch candy if it's in yet, all right? I want to make sure this goes just right, so go ahead and repeat that all back to me."

She did.

Arkadi nodded. "Great, all right, go ahead." She started to back away, ensuring that the snipers would have a clear shot once the shield went down.

Soraya powered down her armor and released it. The whole glittery mess of it retracted down into itself, pooling around her feet. Underneath, Soraya was a skinny wisp of a girl in a soiled tunic, all lanky arms and legs and bony knees. It was clear she hadn't eaten well in a long time, far longer than she and her squad had been on the run. Feeding the soldiers during the war had been difficult enough. Trying to feed them without the help of the enemy food trains they had ransacked all during the war was even harder. There were blackened circles under her eyes, bruising her already dark skin. Her hair had grown in a little, but didn't yet cover all the scars on her skull.

From her research, Arkadi had known the girl wasn't more than seventeen or eighteen, but it was clearer, now. She wasn't a monster or an alien, outside of the suit. She was just another terrified, exhausted human being: a terrified, exhausted human being turning around to switch off the shield over the door, the only thing keeping her alive.

The shield went down.

The girl began to turn again.

Arkadi should have been stepping back. Stepping away.

Instead, she said, "Cover!" and she stepped between Soraya and the light and rushed toward her, arms outstretched.

Mavis the dog reached Soraya before she did, throwing open his paws and enveloping her as he had been trained to do to protect those under fire.

Arkadi did not see the shots, but she felt them as she tumbled into Soraya. A fiery hammer whumped into Arkadi's left shoulder. The dog yelped.

But Arkadi did hear the crack of Soraya's head on the floor.

Arkadi rolled off of Soraya. Mavis still clung to Soraya with his front paws, though there was blood on his rear legs. Soraya's hand was out, reaching for something. Just a few inches from her grasping fingers was a weapon, neatly hidden under the discarded suit.

"Don't!" Arkadi said.

Soraya raised her head. Her eyes were unfocused. "You lied," she said. Blood bubbled from her nostrils.

"I said nobody wanted to hurt you," Arkadi said. "That was true. Nobody wanted this."

"It's not for you," Soraya said, and pointed.

Arkadi followed her arm and saw another soldier on the platform overhead. The soldier tried to bolt, but stumbled.

He was going to run off and blow up the whole Red Secretary. The team wasn't going to be fast enough to stop him.

Arkadi crawled over Soraya and grabbed the weapon with her good hand. She fired at the platform, a wild smear of lights. The soldier rolled up just as she fired again, and then her fire hit him. He tumbled over the railing and crashed to the floor ten paces away.

Arkadi dropped the weapon. Blood ran down her arm. She turned, terrified, staring at her bloody hands.

She raised her head . . . and saw the dog trainer already inside the building, crouching over Mavis the dog.

It should not have surprised Arkadi that the trainer would be first on the scene. Her gaze locked with Arkadi's, but Arkadi could read nothing in the woman's expression. Then the trainer was moving again, back down the rise as Revlan's promised cleanup squad rolled into the room like a tide, precisely two minutes after the shield had gone down.

Arkadi sank to her knees. She clutched at her shoulder as blood pumped over her fingers. A medic near the back of the mass of soldiers rolled her onto a stretcher. Arkadi watched the fallen weapon kicked about the floor, sliding in the dust made muddy with blood.

Another soldier loomed over her from where she lay on the stretcher. Black spots flashed across her vision. She thought the soldier might be Maradiv, then laughed at that idea because the man was the least likely to bother to come up with a retrieval team. The medic jabbed something into her thigh. The pain eased off at the edges, but it still felt like her organs were bleeding out of her shoulder.

"Were there any more?" the soldier said. "More than these?"

"Just us," Arkadi said. "Just us three."

"Two," the medic said. "There are two soldiers here on the floor. Were there three?"

"The dog," Arkadi said. "Will the dog be all right?"

Then the darkness came, and it was blissful, the little death.

Arkadi woke alone in a tent. It took her some time to convince the intern on duty to tell her where she was.

"You're still at the Red Secretary," the intern said. "I'm getting the medic."

The medic came in with Revlan tagging along behind her.

"Did you save—" Arkadi began.

"Both dead," Revlan said. "The girl, we shot. She was out from a head injury. The second was dead when we came in. What happened in there? Did they murder each other?"

"The dog," Arkadi said. "Did you save the dog?"

"The dog's fine," Revlan said. "Tovorov is happy for that."

"She the trainer?"

"Yes. What were you thinking, throwing yourself in front of the snipers?" Revlan said.

"I don't know what came over me," Arkadi said, which was true. It would take her some time to understand that.

"I told them you must have realized there were two in there," Revlan said. "Is that right?"

Arkadi blinked at her. Did Revlan know what had happened? Was she trying to cover for Arkadi, or just guessing? No, Revlan had no reason to cover for Arkadi's violence. Revlan simply needed to fill out the paperwork. If Revlan knew, if any of them knew that she had picked up a weapon . . .

"Ask the trainer," Arkadi said, "she was there." Arkadi put her arm over her face.

"We already asked Tovorov," Revlan said. "I wanted to corroborate her story with you."

"Then you know what happened," Arkadi said. "Put it in the report and get it over with." What did they do to crisis negotiators who committed violence? What order would she go into the incinerators? Before or after the soldiers? After, certainly.

"You did well," Revlan said, "better than any negotiator I've seen. None of them would have taken that bullet. Tovorov says the soldiers shot each other. I admit I'm . . . trying to work that out. Which is why I wanted your help with it."

Arkadi pulled her arm from her face. Her stomach twisted, but she said nothing to correct her.

Revlan continued, "And I said to Tovorov, are you quite certain? Because you're good, Te Avalin, but I didn't think you were good enough to get that soldier to shoot one of her own to save the Red Secretary. Especially considering she had a very serious concussion."

"I didn't either," Arkadi said.

Revlan patted her pillow. "You rest," she said. "Get her some water, will you?" she said to the medic, and the medic took the hint and left them. Revlan leaned over Arkadi and murmured, "Do not think I accept that your hands are clean, negotiator. None of us are. You are as human as me."

Revlan rose.

Arkadi gave her a little two-fingered salute.

"I expect you'll get a medal," Revlan said.

"You will, too," Arkadi said.

"I will," Revlan said, "and I'll be wearing it along with the others when I walk into the incinerator next year. It will be very beautiful, I'm sure."

The lorry came for Arkadi the next day. The medic had stuffed her full of drugs and coagulant, and she was able to limp her way out of the tent. All around her, the soldiers were packing up the command center, carrying supplies back down to the inflatable bridge. Groups of red-liveried scientists were marching up the other way, back to the Red Secretary, presumably to recalibrate it. The Red Secretary would be a weapon no longer. Not for another three hundred years, at least. Arkadi was thankful she would be dead, and all these people either dead with her or incinerated, by then.

But what about those other people? Those future generations, the ones born of those who had committed no violence during this horrible war? Only the peaceful could create a peaceful society, all the holy books said, and this is where it left them in the aftermath of war. She had given them nothing, preserved nothing but a cyclical war as regular as the seasons. Maybe someday they would murder every last one of the enemy. Or maybe someday the enemy would destroy them. One could hope.

As Arkadi reached the fissure in the road, she saw Tovorov there counting out the dog crates and overseeing their transit across the bridge.

Arkadi could not help herself. She limped over to Tovorov and stood a pace distant until Tovorov relented and said, "What do you want?"

"Why didn't you tell them?" Arkadi asked.

"To what end?" Tovorov said. "So you could get incinerated after this, too? No. Someone has to rebuild. Someone has to go on. What you did was not wrong."

"That's not your decision."

"Who else's decision would it be? People make the laws."

"The gods make the laws. People follow them."

"That's a pretty story in the daytime," Tovorov said, "but it doesn't hold up here on the field, when you see night eight times a day."

"You should have told the truth."

"*You* tell the truth," Tovorov said. "I'm damned already. I just want a nice quiet year or two with my dogs before the end. That's all. One more dead out there . . . No point."

"How is Mavis?"

"Alive," Tovorov said. "No thanks to you. But he'll need to be retired."

"We should all be retired."

"Not you," Tovorov said, pointing across the fissure at the lorry. "You have work. My work is done. Soldier work is done."

The driver waved, and Arkadi recognized her. It was the same driver who had taken her up here. She had kept her promise to return.

"When they said the war was over, I was glad," Arkadi said. "I thought it would get easier after that. But it's harder now. It's harder to fight your own people. Harder to see what's right."

"Get yourself a dog," Tovorov said. "They'll keep you straight." When she saw Arkadi staring at the dog crates, she said, "Not one of mine."

"Sorry," Arkadi said. She waved to the lorry driver again, who motioned her over. Arkadi stepped up onto the bouncy bridge, and this time she looked down into the fissure, down and down, past the colorful layers of minerals to the darkness that never seemed to end. It was like looking inside of herself, inside of Soraya. A blackness that would never be filled.

"Come in," the driver said from the other side of the bridge, "Come in," but Arkadi remained transfixed on the bridge, halfway between the driver's open arms and the darkness, halfway between war and peace.

THE SINNERS AND THE SEA

I WANTED HIM the way a sinner wants his feet on solid ground.

I saw him up in the tower of a little shop. His head was bent over his typewriter while the great Mercy Hospital building floated past on its morning flight toward the meatpacking island. The wind brought with it the rancid stink of that district: rancid blood, rotten meat, animal fear. The Mercy Hospital would eventually end up on the second level south, where the techno-babblers waited to stream inside its doors, seeking a remedy for every little injury that had pierced their dirty fingers the night before.

The man looked so studious. So intent on his work, with no care for me or the world outside. I longed for that kind of immersion, but so far could not find it in anything but the contemplation of boys in high windows. I wondered, often, if I could make a living at gawking at pretty boys, but my cousins insisted there wasn't such a job. Last time I was in this quarter of the city, the tower shop had sold crystal recordings and laser players for music that hadn't been banned yet, stuff that folks insisted had come from legal family collections and not stuff hauled up from the sea below. The sign out front now said, "Stationery and Antiquities."

"Stop gaping, Arret," my mentor, Solda, said. She was already ten paces ahead of me, electric truncheon in hand, face masked by her brilliant crimson scarf. My scarf was up too, because we were technically on a Guardian assignment to retrieve a relic. In theory, we couldn't be bothered by vigils, the purity corps, the coven, or even the island Prefect herself, no matter our actions, once the scarves were on.

Solda is generally right, but also old. Your priorities change a lot when you're just a couple years from Reunion.

But me? I wasn't dead yet. Not even close. And that boy was very pretty. The relics could wait.

I pulled the scarf from my own face and stepped into the tower shop. Behind the counter was a plump older woman, the sort who looked like she spent her mornings churning butter or pounding metal or flaying carcasses. She smelled of yeasty wine barrels and old books, which made me want to curl up next to her and stay awhile. Her hands and forearms were massive, and made the stylus she held look dainty by comparison. She had an underbite, and when she turned her doughy face to me, she put me in mind of a bulldog. I'd need to use some charm.

"Fair wind, matron, I'm in a terrible hurry," I said, leaning on the polished counter. It appeared to be real wood, very old. Not surprising, considering she sold antiquities.

"Fair wind ever," she said, and her gaze moved to my red scarf. "There's nothing illegal here," she said. "I have my papers. These are all family relics. Nothing from the sea." She reached beneath the counter.

"Not here for that," I said. "Personal business. Who's the man upstairs?"

"Upstairs?" she said, like a parrot. One of my cousins once had a parrot, which she kept secretly in the barracks for six years. It knew how to say hello in four different dialects. When the head-woman at the orphanage found it, she killed it and made us eat it. We didn't try and sneak in pets after that.

"At the typewriter," I said. "I can see him through the window."

"Ah," she said, and smiled broadly. "You wish to purchase him?"

"You own him?"

"It's all legal—"

"I believe you," I said. "I'd rather romance him."

"That, too, can be arranged," she said, as if the idea amused her.

"The *Priory* docks in fifteen minutes," Solda said from the doorway. "Stop screwing around. I'm not likely to approve your promotion as it is. You're testing my patience."

I tapped the counter and slid over a gold-engraved five-note shell piece. "Pick out something he'd like," I say. "A nice hat. Would look real fetching, with a complexion like his."

She put her meaty hand over the piece and smiled again. "Indeed it would."

"Arret!" Solda, again. "You're the worst apprentice I've ever had—"

"—in a decade," I finished for her. I clucked at her and pulled my scarf back on. "I really want to meet the other bad apprentice from ten years ago. I bet we'd have a lot in common."

"Mooning at a man," Solda muttered, jogging ahead of me. I hurried to catch up. "Shall I tell the coven that's why we were late? That's why this will be a containment and not a retrieval?"

"There are more important things than relics," I said. "I mean, one day one of those things will set the whole city loose and we'll drop dead into the sea. Might as well have fun before then." I spared a look back up at the man. I could no longer see his profile.

"Guardians are supposed to prevent that day," Solda muttered, "not hurry it along."

I couldn't argue with her there. We ran the rest of the way to the *Priory* dock. I could see a flashing hologram blooming up over the island as the ship's great bulk floated over to the dock. The sharp, tangy scent of lemon wafted toward us.

Solda swore. "I told you," she said. "They're getting a message out. This is on you."

We leapt the guardrail before the *Priory* had properly docked. I pulled my own truncheon and raced across Priory Island after Solda. I caught up to her as we heaved over the *Priory* gates and into the great garden where the misty illegal recording dominated the sky. Solda might be old, but I was spry, and I delighted in overtaking her. One thing about growing up an orphan tasked with running messages at six years old—you get fast real quick.

A small crowd had already gathered around the holographic image, mostly pilgrims and nuns who made their living on Priory Island. Few tourists or regular citizens ended up here, which is why it was a strange place to stage a demonstration, but Solda's relic tracker was impeccable, the best one the coven had ever given her, she always said, which almost made up for them giving her me at the same time.

Solda slung her tracker around her neck and waded through the crowd to find the device causing the light show. I loped around the periphery, which was usually where the dissidents would stand around to watch how their demonstrations were received. I ran one hand along the gritty wall, all pocked brick and concrete. Every step I took released the musky scent of decaying leaves.

Above us the image rippled with voices, their tones high and cantankerous. They talked of revolution like it was a great idea that wouldn't lead to the whole city falling into the sea. They talked about a world where people lived on solid ground, and didn't fear the purity corps and Guardians. They talked of some dead world, of the dead past. Most of what they said was stuff any recited text would tell you was a lie, but people loved the idea that there could be some other world but this one we'd made over the drowned carcass of the last one. Here were people like me out here trying to save these folks from themselves, and what thanks did we get for it? The coven telling me I mooned over too many boys.

I tripped over a bit of rubble in the grove surrounding the clearing, and caught myself on a thick tree trunk so large it must have been planted during the Founding. I'd disturbed some duff and dirt, revealing a flat, black projection device. In the stories the school marms all told, glittering jewels and gold were the treasures sought by people of the past. But this was pirate's gold to me. X marks the spot.

I reached for the box just as another figure rushed me from behind. We both went over hard. With the wind knocked out of me, I wasn't much good for anything but flailing. My attacker straddled me and pressed her hands to my throat. Already short on air, I felt my hands go reflexively to her wrists. I should have kept my head and flipped her up and over me, but panic overrides training when you don't have enough of the training part. Blackness juddered across my vision. I freed my right hand and threw dirt in her face. She wore a long coat with a hood, though, and I ended up eating more dirt than she did.

I always heard you think a lot about your whole life before you die. But there I was, getting strangled to death in the Priory Gardens, and the only thing I was thinking about was how I really didn't want to die. I can't imagine having time to think about anything else. Maybe you got more time to think when it all goes black, but I doubted it.

Solda's truncheon thwacked the woman from behind. I had never been so glad to see Solda's scowling face.

The truncheon's current went straight through my attacker and into me. I had a brief moment to watch her seize up before I did, too, losing all control of my body. As I jerked and spasmed, Solda interrogated my attacker, smashing her with the truncheon again and again to emphasize her points. "Where are your collaborators? Where's the other device?"

By the time the pain had passed, for me, I had heard those questions so many times *I* wanted to answer them just to make Solda be quiet. Little bits of spittle flecked her mouth. But my attacker still lay on the ground, curled up, wordlessly absorbing the attacks.

I couldn't help but admire that stupid, thankless little rebel, just a little.

Solda bashed the woman once more, in the head, and her hood came free. My attacker was much younger than I'd thought, maybe sixteen, already old enough to start an apprenticeship. She should have been under some guild's care, working her twelve hours like the rest of us.

"Confine her," Solda told me, and marched off to start on the containment work with the witnesses. Containment was boring, so I was glad to have the more exciting part of the job.

I restrained the girl with a canister of spray-on webbing. It bundled her up in a breathable cocoon. The grunts could come in later and haul her off to the coven for a proper interrogation.

By the time I finished, Solda had already contained the audience. They lay on the grounds, still and beatific as sleeping children. The air still smelled like lemons, an aftereffect of the projection. In a quarter hour the witnesses who'd been contained would get up, shake off a headache, and carry on like nothing had happened. I'd been contained before, back when I was a little kid. I hadn't known what it was at the time, but I remembered the big, kindly face of the Guardian crouching next to me when I came to. I'd been alone, I guess, when I saw whatever illegal tech show it was, and she had stayed with me to make sure nothing happened to me while I was out. When you contain kids too young, sometimes they don't wake up. It's good form to make sure it takes. That was when I decided I wanted to be a Guardian, just like her. She was calm and reasoned and comforting, and she could remember all the world's secrets, all the stuff they made the rest of us forget. I told the coven I wanted to be like her to protect people from the gory technology all the insurgents were bringing up from the dead world below us. But really, it was because I knew she had more knowledge of the real world than I ever would, and I coveted that. I wanted the truth of the world. Turns out, being a Guardian didn't come with as many answers as I'd hoped. Not yet, anyway. The only hope to get more truth was to pass this apprenticeship, and Solda wasn't too keen on seeing me do that.

Solda strode over to meet me. She had the black projection device in her hand; it wasn't much bigger than a heart. She thrust it at me. "Contain that," she said, though she could have just as easily done it herself.

"Sorry," I said, spraying the device with a signal blocker, "I'm not so good once fights hit the ground." I didn't have anywhere to put the device until the grunts arrived, so I slipped it into my pocket.

"You aren't good at defense, period," said Solda. "You aren't good at offense, either." She snapped her mouth shut. I saw the tension in her jaw from the rest of the words she had left unsaid. I could guess at a good many of them.

"Sorry," I said again, but she was already walking away.

"Grunts will be here in two minutes," she said. "You got the number and date for them?"

"This is the eighteenth," I said, "year four hundred and seventy eight. You want me to recite the relic pledge, too?"

Solda snorted at my sarcasm and popped something into her mouth. She went off to wait for the contained people to start waking up.

The grunts arrived a little later, two young men, not much older than the girl in the cocoon, and they hefted her into a nondescript wheeled cart to take her back to the coven. Nobody wanted to see Guardians hauling bodies around the islands. There were rumors enough already about what we did. That was the excuse Solda gave me for divvying up tasks, but I figured it was more likely because it kept all of us knowing pieces about a thing instead of seeing the whole picture. The longer the Guardians had with the rebels, the more we could get out of them. As it was, I'd never see that girl again.

We got off the *Priory* at the next island docking, just as the witnesses were starting to wake up. The island at the dock was the

Seventh Day Restaurant. It wouldn't dock near the coven for at least an hour, so we had some time. The wind was up, buffeting my face, and clouds were speeding past the island, obscuring the long drop between land masses that would, inevitably, lead to the sea.

I went to the edge of the island, to a little park, and Solda followed. I wasn't going to be the one who broke the silence. I knew what was coming.

But when she sat down next to me, she didn't say anything. Instead, she pulled her lunch bar from her pocket and ate it sullenly, staring straight ahead.

"Sorry," I said again, because I really was trying to make amends. When she was angry at me the job was even more miserable.

"Don't be sorry at me," she said. "Be sorry at the coven."

And that's all she would say, no matter how much I wheedled, until we finally docked at the soaring spires of the coven's island ninety minutes later. We didn't even make it to our rooms before a red-liveried little coven's messenger summoned us to a meeting.

That's when Solda finally said something. All she said was, "Shit."

We followed the messenger deeper into the palatial compound until we reached the coven's assembly chamber. The messenger pulled back deep purple curtains and admitted us into the half circle of stone where the five members of the coven stood, draped all in dark purple. At the farthest end of the half circle was the current Coven Senior, Hovana. Tall and plump, all I could see of her was her tawny face peering out at me, the dark eyes squinting out at me from a face with a dimple in the chin so deep that it seemed to split her jaw in two.

"Most apprentices see us just twice in their lifetimes," Hovana said as the messenger closed the curtains behind us, "when they are accepted into service, and when they are removed from consideration or raised to become a Guardian. Yet this is already the fourth time you've sat before the coven. Why is that, Arret?"

"I wouldn't know," I said. "We just disagree about protocol."

Solda wasn't looking at anything in particular, though her gaze tarried a long time on the floor. I could hear her sucking on something, probably one of her hard candies.

"You mean the law," Hovana said. "One cannot disagree with the law. Guardians uphold the law."

"Laws change all the time," I said.

"They aren't changed by apprentices," Hovana said. "That should have been a containment, not a catastrophe. As it was, we had to contain a good many people because you were tardy."

"We can't be everywhere at once," I said. "You want us to take on too many looters with too few hands. The logistics of retrieval—"

"I know very well the logistics of retrieval," she said, and she recited the old code at me.

"I know it," I said.

"Good," she said, "because a Guardian with a poor memory is not suited for the scarf."

I started to recite the full book of lost relics. She stopped me. "That's not the point," she said.

"I spent a year as a librarian," I said. "I can recite ten full treatises on martial law from the founding of the city. I know what I'm about."

"We have enough librarians," she said. "We have enough people around to repeat facts. I need Guardians. I know you have inventory after this, but I want you to give the shift to someone else and cool your head. You're grounded at the coven until further notice. Maybe you'll be a better librarian than a Guardian, you think? This may not be the profession for you. Solda, in the morning I want you to speak to Moravas. The customization of that device was clearly her family's work. I recognized it immediately."

"Then she should be drowned," I said.

"We don't make the rules," Hovana said. "We only enforce them. Got it, librarian?"

I gave her my biggest grin, because I've always found that joviality rankles hard in the face of insult, especially with the coven. "Sure," I said.

"Repeat it back," she said.

"I'm not some first level kid," I said.

"Repeat it," she said, and she even used a teacher's voice, like they all did in the classrooms when we had to give a summary of the day's lessons. The Purity Corps insisted that no knowledge could be permanently marked onto any surface, which left us with our memories. The better your memory, the better you were in school, the better your life. I was lucky, with my memory. There's not much to do in an orphanage after the day's work, so I would spend hours going over lines and stories and formulas until I learned them backwards and forwards.

"Go fuck yourself," I said, and that was the end of that.

They hustled us out of there like I'd set the place on fire. I don't think anyone had ever told the coven to fuck itself. I wasn't even sure why I'd said it. I was tired of being yelled at. Tired of being told I was stupid. Tired of getting only half the truth even though I was training to be a Guardian.

The big doors to the audience chamber closed behind us, and Solda and I stood together in the stillness. Solda put something into her mouth, another hard candy; I caught the faint scent of peppermint. The hall was cold. A couple of other Guardians passed by; neither looked our way.

"You go to the library and fill out the paperwork on today," Solda said. "Then you're suspended, like they said. Archival work. Present yourself to the head librarian after you file the paper."

Solda stepped away.

"Wait," I said, and grabbed for her sleeve.

She yanked her arm back, and when she spoke, her voice was low and gruff. "You listen," she said. "You don't know what I've put on the line for you. Entitled little sinner boys like you come and go around here, thinking they can fuck things up and everyone gives them a pass because there's so few of them. But let me tell you this. We don't need more than a couple boys to keep the world spinning, and the coven is happy to let you fly off the face of the world if you stir the pot here. Your actions are dangerous. Whose side are you on?"

"I'm on the right side," I said. "I know there's no better world than this. I've seen all that rebel propaganda and I know it's shit. But blindly following laws is stupid. I don't like how some things are set up. There's no harm in saying that."

Solda sucked on the hard candy, shaking her head. "Even you don't get it," she said. "You heard it in stories, but you don't know how this world we've made is the end result of thousands of years of trial and error that led to failed civilizations. This society is the pinnacle of social progress. Human beings are naturally prone to chaos. You have to give them structure. You keep prodding at the structure like you're doing, and it tumbles down."

"If it's really that weak," I said, scoffing, "maybe it's not what they say it is."

"You're going to get more than grounded, saying stuff like that," Solda said. "I like you sometimes, Arret, I do. You are smart when you're not distracted. You've got a great memory and a keen sense for how those relic looters think. But you have to bend to order. If you won't bend, it'll break you."

Solda pulled away and moved out into the hallway, back toward the dining area. I was starving, too, but I knew following her would just result in more finger-wagging. I'd do the paperwork like she asked, just this once.

The coven library had its own floating island, connected to the main coven island by a flexible bridge that wasn't for the faint of heart. In bad weather it lurched and juddered and snaked about like something alive. I kept both hands on the smooth, silvery rails, too stubborn to wait for a ferry.

Like the coven, the library was built to impress the weary with the weight of history. All along the path leading up the massive stone steps were twisted human relics that had been dredged up from below. Only the coven and its archivists were allowed to house these sorts of relics, and for good reason. The figures here glistened in the sunlight, their bodies encased in a sheer substance like glass, or clear amber. They were the remnants of the people who had come before, the ones buried by the sea a thousand years ago. They had been petrified and then drowned for their sins. Now they stood here at the archives as a reminder of what excessive hubris and decadence could lead to. Not enough rules destroyed them, the coven would say, but I always thought they were just dumb enough to get caught.

I gave my palm at the library entrance for identification, and the palmist spent her time tracing all the lines to ensure I was who I said I was, which was ludicrous, really. There were only four other men my age who ever set foot in the library, and we looked nothing alike. But we all had to pretend at being useful, so she studied my palm, and I let her, because I'd already yelled at Solda and the coven, and look at where all that had gotten me. But you couldn't have anything outside of the archives written on paper, including identity cards. All the Guardians who had them picked them up at the front desk of the library to use to get into the secret stacks. But outside of the archives, writing stuff down got you thrown into the sea.

I walked up through the stacks. The big wood-and-steel bookshelves were oppressive, stretching up and up for six floors, all connected by the spidery veins of silver catwalks that gleamed in the sunlight streaming in from the multiple glass domes. Marbled light painted rainbows across the floor, intercut by strange, twisted shadows created by the catwalks. Just breathing the air made me cough. The air was clotted with dust and stank of old leather and unwashed old librarians too enamored of their work to pause for hygiene. It was easy to get lost in here. I'd never seen all of it. I still wasn't permitted into most of the rooms, but I could see tantalizing glimpses of them through the stacks. Those were the rooms that housed all the machine recordings, the disks and crystals and lasers and tinny bits of metal and flickering screens and flashy holograms. Would I ever get in there, now?

The head librarian, Juleta, loomed above it all at her great desk, which was perched like a podium atop a slab at the center of the library. She always reminded me of a spider squatting at the center of her web. I went up the seven steps to her, trotting up each one. That's when I finally noticed that there was something in my pocket, because it banged against my thigh as I walked. I reached into my pocket as I came to the top of the pedestal, and my mouth went dry. My fingers touched the cold, webbed coating over the projection device that I'd slipped into my pocket back at the *Priory*. I hadn't turned it in to the grunts when they arrived. I'd completely forgotten. Heat moved up my face. I'd be murdered for this. They'd drown me. How would I explain?

"Have they assigned you over to me yet?" Juleta said, breaking my frozen panic. She fixed her monocle into the deep trough beneath her massive brow. Her black eye swam in the watery lens, three times bigger behind the glass. Strands of white peppered her hair, and she had soft white hair on her chin and cheeks. Her position alone made her one of the smartest people in the world, but in that moment, I loathed the idea of ever coming back here again. At this rate I was going to end up a librarian, not a Guardian, or maybe just a dead criminal, based on what was in my pocket.

I snapped my mouth shut and reconsidered. They were going to drown me anyway when they found out I hadn't turned in the device. There was no way around that. I was a fugitive already. It's just that nobody knew it. I don't even know what came over me, but I said, "I'm here to pick up a file on Moravas." The name just bubbled up, the same one Hovana had told Solda to look into. I was just speeding that along, really. What did it matter, now? All I had to leverage was the case. If I could bring this Moravas in, I could pretend I'd gotten this device from her. Nobody would know. Or maybe I'd get out of here and just stage a relic hunt and tell them this was a new device. Whatever I did, I had to get out of this library, because no one was going to buy that I'd found a projector in here still covered in webbing.

Juleta raised a thick eyebrow. Her eyebrows were still black as pitch, like her eyes. "They letting Solda interrogate that little shit, are they?" she asked. She stuck out her meaty tongue and licked her thumb. She began to page through the massive book at her elbow, making little grunts as she sifted through the information.

Finally she wrote something on a card and handed it over to me. It still got me, watching somebody write something down so casually, even if it was permitted in the library. "Consult that catalog on the name," she said, and went back to her ledgers.

I took the card and hopped down the steps, the device thumping in my pocket as I did. Maybe someone else would worry about getting caught, but what did I have to lose? There's something freeing about knowing you're completely fucked.

I surveyed the great wall of card catalogs, searching for the bank Juleta had written down. There were twenty-eight sets of catalogs, all used for different types of information. I needed the one for whatever it was they filed Moravas under. I'd never searched through it before, which meant she wasn't any type of relic dealer I'd been asked to look up. There was MAA-MAD, and MAE-MAG. I could compare letters, even if I couldn't exactly sound things out very well. So I kept going, down and across, until I got to MOQ-MOR. I pulled open the drawer and found the card with Moravas's name. It listed the full name, which I didn't try and sound out, and gave a number for where the files were held. I could match that number to one of the big secret rooms that I'd never been in before. I knew it because I'd always wanted to go in there. I wrote down the location of the file on the card that the librarian had given me, giving a little illicit shudder as I did, and hustled my way up to the gated entry of that room. Through the slated bars, I could see rows of disks and crystals and baskets full of data drives.

I strode confidently up to the woman sitting at the desk inside the bars and pushed my card under the bars between us. I gave her my best smile. "Librarian sent me your way for this," I said.

"I need your card," she said.

"That's the card."

She smirked. "Your Guardian card," she said. "Unless you have a tattoo?"

"I lost it," I said.

"Is that so? You lost your tattoo?"

I shrugged. "The card. I left it with Juleta up at the front. Listen, if I wasn't authorized, Juleta wouldn't send me up here, would she? Give me back the card and I'll just tell Grand Master Hovana I got pushback. Can I get your name?" I reached for the nub of a much-used pencil sitting on the counter on my side, purely for show. I could read after a fashion, but I wasn't great at writing unless I could copy the forms of the letters exactly.

"It's fine," she said, taking back the card. "Just keep it in the viewing room." When I didn't move, she pointed to the door to the left of me. "I'll let you into the room from my side."

I ambled to the door like I knew what I was doing, and tried the knob. Locked. The clerk came in from the other side and opened it for me. Inside it was even dimmer than the rest of the library, and I had to let my eyes adjust. She led me through a second door into a tiny room muffled by black drapes. There was only a desk and a projection screen on one wall.

"It'll be a few minutes," she said, and left.

I admit I sweated a bit while I waited, but what more could they do to me if they found out I wasn't supposed to be here?

She reappeared with a flat black projection device a lot like the one we had retrieved from the *Priory*, and a sliver of a crystal. "I need to lock you in here while you're viewing the contents," she said, "and I can't permit you to leave until I verify both are back in my possession. You understand?"

"Of course," I said. "Old hat."

A flicker of unease crossed her face, but the truth is that if you're confident and pretend like you know what you're doing, most people will believe anything. She left the two things on the desk and locked the door behind her.

I had dismantled one of these recording devices before while on a retrieval, so I knew where the crystal went. I inserted the crystal and waited, but nothing happened. It took a little poking and prodding, but the thing finally snapped on. A brilliant holographic image burst from the device, nearly blinding me, as I still had my head over the lens. I sat back, and a great jowly face filled the air above the device. The head was nearly as big as the desk. I leapt back, knocking the chair over, to get some perspective.

"This is all a lie," the face said, and as I pulled back it came into focus. I didn't recognize her. Was this the actual relic dealer? Wasn't this supposed to be a file on her? The woman spoke with a heavy accent that I couldn't place. There were different dialects among the floating cities, but she seemed to stumble with basic pronunciation, as if it was a new tongue entirely. She wore her hair in thick black braids wound around her round head. She smacked her lips when she talked, and was looking somewhere to the left of the recording device instead of straight into it.

"This world is a lie," the face said. "I am a lie. My name is a lie. The sea is a lie. Until you accept all of these things, you will find no peace."

I had heard some speeches like this from some of the other relics used to disseminate propaganda. But what the projection said next was odd: "Consider this," she said. "Why is it they don't want you to write anything down? It's because of the dates. They don't want you to realize the truth about the dates, because then the whole story unravels."

I heard a key rattle in the door, and the little desk clerk came in. Her brow was furrowed.

"This must be the wrong recording," she said. "This is not what's on the number, this introduction."

I reached into my pocket then, and tapped the device inside. I don't know why I did it. Sometimes you just have a feeling for these things, maybe because I've been around them so much. The recording in front of us flickered. The gaze was straight at us now, repeating a name and address for Moravas, as well as a lengthy case history. I quickly memorized the data, which was repeated once more before the recording clicked off.

"That was very odd," the clerk said. "I've never seen one do that."

"Oh, these things happen," I said. I checked the materials back in and hurried from the room before she could question me any further. My palms were sweaty, and though I managed to keep from running, my pace was quicker than it should have been in a library.

I descended from the library and out past the palmist, through the forest of petrified sinners, and all but threw myself across the hurky-jerky bridge. What was this device I had in my pocket? Not just a recording or projection device. It did something to other pieces of old relics. It was a key of some kind. Or maybe a trigger. Did it unlock messages in other devices? That was a fancy bit of propaganda.

My heart thudded hard in my chest. I wrapped my red scarf over my face and waited for the next ferry out of the coven. I didn't even look to see where it was going. I just knew I needed to get away as quickly as possible.

The wind whipped at my scarf as I watched coven island float away from us. In a few minutes it was lost to the clouds, and I finally looked up to see my destination. The ferry was headed toward the meatpacking district. From there I could take up another ferry to the lower islands and the traders' square. Lots of techno-babblers down there, pinch pennies, prophets, and other assorted riffraff. I should have expected that this Moravas person would have an address there. I guess it just all seemed too simple, her being there. I mean, where else would she be, up in there with the Noted Families and Safety Custodians? Hardly.

Warm afternoon light turned the world orange as I arrived in the lower islands. The light down there was spotty at the best of times, as the lower islands were often in the shadow of the ones above, which were larger and constantly moving. The ones below were cabled in place in the sea, mounted on giant chains. The lower islands were below the clouds, so from here it was much easier to see the black swath of ocean that had swallowed the rest of the world. Black water for as far as you could see in every direction: the water that ate up all of our ancestors' sins.

I found Moravas's address without much problem. People got out of my way because of the scarf. It wasn't until I reached the slapdash cloth-and-twine flap leading into the shop that I realized I was probably going to scare her off with that scarf, too. I had my truncheon out and ready as I strode in.

An old woman sat behind the counter, winding great lengths of red and black yarn onto paper cards. Antiques stuffed the shelves behind her: cloth toys, wooden clocks that no longer worked, coloring pencils and pens, toy carts, plastic soldiers, bits of foil butterflies, seashell figures, old glass bulbs, buttons, tangles of fishing wire, and other odds and ends that I couldn't name. It smelled of the sea, here, the scent of briny death, probably because it still lingered on all these things she had no doubt illegally brought up from the bottom. The woman was lean, burnished and brittle as a stick. She peered out at me from between tangles of long white hair thick as kelp.

"I'm looking for Moravas," I said.

As I approached the counter, a little light blinked in the belly of a doll just behind her. The woman turned to it, then cocked her head at me. "I'm Moravas," she said.

Then who was on the recording? I thought. I pulled the device from my pocket and set it on the counter with a thunk.

"This is your work," I said.

"Is it?" she said, and her tone was playful.

"Come on, don't fuck around. I saw the hologram over the *Priory*. You tell me who you made it for or I turn you in as the one who pulled off the whole thing."

A smile creased her face. "Will you, now?"

"I won't repeat myself." I set the truncheon on the desk.

She continued carding her yard. "You are a very cute young boy," she said. "I haven't seen a boy down here in weeks. You should stay for a drink."

"You're not taking this very seriously," I said.

"You haven't come here for me," she said.

"What?"

"You have come here for the truth," she said. She tapped the device. "If you were still a Guardian, if you ever were, you would have turned this in. What are you now that you've kept it, now that you've unlocked the message of the world?"

"There was no message," I said, indignant. I stuffed the device back in my pocket.

"You're a sinner, Arret. You always have been."

"How do you know my name?"

"Have you ever been down there, to the sea?" Moravas said.

"No," I said. "That's illegal without a permit."

"I went down often in my youth," Moravas said. Her voice was low, soothing. "We would wing out down over the clouds from the upper islands and dip low, down and down through clouds like silky foam. When we burst free of the clouds, there was the sea, the flat blue sea sparkling with light. The sea, the sea, the world below, for as far as my gaze reached, and for as far as we could power a flying craft."

"A what?" I said. "There are no flying craft." But she continued on as if she hadn't heard me.

"We had circumnavigated the globe and found nothing but sea," she said, "just like they said we would. Oh, certainly, there were areas where the great old rubble of the past jutted up from the roiling sea, but at best what remained was sand bar or marshland, and as the tides went in and out, so too did that mythic thing all the stories called the land. It wasn't so wonderful, I thought. I much preferred the sky."

"What are you reciting from?" I asked.

"My memory," she said.

"There's no land anymore," I said. "Not since the sea buried it a thousand years ago."

"Did you ever wonder why so many of you grew up in orphanages?" Moravas asked. It annoyed me that she was still wrapping the yarn, as if we were having a friendly chat instead of an interrogation.

"No," I said, "I didn't."

"It's easier to tell you all the same story," she said. "The same story of what happened to the ones before you."

"The sinners?"

"We're all sinners," she said.

"I need to bring you in," I said. "You made this device and disseminated propaganda, and that's illegal."

"You're a disgraced Guardian apprentice with no legal authority here," Moravas said, "and that's illegal. So it appears we are at an impasse."

I yanked the truncheon from the table. "What is this? How do you know who I am?" I prided myself on staying calm during terror, but she had unsettled me.

"Tell me the world you know," she said.

"Why?" I said.

"Humor an old woman."

"The world is here," I said. "We are at the very apex of civilization. We rose up over the water and escaped the scourge that killed the sinners. We are God's people. What is there to tell of the world but that?"

"What if I told you the world down there isn't as full of sinners as you think," she said.

"Is this more of your rebel propaganda?" I said.

"Why don't you go down yourself?" she said. "You want the person who made that device? She is down there."

"What . . . in the sea?"

"Yes," Moravas said. "Climb down the chain and follow the red fishing line below the water. It's not deep here. You'll find her and you can bring her to your Guardians, and beg for their approval."

"That's illegal," I said.

"As illegal as all of the other things you've done today," she said.

I gritted my teeth. "There's no way down," I said.

"There's always a way down," she said. "All you have to do is ask."

"If it will get me the person who made this relic, show me the way," I said, because I had come this far, and she was right. What did I have to lose?

She rose from her seat and set the yarn aside. She opened the door behind her and gestured me through. We walked into a dusty, cluttered back room to a trapdoor. She raised it and pointed into the dark. "Follow the stairs down until you reach the light," she said. "Then you'll come to the bottom of the island."

I stuffed my truncheon into the loop at my hip and plunged into the darkness. This whole world is a lie, all their propaganda said. Well, it was time they proved it.

I climbed into the darkness. I glanced up once and saw Moravas gazing down at me. I expected her to be smiling, amused at my misery, but her face was dead serious. Then she closed the trap door, plunging me into absolute darkness. I stared down and saw the tiny pinprick of light that I was supposed to reach, and groaned. What a chase this was.

I don't know how long I climbed, but when I reached the bottom my feet scuffed on solid rock. Someone had drilled a hole through the rock of the island and affixed a rope ladder to the long chain stretching into the sea. Already, I felt like a sinner. There was no greater sin than touching a piece of a world that wasn't yours, the world God had abandoned. We were the people of the clouds, closest to God, and to descend meant hurling ourselves back to some gory, godless past full of heretics and charlatans. The sea was where you threw the cast-offs, the murderers, the unclean, the diseased, the stupid, the malformed. But the sea was where I had to go if I wanted to be redeemed.

So I wiped my hands on my trousers and took hold of the ladder and down I went. It was a good three hundred feet of rope ladder, all twisted with the massive chain that fixed the island in place. For a long time, I didn't look down or up. The ladder was slippery, and I was breathing hard.

After a while, I chanced a look below. From certain angles, one could see the shadowy cities beneath the water on clear days from all the way up in the floating Conservatory. But as I descended, the dark peaks and squiggles resolved into what they were—not craggy rocks or coral or strange alien formations, but wreckage of a past so distant it only existed in story and myth and dusty old archeology manifestos recited from memory.

I turned my face back to the task at hand. I didn't look down again until I found myself out of ladder. I found that I was standing on a floating platform built around a giant buoy to which the chain was attached. Just one link of the chain was as wide as my torso. For the first time in my life, I gazed up at the lower islands and stared at the world from below. Much of the upper cities were covered in clouds, but the lower islands were visible, huge tangled masses of porous stone. Great hanging gardens of vegetation hung off the sides. Strangely, there were what looked like massive fans or portals of some kind in the stone underneath, large as buildings. I had never asked how the world stayed in the air. I wasn't quite sure how it did now, but suspected it was something to do with those huge objects.

I turned then to the sea. From here it did not look as flat and black. Great relics jutted up from it, bits of metal, broken spires, weedy junk that collected mollusks and kelp and other, stranger things. I had expected the sea to be deep, but the old woman was right about it being shallow. I leaned over the platform and saw rocky ground just a few feet below. Real land, right there. The fishing line was easy to see, as well. It ran from the platform out toward one of the big tangled skeletons. It had been an old metal building once, now rusted out and covered in sea creatures.

I tentatively stepped off the platform and into the water, half expecting the sea to open up underneath and swallow me. I held the fishing line like it was some sturdier safety rope. The sea was cool, not as cold as I expected. Little fishes darted all around me in shimmering colors. I knew fish; we ate fish often in the city, but I'd never realized that fish lived in the seas down here, too. I'd assumed everything was dead here. I followed the length of the line all the way out to the structure. As I entered what had once been the grand entrance, I stopped dead.

Inside the structure was a ring of petrified figures just like the ones that lined the path up to the library. And here, too, was a library of sorts. Great rusted metal lockers hung along the wreckage of the walls. Some had been eaten through by rust. Others had tumbled open and surrendered their contents to the sea, or maybe looters.

The red fishing line was attached to the arm of one of the frozen ancestors, her face twisted in misery. There was a device on her wrist that I had no name for, but the display was frozen. I couldn't make out anything on it, though if pressed I would say it wasn't a foreign language at all, but something a lot like ours. Seemed odd, that a language hadn't changed much in a thousand years, since the sea rolled over everything, but maybe that was just the writing that stayed the same. I didn't know enough about writing to judge.

Some joke this was that Moravas had pulled, telling me this would lead to the one who made the device. If it was this woman who'd been dead a thousand years, I couldn't exactly bring her up to pay for it. I thought back to the conversation with the coven, and what Hovana had said. *The customization of that device was clearly her family's work. I recognized it immediately.* That was exactly what she'd said. But if Moravas was stealing these devices from people down here, it couldn't be her family's work, could it?

I stuffed my hands in my pockets and kicked around the little circle of petrified people, these anachronisms from another time. I tapped the device in my pocket and ran my gaze across the metal lockers. I imagined that the lockers were like card catalogs, maybe, or library shelves, everything neatly labeled. I walked up to the lockers and wiped away the rust and grime at the top, trying to match up letters I knew the way I had with the card catalog. But there weren't letters here. These looked more like numbers. Dates.

The dates. Hadn't that hologram said something about dates?

The lockers up top were less damaged. I hauled over a locker already on the ground and stood on it to get a better look at the top row. I rubbed at the top. 425. 426. 427. No, those were too recent to be dates, only fifty years prior to the current date. Were they just locker numbers, maybe, catalog numbers, and not dates?

A deep unease stirred in my belly. I got down and turned back to the group of monuments. The water was starting to pool up higher. The tide was coming in. I had no idea how high the tide reached down here because I'd only ever seen it come in from way up there.

I sloshed closer to the relic people and peered at them. A thousand years underwater, and there was a lot left down here, wasn't there? I shouldn't have come down here. This was a bad idea. I started to feel something about the world tilt in my brain, some core truth. It was so big it took my breath away, and I stumbled in my haste to get back to the platform.

This was foolish.

I scrambled back to the platform and grabbed the rungs of the ladder. I looked up and was overcome with the sheer number of steps it was going to take to get back up. The water curled softly against the platform. I was going to drown down here if I stayed, and likely going to be drowned by the people up there if I went up.

I climbed. God knows I didn't want to, but I did, because the future beneath me was bleak. I climbed and climbed as the world went dark. I had only the sound of my own breath for company. I had to rest often. I slipped, once, dangling there in the salty wind, wondering if I should let go.

The world is a lie, their propaganda said.

God, what a lie.

I crawled back up into the belly of the lower island and collapsed on the soft stone there, desperate to catch my breath. Someone was there holding a lantern, and it hurt my eyes.

When my vision adjusted, I saw that it was Moravas. She knelt beside me and handed me a sling of water.

"Did you get what you came for?" she asked.

"That was a trick," I said. "Those are all ancient people."

"No," Moravas said. "Those are my parents."

"You're a liar," I said.

"Your parents are there, too."

I pressed my hands to my ears. "Stop with this. It's propaganda. It's lies."

"They tell you the world is dead down there," Moravas said,

"but it's not true. It's only sleeping. They put them all to sleep and buried the world so they could make this one. They had no power in the other world, and that frightened them."

My arms were too tired to keep them pressing my hands to my ears. I relented. I gazed at the ceiling. "I'm an orphan," I said. "The relics are a thousand years old. A thousand years ago God punished us and buried the world in water."

"Do you know the power of story?" Moravas said. "It takes only a single generation to change the entire story of a people. Ten years. You take the children off to state schools. You tell them a story. You make it illegal to tell any other. People forget. The world moves on. But I don't forget. I can't forget what was done to the world below us."

"Why?" I said.

"They did what they did because they don't know how to fix things," she said. "So they buried them and started over and told us it was our fault. They said we were lucky humanity had any future at all after they drowned the world."

"The coven?" I said.

"Among others," she said. "Children are easy to manipulate. It's easy to lose your past, to lose your story."

"I won't believe this," I said. "Propaganda."

"Believe what you want," she said, "but it doesn't change the truth. It doesn't change the fact that the device in your pocket is just fifty years old. It wasn't made by a god or a sinner or saint. Just a woman. A human being like you. We can build that world again. We can have that future. But we must spread the real story."

"Propaganda."

"You keep using that word. But do you know it applies just as well to the stories you were told?"

"I have to go," I said. I hauled myself up and onto the stairwell behind me. I expected her to call out, but she didn't.

I spent most of the night wandering the lower islands, trying to dispel the propaganda from my head. A world built on lies, on stories told to children. Did Solda know? Was she old enough to remember something else? She'd never told me. No, no, I was falling for the lies.

But who would I be, if it was true? If I wasn't the story they told me of myself? If I wasn't the orphan of children killed in a fire, if I wasn't special for being a boy who survived the plague, if my memory wasn't a necessity but a convenient tool I had honed for a state that didn't want me to understand the creeping of time?

I couldn't accept it. I couldn't accept that the whole world was a lie, because that left me with nothing. It would leave all of us with nothing.

At dawn, I found myself on the street outside the antiquities shop. I gazed up at the tower room. The man there must have come to work early, because he was already studiously perched behind his typewriter. I could almost hear the clack of the keys. I had stuffed my scarf in my pocket, because I was afraid the Guardians were looking for me. It was only a matter of time before they found me, and I didn't know what I was going to say to them.

Instead, I wanted to see the man, and see if the shopkeeper had bought him a hat. I wanted to know if he liked it. I wanted something real in all this pain and sin and all the gory lies.

I walked inside the shop. A little bell tinkled, one I hadn't noticed before. The doughy woman looked up from her abacus and fixed me with a dark stare.

"What are you here for?" she said.

"I want to see the man upstairs," I said. "Did he like his hat?"

"He's working right now," she said, gaze going back to her work. "Come back tomorrow."

I stepped around her and headed upstairs. She had a lot of bulk to throw around, but I was much faster, even exhausted and sleep deprived. I took the stairs two at a time and came up into the tower room. There were crates and dusty heaps of old-world detritus, harmless trinkets and household items and other, stranger types of things like the ones Moravas had.

And there he sat at the window, still bent over his typewriter. The sun was rising bright in a clear blue sky, shining right through the window, and I squinted as I rushed forward. I saw him only in outline.

"I had hoped to find you here," I said.

As I approached and my angle to the sun shifted, I noticed something uncanny in the way he sat. He was hunched over working, yes, but there was no liveliness to his limbs, no sheen to his dark skin. He glistened softly in the light. It was not his clothes that shimmered, but his skin, because he wasn't a man, but a relic, an anachronism. He was one of those dead ancestors hauled up from the depths of the sea for us to gawk at and second-guess. He was not a man, not a man, not a man . . . The world is built on lies.

I sank to my knees and stared at him.

"You wish to buy him?" the store keeper said, huffing up the stairs.

"Please leave me alone," I said softly.

I heard her breathing behind me for a moment more. Then the stairs creaked, and she headed back down.

I got up and sat on a box next to the relic. He had been frozen here in this pose, slightly hunched as if at a typewriter, and the shopkeeper had put an antique typewriter there in front of him. It might be illegal to use a typewriter, but it was fine to own one, and she probably hoped to sell the two as a pair. She had hidden this relic in plain sight, and avoided people like me who would have confiscated it.

We built this world over the bones of lies. It's fake, just like the man in the window. It put bitter, angry, violent people in power, and now here we are, living in a whole world of lies built around a cold, hollow core.

We are sinners. And I am the worst kind. Because I did not cry out, or yell about a better story, or take up arms, or resist. I wanted my old story back, the one about the world where I was so very special, and we were the chosen of God, not the detritus of some great greedy coup. Instead, I dug around in the crates up there until I found a hat, and I placed it at a jaunty angle atop the relic's head, and I sat there next to him as the sun rose again over the world. I thought about how I had become the worst sort of sinner. Not just one who steals relics or defies the coven.

I'm a sinner who wants his feet on solid ground.

THE WOMEN OF OUR OCCUPATION

THE DRIVERS WERE BIG WOMEN with broad hands and faces smeared with mortar grit, and they reeked of the dead. Even when we did not see them passing through the gates, ferrying truckloads of our dead, they came to us in our dreams, the women of our occupation.

My brother and I did not understand why they had come. They were from a far shore none of us had ever seen or heard of, and every night my father cursed them as he turned on the radio. He kept it set to the resistance channel. No one wanted the women here.

My brother got up the courage to ask one of the women, "Who stays at home with your kids while you're here?"

The woman laughed and said, "You're our children now."

But I knew the way to conquer the women. When I was old enough, I would marry them. All of our men would marry them, and then they'd belong to us, and everything would be the way it was supposed to be.

We woke one night to the sound of a burst siren. The scream was only a muffled moan in the heavy, humid air.

My mother bundled up my brother and grabbed the house cat.

My father made me carry the radio. We hid in the cellar under the house, heard the dull thumping of bursts.

"They're looking for insurgents," my father said. He turned on the radio, got only static. "You know they castrate them."

"Hush, Father," my mother said.

My brother started crying.

The death trucks and the mortar trucks came the next morning. The women loaded up the bodies. They shoveled away the facades that had come off the houses. Our house was all right, but the one next door had been raided. The yeasty smell of spent bursts clung to everything. The house had fallen in on itself.

I saw them bring out a body, but I couldn't tell who it was. My mother pulled the curtains closed before I could see anything else. She told me to stay away from the windows.

"Why are they here?" I asked her.

"I don't know," she said. "No one knows."

One night, many months into the occupation, two women came to our door.

My mother answered. She invited them in and offered them tea and bloody sen. The sen would stain their tongues and ease their minds, and the tea was said to warm women's souls. If they had them.

The women declined.

I stood in the doorway of the kitchen and peered out at them. My brother was at the table eating cookies.

The women asked after my father.

"Working," my mother said. "Men's work. He's an organic technician."

One of the women stepped over to the drink cabinet. She flicked on the radio.

My mother stood very still. She gripped her dishrag in one hand, so tightly I thought her fingernails would bite through it and cut her palm.

The radio played—a slow, easy waltz. Someone had tuned it back to the local station.

"Your husband's study, where is it?" the other woman asked.

"This way," my mother said. My mother looked straight at me. They would have to come through the kitchen.

I ducked back into the kitchen and slipped into the study. I pulled open the top drawer. My father's gun was heavy. Blue and green organics sloshed in the transparent double barrels. I'd never held it before. I didn't know where to put it. Father's papers were there, too, papers about the resistance that he said we weren't supposed to touch.

My brother had followed me in. He waddled up to the desk, stared at the gun.

"You're in trouble," he said.

"Quiet," I said. "We'll play a game. Sit here. I'll give you more cookies."

When the women came in behind my mother, my brother and I were sitting up on the big leather sofa by the window. I opened up Father's screes board. My brother stared at the women.

The women went right to the desk. I tried not to look at them. They opened up the gun drawer.

The largest woman turned to me. She wore a long dark coat, even in all the heat. Sweat beaded her big face.

"Come here," she said.

"He's only—" my mother began.

"Here," the woman said.

I got up. She put her big hands all over me, patted me down. She looked around the room. Looked back at us.

"Get out," she said. "We're cleaning this room."

I took my brother by the hand. The three of us went to wait in the living room. My mother kept staring at me. I gave my brother more cookies. We sat and listened to the sounds of the crashing and tearing coming from my father's study.

After a long time, the women came out. They stood in front of us and put their hats back on.

"Good evening," they said.

"Good evening," my mother said.

When they were gone, my mother held out her hand to me. I pulled up the back of my brother's shirt and took out the gun and the papers. My mother cried. She pulled us both into her arms.

My father did not come home that night. Or the next night. We got a telegram from the women. They had taken my father away for questioning. He would be kept for an undefined period.

We were alone.

With father gone, we had no money. The lab he worked for wouldn't send us anything. They were afraid that the women would accuse my father of something.

The neighbors came and brought over food and ration tickets. My mother went to each house afterward and asked if they needed laundry done, or shirts mended, but they all said the same thing. They were saving their own money. No one could help us.

"What about the women?" I said. "Who mends their shirts?"

My mother frowned at me. "Certainly not their husbands," she said.

So my mother allowed the women into our house, and she mended their shirts. She cleaned and pressed their dress pants, their stiff white collars. My brother and I shined their boots.

It was strange, to have the big women in the house, wearing their long dark coats and guns. My mother did not speak to them any more than she had to. When they came in she held herself very stiffly. She pursed her mouth. Her eyes seemed very black.

I tried to hate the women, too. They always greeted me like the man of the house, because they had taken my father. If I was the one who answered the door, they always asked my permission to see my mother. They were very polite. Sometimes they would talk to each other in low voices, in their own language. It was soft and rhythmic, like the memory of my mother's voice before I could understand the words.

After a month of this, one of the women said to my mother, "It will be a shame when your husband returns. We will have no clean shirts."

My mother just stared at her. I had never seen her look so angry.

When my father did come back, red dust filled the seams of his face. His hair had gone white. The spaces under his eyes were smeared in sooty footprints, a dark wash against his sallow skin.

He had no marks or scars that I could see. He still had all of his fingers. But he walked with a limp that he had not had before, and he could not close his left hand into a fist. He became very quiet. He spent most days sitting in a chair by the big window, staring out. He did not speak to us. He could not go to work.

My mother had to keep mending shirts. When the women came, my father moved his chair into his study and shut the door. He started smoking opium.

The air inside the house was heavy all the time. My mother sent me out more often to run errands for her. She didn't have time to go to the market herself. Father never left the house. My brother tried to go with me, but mother made him stay behind to shine the boots.

On the street, I met other boys with homes like mine. Their fathers had all been taken in as well. I went out with a group of them to throw rocks at the windows of a women's barracks. But the women were waiting for us. They grabbed the oldest boys. They shot them in the head.

I didn't leave the house for a while, after that. I hated the women. I hated them, and I dreamed of them.

The women were making changes. They draped their country's colors over ours. They did it first at the police buildings, then the government buildings. Fewer trucks of bodies and mortar rubble passed through the gates. There were fewer night sirens.

After a year, I noticed something else, though my mother said I imagined it, said I was giving the women more power than they had. The summers were not as hot. The air wasn't as humid. The women were changing the weather, too.

My mother tried to make things normal. She tried to get me and my brother to go to the new schools, the ones the women opened after shutting down ours. In those schools, all of the teachers were teenage girls. Our girls, but girls just the same.

What were we supposed to learn, from girls?

The women in our house kept coming. Some of them lived just down the street now, in houses where the owners were killed or deported for being part of the resistance. When I asked one of the women if she ever got lonely in the big house, she said no, she never got lonely.

"I live with my sisters," she said.

"Why don't they do your laundry?" I said.

My brother was shining her boots. My mother looked up sharply, but I didn't care. I was the man of the house. I could say what I wanted.

The woman just laughed like it was the funniest thing she'd ever heard.

Some time later, I met a girl at school I liked, and she liked me, I think. But the next year, she left school because she wanted to join the new fighting squad that the women had started. Girls were allowed to join when they were fourteen. I got angry when she told me she was going.

"What," I said, "you want to learn how to kill people like those women do? You'll be just like them."

She glared at me. Black eyes, like my mother's. "They won," she said. "It won't be so bad to be like someone who wins, will it?"

"Won? What did they win?"

"Everything," she said.

I left school, even though it made my mother angry. I got a job unloading fishing boats in the bay. There were mostly men down there, though the women were posted around as guards and they had put a bunch of girls in charge of customs. Those women made a lot more money than any of us working the boats.

I once heard one of the men say something nasty to the customs girls. He called them whores, and traitors, and said he could fuck the traitor out of them. He said it in front of two women working as customs guards. One of the women pulled out her gun and shot him. I still stayed on in my mother's house. Father's health got worse. We lost more and more of him to opium.

I sat with him one hot night during the monsoon season. All of the windows were open, letting in the rain, but he wouldn't let me close the house up. Mother had taken my brother to the hospital. He had an infection in his lungs.

"I have such dreams," my father said. He reached for my hand. I let him take it. His hand was cold and clammy in mine, despite the heat.

"I dream that the women came from another world," he said. "They came on boats made of spice and spun sugar. We disappointed them. They're too hungry for us." He turned his blank stare to me. "They're going to eat us."

There was a new woman on watch at customs. She looked at me only once, but I couldn't help but follow her with my eyes. She was big and tall like the others, and her face and hands were broad. She had a dark complexion and tilted green eyes, like jade. She looked twenty. I wasn't even sixteen. I didn't think she noticed me. But she caught me heading home and said, "The streets are not safe for boys. I'll bring you home."

She was a head taller than me, but she moved like water. We walked through the maze of deserted streets bordering the harbor and passed under a gaslight. She suddenly took me by the arm and pulled me into a dark alley. I choked on a cry. She pressed me against the gritty wall of an abandoned warehouse and shoved her hand down the front of my trousers. I struggled, but didn't say anything. Her big body and long coat shielded me from the street. No one could see me. No one at the dock. Not my mother. Not my father.

I gripped the back of her neck, dug my fingers into her hair. She pulled me into her.

When I saw her again, she was with a group of women by the customs house. I nodded at her. She turned to the other women, said something in their language.

The women all looked at me. They laughed.

All of the women kept looking at me. They kept laughing. I had to leave the docks.

I got a job driving mortar trucks through the gates. Most of the women had given up those jobs by then. They were all working in government and security positions.

During the day, I went to the ruins of old houses. I could still smell the yeast of old bursts. I shoveled up all the raw material and loaded it into the truck. I met other young men like me. I met men who had wanted to be teachers and doctors. It was the women, they said, who held them back. The women took all of the jobs. The women were too intimidating. The women owned the world.

One night, I drove my mortar truck through the gate and stopped at the big pit where the bodies and rubble were heaped. The women had bombed out the original government offices, long before. They used the deep pit left behind as a waste dump. I sat in the truck and stared out at the pit for a long time.

I got home sometime just before midnight.

My mother sat alone in the dark living room. She sat staring into the empty fireplace. A pile of neatly folded laundry sat at her hip. Shirts hung on the line in the kitchen.

"Do you want some light?" I asked her.

She was very still.

"Is father all right?" I asked.

"He's passed," she said. Her dishrag lay in her lap. She did not touch it.

I went upstairs. Father lay in bed. A single gas lamp flared, casting dark shadows. There was a bloody, clotted smear against the far wall. Half of father's head was gone. I saw the gun near his limp hand. His eyes were still open.

He had left no note.

Some women came to collect the body, though a man drove the body truck. One of the women turned to me just before they left. "We all battle dragons," she said. "There's no shame in losing."

"There'd be no battle," I said coldly, "without the dragons."

She grinned, slid her hat back on. "There will always be dragons," she said. "It's only a matter of who plays the dragon, who plays the sheep. Which would you rather be?"

I spent the rest of the night in the market square, watching the women. Sunrise rent the sky like the remnants of a red dress. I couldn't remember the last time I'd seen a red dress. I didn't miss them.

I watched the changing of the guard. I bought a newspaper. It was in two languages now, ours and the women's. I kept turning the page back and forth, back and forth, but I could see no difference between one and the other.

All the news was the same.

THE FISHERMAN AND THE PIG

NEV SAT ON THE END of the charred pier, casting his line again and again into the murky water in the hopes of catching a corpse.

A new war raged thirty miles upstream, and if Nev was patient, he could often hook one of the bodies that washed down the river. Beside him, Pig, a little pot-bellied pig, lay snoring softly in the folds of the cloak he had shed as the suns rose over the gray water. Mist still clung to the water's edge, and he caught a glimpse of crested herons poking around in the shallows for breakfast.

The rise of the suns made the horizon blaze red-orange. Nev felt a tug at his line and reeled in his catch. It was not a body, alas, but a little trout with a pouting face. He tossed it into the basket beside him with the others. Today's catch wasn't good; the river had been fished out upstream, or maybe there had been a change in the fish runs. They came and went, those runs. He only had about six small fish to sell at the market this morning. He might as well just eat them.

Nev packed up his gear, eager to get to the market before the last of the stalls was taken. He poked Pig in his belly to get him to wake. Pig gave a little snort and rolled back over and went back to sleep. Nev gently pulled the cloak out from under him, dumping Pig on the pier, and that woke him properly. Pig rolled to his feet and regarded Nev with a perturbed look.

"You're the lazy one," Nev said, and shook out the cloak and wrapped it around his shoulders. He grabbed the basket of fish and threaded his pole through the top and turned back up the smoky pier. Mist made it difficult to see more than three paces ahead, but Nev spent every day but Prayer Vigil on this pier, and he knew how to avoid the worst of the cracked and worn boards. Pig followed, so close Nev felt the whisper of Pig's little breaths on his ankles.

As he walked off the pier and onto the road, two men waiting there moved into his path, effectively cutting him off from transitioning from pier to boardwalk. Nev tensed. They didn't have the look of government people, or Body Guild enforcers, but times changed quickly, and he couldn't be certain what agents of either were like anymore. He had lived out here in this backwater town for eight years. The death of his body manager, Tera, had left nothing for him in the cities. Tera had died in her sleep a year before she turned seventy. She had a little smile on her face and a bottle of her favorite bourbon in her hand. If he were to ever die, really die, he hoped to go the same way.

Tera had preferred to be near people and public houses. He hadn't. So, he had packed up himself and his pet turtle and come out here. The morning he arrived, the little pot-bellied pig had burst out of the butcher's door and squealed across his path. Nev had bought the pig, and called him Pig, because he had expected he'd eat it himself, eventually. Eight years on, that seemed less likely. Between the turtle and the pig, that was company enough for Nev.

These men were not welcome. And by their aggressive postures, they knew it.

"How's your catch today?" the one on the left asked. He was a beefy man, without tattoos or piercings, lean and brown, with an unremarkable complexion and a forgettable face.

"Not well," Nev said. He did not attempt to summon a smile, but he held out the basket for inspection.

The man on the right leaned over, though he was barely tall enough to clear the basket's rim. "You sell these?" the man asked.

"I suspect you know I do," Nev said. "I have a stall reserved in the market."

"We don't, sad to say," the short man said. He nodded at the railing behind them where two large baskets overflowing with fish were just visible through the mist. "My name's Parn, and this is Shotsky. Think you can help? These will just go bad. You can keep a good cut. Say, seventy percent."

"Eighty," Nev said.

"Sure," the one called Parn said, and that made Nev's spine tingle, just a little. They had offered too high, and not bothered to haggle. Bad sign on top of bad sign.

Nev glanced down at Pig, who was snuffling at the men's bell-shaped trouser hems.

"I'll take a basket," Nev said. "To see how it goes."

"Sure, sure," Parn said. "Shotsky here will carry them for you, eh, old man?"

Nev grimaced at being called "old," though by every measure he was certainly old. The body he currently wore was the sort that accumulated a great deal of hair, from bushy white head to busy white toes. He had tried, in vain, to tame some of it but had given in and grown it out long and scraggly. His beard ended in a little tail that nearly reached his belly button, and the braided rope of his hair was the same length in the back. He had longed for some of the spry, smoother-skinned bodies of his youth for years, until he remembered that no one would even think to look for him in a skin as foreign to his people as this one.

Unless these men had?

You are too distrustful, Nev thought, but it was that distrust of and disappointment in people that had kept him alive this long. He had learned to measure time in bodies instead of years, until he lost count of the bodies, too, sometime after the third war he'd fought in for the Body Mercenary Guild.

Nev called Pig back to him and waved at the men to follow him to the market. The entire enterprise was not auspicious, but he couldn't figure out their game. What did he have to lose if this was legitimate? Perhaps the fish were bad. If the fish were bad, no one would buy them anyway, and he could say so honestly. There were some criminal enterprises making their way down the river, and if this was the first foray of such a family into town, he didn't want to be on their bad side. What bothered him was why he had stood out to them at all. Was it the age of the body? He must look old and feeble to them, an easy mark.

The man called Shotsky put the big basket of fish in the middle of Nev's stall. Now that the suns had fully risen and he could see the fish properly, Nev saw that they were fresh, gleaming things, so radiant and dewy-eyed one could almost believe they were alive. Early morning shoppers were already moving to the stall, drawn by the beautiful fish.

"We'll come back tomorrow," Parn said, and winked. "Good luck!"

Nev had no trouble selling the fish. They were lovely, cool, and intact. They didn't appear to have been tampered with and bore only the usual damage to fins and scales that one would see from wild trout. Nev decided the fish must be stolen goods, something the men had taken out of the back of a cart and didn't want to be found with. The sooner Nev sold them all, the better.

The fish were nearly all gone by mid-afternoon when the market closed for the hottest part of the day. Only two remained in his basket, and those were the smallest of the bunch. He added them to his own catch. What he didn't eat for dinner, he could cook up for breakfast for him and Pig.

Nev trekked across the thinning market and out of the village square. He lived up on a little rise about a mile outside the village in the rough-hewn cottage that the man who inhabited the body before him had built, likely with the two well-worn hands that Nev used to open the door.

The coals from the morning fire still smouldered in the stove. He went out to the little pond in the back where his pet turtle lived. The little turtle had grown large over the years and was now as long as Nev's arm. It surfaced in front of Nev, and Nev fed it one of the little fish. He watched contentedly as the turtle ate, then went inside and stoked the fire and cooked up his little fish.

He left the door open in the front and the back to invite a breeze. While the village was small, his neighbors had learned to leave him be. He had found this body much farther up the mountains, dead for a few hours, no more, because the beasts up there had yet to tear it apart. Nev had been ready for a change, then. When he came back into the village, he found that the man had been a hermit, and that suited Nev just fine. He could pretend at being an old, mad hermit. He had been pretending at that most of his life.

Pig sat at the base of the table where the two large fish remained, snorting his complaints about not being able to eat them. Nev got up and took one from the table and tossed it to him. Pig squealed and pawed at it.

He noted some movement outside and peered out. Shotsky was making his way up the path to the house. Nev felt a chill, though surely, the man was just coming for his money?

A sharp, familiar scent caught Nev's attention. He scrambled back to the table where Pig was tearing into the fish and snatched the fish away from him. He grabbed its body so hard that its guts escaped through the tear Pig had made in its belly, and the tangy scent of cloves and lemon assaulted his nose.

The gooey insides splattered all over Nev's hands, and in that moment he was transported to a battlefield eighty years back, when he bore some other body. The air smelled just like this, and all around him were the dead and dying. A woman on the ground reached out to him, her fingers grasping for him, and he had scrambled away from her, shrieking, because he knew she wanted to kill him and take his skin, the way he wanted to kill her and take hers, because the bladders full of toxic goo that had exploded on the field were murdering them all . . .

Nev gasped and wiped the toxin off on the table. He hurled the fish into the sink and scrubbed his hands, knowing already that he was far too late. His flesh puffed up around where the liquid had touched him, and his tongue went numb. He turned just as Shotsky entered.

"You sell them all?" Shotsky said, and then he stopped still, because he must have smelled it too.

The toxin was rushing through Nev's bloodstream now, and in his experience, that meant he had about two minutes on his feet before his organs failed.

Shotsky folded his arms and shook his head. "Shouldn't have opened those up, old man," he said.

Nev knew for certain, then, that this man had no idea who Nev was. If the man had known, he would not have stood so close to him. The man would have run.

Nev did not like violence, as a rule. He knew too much of bodies. But violence was his profession, had been since he was just a young girl in a rural little wastewater like this one. Eight years, and the outside world had let him alone. They had been good years. But the outside always intruded, eventually.

Nev kicked Shotsky in the kneecap. The man howled. Nev thrust a palm into his face and felt his own bones jarring in protest. His mind knew how to fight, but this body was not fit for it.

Shotsky pinwheeled back and tripped over Pig. Pig squealed and ran behind the loft ladder, shrieking.

Nev picked up his stool and bashed Shotsky over the head with it. A sharp pain ran up Nev's arm, causing him to drop the stool. He hissed and clutched at his arm. Tingling numbness was already running up his hand and into his shoulder; the toxin doing its work. He grabbed the fish from the sink and sat on Shotsky's chest and shoved the fish into his throat. Shotsky's eyes bulged. He flopped on the floor, clawing at his own face.

Nev suspected he would regret doing this, later, but all he could think about now was murdering this man as quickly as possible. Nev had fished no corpses from the river this morning. He had no fresh bodies to save him. The only corpse he could jump into today was one he made himself.

Shotsky choked and swung hard. The punch took Nev clean off him and onto the dirt floor. Nev saw blackness, heard a terrible crunch. Something felt strange in his mouth, and he knew his jaw was broken. Shotsky came up spitting toxic fish mush, yowling at Nev in some language he didn't know.

Nev drooled blood and spit. The numbness had moved into his chest now, and into his other arm. He could only kick his feet helplessly against the floor.

Pig romped over to him. Nev tried to yell at him to go back, to stay away or he was going to become Shotsky's dinner, but he couldn't form any words. It all came out a garbled moan.

"You have killed us, you stupid little man," Shotsky said, and slapped Nev. The pain was so intense that Nev saw a brilliant, glaring light spill across his vision. Heard his bones grating against one another. "We are lost," Shotsky said, "lost to the God of Light. Lost to the cause of the righteous, you foolish old man."

Shotsky fell heavily onto his side. He gasped and clawed at his face, which was likely going numb.

Nev tried to reach out a hand to him, for his own comfort

more than any other, but neither arm worked. Pig clammered up on top of Nev, pushing his snout into Nev's hair. All that gory hair. Nev would miss the hair. He stared into Shotsky's bullish face, wondering which of them would die first. Nev had more experience at holding it at bay, but death came to every body sooner or later, even body mercenaries.

Pig snuffled and pressed himself into the crook of Nev's neck. Nev wanted to comfort him. *It's all right, little pig*, he wanted to say, it's all right. But it was not all right.

Shotsky huffed out a breath. His eyes went still.

I beat you, Nev thought, grimly. I outlasted you. He said a prayer to God's eye, out of habit.

And then, he leaped.

Nev experienced a moment of darkness, then a buzzing softness, like that muzzy place between sleep and wakefulness. And suddenly: blazing consciousness. It was always shocking to come awake inside a new body. Nev gasped. He tasted fish, and the tangy acid of the toxin still swimming in the body's throat. His throat. My throat, he thought, because the sooner he claimed the body as his, the easier it was to use it.

Nev heaved himself up and stumbled to the sink. Shotsky's body—my body, Nev amended—was tall and beefy. It had been a long time since Nev had been in such a body. He pushed his hands into the sink and turned on the tap that ran water down from the cistern on the roof. He scrubbed his hands and washed out his mouth. He vomited, then, fish and toxic goo and whatever the body had last eaten. His bowels loosened, and he shat and pissed himself. His limbs felt like dead meat, but that would pass. His second wind would come soon, the wind that burned out whatever ailed this body and refreshed it for its new host.

He stood over the sink, breathing heavily, until his new body filled with a cramping, searing pain, like birth. His legs buckled, and he fell to his knees, big hands gripping the edge of the sink. This was how he had been reborn a thousand times, a mercenary who would never die, leaping from body to body as long as there were fresh bodies on the field that he could put his hands on. He had fought this way for so long he hardly remembered who he was or where he had come from.

But the toxin, he knew. The toxin had murdered a good many people. Soldiers he loved as brothers and sisters, back in those days when he could still care for anything human.

Nev pulled himself upright and peeled off his clothes. They had been filthy before he soiled them. Nothing he had here would fit this new body, so he would have to wash them.

He balled up the clothes and washed his body as best he could in the sink. When he was clean, he turned.

His former body was curled on its side. It looked vulnerable and delicate, like a twisted flower. And there, tucked into the crook of the neck, was Pig.

Nev approached the body, still naked, calling to Pig. "Can you come here, Pig?" he said. "It's me, Pig!" His voice sounded strange, because of course, from inside this head, the voice that he had heard as Shotsky's sounded very different.

Pig raised his head and peered at him, then buried his face back into the comforting braid of hair that had fallen across his former body's shoulder.

Nev knelt next to the body. Blood pooled from the mouth. He was careful not to touch anything, as some of the toxin could still be on the floor and on the body's skin. "Come, Pig," he said softly, but still, his voice sounded deep and gravelly.

Pig did not stir.

Nev didn't want to leave Pig alone with the body because it could still be contaminated. So though it pained him, he pulled on a pair of old gloves and picked Pig off the body and rolled the body up in an old sheet. He hauled the body up into the loft, grateful for this new body's strong arms and legs. Nev avoided looking into the face of his old body. When he was done with a corpse it became a thing, a tool, like a pen or an ax.

Pig squealed at him throughout the ordeal. He ran around in circles, irate at what was being done to the body it knew and loved.

"Come, Pig," Nev said one last time as he moved to the threshold. But Pig trotted up to the end of the ladder and lay down and gazed up at the old corpse there in the loft.

Nev rubbed at his eyes. He needed to keep moving, because if he paused to think about what he needed to do now, he would lose heart. Someone had deliberately used him to offload those fish; even many buyers were likely in on what he was selling. Maybe they had even meant for him to die, too, and he didn't take kindly to that. People who tried to kill him often came back to finish the job. He took his cloak, which was a cast-off large enough to cover him, from the wall, and knotted it around his thick waist with an old length of rope.

Nev walked outside, shielding his eyes in the low afternoon light. At the bottom of the path leading up to his house was a llama. Two llamas, in fact, hitched to a small cart filled with empty baskets. Llamas. It had to be llamas.

"You know where you're going?" he asked the llamas. One of them bared its teeth at him. "Good," Nev said, "because I don't."

Nev climbed up into the seat of the cart and took up the reins. He had seen a few llamas around the village, but never driven a cart pulled by them.

"Forward," Nev said. "Go?" He flicked the reins.

The llamas looked back at him sedately. "Dinner?" Nev suggested. "I'd like to have a word with Parn."

That seemed to spur some latent memory, and the llamas trundled up the path and around Nev's house, heading back toward the village. Nev held the reins loosely, hoping they knew where they were going. If nothing else, maybe they would take him to a tavern where he could drown out his memory of this whole day.

But the llamas took him instead through the village and halfway to the next, down a little pebbled path to a dilapidated wreck of a mill along the waterfront. They halted in front of a big, empty feed trough and made a little humming sound, oddly soothing after Nev's day.

Nev got down from the cart and turned just as little Parn came out from the mill, wiping his grimy hands on a leather apron.

"Where in the seven hells have you been?" Parn said. "What happened to your fucking clothes?"

Nev considered his options. He walked toward Parn, the mud squelching pleasingly between his toes. Nev took Parn by the throat and lifted him. It had been a long time since he could do something like that, and he reveled in it.

Parn kicked and gurgled.

"What's the game?" Nev said. "Who's handing that weapon out?"

Parn moved his lips. No sound came out.

Nev lowered him so his toes touched the ground, and eased up his grip. Parn gasped. "The fuck are you?"

Nev tightened his grip again. "I had a very happy life here as a very happy hermit, and you've fucked it up."

"Just a job," Parn sputtered. "Who the fuck . . . oh fuck . . . fuck . . . you're . . . you're a corpse jumper! Corpse mercenary! Fuck you! Fuck!"

"Let him go!"

Nev turned. A young woman was scrambling out from underneath the musty blanket in the back of the cart. She was in her late teens, all knees and elbows. Her dark hair hung into her face. She leveled a crossbow at Nev; not a homegrown version, either, but the sort carried by soldiers. Her clothing was torn and filthy; it was a wonder he hadn't smelled her from his place at the front of the cart, but his senses were imperfect when he was still getting used to a body.

"This doesn't concern you," Nev said.

"It sure as shit does!" she said. "He murdered my sisters with that shit in the back."

"There's a great deal of filthy language being bandied about," Nev said. "Is it necessary?"

Color flooded her already dark face. "I've been at the front," she said. "I can skewer you through the eye."

"To what end?" Nev said. "You can murder him when I'm done."

"You can't murder him," she said. "He knows where the necromancer is."

"Necromancer?" Nev said, because he had not heard that word, in any language, in decades.

"Necromancers make that shit in the fish," she said. "It brings the dead back to life."

Nev had a moment of dissonance. "It . . . does what?"

Parn was still struggling, limply. Nev released him. Parn tumbled to the ground, gasping and clawing at his throat.

Nev turned to the girl. "I know that toxin," he said. "It murders people."

"Sure it does," she said. "Then it brings them back to life. They're testing it up there at the front, and out here, because no one gives a shit about backward people out here."

Nev said, "I think I need to find this necromancer." He couldn't help but put a hand to his own throat. This body had swallowed the fish, and the toxin it contained. So had his prior body. But if it brought the dead back to life . . . which dead was coming back into this body? Nev broke out into a cold sweat.

He kicked over Parn and pressed his bare, muddy foot to the man's throat. "You heard the girl," Nev said. "Where's the necromancer?"

The girl's name was Branka, and according to her she was seventeen, "nearly eighteen," and had enlisted the year before to fight in "the war." Nev did not ask what the war was about because it was assumed, in every age, that when one spoke of "the war" everyone else knew exactly which war they were talking about.

Branka insisted on coming with him, though he tried to dissuade her. She did know how to use a crossbow, and that seemed handy. Nev found some clothes inside the mill that fit him, though no shoes. Nev took it upon himself to drag Parn up into the mill and strangle him. It was done cleanly and without malice. A body mercenary needed a body. It was quite possible he would need this one later.

Branka saw him come out alone but did not ask about Parn.

"If he was telling the truth," she said, "the necromancer's only four days away by cart. We can do that faster, in two days maybe, if we take turns driving."

"Llamas need rest," Nev said, "like people. You can't drive them into the ground."

"Sure, sure," Branka said. "I knew that, you know? I'll drive first."

Nev said nothing, but neither did he protest as she got up into the cart. He spent some time gathering a few supplies around the mill, and then they were out onto the road again, bumping along.

"So you're really a corpse mercenary?" Branka said. She glanced at him out of the corner of her eye. The world lay at the cusp of evening, but it was nearly summer, and the day would stretch on another couple of hours. Nev wanted as many miles between them and the mill as possible before dark.

"We called ourselves body mercenaries," he said, "back when we did that."

"I wondered," she said, "when I saw you come out of that house.

I mean, a guy went in, but it was clear some other guy came out. I thought maybe that old man put a spell on you."

"Not far off, really."

"Yeah, I guess. So you could jump into my body, then?"

"Only if you were dead."

"Was that meant to be comforting? Because it wasn't."

"I'm simply clarifying," Nev said. "It's not as if I cast out your soul. Your soul is already gone when I inhabit your body."

"Like a parasite," she said.

"I prefer to think of myself as a snail," Nev said.

Branka nodded. "Sure. A worm."

Nev sighed. "What are you intending to do when you meet this necromancer?"

"Same as you, I expect," Branka said. "I'll kill him."

"Because he killed your family?"

"Sure," she said. "You?"

"He murdered my life," Nev said, and he thought of Pig. "This life, anyway."

"There's always some other life for you, though, isn't there?" Branka said.

Nev shrugged his broad shoulders. He was beginning to get used to this body. He enjoyed the heft of it. He rubbed at the stubble on his face. "I liked my life," he said. "I don't always like the lives I have."

"So why not just jump into some other one? You know, I thought all you guys were extinct. Burned out. Hunted down. I've never met a real corpse mercenary."

"I haven't met another one like me in a long time," Nev said. "The world was different then."

They rode on in silence until dark. They didn't make camp so much as simply halt. Nev wrestled with the harnesses for the llamas and let them graze. After a time, they started up their humming, which he hoped was a good sign.

Then he lay in the back of the cart with Branka and pulled his cloak up over them both. They lay pressed together, warmed mostly by the heat of their bodies. Above them, the great spinning orbs of the God's wheel tracked across the sky. Nev was reminded of the night before, when he had sat out under the stars with Pig and his turtle and breathed in the scent of the new grass and been still, so very still.

"Can you have sex?" Branka asked. "I mean, not now, but just . . . generally?"

Nev started. "What sort of fool question is that?"

"I mean . . . do you shit like other people?"

"You've seen me piss. These are very personal questions."

"I'm a curious person," Branka said. "Plus, if we're going to fight a necromancer together, I want to know something about you."

"Better not to," Nev said. "I haven't asked about you."

"I noticed," Branka said. "It's polite to ask people questions."

"I find it rude," Nev said.

"Not me," Branka said.

"Clearly," Nev said.

She sighed heavily. "My sisters raised me," she said. "I was the youngest. I enlisted last. My brothers stayed home and made some good matches, you know, but we all had heads for tactical stuff. Well, my sisters did. Not me, so much. They looked out for me. But on the field, that day, this same smell . . . like rotten lemons . . ."

"I know it," Nev said.

"Everyone died," Branka said. "I saw them die. I was up a tree, though, acting as lookout, trying to get us back on the road. Navigating from maps is shit, you know? I don't know how they got us. Catapults? From where? But that stuff ended up in the air. Pretty big wind. I guess it all blew out when I came down. But that guy came by later, Parn. And I followed these guys for weeks. Weeks! And I heard about the necromancer when they talked at night."

"Long time to track them," Nev said, because she seemed to want some kind of human response. It had been so long since he'd engaged in a sustained conversation that he had the urge to flee.

"They were my sisters," Branka said.

Nev had a fleeting moment where he remembered his own sisters, all older, all dead now. "I understand," he said.

"Have you ever fought a necromancer?" Branka said, and he heard the hopeful expectation in her voice.

"No," Nev said, "but there's a first time for everything."

Four days later, they wound their way into the little green valley that Parn had told them about before Nev wrung his neck. Torture, as a rule, did not work often, but Branka's earnestness had helped. Parn might not have believed that Nev would spare him, but he hoped Branka might. It had been enough.

The valley was lovely; a little crease in the world, set against the sparkling, wine-dark sea. At the center of the valley was what had once been a little village, now just a charred ruin. The only building that still stood was the silver temple to the Eight Sisters of God.

Nev reined in the llamas beside the temple and tied them to the hitching post outside.

"Now what?" Branka whispered. She had her crossbow out.

"First," Nev said, "put that fool thing away."

Nev stepped up into the temple and pushed open the double doors. The benches were all focused around the center of the room. There, an altar stood with a great orb fixed atop it. The light of the suns drenched it from a hole in the roof, sending dazzling little colored spots of light dancing around the room.

A woman sat at the farthest seat from the door, head bent over a book. She was an old plump woman with a cloud of white hair and a kind face. She reminded Nev at once of his grandmother on his mother's side. He remembered his grandmother braiding back his hair and telling him to be a good strong girl.

The woman raised her head from her book and smiled at them.

"You must be the corpse mercenary," she said.

"Everyone keeps calling me that," Nev said. "I'm a body mercenary."

"New words, same profession," the woman said, and stood.

"Are you the necromancer?" Nev asked.

"I prefer the term 'knowledge seeker.'"

"New words, same profession," Nev said.

She laughed at that. "Oh, you are clever," she said, "but I suppose one has to be, to survive as long as you have."

"You don't know me," Nev said, with more conviction than he felt. It was impossible that he had given away who he was. He could be any number of body mercenaries. They had fled like insects after the last great war, set loose by a terrible act.

"I know your type," the woman said, and she began to walk toward them.

Nev raised a hand. "That's far enough," he said. "I'm inhabiting a body killed with your serum. I need to know what happens when it comes back to life."

The woman raised her brows. "Indeed," she said, "so do I."

"You don't know?" Nev said.

"Of course not," she said. "Why do you think we've been testing it? Many governments have been working together over the last fifty years to eradicate the last of the rogue corpse mercenaries. The body-hopping must stop. You must rest."

"I decide when I rest."

"That's a selfish thing," she said.

"Hold on here," Branka said, and out came the crossbow, too fast for Nev to bat it back down again. "You're murdering people. You murdered my sisters."

"I murder a lot of people's sisters," the woman said. She pointed at Nev. "He has murdered more. He has even murdered himself."

"She doesn't have any answers," Nev said. "Let's go." He would find out soon enough what would happen to him.

He turned just as he heard the clink and hiss of the crossbow bolt.

"Dammit, Branka!" Nev said as the crossbow bolt thumped into the necromancer's chest. She grabbed at the bolt and grimaced.

"Foolish," the necromancer said. "Foolish."

The air around her began to darken. Nev thought it was a trick of his eyes, but no. A swirling mist kicked up around her, darkening the room.

Branka yelled and barreled toward her.

Nev called after Branka. The air filled with a low buzzing sound—flies. They seemed to burst out of the mist, made from motes of dust. The flies clogged his mouth and eyes, and he began to scream. He had woken up like this many times, covered in flies, screaming.

Branka was tangling with the necromancer, using her crossbow like a bludgeon. The waves of flies pelted her, buffeting her away from the necromancer like a strong wind, but she was persistent.

Nev clawed his way through the swarm of flies. He gripped the necromancer by the collar and head-butted her in the face. Blood burst from her nose. Her legs buckled. She collapsed. The wall of flies collapsed with her, becoming a misty cloud, like smoke, that dissipated.

Nev let himself collapse on one of the benches, spent. He was trembling.

Branka stood over the body of the necromancer, crossbow still in hand. "Is that it?" she said.

Nev coughed. He spit up a couple of flies. Grimaced. But there was something deeper, something caught way down. He coughed again, harder this time. Again. He had trouble catching his breath.

"Are you all right?" Branka asked.

Nev heaved. His whole body trembled. The world began to feel fuzzy, and he was filled with the blazing warmth that suffused him each time he came awake in a new body.

"Go," Nev said. "He's coming back, Branka. Go."

"What about you?" Branka said.

Nev showed his teeth. "There is always another body."

The darkness took him.

Nev woke in the loft of the mill, gasping and screaming. He rolled over and vomited and gazed at the little hands that had once been Parn's.

The necromancer had done it. She'd thrown him out of a body. If he hadn't had another backed up somewhere/here . . . If he had only relied on the others from the battlefield, dead and contaminated . . . He shivered. They were coming for him, and people like him. He had been foolish to think that if he lived a peaceful life, they would forget about him. People like him could never be peaceful. The world didn't let them.

Nev walked all the way back to the hermit's cottage, unsure of what he would find there.

When he stepped up to the door, it was already open. He gazed up into the loft and saw the sheet he had used to cover his former body. But the body was gone.

The old hermit was alive again, brought back from the dead. He shivered.

Nev walked into the back. He didn't see the turtle anywhere, but the turtle was likely as safe here as he would ever be. And there, at the corner of the house near a rain barrel, he saw Pig.

Pig lay there in the mud, very still.

Nev approached, resigned. They took everything, all of them.

The little pig stirred, then, and Nev's heart leaped. "You silly pig," Nev murmured. "He didn't know what to do with you either, eh?"

He knelt beside Pig. "It's me," he said. "It's me, Pig."

Pig snorted and shook his head and trotted away a few steps. He cantered around the yard. Pig came to rest in the doorway to the house, legs splayed, and stared at Nev.

Nev sighed and leaned back on his heels. "You can't stay here," he said.

Nev took up a sack on top of the rain barrel and managed to corner the little pig in the kitchen and scoop it up. Pig shrieked and flailed inside the sack. Nev always hated the sound of pigs shrieking. It sounded too human. He knotted some twine around the top of the sack and collected a few other things.

He didn't like to take much when he moved from town to town. Too many unique items could identify him from body to body, and then it was only a matter of time before someone from the Corpse Guild caught on and captured him, and that would be the end of his very long travels. As much as he wanted closure some days, the deep fear of death, of going where he had watched so many others go, won over every time.

Nev knotted the sack of his belongings to the end of the sack with Pig in it and slung both over his shoulder. It would be dawn soon, and he wanted to be well clear of the town by then.

As the suns rose, he traveled up and up into the hills, mile after mile. The way was rocky, churning with mud. Finally, they came to a little clearing. Light brightened a soft blue puddle way back in the woods, and on the other side of that, Nev saw a little family of wild pigs snorting around in the undergrowth.

Nev untied the sack with Pig in it and gently released him.

Pig cantered out into the light, kicking up his heels. He trotted away from Nev a few paces, turned back.

Nev was down on one knee in the mud, the sack in one hand and an apple in the other. He tossed the apple to the pig.

"I know I don't look like him," Nev said, "no beard. Not enough hair, eh? That's all right. You take care, little pig. You're more human than any of us."

Pig snorted at him.

Nev got up. He shook the filth from the sack and tied it back up with his other belongings. All he had in the world, again. On to the next town, again.

Where to, next? War upriver, death downriver. It was time to cross the river.

Nev headed farther up the path, kicking up dirt and loam as he went. He wondered if Branka had heeded his warning or murdered the body he had left behind in the temple, the one that no doubt now housed Shotsky's soul again. No matter how far Nev ran away from the world, it always came back for him.

He heard a little snort behind him, and turned.

Pig had come forward a few paces. He stood there, head cocked, snorting.

"What is it, Pig?" Nev said. "Pig?"

Pig kicked up his legs and barreled toward Nev. Nev got down on his knees and opened his arms, and the little pig hopped into his lap and pressed his nose to Nev's face, snorting and snuffling all the while.

"Are you coming then?" Nev said. His throat closed, and his voice shook. He cried as he rubbed the little pig's waggling butt.

After a time, Nev stood. Pig gazed up at him adoringly. Nev took a few hesitant steps forward. He called for Pig, still afraid he would not come. But Pig trotted after him, content to follow his new family. Together they forged across the road as the suns broke through the trees.

GARDA

DEAD YOUNG MEN kept washing up on the crooked sandbar that abutted the black ruins of the palace on the pier. The body lying now at the feet of Inspector Abijah Olivia was positioned facedown in the sharp black glass of the beach. Abijah wore heavy boots to protect her from the sand, but the body was not so lucky. Barefoot and mostly naked, thousands of tiny lacerations peppered its sallow grayish skin. Tattered remnants of black and gray clothing still clung to the body in places, giving the impression that the corpse was an old, ancient fish that had fought throughout its ascent into the air, then was abandoned here in the ruin of some net. The lower half of the corpse lay at an awkward angle, as if the torso and legs had been twisted in opposite directions. Clumps of black hair still clung to the head, but Abijah noted two chunks of scalp missing just above the neck, as if he had been yanked by the hair so hard that it had come free. The great hooked-beak birds patrolling the coast could have done that after the body washed up, she supposed, hoping to snag the long hair for their nests. More answers would come from the medical examiner.

"Sorry catch, you are," Abijah muttered, squatting next to the body. She poked at the left wrist with a stylus, pulling up a necklace of pink kelp to reveal a work tattoo. Like the other dead men she had seen on this sandbar, this young man appeared to have been employed at the wight factory upriver, which was run by the last of the operations that accepted off-world labor. Being off-world would account for the body's tall, slender frame and weak bones. The twist to the lower body could have just as easily happened postmortem, when the corpse hit the water. If he'd already been a corpse, at that point. One of the previous young men had actually drowned; the others had been dead hours before meeting the salty water.

The crunching of boots across the volcanic glass alerted Abijah to the arrival of what was most likely the garda assigned to the case. Abijah turned to see the woman duck beneath the webbing that secured the scene. She fixed Abijah with a wintry look. Abijah knew the stout little woman, all hips and ass, who shoveled toward the body like a rugby forward prop ready to hit the opposition at pace.

"You're not assigned to this case," Garda Katya Sobrija said. Behind her, the yellow lights of the garda ambulatory unit blinked muzzily through the mist. This far south, the sun never really set; this moody, yellow-ochre dusk was as dark as the island would ever get.

Abijah offered up her wrist, and a blooming insignia and the relevant signatures misted up from the interface written into her skin. "Not doing it for the garda," Abijah said. "Private contract."

"You've got to be kidding me," Katya said, pointing her fingers at the projection and accepting the data transfer. Her eyelids flickered as she reviewed the data privately, streamed onto her retinas. "Fuck's sake."

"The garda had three chances to solve this one," Abijah said. "Now it goes private."

"Provided somebody pays for it," Katya said. "Who's paying?"

"That's confidential," Abijah said. "You saw it's been sealed."

"Concerned citizen, huh?" Katya said, stuffing her fists against her waist. "Who else you working with?"

Abijah shrugged and gave a little smile. She turned her attention back to the body.

"Oh no, fuck," Katya said, pulling at the cigarette case in the front pocket of her slick. "I have six complaints out against that—"

"She'll be fine," Abijah said. "She's been sober a month."

"And you?" Katya said, tapping out a cigarette.

"Gave it up," Abijah said, "the way you gave up smoking last summer."

Katya grimaced and popped off the tip of the cigarette to light it. "Simple pleasures," she said.

"You're contaminating the scene."

"Not my scene anymore, is it?" Katya said. "How's Maurille and Savida?"

"Divorcing me," Abijah said. "Said they were happier with each other."

"Sorry to hear it. The kids?"

"Already on the continent for the exams," Abijah said. She rose and tucked away her stylus. "Hold the scene for the medical examiner. Bill your time to the account."

"This is the biggest shit," Katya said.

"Definition of insanity is doing the same old thing, expecting a different result. You need fresh eyes on the case."

"You don't even know it's connected to the other boys."

Abijah snorted. "I don't know if the sun will come up over that horizon today either," she said, "but I can tell you that it's pretty likely." She crunched back across the sand, moving past Katya, and noticed a gleaming bit of detritus at the edge of a large, smooth hunk of volcanic glass. She stooped to pick up the object, and hooked it with her stylus. It was a gold-plated button stamped with a grinning round head fitted with a monocle. Abijah knew the farcical design immediately, because it was used on the all-weather coats issued to garda when they reached the Inspector level and above. She had one herself.

Abijah pulled out a bit of sticky evidence gum and gobbed it over the button, then slipped it into her pocket.

"What's that?" Katya said, coming up behind her just as she hid the button from view.

"Bit of pretty flotsam," Abijah said.

"You're a terrible liar," Katya said, and flicked her cigarette butt onto the glittering beach.

"Sorry about your pasties," Pats said, chomping on the last two bites of something flaky with a gooey center as she pushed inside Abijah's apartment door.

"Thanks for saving me some," Abijah said.

Pats licked her fingers. She was missing the ring and pinkie fingers on her left hand; both ended cleanly at the knuckle. "Just making sure they aren't poisoned," Pats said. "I got your back. And your guts. Such as they are. Used to be my guts, some of them."

"You get the files?"

"Sure," Pats said. She set the pastry box on the divan and pulled a green folder from inside of her long black coat. Pats sank into the divan and put her muddy boots up on the rock table. She wet her fingers and opened the folder.

Abijah sat beside her. The folder contained several pages of sketches depicting the park and gardens nearest the local garda station.

"You're getting better," Abijah said, pulling out one of the slippery pages. The ink could be wiped away with a simple solvent and the pages reused.

Pats peeled back the inside front cover of the portfolio, revealing a double helix-shaped strand of green code. She pulled it free and it floated up into the air, untangling itself.

Abijah set her interface to receive mode and downloaded the data before it self-destructed, breaking apart into a fine mist and blowing away under the strength of her breath. Abijah quickly streamed the data across her vision: case notes, snaps, crime scene recordings, reports, for all three of the previous murder cases for the off-worlders who had washed up on the sandbar.

"This everything?" Abijah asked.

"Everything stored in the general case file," Pats said. "It hasn't been secured. So, yeah, if there's anything else related to the case that they've got, it's not linked to these cases in the server. Always a chance there's something buried in a file another some code name. But I just don't get that anyone cares enough about these cases to go to the trouble."

"'Cause they're off-world?"

"Sure," Pats said, reaching forward to dig out another pastry. It oozed raspberry filling that glopped onto her fingers. "These are good."

"Who left these?" Abijah said, pulling at the top of the box.

"They're for Maurille," Pats said, "from that bakery she sponsors."

"Shit, Pats, I'm already on the outs with Maurille."

"All the more reason to eat her pasties." Pats grinned wolfishly. "When they kicking you out?" Her gaze moved to the tubs and plastic barrels half-full of Abijah's belongings.

"Had the talk last week," Abijah said.

"You don't sound surprised."

"Been bad awhile."

"What they tell you?"

Abijah popped open the top of the box and grabbed the last pastry; strawberry. Maurille's favorite. "They told me I'm too emotionally unavailable," Abijah said.

Pats guffawed and slapped her own knee. "That's a great one! Youse hooked up during the war! They expect you to change?"

"Guess so," Abijah said, and bit into the pastry. "You miss living on the continent?"

"Nah," Pats said. "I live on a good disability pension." She cocked her finger against her head. "Upside to being a nut. But I do miss the war."

"You miss killing."

"Eh, well, that too. Garda get touchy about that, way touchier than in the war, you know? Bad sports." Pats stood and wiped her hands on her coat. "You let me know if you need anything else."

Abijah dug into her pocket and pulled out the button in its clear webbing. "You take that to the medical examiner, have her look at it? She's on your way home."

"Sure," Pats said, shrugging.

"Kids all worked at the same factory," Abijah said, "judging by the tattoos. Can you confirm that, too?"

"Those reports should."

"I need to know about this fourth one, though. Can you look into his family?"

"Aw, you always want me to do the messy people shit."

"It's because you're so personable," Abijah said.

"Blah, blah," Pats said, and waved her fingers at her. "Ah, before I forget!" She reached into her coat pocket and pulled out a large, copper-colored can of rum, then winked. "A divorce gift!"

"I'll need a lot more of those," Abijah said.

Pats grinned triumphantly and pulled a second can out of her other pocket and thunked it down on the table with satisfaction. "One for each spouse!" she crowed, and flounced out the door.

Abijah popped open the can before the door had closed and took a long drink. Private work had its benefits. Sobriety was not regulated, and certainly not expected, when someone hired her. Her window screen covered the entirety of one wall, though a large section on the far left was glitchy, which meant the beachy scene she had programmed into it appeared to have a massive black hole zigzagging along the boardwalk through which tourists disappeared as they rambled out of the frame. She opened her interface and ordered up a wintry scene from the continent, something recorded in the Black Hills before the shelling of Solosia. Everything existed in some bio-digital memory these days, even the places long dead—countries, continents, starships, whole worlds, entire systems, so many one could get lost trying to count them, like trying to make a map of the stars from a starship heading out for the edges of a universe that was still expanding, stars blooming ahead and dying behind, endlessly.

She asked for one of her favorite curated news channels and watched the headlines streaming to the right of the projection. She could just as easily have played it all across her retinas, but when she was home she preferred to switch off. Boots on the table, drink in hand, she asked for the highlights of a few headlines about the case, mostly nonprofessional takes on the recent murder and the usual half-dozen conspiracy theories from unhinged folk on the edges of the colony. To each their own, she supposed.

Abijah finished her first can of rum as the world began to grow more bearable at the edges. A persistent message tap-tapped at the edge of her vision, a little red arrow indicating a conferenced call from Maurille and Savida. She brooded on it a long moment, then popped open the other can and accepted the call. The safety notification asked her to confirm she was not currently mobile or operating any type of machinery. She checked "no" and her wives' faces filled her vision.

Maurille and Savida projected an image of themselves that was certainly far removed from wherever they were currently holidaying on the continent. They both looked severe and buttoned up, as if expecting a business negotiation to break out at any moment. Maurille, tall and lean, like an exceptionally well-bred tree, was older, her face softer now around the edges. Maurille and Abijah had married first, and Savida had come later, a slim woman a decade their junior whose fisher-family had supported her schooling in bio-environmentalism on the continent and then welcomed her back as a local government resource steward. Somehow the two of Abijah's spouses grew more serious, brought together, no doubt, when Abijah had gone away to the war. When Abijah came back, maybe, there had been time to repair what the three of them had, but she hadn't been ready back then. Wasn't ready now.

"Are you drinking?" Maurille asked, softly concerned.

"Nah," Abijah said, sipping her rum.

Savida made a face, because though Abijah had chosen a fine upstanding image of herself to project to them, they could certainly hear everything.

"We're calling about the dog," Maurille said.

"What dog?" Abijah said.

"There was a dog in the apartment," Savida said, "when we came to get our overnight bags for the trip up. Did you get a dog?"

Abijah turned to look around the room; the motion of her head flipped the full-screen of the faces to the bottom left corner of one eye, letting her get a view of her actual surroundings instead of the projected ones. "No dog here," Abijah said, but she got up anyway, sipping the rum as she did, and checked the two bedrooms, the closet, and the little balcony, just in case.

"No dog," Abijah said. "No paw prints. Not even a shit."

Maurille said, "It was quite clearly in the apartment."

A knock came at the door. Distracted, Abijah wondered if Pats had come back to try and lick the inside of the pastry box. She opened the door, hoping for a distraction from her wives—and got a fist in her face.

The blow was so unexpected it took her right off her feet. She sat back hard on her ass, black spots juddering across her vision. The can of rum sailed off to her right and collided with the cold box in the kitchen. The call with her wives went dead; their faces disappeared. Her window blinked dark, and then lights cut. She had already pulled her blackout curtains, so she couldn't see anything at all. She had time to note three figures advancing, one of them with a six-legged dog on a leash, before they swung the door into the hall shut, completing their cover.

Three against one was bad odds sober during a fair fight, let alone drunk while on the floor and parted from her interface. At least it solved the question about the dog. These folks had been casing her place earlier. Thank fuck they hadn't touched Maurille or Savida.

They proceeded to beat the ever-loving shit out of Abijah. They wore heavy, steel-toed boots that landed hard, savage blows to her chest and stomach and back. One mashed her in the face, dazing her. She wished, then, that she had finished the second can of rum, because she would have felt less and blacked out sooner. Instead, she went limp, letting them think she was down and out for good. The boots gave them away. This was a small town, and only garda wore boots like that.

As Abijah squinted at them through her one good eye, blood leaking down her face, one of her attackers opened the door, and in that slanted light from the hall she saw one of them, a squat figure, put her fists to her broad hips, and then self-consciously pat at her left breast pocket for a cigarette case.

"Little fucking weasel," Abijah muttered, or tried to. Her face wouldn't cooperate, which was just as well.

They gave her a couple more kicks, and then the combination of pain and drink finally took her away, mostly.

Abijah dragged herself into proper consciousness only to find she had a dry mouth and painfully empty stomach. She wanted to eat a whale. She gagged and heaved, but only drooled saliva onto the floor. She wasn't sure how long she'd been out, because her curtains were still drawn and her interface still wasn't back online. She crawled to the door and planted her hand in something soft and foul. Dog shit. The fucking dog had shit in her fucking apartment.

She snarled and flailed to her feet, fumbling her way to the wash room with her non-befouled hand. The lights were still off—nothing came on as she entered the room—but the water worked, and she scrubbed her hands and face clean. She put some pain-killers in via fast-acting eye drops and pocketed a vial for later. They were prescription-only drugs, but she didn't technically have her own prescription for them.

Abijah tripped the emergency generator, cycling the power back on, and tromped down the stairs to the pub to get a drink, because sometimes that was the only thing that solved her problems. Certainly calling the garda to report being beat up by gardai wasn't going to further her cause. The stiffness and pain bled out of her with every step as the drugs did their work, fuzzying the edges of her discomfort until she felt tired more than anything else.

She pushed open the door to the pub and found the pub owner, Maliki, engaged in an engrossing game of some kind on her interface.

Abijah waved a hand at her and called out, breaking Maliki's concentration. Maliki blinked and focused on her. "Where the fuck you been?" Maliki said. "Been trying your interface for an hour. Maurille called and said you cut out."

"Need a reboot," Abijah said. "Got a juicer in the back?"

"Sure, the kid's back there. You in trouble with the law again?"

"Pour me a drink and I'll tell you," Abijah said.

"Pay your tab and I'll pour a drink!" Maliki called after her, but Abijah was already through the heavy curtains into the sprawling muck of the back room. Maliki's kid, Popsy, bore a huge monocle over one eye, surgically implanted more for show and shock value than practicality. Popsy sat hunched at a loom full of disembodied interfaces. She swung her massively magnified brown eye in Abijah's direction. Her hair was bright green, shaved on both sides and curled up on top into delicate ringlets like a fancy sea anemone.

Abijah sat next to her on the skull of a whale and held out her blank arm. "Garda wipe," she said.

Popsy clucked at her. "In deep already? Didn't you take the case yesterday?"

"Always been popular with the garda. Bestest friends."

Popsy rebooted her interface and got it blinking at her again. There were two messages already from her wives, one from Pats, and one from her client.

"Thanks," Abijah said, blinking open the message from her client as she headed back out to the bar and initiating a call before it had even started replaying.

"You owe me another favor!" Popsy said.

"Sure!" Abijah said. "I'll pretend I didn't see all those illegal interfaces."

Popsy spit at her.

Abijah settled up at the bar. She and Maliki were the only ones up. Her interface told her it was only three hours after dawn. Good a time as any, she supposed, and chugged the beer Maliki had left on the bar.

Rylka vo Morrissey dominated her vision as the call connected, and Abijah blinked her back to her left eye only. Rylka sat out in her garden in a little automatic chair, or was projecting herself that way, surrounded in white and red roses with little purple tongues and waspish petals. During very wet seasons, roses often bred wasps, which made them the sort of hobby only those with a lot of time and maybe some masochistic tendencies got into. In the garden behind her, Abijah glimpsed a few laborers' heads bowed to the task of cutting back the roses and watering their little flickering tongues. Rylka, like most of the vo Morrisseys, had a degenerative condition caused by chemical bursts during the war that limited her mobility. Abijah had the same thing, from the same cause, the doctors all said, but it was curled up in her like a serpent, waiting for some external condition to trigger it, like a bomb waiting in her body.

"Your interface went down last night," Rylka said. "Is everything all right?" She was young, slender and reed-like, with bold features and a full mouth that lent her otherwise willowy appearance some gravitas.

"Got beat up by some garda," Abijah said, "so your instincts were right. They're certainly eager to keep me from finding anything out."

Maliki reappeared with a cold pack and bashed it on the counter to activate it, then handed it over to Abijah. Abijah gratefully pressed it to her throbbing head.

"You're continuing the search?" Rylka asked, and her eyes got all big and dewy. "I'd hate to think—" Rylka was descended from some of the founding families. While terms like *rich* and *wealth* weren't really in vogue out here where everyone was supposed to toil alongside each other and share in the world's prosperity, she was certainly well insulated and . . . well-gifted by her colleagues in exchange for political favors. Abijah was counting on being well-gifted for her own services, too. Everybody needed a good word at the council when shit went down.

"Following up with the medical examiner today," Abijah said.

Rylka let out her breath. "Good," she said. "These deaths are worrying to me personally, and to the council. If they get the attention of the continent, we could very well find ourselves occupied by their police forces. Our garda should be able to handle this issue. My family has proudly served among the garda for generations, and I won't have a small crop of bad actors open us up to injury from the continent."

"If they come down here, it'll be shit trying to get them to go back," Abijah said. "I get it."

"Thank you, Abijah," Rylka said, and ended the call.

Abijah finished her beer and left a digital IOU on Maliki's public message board.

She caught a trolley out front and took it up north toward the forensics and medical research buildings while reviewing the message from Pats.

"Confirmed the kid works up at the wight factory," Pats said. "Meet you there after lunch. You'll love the dirt I've got on the owner. Real piece of war work, that one."

Abijah confirmed the post-lunch date and stepped off the trolley at the medical examiner's building. She transferred her credentials to the desk, which was automated, and it admitted her into the building.

When she got upstairs, the medical examiner, Bataya, was waiting for her.

"How's your sister?" Abijah said.

"Still annoyed you haven't called," Bataya said. "How are your wives?"

"Still in love with each other," Abijah said. "What do you have for me?" She moved past Bataya and into the morgue. The young man's body lay atop a grooved stone slab. Without the tatters of his clothes, he looked even more diminutive and sad, a shriveled flower. Abijah ran her hands under the protective glove sprayer and shook the film on her hands dry, then approached the edge of the table. He had already been cut open; just a small incision in the chest and on the inside of the thigh where he was pumped full of recording devices that traveled throughout his body taking recordings, tiny and mobile as his blood had been.

His face was lacerated; he had been lying on it when she last saw him.

"You must have his name," Abijah said. "Pats verified where he was working."

"Yes," Bataya said, moving to the other side of the table. "Turns out this one didn't drown either, just like the last one. He was dead of head trauma before being dumped." Bataya was a small woman, nimble, with luxurious purple-black hair and faux gray eyes. She was studying for a certificate in combat yoga and advanced reiki; maybe she'd already earned them. It had been months since Abijah was last in here. They had only almost slept together once, or as Abijah had explained it to Pats, "We were going to have sex . . . but then we decided not to." And Abijah blamed that on the alcohol. Or perhaps her own fascination with what a woman trained in both reiki and combat yoga would be like in bed.

"Did Pats give you the button?" Abijah asked.

"Yes," Bataya said, and her mouth thinned, and Abijah wondered if she'd done something wrong. Bataya went over to the counter and fished out the button, which rested now in a glass dish. The evidence webbing had been removed from it. Bataya set it directly on top of the body's chest.

"It's a garda Inspector-class, all-weather coat button," Bataya said, "which I assume you knew. The rest—there's no evidence on it. No fingerprints. No DNA. No unusual organic material. It's possible this was just something washed up on the beach near the body."

"How'd you know it was near the body? I didn't tell you or Pats that."

She smiled thinly. "Particles," she said. "That beach has a very unique signature because of the burning of the palace. Lots of base metals, including mercury, after it got blown up during the war, settled into the sand there. It was toxic to swim there until twenty years ago."

"So the body had these same particles, then?"

"Of course. I mean, it was found there."

"Both sides, clothing too, I mean. Nothing out of the ordinary there? Let's say the body had been dropped upriver, say, near the factory? Would it bear traces of other particles from its journey downriver that could help us identify where it came from?"

"I see," she said. "Well it did, yes. The fingernails tend to be good for that. No human DNA under them, but there was silt, and it's not a match for the beach near the pier. That's all glass. That beach is glass all the way up to the factory."

"So the body was dumped no further south than the factory."

"A reasonable conclusion. But that leaves a hundred kilometers of river." She pursed her mouth. "I was getting to the silt under the nails, you know. But you started with that banter about the button."

"Entirely my fault."

"Just so," she said, and sniffed.

"Any way to match the silt to a smaller patch of river?"

She sighed. "We can try, but you should know that the garda aren't happy about me running these tests."

"It's a private contract," Abijah said, "from Rylka vo Morrissey. They can be unhappy all they like, but the job is legitimate."

"I've seen the order," Bataya said, "or I wouldn't have let you in."

"It's good to see you again too," Abijah said.

"You didn't have to call me," Bataya said, "but you should have called my sister."

"I've been—"

"Drunk?" she suggested.

"That too. But . . . on a case, so."

"On a case for a day," Bataya said. "Sorry, you just . . . disappoint me a lot. All the time."

"We'll keep things professional, then. I promise."

Bataya sighed. "I'll buy you a drink."

"One drink," Abijah said. "But later. I'm meeting Pats at the factory to ask about the boys."

"Boys," Bataya said, shaking her head. "We had no word for such a thing, sixty years ago."

"We did," Abijah said, "it just wasn't very polite."

Pats waited outside the factory gate, chewing on betel nut leaves and scratching at what Abijah confirmed were mosquitoes as she stepped off the trolley and onto the packed gravel of the factory road.

"You look like shit," Pats said. "Garda?"

"Katya was with them," Abijah said, "if you can believe that."

"No shit? Cheeky weasel."

"That's what I said."

Abijah presented her credentials at the gatehouse and asked to see the factory supervisor. There was a human attendant here, and she closed up the door and conferred with a superior for a few minutes before admitting them. Abijah fixed her with a grin, but the woman only glared at her.

Inside, they were met by one of the owner's aides, maybe a secretary or a deputy, who warbled on the whole time as if they were there for a public investor tour.

"We employ over six hundred people here," the little birdish woman said; she was approaching fifty, and she zoomed about in a little chair like Rylka vo Morrissey's, no doubt afflicted by the same ailment. Nobody asked about injuries much, after the war. Not sober, anyway.

"All off-worlders?" Abijah asked.

"The floor workers, yes," the woman said. Which meant most everybody. "Management and skilled labor are all local. You can see our public safety records. We abide by all treaties and accords. Getting placed here is considered a boon for off-worlders."

"No doubt," Abijah said, "when the alternative is living three thousand to every cramped can in the sky."

"Certainly we provide them with many opportunities!" the woman said, and showed them into the factory owner's office.

The desk was clear of all items except a single nameplate, which read, "Ofram Fucking vom Amadson." One wall was projected with a view of the factory floor, a teeming morass of bio-machines and humanity merged to perform complex manufacturing tasks. The woman behind the desk blinked and rose as they entered, no doubt immersed in some real-time shooter on her interface. She was a top-heavy woman with razor-cut hair dyed a bright red; the fringe was long and hung into her eyes. The haircut made her look young, but if Abijah had to guess, she'd say the woman was forty.

"You own the place?" Abijah said.

"Can we call you 'Fucking'?" Pats said, and that elicited the smallest moment of confusion for Ofram, who seemed to have momentarily forgotten about the nameplate.

"Ah," Ofram said, giving a smile that was so obviously forced it hurt Abijah's own pride to watch it. "The nameplate, yes. A joke from my mother. Can I help you? I read over your credentials. You're looking into the death of the workers? A tragic case."

Ofram didn't invite them to sit, but Pats did anyway, and Abijah followed. She tracked the movement of the workers on the floor as she did. "You all made weapons here during the war," she said. "What you make now?"

"Fertilizers, cleaning products," Ofram said, settling into her own seat again. Behind her was a stretched canvas banded in several colors. Abijah couldn't figure out the medium, but it seemed like a freshman effort.

"You play rugby?" Pats asked. She had brought out a little switchblade knife and was cleaning her fingernails with it.

"No," Ofram said. "Did the boys play rugby?"

"We're here about the latest one in particular," Abijah said. "Name was—" She glanced at Pats, realizing she never had gotten around to getting his name from Bataya. Shit, she was as bad as all of them.

"Sam Kine," Pats said. "I have his little tin pod number here"—she tapped her head—"which I'm sure you used to tell his family he's not coming back."

"That's correct," Ofram said. "We were given permission to beam out that message."

"And you're getting a replacement sent down, then?" Abijah said.

"Per the treaty," Ofram said, "yes. It's protocol. There's really nothing strange about it. The boys here get lonely and stupid. They don't understand water. They never see much of it up there, and when they get here they get dangerous in it. Go paddling around, and the little fucks can't swim, and they drown."

"Three of the four didn't drown," Abijah said. "They were dead before they hit the water."

"There is disagreement among the boys," Ofram said. "They fight a lot in those cans up there. Hard to break them of it once they're here in a civilized place."

Pats snorted.

"I've told the gardai all of this," Ofram said. "You can read it in the report."

"Seems the kids would be happy here," Abijah said, and her gaze moved again to the projection window. It immediately turned off, then flickered again and showed an image of a massive red cherry tree blowing in the breeze. Abijah raised her brows and regarded Ofram.

"They're never satisfied," Ofram said.

"That why you sell them out?" Pats said casually. "Got some reports that boys here get sold out for labor, the ones that don't do what they're told."

"Where did you hear that?" Ofram said. "That's against the treaty."

Abijah cocked her head at Pats. "Where *did* you hear that?"

Pats shrugged, but a message pinged at the bottom left of Abijah's vision, and she blinked it open. It was from Pats, and read,

"Maliki hears the best shit at the bar. Listen more than you talk over there, lushie."

Ofram leaned over her desk. "These people are trash," she said. "You know what we called them when they first started coming here forty years ago, twenty years after those blasted space boats got stuck in orbit on the way to some exploded star? 'Not-people.'"

"I know."

"Then you understand."

"Do I?"

Ofram said, "These people, you call them, they're aliens. Alien biology, alien urges, alien customs."

"So that justifies their treatment?"

"What do you think?" Ofram said. "Dogs are tools. These boys are tools, too. Companion animals. They send us these ones because they're useless to them. They don't bear babies. They can't feed babies. At best, they're useful for brute labor, and that's what we use them for too. Maybe it's not us you should be questioning, but the sort of people that send their own down here to dig shit and die."

"One last question."

"Quickly, now. This factory doesn't run itself."

Could have fooled me, Abijah thought. "You ever been a garda? Anyone in your family served civilian?"

"Certainly," she said, "my grandmother was Inspector Sixth Class."

"You have her coat?"

"What?"

"The all-weather regulation coat everyone above Inspector gets. You have it?"

"Those have to be returned to the garda on retirement," she said. "So no, I don't expect so."

"Not in any storage cellar somewhere? Maybe reported lost so a kid or a cousin could have it as a memento?"

"Not that I'm aware, no. Why?"

"Just tying up some loose ends."

Abijah ended the interview, and Pats followed her out.

"That woman's a piece of shit," Pats said.

"You don't know that Maliki's information is good," Abijah said. "If we ran every investigation on tips from the bar we'd have half the island in rehabilitation."

"Let's come back tonight," Pats said, "when she gets off. Someone has the grandma's coat. We soften her up, ransack her place for the coat. C'mon, what else are you doing tonight?"

Abijah thought about lean little Bataya, and combat yoga. She sighed. "Not a damn thing," Abijah said. "But I'll need a drink first."

Unsurprisingly, Ofram quit work early, heading out across the road to the trolley. Abijah waited in the shadow of the station in case Ofram slipped away from Pats, but Pats was an old hand at kidnapping, and Ofram was unprepared.

Pats pressed her switchblade directly behind Ofram's left kidney and walked her back around the side of the factory to a rear entrance. Abijah had pulled up a schematic of the place and found a little abandoned room at the top of a rickety set of metal stairs. Abijah took up the rear, ensuring they weren't followed as they trod across the catwalk that overlooked one of the abandoned factory floors. No doubt this wing had been used in the heyday of the factory when it manufactured the sort of weapons that had made toxins like the ones that were ticking away inside Abijah.

Pats sat Ofram down on a crate and pulled up another one in front of her.

"I've done nothing wrong," Ofram said. She was sweating heavily. "You ask anyone here. Everything is regulation."

Abijah leaned against the wall by the door. This one was up to Pats.

"Listen," Pats said, "I don't like the idea of you all dumping aliens in a river 'cause they won't work themselves to death here. I've seen labor camps. Not a fan."

"That's not what this is," Ofram said. "It's all regulation. Public files! You can access it all right now."

There was a banging outside on the catwalk. Abijah ducked out, quickly, to see what the noise was. One of the overhead lights had fallen against the wall.

Behind her, Abijah heard Ofram make a break for it. She whirled around just as Ofram careened out the door, Pats hot on her heels.

"Little fuck!" Pats yelled. She ran with her switchblade out. Ofram was shrieking.

Abijah ran after them. Ofram tripped and stumbled onto the catwalk below them. Pats pinned her in on the other end. As Abijah rushed after them, Ofram pressed herself against the railing. The whole catwalk creaked and juddered.

"Don't move!" Abijah yelled.

Ofram screamed. The railing gave way and Ofram tumbled, arms pinwheeling as she fell, her mouth a shocked, terrified O.

She hit the rock floor with a heavy, wet thud, like a melon.

Abijah rushed down the stairs to the musty floor and picked her way to Ofram, but it was a wasted effort. Ofram's head was split clean open, blood pouring all around her. Abijah looked up and saw Pats gazing over the broken railing, knife still out.

"Ah, well," Pats said.

It wasn't the first time an interrogation had gone wrong. Fuck, Abijah thought. "Clean it up," Abijah said. "Don't tell me anything more about it."

"Thanks, Jeesmo. You've not gone totally soft," Pats said.

Abijah grimaced at the old nickname. "Clean it the fuck up," she said.

She didn't start shaking until she reached the trolley station. Public contracts didn't excuse her for murder, even an accidental one. She waited out by the trolley station until Pats was done, and they traveled back into town sitting side by side. Pats was animated and chatty, giddy about old times. The death and cleanup had no doubt reawakened her love of wet work.

"We all come back after they train us to get good at stuff," Pats said. They were alone in the trolley car, but she knew better than to speak in specifics. "Then they tell you not to do it. Like telling you sex is great, sex is fun, have sex, and you have a lot of sex, and then they say, you know, stop. Just like that. Like, stop drinking water."

"I need a drink," Abijah said.

"Good call, Jeesmo," Pats said, thumping her on the back.

"Don't fucking call me that."

"Those were good times, Jeesmo. Good, good times."

They stopped along the way to Pats's place and picked up four cans of rum apiece and cracked them open on the walk along the canal and down to Pats's one-room garden flat. The door squeaked. The place smelled of mildew. Abijah was already good and tipsy when Pats yelled for the lights and Abijah found herself staring right at an Inspector-level, all-weather coat slung over the tatty divan.

Abijah narrowed her eyes. She snatched the coat off the divan and dropped her bag of rum. She counted the buttons. And there it was. A little tangle of synthetic thread was all that was left of the last button on the front of it.

"Where the fuck did you get this coat?" Abijah said.

"What?" Pats said, thunking her bag on the counter. "Fuck's sake, Abijah, it's mine. It's regulation."

"There's a button missing!" Abijah said. She shook the coat at Pats.

Pats's face got dark. A vein throbbed in her temple. "You think

I murder little boys?" she said. "Helpless little alien boys? I'm not you, Jeesmo."

"That was different! That was war! And this is your coat!"

"You have one just like it," Pats said, low.

Abijah huffed out a long breath. Pats was crazy, nuttier than most, but Abijah was not a paragon of sanity either. War twisted people in fucked up ways. You were never quite the same, after. "You killed Ofram back there," Abijah said. "How the fuck do I know what you're capable of? I saw you murder little kids right in front of me."

"Those kids who gave us glass mixed with ice?" Pats said. "Those cute little girls from the continent who set homemade traps that blew off my fingers and made you deaf in one ear for two years? Those sweet little things? It was a fucking war, Abijah!" Pats stormed over to her bedside table and dumped out the drawer. She grabbed something shiny from the pile of junk and threw it at Abijah's head, hard.

Abijah ducked. The gold-plated button bounced off the wall and landed heavily at her feet, the little round face with the monocle peering up at her, smiling broadly.

"Don't forget that you're no fucking saint, Jeesmo," Pats said.

It was the last thing said by the enemy captive that Abijah had skinned alive, all those years ago during the war. "Geez . . . mo . . ." What the second word was going to be, none of them would ever know, but they had found it hysterical at the time. The whole squad had laughed about it for months, probably because they were sleep deprived and high as fuck at the time.

"Get the fuck out of my place," Pats said.

Abijah stumbled outside. Her head throbbed. She needed another drink, soon, maybe all the drinks. Easy fucking case was going way too fucking wrong. She grabbed a trolley and took it uptown to Maliki's bar. By the time she got there, she had a call from her client blinking at the edges of her eyes. She slid up to the bar like a drowning woman alongside a life raft, and ordered three shots of rum in quick succession. Popsy was behind the bar, and she served up the drinks without a word, only that one glaring eye, judging.

"Rough night?" Popsy said.

"Rough fucking life," Abijah said. "What do you know about this story, that the factory workers are getting sold off for day work?"

"Sure," Popsy said. "Mostly to hoity families, you know, folks that can't get touched. They do it on the contractual day off, and after hours. Some of those kids do twenty-hour days."

"That's shit," Abijah said.

"But profitable," Popsy said.

"Profitable enough to kill kids who wanted to blow it open?" Abijah said, and her client's call was blinking still, shit, leave a fucking message . . . And then Abijah sat straight up. She remembered the heads of the workers in the gardens, and vo Morrissey's garda family.

"Fuck," Abijah said, and fled the bar.

"Hey!" Popsy said. "You owe us three eggs for those!"

Rylka vo Morrissey lived up in the rolling hills that overlooked the black coast to the south and the factory to the north. The gardens grew densely, mostly food crops, as every tended garden had to give over eighty percent of its footprint to food production. The trolley line ended at the bottom of the hill, so Abijah had to trudge up by foot, as anyone without a licensed personal flying vehicle would have to do. It was a good way to reduce visitors. And prying eyes.

In truth, Abijah had taken this job without ever visiting Rylka's sprawling estate. Rylka was only allowed to live there because the grounds were technically publicly owned. She was listed as a "public caretaker." When the people had taken back the land from private families and corporations hundreds of years ago, her family and a few others had held on this way, arguing that they were the perfect, most invested stewards of such lands. Many of them, like Rylka, could continue to build private empires beyond the walls.

Abijah had let Rylka know she was on her way with information vital to the case, so the big gates opened for her. There were no human attendants at the gates, and she saw no one as she approached, though the gardens were, as she had seen in so many projections, immaculate. They wouldn't get that way without a lot of people working there, and according to Abijah's quick search of the public employment database, Rylka's estate provided her with only four publicly funded employees.

Rylka herself opened the door. She leaned on a sturdy wooden cane, and the smile she had for Abijah nearly made Abijah quit her resolve.

"What have you discovered?" Rylka said.

"Where's the coat?" Abijah said.

Rylka cocked her head. "The coat? Are you cold?"

Abijah strode inside and went to the hall closet. She tore it open and went through the hanging garments. No, too easy. She wouldn't keep it here. The whole house was massive, quiet, immaculate.

"What are you doing?" Rylka said, limping inside.

Abijah took the stairs two at a time, heading up to the master suite. She opened the door, prepared to overturn everything in the room. But there the coat hung, right there next to the head of the bed, as if it were the most normal thing in the world. And, of course, it was—they were all tied to the garda in some way on this little island.

She felt along the front of the coat. There was not one missing button but two, right up near where it would close over the breast, and one of the buttons on the cuff was gone, too. Abijah turned over the inside of the left coat sleeve and saw a single long, black hair curled upside of it, like something a nesting bird would retrieve from the head of a bloated body washed up on the beach.

Abijah heard Rylka on the steps. "You were a fool to keep the coat," Abijah said.

Rylka limped into the doorway, casually holding an electric pistol ahead of her. "Not at all," she said calmly. She settled into a chair near the doorway, gun trained on Abijah, and shifted into the chair with a little wince. "What better way to ensure you are left alone while carting around a body than to wear a garda coat?"

"But you weren't the one wearing it."

"No."

"Ofram."

"Ofram was stupid," Rylka said, "but loyal. She did as I asked in all things. Which, honestly, could also be said of you."

"I don't get it," Abijah said. "Why hire me to dig into your own business, your own murders? You wanted to frame Pats and get me to turn her in? You must have known that wouldn't happen."

Rylka smiled thinly.

"Right," Abijah said. "That wasn't it, was it? You wanted us both implicated. With us out of the way and the garda already in your pocket there's nobody on this island to investigate you and your little off-world labor camp. Nobody from the continent will come down here unless you get too wild, and you're a long way yet from wild, aren't you? Lots more time to exploit and murder boys."

"All superior guesses," she said. "I was told you were fairly good."

"Then you should have dumped the coat."

"Ofram was to come for it after one final job for me," Rylka said. "You mucked up our plans to silence a few more choice voices."

"And saved some kid's life."

Rylka waved the gun. "Life, life, life, that's all anyone talks about. Life isn't so special. They breed like parasites on the neighboring worlds and they toss all their filth out into the blackness in big cans bursting with human filth. They breed so many they don't know what to do with them. There are people and not-people, and not-people have no place here."

"The law doesn't make that distinction anymore." A call tapped its attention at the edges of Abijah's vision. Maurille and Savida. Of course.

"Maybe it should," Rylka said.

"You don't make the law," Abijah said. She twitched her fingers, opening and streaming the call.

"Not yet," Rylka said, and raised the gun.

"Real-time," Abijah said, and blinked her emergency broadcast code.

The gun went off just as Maurille and Savida's faces popped up at the bottom left of her vision. Abijah had set the call to record what she saw, so what Maurille and Savida witnessed was Rylka vo Morrissey holding a still-glowing electric gun, her image juddering and twisting as Abijah flopped on the floor like a fish, jolted by electric current.

Abijah had time to note that both of her soon-to-be ex-wives were dressed in festive swimwear, like they were about to head out to some northern water festival. Maurille held a fruity drink in a bobonut shell, the top of it frothing over onto her fingers. Even in her distress, Abijah experienced a moment of longing and nostalgia. She and Maurille had loved those fucking drinks.

The wailing of the emergency sirens split her skull, then. Outside in the misty dusk, she saw the blaring of the garda first-responder lights. Garda. Well, that wasn't going to go well.

Rylka, her face triumphant and unaware that she was still being recorded, fired again.

The wedding announcement showed up in Abijah's curated newsfeed alongside a headline about the Inspector General from the continent arriving on the island. It was only a matter of time, Abijah figured, for both of those things to come to pass. It was a welcome distraction from the divorce paperwork she had finished the day before.

"So Bataya's getting married after all," Pats said, setting a bowl of crisped yams into Abijah's lap.

They sat on Abijah's divan in her new apartment, facing a projection screen that was half the size of her last one, but less glitchy. No one was falling into a digital black hole. The newsfeed, sensing their interest based on eye contact, popped out the wedding announcement.

Abijah didn't know the couple Bataya was marrying, but they looked like all right people. She maneuvered her bandaged hands around the bowl of crisped yams and levered it up to her face, where she could catch one of the crispy little wafers with her tongue. She hadn't been able to taste anything but metal for a week after the incident with the electric gun. Luckily Rylka had it on a low setting, or Abijah would be dead. Better still, Maurille and Savida had sent her public recording out to the police on the continent. For better or worse, those meddling little fucks on the continent were headed down to the island to clean out the gardai. Abijah's feelings remained intensely mixed about that, especially knowing the shit the continent had bombed them with still stirred in her own guts.

Pats punched her gently in the arm. "Hey, you know, we're alive for it, huh?"

"What, alive for the conquering of our country?"

"Eh," Pats said. "We were already conquered in all but name. Treaties are shit. Ask the aliens about treaties and contracts. It was all in name only to make people feel better about giving up. At least it's real now."

"Going to be real blood," Abijah said.

"Already real blood," Pats said, popping one of the crisps into her mouth. "I like the new place."

Abijah set the bowl between them and reached forward to cup her beer can in her hands. She worked to position her mouth in front of the straw.

"What you giving up for the feast of Saint Saladin?" Pats said.

"Drinking," Abijah said, and finally got the straw in and slurped her beer.

"Good, good," Pats said. "I'm giving up killing!"

"Turn off the news," Abijah said, "and let's watch something that doesn't make a difference to anything."

Pats changed the programming.

THE PLAGUE GIVERS

I.

SHE HAD RETIRED to the swamp because she liked the color. When the Contagion College came back for her thirty years after she had fled into the swamp's warm, black embrace, the color was the same, but she was not.

Which brings us here.

The black balm of dusk descended over the roiling muddy face of the six thousand miles of swampland called the Freeman's Bath. Packs of cannibal swamp dogs waded through the knobby knees of the great cypress trees that snarled up from the russet waters. Dripping nets of moss and tangled limbs gave refuge to massive plesiosaurs. The great feathered giants bobbed their heads as the swamp dogs passed, casual observers in the endless game of hunter and hunted.

Two slim people from the Contagion College, robed all in black muslin, poled their way through a gap in the weeping moss and brought their pirogue to rest at the base of a bowed cypress tree. Light gleamed from openings carved high up in the tree trunk, far too high to give them a view of what lay within. There was no need.

This tree had been marked on a map and kept in the jagged towers of the Contagion College in the city for decades, waiting for a day as black as this.

"She's killed a lot of people," the smaller figure, Lealez, said, "and she's been wild out here for a long time. She may be unpredictable." The poor light softened the contours of Lealez's pockmarked face. As Lealez turned, the lights of the house set the face in profile, and Lealez took on the countenance of a beaked fisher-bird, the large nose a common draw for childhood bullies and snickering colleagues at the Contagion College who had not cared much for Lealez's face or arrogance. Lealez suspected it was the arrogance that made it so easy for the masters to assign Lealez this terribly dangerous task, rushing off after some wild woman of legend at the edge of civilization. They were always saying to Lealez how important it was to know one's place in the order of things. It could be said with certainty that this place was not the place for Lealez.

Lealez's taller companion, a long-faced, gawky senior called Abrimet, said, "When you kill the greatest sorcerer that ever lived, you can live wild as you like, too."

Abrimet's hair was braided against the scalp in a common style particular to Abrimet's gender, black as Lealez's but twice as long, dyed with henna at the ends instead of red like Lealez's. Lealez admired the shoman very much; Abrimet's older, experienced presence gave Lealez some comfort.

Full dark had fallen across the swamp. Swarms of orange fireflies with great silver beaks rose from the banks, swirling in tremulous living clouds. Far off, something much larger than their boat splashed in the water; Lealez's brokered mother had been killed by a plesiosaur, and the thought of those snaky-necked monsters sent a bolt of icy fear through Lealez's gut. But if Lealez turned around now, the Contagion College would strip Lealez of title and what remained of Lealez's life would be far worse than this.

So Abrimet called, "We have come from the Contagion College.

We are of the Order of the Tree of the Gracious Death! You are summoned to speak."

Inside the tree, well insulated from the view of the two figures in the boat, a thick, grubby woman raised her head from her work. In one broad hand she held the stuffed skin of an eyeless toy hydra; in the other, a piece of wire strung with a long white mat of hair. An empty brown bottle sat at her elbow, though it took more than a bottle of plague-laced liquor to mute her sense for plague days. She thumbed her spectacles from her nose and onto her head. She placed the half-finished hydra on the table and took her machete from the shelf. The night air wasn't any cooler than the daytime shade, so she went shirtless. Sweat dripped from her generous body and splattered across the floor as she got up.

Her forty-pound swamp rodent, Mhev, snorted from his place at her feet and rolled onto his doughy legs. She snapped her fingers and pointed to his basket under the stairs. He ignored her, of course, and started grunting happily at the idea of company.

The woman rolled her brown, meaty shoulders and moved up to the left of the door like a woman expecting a fight. She hadn't had a fight in fifteen years, but her body remembered the drill. She called, "You're trespassing. Move on."

The voice replied—young and stupidly confident, maybe two years out of training in the city, based on the accent, "The whole of this territory was claimed by the Imperial Community of the Forked Ash over a decade ago. As representatives of the Community, and scholars of the Contagion College, we are within our rights in this waterway, as we have come to seek your assistance in a matter which you are bound by oath to serve."

The woman did not like city children, as she knew they were the most dangerous children of all. Yet here they were again, shouting at her door like rude imbeciles.

She pushed open the door, casting light onto the little boat and its slender occupants. They wore the long black robes and neat purple collars of the Order of the Plague Hunters. When she had worn those robes, long ago, they did not seem as ridiculous as they now looked on these skinny young people.

"Elzabet Addisalam?" the tall one said. That one was clearly a shoman, hair twisted into braided rings, ears pierced, brows plucked. The other one could have been anything—man, woman, shoman, pan. In her day, everyone dressed as their correct gender, with the hairstyles and clothing cuts to match, but fashions were changing, and she was out of date. It had become increasingly difficult to tell shoman from pan, man from woman, the longer she stayed up here. Fashion changed quickly. Pans dressed like men these days. Shomans like pans. And on and on. It made her head hurt.

She kept her machete up. "I'm called Bet, out here," she said. "And what are you? If you're dressing up as Plague Hunters, I'll have some identification before you go pontificating all over my porch."

"Abrimet," the shoman said, holding up their right hand. The broad sleeve fell back, exposing a dark arm crawling in glowing green tattoos: the double ivy circle of the Order, and three triangles, one for every Plague Hunter the shoman had dispatched. Evidence enough the shoman was what was claimed. "This is Lealez," the shoman said of the other one.

"Lealez," Bet said. "You a shoman or a neuter? Can't tell at this distance, I'm afraid. We used to dress as our gender, in my day."

The person made a face. "Dress as my gender? The way *you* do? Shall I call you man, with that hair?" Bet wore nothing but a man's veshti, sour and damp with sweat, and she had not cut or washed her hair in some time, let alone styled her brows to match her pronouns.

"It is not I knocking about on strangers' doors, requesting favors," Bet said. "What am I dealing with?"

"I'm a pan."

"That's what I thought I was saying. What, is saying neuter instead of pan a common slur now?"

"It's archaic."

"We are in a desperate situation," Abrimet said, clearly the elder, experienced one here, trying to wrest back control of the dialogue. "The Order sent us to call in your oath."

"The Order has a very long memory," Bet said. "I am sure it recalls I am no longer a member. Would you like a stuffed hydra?"

"The world is going to end," Lealez said.

"The world is always ending for someone," Bet said, shrugging. "I've heard of its demise a dozen times in as many years."

"From who?" Lealez grumbled. "The plesiosaurs?"

Abrimet said, "Two rogue Plague Givers left the Sanctuary of the Order three days ago. *Two* of them. That's more than we've had loose at any one time in twenty years."

"Sounds like a task that will make a Plague Hunter's name," Bet said. "Go be that hero." She began to close the door.

"They left a note addressed to you!" Abrimet said, gesturing at the pan.

"I have it," Lealez said. "Here."

Bet held out her hand. Lealez's soft fingers brushed Bet's as per put the folded paper into Bet's thick hands.

Bet recognized the heavy grain of the paper, and the lavender hue. She hadn't touched paper like that in what felt like half a lifetime, when the letters came to her bursting with love and desire and, eventually, a plague so powerful it nearly killed her. A chill rolled over her body, despite the heat. The last time she'd seen paper like this, six hundred people died and she broke her vows to the Order in exchange for moonshine and stuffed hydras. She tucked the machete under her arm. Unfolded the paper. Her fingers trembled. She blamed the heat.

The note read: *Honored Plague Hunter Elzabet Addisalam, The great sorcerer Hanere Gozene taught us to destroy the world together. You have seven days to save it. Catch us if you can.*

The note caught fire in her hands. She dropped it hastily,

stepped back. The two in the boat gasped, but Bet only watched it burn to papery ash, the way she had watched the woman with that same handwriting burn to ash decades before.

The game was beginning again, and she feared she was too old to play it any longer.

II.

Thirty years earlier . . .

The day of the riots, Hanere Gozene leaned over Bet's vermillion canvas, her dark hair tickling Bet's chin, and whispered, "Would you die for me, Elzabet?"

Bet's tongue stuck out from between her lips, brow furrowed in concentration as she tried to capture the sky. For six consecutive evenings she had sat at this window, with its sweeping view over the old, twisted tops of the city's great living spires, trying to capture the essence of the bloody red sunset that met the misty cypress swamp on the city's far border, just visible from her seat.

The warm gabbling from the street was a prelude to the coming storm. Tensions had been hot all summer. The cooler fall weather moved people from languid summer unrest to more militant action. Pamphlets littered the streets; the corpses of dogs had been stuffed with them, as protest or warning, and by which side, Bet did not know nor care. Not then. Not yet. She cared only about capturing the color of the sky.

Bet was used to Hanere's flair for the dramatic. Hanere had spent the last year in a production of *Tornello*, a play about the life and death of the city's greatest painter. She had a habit of seeking out and exploiting the outrageous in even the most mundane situations.

Hanere twined her fingers into Bet's apron strings, tugging them loose.

Bet batted Hanere's hands away with her free one, still intent on the painting. "You want to date a painter because you're playing one," Bet said. "I have to give you the full experience. That means I work in this light. Just work, Hanere."

"Sounds divine," Hanere said, reaching again for the apron.

"I'm working," Bet said. "That's as divine as it gets. Have some cool wine. Read a book."

"A book? A book!"

Bet would remember Hanere just this way, thirty years hence: the crooked mouth, the spill of dark hair, eyes the color of honey beer widened in mock outrage.

The lover who would soon burn the world.

III.

"Hanere Gozene," Bet said, waving the two Plague Hunters inside. The name tasted odd on her tongue, like something both grotesquely profane and sacred, just like her memories of that black revolution.

Mhev barked at the hunters from his basket. Bet shushed him, but his warning bark convinced her to look over her young guests a second time. The appearance of Hanere's letter had shaken her, and she needed to pay attention. Mhev didn't bark at Plague Hunters, only Plague *Givers*.

"Neither of us is used to company," Bet said. When she was younger, she might have forced a smile with it to cover her suspicions, but she had given up pretending she was personable a long time ago.

Abrimet sat across from her at the little table strewn with bits of leather and stuffing from her work on the hydras. The younger one, the pan, stood off to the side, tugging at per violet collar. Bet slumped into her seat opposite. She didn't offer them anything. She picked up the half-finished hydra and turned it over in her hands. "City people buy these," she said. "I trade them to a merchant who paddles upriver to sell them. No back country child is foolish enough to buy them and invite that kind of bad luck in, like asking in a couple of Plague Hunters."

Lealez and Abrimet exchanged a look. Abrimet said, quickly, "We know Hanere left twelve dead Plague Hunters behind her, when she last escaped. If she's out there mentoring these two rogues—"

"I'm over fifty years old," Bet said. "What is it you hope I'll do for you? You're not here to ask me to hunt. So what do you want?"

Mhev stirred from his basket and snuffled over to Abrimet's boots. He licked them. Abrimet grimaced and pulled the boots away.

"Did you step through truffled salt?" Bet asked, leaning forward. She used the shift in her position to push her hand closer to the hilt of the machete on the table. They were indeed Givers, not Hunters. She should have known.

Abrimet raised hairless brows. "Why would—"

"It is a common thing," Bet said, "for Plague Givers to walk through truffled salt to neutralize their last cast, or to combat the plain salt cast of a Plague Hunter, which of course you would realize. It ensures they don't bring any contagion from that cast with them to the next target. Mhev can smell that salt on you. It's like sugar, to him. Regular salt, no. Truffled salt? Oh yes."

"Abrimet is a respected Hunter," Lealez said, voice rising. "You accuse Abrimet of casting before coming here, like some rogue Giver? Abrimet is a Hunter, as am I."

"You're here for the relics," Bet said, because most of the company who came here wanted the relics, and though these two had a fine cover story and poor ability to hide what they were, they would be no different.

"You *did* use them, then," Abrimet said, leaning forward. "To defeat Hanere."

Mhev nosed under Abrimet's boot. Abrimet toed at him.

"Not every godnight story is entirely rubbish," Bet said. She still held the bottle, though it was empty. Flexed her other hand, preparing to snatch the machete. "We went south, to the City by the Crushed Lake, where Hanere learned all of her high magic. The relics assisted in her capture, yes."

"We'll require the relics to defeat her students," Abrimet said, "just as you defeated her."

Mhev, sated by the salt, sat at Abrimet's boot and barked.

Bet made her choice.

She threw her bottle at Abrimet. It smashed into Abrimet's head, hard. Bet grabbed her machete and drove the machete through Abrimet's right eye.

Lealez shrieked. Raised per hands, already halfway into reciting a chant. Mhev's barking became a staccato.

Bet grabbed one of the finished hydras on the shelf and pegged Lealez in the head with it. A puff of white powder clouded the air. Lealez sneezed and fell back on the floor.

"No spells in here," Bet said to her. "That's six ounces of night buzz pollen. You won't be casting for an hour."

Bet pulled the machete clear of Abrimet. Abrimet's face still moved. Eye blinked. Tongue lolled. The body tumbled to the floor. Mhev squeaked and went for the boots.

"How were you going to do it?" she asked Lealez.

"I don't, I don't understand—" Lealez sneezed again, wiping at per face.

Bet thrust the bloody machete at per. "I have hunted Plague Givers my whole life. You thought I could not spot one like Abrimet? Did you know they cast a plague before they came here? Why do you think they stepped through truffled salt?"

Lealez considered per position, and the fine line between truth and endangering per mission. Bet's face was a knotted ruin, as if she had taken endless pummeling for decades. Her twisted black hair bled to white in patches. She was covered in insect bites and splattered blood. The spectacles resting on her head were slightly askew now. She stank terribly. The little rat happily gnawed at Abrimet's boots. Lealez had a terrible fear that this would all be blamed on per. Cities would die, the Order would be disbanded, because per had been too arrogant, and gotten perself into this horrible assignment. Abrimet, a Plague Giver? Impossible. Wasn't it? Lealez would have seen it.

"I didn't know what Abrimet was," Lealez said. "I just want to make a name for myself the way you did. I was the best of my class. I've . . . I've already killed three givers!"

"If that's true you should have a name already," Bet said.

"If they find that you killed Abrimet, you will be stung to death for it."

"A very risky venture, then, to let you go," Bet said, and was rewarded with a little tremble from Lealez.

Lealez wiped the pollen from per robe. It made per fingers numb. As per straightened per robe, Lealez wondered if Bet knew per was stalling, and if she did, how long she would let per do it before stabbing Lealez, too, with a machete. "I can speak for you before the judges, in the end," Lealez said. "You'll need someone to honor you. Another hunter. We can't hunt alone."

"A smart little upstart with no talent," Bet said.

"It's true I'm an upstart," Lealez said, "but you can't legally hunt without another hunter." Per smirked, knowing that even this old woman could not stand against *that* law.

Bet lowered her machete. "I'd have guessed the story you sold me was as fake as your friend, but I knew the paper, and I knew the signature. If I find you faked that, too, you'll have more to worry about than just one dead Plague Hunter."

"It's very genuine," Lealez said. "We only have four days. They'll kill tens of thousands in the capital."

"The note said seven days."

"It took us three days to find you."

"I'll hide better next time."

Lealez got to per feet. Lealez found per was trembling, and hated perself for it. A woman like Bet looked for weakness. That was Abrimet's flaw; their fear made them start to cast a plague, instead of waiting it out. A dangerous tell in front of a woman like this. Lealez needed to seal perself up tight.

Insects whispered across the pier. "Bit of advice," Bet said. "The Order forgives a great deal if you deliver what it wants."

"You need me."

"Like a hole in the head," Bet said. "But I'll take you along. For my own reasons."

"What's more important than eliminating a threat to the Community?"

"There must be any number of stationery shops where—"

"That was Hanere's handwriting."

"That isn't possible."

"I turned Hanere over to the Order three decades ago, and read about her death on all the news sheets and billboards."

"She was drawn and quartered," Lealez said.

"And burned up in the searing violet flame of the Joystone Peace," Bet said. "But here she is. And why do you think that is, little upstart?"

Lealez shook per head.

"Somehow she survived all that, and now she's back to bite the Community."

"So where do we start?" Lealez asked.

"We start with the sword," Bet said. "Then we retrieve the shield. Then we confront Hanere."

"How will we know where to find her?"

Bet pulled her pack from a very high shelf. "Oh, we won't need to find her," she said. "Once the objects of power are released, she'll find us."

IV.

The Copse of Screaming Corpses loomed ahead of Bet and Lealez's little pirogue. Great, knotted fingers, black as coal, tangled with the fog, poking snarling holes in the mist that hinted at the massive shapes hidden within. Sometimes the waves of gray shifted, revealing a glaring eye, a knobby knee, or the gaping mouth of one of the twisted, petrified forest of giants, forever locked in a scream of horror.

The copse was a good day's paddle from Bet's refuge. When she told Lealez the name, Lealez thought Bet was making fun.

"That isn't the real name," Lealez said. The dense fog muffled per words.

"Oh, it is," Bet said. "It's aptly named."

"Does the name alone scare people off?"

"The smart ones, yes," Bet said.

Ripples traveled across the bubbling water.

"What are these bubbles?"

"Sinkhole," Bet said. "They open up under the swamp sometimes. Pull boats under, whole villages. We're lucky. Probably happened sometime last night."

"Just a hole in the world?"

"Had one in the capital forty years ago," Bet said. "Ate the Temple of Saint Torch. Those fancy schools don't teach that?"

"I guess not," Lealez said. Per gazed into the great canopy of dripping moss that covered the looming giants above them. Their great, gaping maws were fixed in snarls of pain, or perhaps outrage. Lealez imagined them eating per whole. "Why put it here?" per said. "This place is awful."

"Would you come here for any other reason but retrieving an object of power?"

"No."

"You have your answer."

Bet poled the pirogue up to the edge of a marshy island and jumped out. She tied off the pirogue and pulled a great coil of rope over her shoulder. She headed off into the misty marsh without looking back at Lealez. Lealez scrambled after her, annoyed and a little frightened. Bet's generous shape was quickly disappearing into the mist.

Lealez yelped as per brushed the knobby tangle of some giant's pointing finger.

When Lealez caught up with Bet, she was already heaving the large rope over her shoulder. She sucked her teeth as she walked around the half-buried torso of one of the stricken giants. Its hands clawed at the sky, and its face was lost in the fog.

Bet tossed up one end of the rope a couple of times until she succeeded in getting it over the upraised left arm of the giant. She tied one end around her waist and handed Lealez the other end.

Lealez frowned.

"Hold on to it," Bet said. "Pull up the slack as I go. You never climbed anything before?"

Lealez shook per head.

Bet sighed. "What do they teach you kids these days?" She kicked off her shoes and began to climb. "Don't touch or eat anything while you're down here."

Lealez watched, breathless. Bet seemed too big to climb such a thing, but she found little hand- and footholds as she went, jamming her fingers and toes into crevices and deviations in the petrified giant.

Lealez held tight to the other end of the rope, pulling the slack and watching Bet disappear into the fog as she climbed up onto the giant's shoulder. Lealez glanced around at the fog, feeling very alone.

Above, Bet took her time climbing the monster. She had been a lot younger when she'd done this the first time, and she was already resenting her younger self. Warbling hoots and cries came from the swampland around her, distorted by the fog. Her breath came hard and her fingers ached, but she reached the top of the giant in due course.

She knew there was something wrong the moment she hooked herself up around the back of the giant's head. The head was spongy at the front, as if rotting from within. The whole back of it had been ripped open. Inside the giant's head was a gory black hole where the sword had been.

She pulled the knife from her hip and hacked into the back of the head, peering deep inside, scraping away bits of calcified brain matter. But it was no use. The head was empty. She traced the edges of the hole carved in the giant's head. Someone had hacked out the great round piece of the skull that she had mortared back into place with a sticky contagion years ago. Only she and her partner, Keleb, had known about the contagion. They would be the only two people capable of neutralizing it before removing the relic.

"Briar and piss," she muttered.

Below, Lealez screamed.

Bet sheathed her knife as she scrambled back down the giant, aware that her rope had gone slack. Foolish pan, what was the point of a rope if Bet cracked her head open on the way down?

Lealez screamed and screamed, horrified by the rippling of per skin. Lealez had tilted per head up to follow Bet's progress and left per mouth open, and a shard of the great giant's skin had flaked off and fallen into per mouth.

Lealez gagged on it, but it went down, and now per body was . . . growing, distending; Lealez thought per would burst into a thousand pieces. But that, alas, did not happen. Instead, Lealez grew and grew. Arms thickened with muscle. Thighs became large around as tree trunks.

When finally Lealez saw Bet sliding down the tree, Lealez's head was already up past Bet's position.

Bet swore and leapt the rest of the way down the face of the giant. She took a fistful of salt from the pouch at her hip and threw it in a circle around Lealez's burgeoning body. Lealez's clothes had burst, falling in tatters all around per. Bet muttered a chant, half-curse, half-cure, concentrating on the swinging arms above her. Bet pulled a bit of tangled herb from another pouch, already laced with contagion. She breathed the words she had last spoken in a dusty library in the Contagion College and let the plague free.

All around them, biting flies swarmed up from the swampland, drawn by her cast. They ate bits of the contagion and landed onto Lealez's body, which was now nearing the height of the petrified giants around them. Per skin was beginning to blacken and calcify around per ankles.

The swarm of flies covered Lealez's body like a second skin. Lealez squealed and swatted at them, per movements increasingly slow. The flies bit Lealez's flesh again and again while Bet squatted and urinated on the salt circle.

All at once the flies fell off Lealez. The pan's skin began to flake away where it had been bitten. The body contracted again, until it was half the size it had been, still giant. Then Lealez fell over with a great thump.

Bet ran to Lealez's side. The skin had turned obsidian black, hard as shale. Bet took her machete from her hip and hacked at the torso until great cracks opened up in the body. Then she pulled the pieces away.

Lealez was curled up inside the husk of per former self, arms crossed over per chest, shivering.

"Get out of there now," Bet said, offering per an arm.

Lealez tentatively took her hand, and Bet pulled per out. "Dusk is coming soon," Bet said. "I don't want to get caught out here."

It was warm enough that Bet wasn't too worried about Lealez being naked, but Lealez seemed to mind, and went searching for per pack, which had been ripped from per body. It was a stupid search, Bet thought, because the fog was getting denser, and they were losing the light, and Lealez's things could have gone anywhere.

Finally Lealez found the remains of per haversack, and pulled on a fresh robe. But the rest of per things were scattered, and Bet insisted they move on and not wait.

"The college will be angry," Lealez said. "My books, my papers—"

"Books and papers? Is that all you can think about? Hurry. Didn't I tell you not to touch or eat anything?"

"You didn't say why!"

"I shouldn't have to say why, you dumb pan. When I was your age I did whatever my mentor said."

"Are you my mentor now? You aren't even officially a Hunter. You would never be approved as a mentor by the college."

"Is everything joyless and literal with you?"

"You don't know how the college is now," Lealez said. "Old people like you tell us how things should be, how we should think, but this is a new age. We face a different government, and new penalties after the Plague Wars. We can't all go rogue or shirk our duties. We'd be kicked out. The college is very strict these days. People like you would never make it to graduation. You would end up working in contagion breweries."

"I'm sure you'd like to continue on with that fantasy a while longer," Bet said.

Once they were in the pirogue and had cast off, Lealez finally roused perself from misery and asked, "What about the artifact?"

"Someone got to it first," Bet said.

"Hanere?"

"Only one other person knows where these are. I expect they was compelled to get it."

"Your partner?"

Bet nodded.

"You think they are still alive?"

"No," Bet said.

At least Lealez said nothing else.

V.

Bet's partner, Keleb, too, had retired, but had chosen a canal that acted as a main trading thoroughfare into the city instead of a hard-to-find retreat like Bet's. It took a day and a half to reach the shoman's house, and Bet found herself counting down the time in her head. Lealez, too, reminded her of the ticking chirp of time as they poled downriver. The current was sluggish, and the weather was still and hot.

Despite the stillness, Bet smelled the smoke before she saw it. Lealez sat up in per seat and leaned far over the prow, knuckles gripping the edge of the craft.

The guttered ruin of Keleb's house came into view as they rounded the bend. The shoman had built the house with Bet's help, high up on a snarl of land that hardly ever flooded. Now the house was a charred wreck.

Bet tied off the pirogue and climbed up the steep bank. She counted three sets of footprints along the bank and around the house. They had stayed to watch it burn.

Bet poked around the still smoking house and found what was left of Keleb's body, as charred and ruined as the house.

"Help me here," Bet said to Lealez.

Lealez came up after her. "What can we do?" Lealez said. "The shoman is dead."

"Not the body I'm here for," Bet said. She walked off into the wood and chopped down two long poles from a nearby stand of trees. She handed a pole to Lealez. "Help me get the body rolled back, clear the area here."

Lealez knit per brows, but did as per was told. They heaved over Keleb's body to reveal a tattered hemp rug beneath. Bet yanked it away and used the pole to lever open a piece of the floor. Peeling back the wood revealed a long, low compartment. Lealez leaned over to get a better look, but it was clearly empty.

Bet sucked her teeth.

"What was here?" Lealez asked.

"The cloak," Bet said.

"I thought there were two relics, a sword and a shield."

"That's because that's all we reported," Bet said. "Because we knew this day would come." Bet saw the edge of a piece of paper peeking out from the bottom of the cache and picked it up. It was another note, made out to her in Hanere's handwriting.

"What does it say?" Lealez asked.

Bet traced the words and remembered a day thirty years before, rioting in the streets, a plump painter, and a future she had imagined that looked nothing like this one.

Bet crumpled up the note. "It says she will trade me the objects in return for something I love," Bet said. "Good thing I don't love anything."

Nothing but Hanere, of course. But that was a long time ago. Bet hardly felt anything there in the pit of her belly when she thought of Hanere. It was the time in her life she longed for, not Hanere. That was what she told herself.

"What a monster," Lealez said, staring at Keleb's charred body.

"None of us is a sainted being, touched by some god," Bet said. "But she's missing the third relic. She'll need that before she can end the world."

Lealez shivered. "We don't have much time left."

"There's a suspension line that runs up the river near here," Bet said. "Let's see if we can find you some clothes."

"There are only shoman's clothes here," Lealez said.

"We all have to make sacrifices," Bet muttered.

They walked away from Keleb's house; two people, a woman and a pan dressed in shoman's clothes, the vestments smoky and charred. Bet expected Lealez to talk more, but Lealez kept the peace. Lealez found perself following after Bet in a daze. For years Lealez had wanted nothing more than to prove perself to the Contagion College. It was beginning to dawn on Lealez just what per had to do to achieve the honor per wished for, and it was frightening, far more frightening than it had seemed when Lealez read all the books about Plague Hunters and Plague Givers and how the Hunters tracked down the Givers and saved the world. No one spoke of charred bodies, or what it was like to be cut out of one's own plague-touched skin.

The great suspension line ran along the Potsdown Peace Canal all the way to the Great Dawn Harbor that housed the city. Bet sighed and paid their fare to the scrawny little pan who lived in what passed for a gatehouse this far south of the city.

"College better reimburse all this," Bet said, and laughed, because the idea that she would be alive to get reimbursed in another day was distinctly amusing.

Bet and Lealez climbed the stairs up to the carriage that hung along the suspended line and settled in. Lealez looked a little sick, so Bet asked, "You been up before?"

"I don't like heights," Lealez said.

The gatekeeper came up and attached their carriage line to the pulley powered by a guttering steam engine, which the pan swore at several times before the carriage finally stuttered out along the line, swinging away from the gatehouse and over the water.

Lealez shut per eyes.

Bet leaned out over the side of the carriage and admired the long backs of a pod of plesiosaurs moving in the water beneath them.

After a few minutes, Lealez said, "I don't understand why you didn't tell the college there were three objects."

"Of course you do," Bet said.

"It doesn't—"

"Don't pretend you're some fool," Bet said. "I haven't believed a word you've said any more than I believed your little friend."

Lealez stiffened. "Why keep me alive, then?"

"Because I think you can be salvaged," Bet said. "Your friend couldn't. Your friend was already a Plague Giver. I think you're still deciding your own fate."

They rode in silence after that for nearly an hour. Lealez was startled when Bet finally broke it.

"Keleb and I couldn't defeat Hanere ourselves," Bet said. "I'd like to tell you we could. But she's more powerful. She has a far blacker heart, and a blacker magic. We went south, Keleb and I, and got help from sorcerers and hedge witches. They were the ones who created the objects of power. The sword, the shield, and the cloak."

"How do they work?" Lealez asked.

"You'll know soon enough," Bet said. "Not even Keleb knew where I kept the shield, though."

"But, the other weapons—"

The carriage shuddered. Lealez gave a little cry.

"Hold on, it's just—" Bet began, and then the carriage hook sheared clean away, and they plunged into the canal.

VI.

Thirty years earlier . . .

Hanere had always loved to watch things burn. Bet sat with her on the rooftop while riots overtook the city. They sipped black bourbon and danced and talked about how the world would be different now that the revolutionaries had done more than talk. They were burning it all down.

"If only I could be with them!" Hanere said.

Bet pulled Hanere into her lap. "You are better off here with me. Out there is a world of monsters and mad people."

Hanere waggled her brows. "Who's to say I'm not a bit of both? Come with me, we are out of bourbon!" She held up the empty bottle.

"No, no," Bet said. "Stay in. We'll sleep up here."

Bet had gone to sleep while the world burned. But that wasn't Hanere's way. While Bet slept, Hanere went out into it.

It was the edge of dawn when Bet finally woke, hungover and covered in cigarette ash, hands smeared in paint from her work earlier in the day. It was not until she sat up and saw the paint smearing the roof that she thought something was amiss. Her gaze followed the trail of paint that was not paint but blood to its origin. Hanere stood at the edge of the rooftop, wearing a long white shift covered in blood.

Bet scrambled up. "Are you hurt? Hanere?"

But as Hanere turned, Bet stopped. Hanere raised her bloody hands to the sky and her face was full of more joy than Bet had ever seen.

"The government is nearly toppled," Hanere said. "We will be gods, you and I, Bet. There's no one to stop us. It's delightful down there. You must come."

"What did you do, Hanere?"

"I am alive for the first time in my life," Hanere said. She opened her hands, and salt fell from her fingers. She murmured something, and little blue florets colored the air and passed out over the city.

"Stop it," Bet said. "What are you doing? You can't cast in the city outside the college!"

"I cast all night," Hanere said. "I will cast all I like. Come with me. Bet, come with me, my Elzabet. My love. We can take this whole city. We can burn down the college and those tired old people and repaint the world."

"No, Hanere. Get down from there."

The joy left Hanere's face. "Is that what you wish for us?" she said. She came down from the rooftop and walked over to Bet. She placed her hands on Bet's stomach. The blood on her hands was still fresh enough to leave stains. "Is that what you wish for our child?"

VII.

Bet sucked in water instead of air, and paddled to the surface, kicking wildly. She popped up in the brown water and took in her surroundings. Lealez was nowhere in sight. She dove again into the water, feeling her way through the muck for Lealez. Opening her eyes was a lost cause; she could see nothing. Her fingers snagged a bit of cloth. She grabbed at it and heaved Lealez to the surface.

Lealez coughed and sputtered. Bet kept per at arm's length, yelling that all per splashing was going to drown them both.

"Head for the shore," Bet said.

Lealez shook per head and treaded water using big, sloppy strokes. Bet followed per gaze and saw the hulking shapes of the plesiosaurs circling the carriage.

"They eat plants," Bet said. "Mostly."

Bet hooked Lealez under her arm and paddled for the shore. The plesiosaurs kept pace with them, displacing great waves of water that made it more difficult to get to the shore.

Lealez gasped. "They'll crush us!"

"More worried about the lizards on the shore," Bet said.

"What?"

Two big alligators lay basking along the shore. Bet made for another hollow a little farther on, but they were closer than they should be.

"They only eat at night," Bet said, reassuring herself as much as Lealez. "Mostly."

Bet and Lealez crawled up onto the bank and immediately started off into the brush. Bet wanted to put as much distance between her and the lizards as possible. Massive mosquitoes and biting flies plagued them, but Bet knew they were close enough to the city now that they might find a settlement or—if they were lucky—someone's spare pirogue.

Instead, they found the plague.

The bodies started just twenty minutes into their walk to the shore, and continued for another hour as they grew nearer and nearer the settlement. Soft white fungus grew from the noses and eyes and mouths of the dead; their fingers and toes were blackened. Bet stopped and drew a circle of salt around herself and Lealez, and sprinkled some precautionary concoctions over them.

"Do you know which one it is?" Lealez whispered.

"One of Hanere's," Bet said. "She likes to leave a mark. She's expecting us."

"Is this where you left the shield?"

"Hush now," Bet said as the swampland opened up into a large clearing. Nothing was burning, which was unlike Hanere.

Bet stopped Lealez from going farther and held up a finger to her lips. Two figures stood at the center of the village, heads bent in deep conversation. One wore a long black-and-purple cloak. The other carried a sword emblazoned with the seal of the Contagion College.

"Stay here," Bet said to Lealez. She pulled out her machete and stepped into the clearing.

The two figures looked up. Bet might have had to guess at their gender if one of them wasn't so familiar. She knew that one's gender because she'd been there during the ceremony where he'd chosen it. It was her and Hanere's own son, Mekdas. The other was most likely female, based on the hairstyle and clothing, but that didn't much concern Bet.

A trade for something Bet loved, that's what Hanere had written.

"So it was you who broke away from the Contagion College," Bet said.

Mekdas stared at her. He was nearly thirty now, not so much a boy, but he still looked young to her, younger even than Lealez. He had Hanere's bold nose and Bet's straight dark hair and Hanere's full lips and Bet's stocky build and Hanere's talent and impatience.

"I left you with the college so you could make something of yourself," Bet said. "Now here you are disappointing me twice."

"That's something Hanere and you never had in common," Mekdas said. "She was never once disappointed in me."

Bet searched the ground around them for the shield. If they had gotten this far they must have found that, too, no matter that Bet was the only one who was supposed to know where it was. Had Hanere used some kind of black magic to find it?

"Give over the objects," Bet said, "and we can talk about this."

"Have you met my lover?" Mekdas asked. "This is Saba."

Saba was a short waif of a woman, a little older than Mekdas. As much as Bet wanted to blame this all on some older Plague Giver, she knew better. She had done her best with Mekdas, but it was all too late.

Bet held out her hand. "The cloak, Mekdas."

"You're an old woman," Mekdas said. "Completely useless out here. Go back to your swamp. We are remaking the world. You don't have the stomach for it."

"You're right," Bet said. She didn't know what to say to him. She had never been good with children, and with Hanere dead, she had wanted even less to do with this particular child. He reminded her too much of Hanere. "I don't have the stomach for many things, but I know a plague village when I see one. I know where this goes, and I know how it ends. You think you can take this plague all the way to the city?"

Saba raised the sword. "With the relics, we will," she said, and smirked.

"Hanere tell you how they work, did she?" Bet said. "The trouble is Hanere doesn't know. There is one person alive who knows, and it's me."

"Hanere will show us," Saba said.

"You shut the seven fucking hells up," Bet said. "I'm not talking to you. Mekdas—"

"Why are you even here?" he said.

"Because Hanere invited me," Bet said.

That got a reaction from him. Surprise. Shock, even.

Bet already had a handful of salt ready, but so did they. The shock was all the advantage she had. Bet flicked the salt in their faces and charged toward them. She bowled over Saba and snatched the sword from her. They were Plague Givers, not warriors, and it showed.

Mekdas had the sense to run, but Bet stabbed the sword through his cloak and twisted. He fell hard onto a body, casting spores into the air.

Bet yelled for Lealez.

Lealez bolted across the sea of bodies, hand already raised to cast.

"Circle and hold them," Bet said.

Lealez's hands trembled as per made the cast to neutralize the two hunters.

Bet tore the cloak from Mekdas's shoulders and wrapped it around her own. She dragged the sword in one hand and crossed to the other side of the village. Bet found the tree she had nested her prize in decades before and hacked it open to reveal the shield, now buried in the heart of the tree. Sweat ran down her face so heavily she had to squint to see. She picked up the shield and marched back to where Saba and Mekdas lay prone inside the salt circle.

"Now you'll see all you wanted to see," Bet said to Mekdas. "You will see the world can be made as well as unmade, but there are sacrifices." She raised the sword over her head.

"No!" Lealez said.

"Please!" Mekdas said.

Bet plunged the blade into Saba's heart and spit the words of power that released the objects' essence. A cloud of brilliant purple dust burst from Saba's body and filled the air. Lealez stumbled back, coughing.

Bet quickly removed the cloak and draped it over Saba. All around the village, the bodies began to convulse. White spores exploded from their mouths and noses and spiraled toward the cloak, a great spinning vortex of contagion.

Lealez watched the cloak absorb the great gouts of plague, feeding on it like some hungry beast. A great keening shuddered through the air. It took Lealez a moment to realize it was Saba, screaming. And screaming. Lealez covered per ears.

Then it was over.

Bet stepped away from Saba's body, but tripped and stumbled back, fell hard on her ass. She heaved a great sigh and rested her forehead on the hilt of the sword.

"What did you do?" Mekdas said. His voice broke. He was weeping.

Bet raised her head.

All around them, the plague-ridden people of the village began to stir. Their blackened flesh warmed to a healthy brown. Their plague-clotted eyes cleared and opened. Soon, their questioning voices could be heard, and Bet got to her feet, because she was not ready for questions.

"They're alive!" Lealez said, gaping. "You saved them."

Bet pulled the cloak from Saba's body. Saba's face was a bitter rictus, frozen in agony. "They only save life by taking life," Bet said. "Now you know why I separated them. Why I never kept them together. Yes, they can give life. But they can take it, too. It's the intent that matters."

"We have one of them, at least," Lealez said. "We can take him to the Contagion College."

"No," Bet said. She raised her head to the sky. "This is not done." While the people of the village stirred, the insects in the swampland around them had gone disturbingly quiet.

"What is—" Lealez began.

"Let's get to the water," Bet said. "Take Mekdas. We need to get away from the village."

"But—"

"Listen to me in this, you fool."

Lealez bound Mekdas with hemp rope rubbed in salt and pushed him out ahead of them. Lealez had to hurry to keep up with Bet. Carrying the objects seemed to have given her some greater strength, or maybe just a sense of purpose. She forged out ahead of them, cutting through swaths of swampland, cutting a way for them all the way back down to the water on the other side of the river.

Lealez stared out at the water and saw two pirogues attached to a cypress tree another hundred steps up the canal. "There!"

"Take my machete," Bet said. "You'll take one boat on your own. Follow after Mekdas and I."

Lealez took the machete. "You're really going to turn him in?"

Bet glared at per so fiercely Lealez wanted to melt into the water.

"All right," Lealez said, "I wasn't sure what I was thinking." Lealez waded out toward the pirogue. Lealez noticed the ripple in the water out of the corner of per eye and turned.

Bet saw the ripple a half moment before. She yelled and raised her sword, but she was too slow.

A massive alligator snatched Lealez by the leg and dragged per under the water. Bet saw Lealez's upraised arms, a rush of brown water, and then nothing.

Mekdas ran.

Bet swore and scrambled after him. She fell in along the muddy bank, and then something else came up from the water for her.

Hanere emerged from the depths of the swamp like a creature

born there. She head-butted Bet so hard Bet's nose burst. Pain shattered across her face. Bet fell in the mud.

Muddy water and tangles of watercress streamed off Hanere's body. Her hair was knotted, and her beard was shot through with white. She grabbed hold of Bet's boot and dragged Bet toward her.

Bet held up the sword. "Revenge will get you nothing, Hanere!"

"It got me you," Hanere said, and wrenched the shield from Bet's hand and threw it behind her.

"You feel better with me here?" Bet said, gasping.

"A bit, yes."

"And when your son is dead? If I don't kill him, someone else will."

"They were in love, like we were," Hanere said. "It was easy to convince them to burn down a world that condemned them, and me. Even you. This world cast even you out, after all you did."

"Not like us. They're both criminals."

"You became a criminal when you fucked me, and kept fucking me, even when you told them you were hunting me. You and your soft heart."

Bet kicked herself farther down the bank, holding the sword ahead of her. "I thought you dead," Bet said. "For thirty years—"

"That's a bunch of shit," Hanere said. "You know they'd never kill someone like me. You know what they did to me for thirty years? Put me up in a saltbox and tortured me. Me, the greatest sorcerer that ever lived."

"How did you—"

"Does it matter?" Hanere said, and her tone softened. She crawled toward Bet and took hold of the end of the sword. She pressed it to her chest and said, "Is this what you wanted? To do it yourself? Or did you wait always for this day, when we could take the world together?"

Tears came, unbidden. Bet gritted her teeth in anger. Her own soft heart, betraying her. "You know I can't."

"Even now?" Hanere said softly. "After all this time?"

Bet shook her head.

Hanere reached out for Bet's cheek, and though it was mud on Hanere's fingers and not blood, the memory of Hanere's bloody hands was still so strong after all these years that Bet flinched.

"We are done," Bet said, and pressed the sword into Hanere's heart.

Hanere did not fight her. Instead, she pulled herself forward along the length of the blade, closer and closer, until she could kiss Bet with her bloody mouth.

"I will die in your arms," Hanere said, "as I should have done."

Mekdas screamed, long and high, behind them.

Bet sagged under Hanere's weight.

Mekdas bolted past her and ran toward the two pirogues.

Bet turned her eyes upward. Soft white clouds moved across the purple-blue sky. She wanted to be a bird, untethered from all this filth and sweat, all these tears. Thirty years she had hidden, thirty years she had tried to avoid this day. But here it was. And she had done it, hadn't she? Done everything she hoped she would not do.

She heard a splashing from the water, and heaved a sigh. The lizard would take her. Gods, let the lizard take her, and the relics, and drown them for all time.

When she opened her eyes, though, it was Lealez who stood above her, dripping water onto her face. The pan was covered in gore, and stank like rotten meat. Lealez held up the machete. "Told you I was the best in my class," Lealez said.

"Didn't know you learned how to kill lizards," Bet said.

Lealez gazed at Hanere's body. "Is she really dead?"

"I don't know that I care," Bet said. "Is that strange?"

Lealez helped her up. "The boy is trying to figure out the pirogue," Lealez said. "We aren't done."

"You take him."

"He's your family," Lealez said.

"My responsibility?"

"I just thought . . . you would want to take the credit."

Bet huffed out a laugh. "The credit? The *credit*." She heaved herself forward, slogging toward the pirogue.

Mekdas saw her coming and pushed off. As she approached he stood up in the little boat, unsteady already on the water.

Behind him, Bet could just see the lights of the city in the distance. Did they all know what was coming for them? Did any realize that there were Plague Givers out here who wanted to decimate the world and start over? Would they care, or would they be like Hanere, and wish for an end?

"You must kill me to save that city, then, mother," Mekdas said. "Will you kill me like you did Hanere? You won't bring me in alive. You must make the—"

Bet threw her sword. It thunked into her son's belly. He gagged and bowled over.

Lealez gaped.

Bet waded out to the pirogue and pulled it back to shore.

"You killed him," Lealez said. "I thought—"

"He's not dead yet," Bet said, but the words were only temporarily truth. He was gasping his last, drowning in his own blood.

"I've heard ultimatums like that before," Bet said. "Hanere gave me one, and when I hesitated, I lost her. You only make a mistake like that, the heart over reason, once. Then you take yourself away from the world, so you don't have to make decisions like that again."

"But—"

"Blood means little when there's a city at stake," Bet said. She gazed back out at the city. "Let's give them to the swamp."

"But we have to take the bodies back to—"

Bet raised the sword and pointed it at Lealez. It was only then that she realized Lealez was favoring per right leg; the lizard had gotten its teeth in per, and Lealez would get infected badly, soon, if they didn't get per help in the city.

THE PLAGUE GIVERS | 183

"We do the bodies my way," Bet said, "then we get you back to the city."

When they came back to Hanere's body, it was encircled by a great mushroom ring. Green spores floated through the air.

"Is she dangerous?" Lealez said.

"Not anymore," Bet said.

Together, they hauled the body through the undergrowth, avoiding the snapping jaws of swamp dogs and startling a pack of rats as big as Bet's head. Bet was aware of Hanere's stinking body, the slightly swelling flesh. When they dumped her into the hill of ants, Bet stood and watched them devour the woman she had spent half her life either chasing or romancing.

"Are you all right?" Lealez said.

"No," Bet said. "Never have been."

Mekdas was next.

While they stood watching the ants devour him, Lealez glanced over at Bet and said, "I know this is a hard profession, but there's honor in it. It does a public good."

"No, we just murder people."

"We eliminate threats to—"

"Can you even say it? Can you say, 'We murder people'?"

"This is a ridiculous conversation."

"On that, we can agree," Bet said. She glanced over at Lealez. "Something I noticed back there, in the Copse of Screaming Corpses. You never showed me your credentials."

"Don't be ridiculous."

Bet grabbed per arm and yanked back per sleeve before Lealez could pull away. There was the double ivy circle of the order, but no triangles.

Bet released her, disgusted. "What happened to being best in your class? Apprehending three Plague Givers? That's what your duplicitous friend Abrimet said, wasn't it?"

"I came out here to make a name for myself."

Bet stared down at the little pan, and though she wanted to hate Lealez more than anything, she had to admit, "I suspect you have indeed done that."

VIII.

Lealez smoothed per coat and mopped the sweat from per brow. The great Summoning Circle of the Contagion College was stuffed to bursting with fellow Plague Hunters. The map case Lealez carried over per shoulder felt heavier and heavier as the afternoon wore on to dusk. The initial round of questions had worn down into a second and then third round where Lealez felt per was simply repeating perself. Not a single apprentice or hunter with fewer than three triangles was allowed into the space. By that measure, Lealez wouldn't have been able to come to per own trial just a few days ago. Lealez swallowed hard. In front of per lay the relics per and Bet had spent so much effort retrieving.

Lealez knew it was a betrayal, but per also knew there was no triangle on per arm yet, and this was the only way.

The coven of judges peered down at Lealez from the towering amber dais. The air above them swarmed with various plagues and contagions, all of them meant to counteract any assaults coming from outside the theater. But the swarm still made Lealez's nose run and eyes water. Lealez felt like a leaky sponge.

"Where are the bodies?" Judge Horven asked, waggling her large mustache.

"We disposed of them," Lealez said. "Elzabet was . . . understandably concerned that Hanere Gozene could rise again. As she had risen once before."

"Then you have no proof," Judge Horven said.

Lealez gestured expansively to the relics. "I have brought back the relics that Elzabet Addisalam and Keleb Ozdanam used to defeat Hanere Gozene," Lealez said. "And you have the testimony of the two of us, of course."

Judge Rosteb, the eldest judge, held up their long-fingered hands and barked out a long laugh. "We are former Plague Hunters, all," they said. "We know that testimony between partners can be . . . suspect."

"I stand before you with all I have learned," Lealez said. "Abrimet was unfortunately lost to us along the way, through no fault of either Elzabet or myself. Their death was necessary to our goal. I regret it. You all know that Abrimet was my mentor. But we did as we were instructed. We stopped Hanere and the other two Plague Givers. I retrieved the relics. Both of those things cannot be contested. Because even if, as you say, you see no body, I can tell you this—you will never see Hanere again upon this soil. That will be proof enough of my accomplishments."

The judges conferred while Lealez sweated it out below them. Not for the first time, Lealez wished they had let Bet inside, but that was impossible, of course. Bet had murdered Abrimet, and done a hundred other things that were highly unorthodox in the apprehension of a Plague Giver. The judges would already worry that Bet had been a terrible influence on Lealez. Lealez would be lucky to get through this with per own head intact. At least Lealez would die in clean clothes, after a nice cold bath, which was the first thing per had done on entering the city.

Finally, the judges called Lealez forward.

"Hold out your arm," Judge Rosteb said.

IX.

Bet waited for Lealez outside the great double doors of the theater. Plague Hunters streamed past Bet as they were released from the meeting, all pointedly ignoring her. No one liked a woman who could kill her own family, no matter how great a sorcerer she was. The better she was, the more they hated her.

And there was Lealez. Lealez walked out looking dazed. Bet frowned at per empty hands. Lealez had gone in with the relics to make per case for destroying them, but Bet had a good idea of what had happened to them.

"Let's see them," Bet said, and snatched Lealez's arm. They had tattooed the mark of three successful hunts there. Bet snorted in disgust. "All three, then. You really learned nothing at all, did you? I could kill you, too, but there are hundreds, thousands, just like you, crawling all over each other to do the bidding of the City Founders. You're like a hydra, spitting up three more scaly heads for every one I hack off."

"You don't know how difficult it is to rise up through the college now," Lealez said.

"You kids talk like it was any easier. It wasn't. We got asked to make the same stupid choices. They wanted the relics when Keleb and I came back, too. But we held out."

"You were already famous! Your reputation was secured!"

"Shit talk," Bet said. "You're just not tough enough to give up your career so young. I get that. But think on this. It's easy to destroy a country with plague, but how do you save your own from it? You'll all unleash something in the far empires and think we're safe, but we aren't, not with a thousand relics. All killing gets you is more killing. You pick up a machete, kid, and you'll be picking it up your whole life."

"None of it matters now," Lealez said, and sniffed. Lealez pulled a cigarette from a silver case, but for all per insouciance, Bet noted that per hands trembled. "They have the relics. What they do with them now doesn't concern me."

"Dumb kid," Bet said.

Lealez lit per cigarette with a clunky old lighter from per bag, something that would have weighed per down by an extra pound in the swamp. Lealez took a long draw. "I gave them the sword and the shield," per said, "just so you know."

"The . . . sword and shield. That's what you gave them?"

"Yeah, like I said." Lealez pulled a leather map case from per shoulder. "Here's the thing I promised you," Lealez said.

"I see," Bet said. She took the case from per. "You know the relics don't work unless they're all together?"

"Don't know about that," Lealez said. "I'm just a dumb kid, re-member?"

"I'm sorry," Bet said.

Lealez shrugged. "Just get out of here. You aren't suited to the city."

Bet tipped her head at Lealez. "I don't want us to meet again," Bet said. "No offense meant."

"None taken," Lealez said. "If we meet again it means I'm not doing my job. I know how to play this game, too, Bet." Lealez handed Bet the lighter and walked back into the college.

Bet pocketed it and watched per go. Lealez did not look back. When Lealez opened the great door of the college to go back inside, per hand no longer trembled. That pan was going to make a good Hunter someday, like it or not.

Bet shouldered the map case and began her own long walk across the city. It took nearly two hours to cross the dim streets, navigat-ing her way based on which roads had functioning gaslights. She went all the way to the gates of the city and into the damp mud of the swamp before she risked opening the map case.

Inside, the cloak artifact was rolled up dry and tight. Bet rented a skiff upriver and spent the next week trudging home on foot and by whatever craft she could beg a ride upon.

When it came time to do what needed to be done, she wasn't sure she could do it. What if there was another Hanere? But so long as the relics existed, the world wasn't safe.

Bet burned the cloak there in the canopy of the cypress trees while swamp dogs snarled and barked in the distance. She watched the smoke coil up through the dense leaves and moss, and let out a breath.

It was decided. For better or worse.

X.

She had retired to the swamp because she liked the color. The color was the same, but she was not.

Bet leaned over the dim light of her firefly lantern, pushing her stuffed hydra into its glow. She eased the big sewing needle through its skin with her rough, thick fingers. On the shelves behind her were dozens of cast-off hydras, each defective in some way that she could not name. The college knew where she was now, and it made her work more difficult to concentrate on in the many long months back at her damp home. She sweated heavily, as the sun had only just set, and the air would keep its heat for a long time yet. She was tired, but no more than the day before, or the day before that. She had made her choices.

Mhev snorted softly in his basket with a litter of four baby swamp rodents, all mewing contentedly out here in the black. She wished she could join them, but her work was not done.

Outside, the insects grew quiet. Bet had been waiting for them. The waiting was the worst part. The rest was much easier. Whether it was child or Hunter or Giver or beast who stilled their call, she had made her choice about how to defend her peace long before, when she first condemned Hanere to death. She had already killed everything they both loved then.

That left her here.

Bet took hold of the machete at her elbow, the machete she would be taking into her hands for the rest of her life, and opened the door.

TUMBLEDOWN

IT WAS TOO EARLY in the season for a plague, but plague never waited on the turn of the seasons. Sarnai knew that as well as anyone.

From inside the tram, Sarnai saw wan winter light trickle across the northern horizon like whisky from the bottom of a glass. A flat-faced white fox made its way across the tundra, shaking its mane of feathers. It left a trail of purplish blood across the snow; its rear paw had been mangled by some predator, or perhaps a trap left out by an illegal feather dealer. There were larger predators out there, ones suited to hunting down that little fox with ease. The fox raised its head and met her look, then began digging into a pillowy hillside, shaking its mane of feathers once again. Only the very smartest and most persistent survived out here.

As the tram picked up speed, the landscape bled into a single smear of flickering white, and Sarnai had to look away to keep her headache at bay. Bright light triggered migraines. She passed her hand over the tram window, but the dimmer was broken. No relief there.

The tram slowed as they reached the research station.

While the others got their things and stood, Sarnai waited

impatiently for the full stop. The flickering sign outside the station came into focus as the train came to a halt. The sign swung in the heavy wind, buffeted by a slurry of snow made from frozen water and mercury. Sarnai clipped her respirator back on, sealing her environmental suit once again, and used the bar next to the window to heft herself up onto her blocky mechanical leg braces. She didn't like the braces. They were for the comfort of others. She could stand upright and shift the weight of her torso to control the movement of her legs. It made it easier for people to forget her difference. In a little settlement like this, other people's discomfort could be deadly. So she wore the fucking braces, though they were a lie. She preferred being in her chair at home where she could haul herself around using her upper body. She took great pride in her massive shoulders and forearms.

Sarnai slung her emergency bag over her shoulder and picked up her cane. She didn't need the cane to walk, but it was good to have in case of a stumble. It had saved her from a lot of embarrassing falls. She followed the others onto the platform, clacking onto it in her custom ice shoes, which left little pinpricks in the snow and ice as she walked.

Sarnai went through the airlock, which cycled through with a hissing whoosh. Little particles of frozen mercury were pulled away from the skin of her environmental suit by powerful magnets, redistributing the mercury into containers beneath the station that would later be traded off-world. The doors in front of her opened. Sarnai peeled off her respirator and slung it over her shoulder. She pushed back her hood and entered the station.

Sarnai made her way straight ahead to the moving escalator that went up to the health labs. The research station was the only one on Narantu, and it clung stubbornly to the outer ring of settlements huddled around the equator. The population had swung rapidly over the last seventy years, brought low by plague, famine, and extreme weather that threatened settlements that crept too far north or south from the core. Trams connected a few of the population centers to the community-owned resource centers, mining facilities, and public harvesting hubs, but most travel was still done by sled. The thick air, paired with strong gravity and a preponderance of dust made of volcanic grit, and toxic mercury, made flight cost prohibitive. Every form of travel was dangerous, here, but flight most of all.

Enkh, Sarnai's boss, waited for her at the top of the escalator. Enkh's doughy face was pained. Enkh was over fifty, one of the first generation to grow up on Narantu, and she wore her thick black hair braided back into double bows on the side of her head. She closed her fist when she saw Sarnai, extinguishing the pop-up display projected from the tattoo on her forearm.

"I heard," Sarnai said as Enkh opened her mouth. Sarnai would not have come into work this early unless she had heard.

"It was Erdene," Enkh said. "I don't know what she encountered out there, but she had taken off half her suit. Came in sunburned and emaciated, half an arm gone, crawling with the spinal plague. We're meeting in the conference room to discuss how to get the antibodies sent out to Batbayer. It's a full-blown epidemic."

"Batbayer is three thousand kilometers out," Sarnai said. "Making a run like that this time of year is impossible."

"Let's see what Khulan has to say," Enkh said.

Enkh and Sarnai made their way to the conference room where the rest of the team was already gathered. The head of the research facility, Otryad, was a lean, birdish woman with a long nose that nearly touched her upper lip. Batu and Temujin, the heads of the health and disease control labs, respectively, sat with heads bowed over their pop-up displays. Old Khulan was muttering to himself in front of the projection wall.

Sarnai limped over to him and pressed the patterned sequence on his display to synch up the dual projected screen and his personal one. A grin split Khulan's bearded face, and he thumped her arm firmly. She was glad for the grip of her shoes. Sarnai sat in the seat closest to the projector and caught her breath as the others settled down.

"You've all heard about Batbayer," Otryad said.

"We've lost settlements to tumbledown before," Sarnai said, using the colloquial name for the spinal plague. She wanted to be the first to say it out loud because everyone was pointedly not looking at her. "Those in Batbayer chose to live on the edge, just as my own parents did. That far out, they know the risks."

"We owe it to Erdene to listen to what she has to say," Khulan said. He fiddled with his display and projected a frozen recording onto the screen.

Sarnai did not want to watch any recording from out there. She had already lived that. Sarnai turned to the screen to avoid others' stares but lowered her gaze so all she saw was the bottom of the image and Erdene's red-striped environmental suit. Unfortunately, Sarnai did not cover her ears.

Erdene was coughing, a hack-hack-hoop sound that made Sarnai shiver. The hissing of the sled over the snow and the jingle of the dogs' tack sounded dully behind her.

"Confirmed the first incidence of spinafalia," Erdene rasped. Sarnai watched the creases in Erdene's environmental suit rise and fall and ripple like some fabulous mountain range. "Zero patient was a trader. Says he came through Tetseggai twenty days ago, and Asharaanti thirty days before that. They may already be gone. No time to get lorphor there. All falling down." She paused to hack again.

Sarnai's gaze dipped below the projection into the dark crease between the wall and the floor. There had been no lorphor, no cure when tumbledown came to her home settlement in Ganzor. Her mother hadn't survived it. Nor had either of her fathers. Eighteen of the twenty-six people in their township had died. It had all started the same way, with the cough. At night, still, Sarnai would lie awake and press her ear to the wall and listen hard for it, determined that it was real and the plague had come to the station and was going to kill every last person she knew or break them into pieces.

Eight people from her settlement had lived, including Sarnai. But living came with a cost. One little girl had lost all feeling from the left side of her cheek down through her left arm. Another felt nothing from the thighs down. Three were quadriplegics. Her cousin could move the right side of his body, but not the left, and he had not survived when they worked together to board a sled and head toward the core settlements sixty days after the last person died of the plague. She had watched her cousin freeze to death when their sled tipped over.

She was lucky, they all told her. Lucky because though she would never walk with her own legs again, she could still make herself useful. Technology had come so far, they all reassured her. She would walk, walk walk walk. That's all they ever talked about, her walking. It would be some time before they broke the news about the catheter, and installed the holes in her guts so she could relieve herself on her own. And nobody mentioned sex to a seven-year-old. Walking was all anyone talked about, but getting around was the least of her everyday concerns.

Erdene's coughing brought her back to the present.

Sarnai made herself look at Erdene's broad, shiny face this time. Erdene wore her respirator and hood, but Sarnai could see her eyes behind the dim film, and she recognized the fear in them.

"We have to catch it here," Erdene said. "If we don't catch it here, it will spread." One of the dogs yowled. A chorus of others took up the yelping and squawking, and there was a hiss and thump and a barely audible, "Oh shit!" from Erdene, and then the recording stopped.

Khulan waved his hand to brighten the lights and regarded them all. "I volunteer to go," he said. "We've taken huge population losses to the south. Having this come down from the north will be . . . Well."

"Catastrophic," Otryad said.

"Khulan can't go alone," Enke said. "It's perilous even for an experienced runner."

"The lorphor serum won't last that trip," Sarnai said. She could not keep the irritation from her voice. "I've tested the stability of the serum in thousands of different conditions. Three thousand kilometers is too far. It will take too long and it'll be bad when it gets there. Even if you survive, Khulan, you'll get the plague and die up there."

Otryad peered at Sarnai, head slightly tilted. "That's right. You and . . . that intern last year, you made sixteen sled runs up to the coast and back."

Sarnai said, "And that was three hundred kilometers, not three thousand." And her leg braces had frozen and the intern had nearly died from mercury poisoning, but she didn't want to remind anyone of that because she would need funding for the next round of testing. "Visibility out there is near zero. That, and the level of mercury in the air this time of year, makes flight impossible. It has to be the sleds, and that means we need more time to ensure the serum is stable across that distance. Wait the extra days and send in someone for the survivors."

"Are you volunteering?" Otryad said. "I thought you would be the first, after what happened to your family."

"Fuck you," Sarnai said. Everyone went very still. It wasn't just an inappropriate outburst; it was a serious breach of etiquette, to speak that way to a superior. "You want to send me because I'm expendable. An old man and a cripple. We'll die out there, and the serum will go bad, but you'll be able to tell the community you did all you could against the plague, against tumbledown, then you'll quarantine them and cut off supplies and hoard it here in the core."

"There is hope in us going," Khulan said, firmly. "Think of those children who survived, like you. Even if the serum doesn't survive, they should know we care for them. That's the covenant we all made here, to care for one another. We can't abandon them, even if—"

"Even if they end up like me," Sarnai said, "but you know, except for all of you, my life isn't that bad. It's not a horror story. You all just keep making it one with your fear and your pity, holding me up like some kind of totem against what's happening out there. It will come for you, too. It's coming now. You can throw me at it, but—"

"No one will make you do anything," Otryad said. "I'm sorry you feel this way about the mission, but we are not making you do anything. Batu, Temujin, stay here. As Sarnai pointed out, we'll need to discuss quarantine procedures. There will be survivors making their way here, whether Khulan is successful or not. That's all, thank you."

Enkh shot Sarnai a long look as she hustled from the room. Sarnai pushed herself up, using the table for leverage, and grabbed her cane. When she limped out into the hall, Khulan was waiting for her by the oxygen bar.

Khulan fell into step beside her. "There is no shame in being afraid," he said, "but you did not have to be rude."

"I'm not fit to go on that journey," Sarnai said, "and neither are you. And you know it."

"What does that mean, fit?" Khulan said, spreading open his palms. "You think it means you have a perfect body, one that makes sense? We would be more effective creatures with bigger eyes, more hands, tougher skins. But we are what we are because that's what was best suited to the place and time where we evolved. Out here, we need different things. Smarts, guts, tenacity, certainly." He patted his belly. "Fat, absolutely. But most of all, yes, we need hope instead of despair. The first to go are those who despair. They cannot stand all this darkness, this madness." He pressed her sternum with his finger. "But you are still here." He tapped his chest. "I am still here." Huffed a breath that smelled of tobacco and peppermint. "We are best suited to the task ahead."

"I'm not as fat as you," Sarnai said.

"We're not all perfect," he said, patting her tummy. She could not feel it.

"If the serum goes bad," she said, "and it will, then . . ."

Khulan sighed. "If it goes bad, then there is only you, but I prefer hope over despair."

Sarnai closed her eyes. She heard the coughing again. The death of ghosts. "We're all going to die out there," she said.

"If that plague reaches the core communities, we're all going to die in here, too," Khulan said.

Sarnai opened her eyes. "Shit," she said.

"That's my lead dog's name," Khulan said.

The sled was a smooth, rocket-shaped slab of metal, one of many parts of the old colonial ships that had been refitted for a more useful purpose. The dogs had been bred from various strains that had arrived in embryonic form on the ships and mixed with local creatures to create a hybrid capable of breathing the atmosphere unaided and scrabbling through ice laced with sharp volcanic rock and pools of frozen mercury. They had dual coats: fur and feathers, and giant beaks with forked tongues. Their ears were large and pointed; they could hear even the tiniest sound miles away, and it made them excellent for detecting approaching predators, of which there were many on the open tundra.

Sarnai rode in the right side of the sled's tube with Khulan on the left. The tube was snug and warm inside and could be sealed against cold for the night, but not pressurized. Their environmental suits had to stay on. They were insulated by their supplies and the six cases of serum at their feet. Why Khulan insisted on them when Sarnai knew they would go bad was beyond her.

Sarnai didn't look back until they were already fifty kilometers from the research station, the dogs squawking out a warning to passersby to clear the sled way for their passage. The core settlements were densely populated. The houses had all been made from prefabricated parts printed out by one of the many structural printers. On the horizon to the north, Sarnai saw the unfinished peak of the colony's first major air purifier, still two years away from completion. It would effectively remove the mercury from the air and add oxygen, then remix that with the existing air to make it more palatable for humans. The mercury it collected was stored in great vats beneath it, ready for transport and sale off-world.

The wind was already bitter cold. Sarnai ducked back into the tube of the sled and out of the gale. She pushed her personal pack into her lap. She could feel nothing from her sternum down, so she had learned to check all of her movements by sight to ensure she didn't injure herself.

Sarnai and Khulan did not speak until they broke for their first rest of the day after one hundred kilometers. The dogs could do about two hundred kilometers a day if pushed, which meant it would take fifteen days, at the very least, to get to Batbayer. If Sarnai didn't die on the way there, she imagined dying of some infection on the way back from having to reuse her catheters.

They camped against a massive snowdrift hulked up behind a hill, circling the dogs for protection against the wind. Khulan volunteered to clean the dogs' taloned feet of snow and ice. Sarnai clunked around in her leg braces, keeping her balance with a ski pole as she kicked out a place to set up the heat source. She and Khulan hunched over the heat-emitting blue orb and warmed their tea pouches. She sucked hers down without ceremony through a straw that clipped through her respirator.

Khulan reached into his environmental suit and handed her a bottle of whisky.

"Those best prepared survive out here," he said, and chuckled.

A cawing sound came from the west, and the dogs' ears perked up.

"Sounds like stinging lilies," Sarnai said.

"Too close to the core settlements," Khulan said, but he peered to the west.

"How long do you give us?" Sarnai said. "Two hundred kilometers?"

"A thousand, at least," he said and held out his hand to get the whisky back. "If you won't drink that, I will."

She snorted and handed it over. "I prefer red wine," she said. In truth, she didn't want to drink any alcohol on this trip because the more she drank, the more she'd have to cath out through the stoma in her abdomen. But then, if she was going to die anyway, who cared if she had to cath out every three or four hours instead of every six? She very nearly snatched the whisky back.

The cawing sound crackled across the sky again. It was already dusk; days were about six hours long on Narantu during the long winter season. In the summer, the small red eye of the second sun would appear and give them a little more light for an additional six hours while they danced through one another's orbits, but not much more heat. Already Sarnai could see the brightest stars peering down at them through the darkening sky.

After they ate, Khulan went off to urinate, and Sarnai changed her colonoscopy bag, then they were lining up the dogs again and mushing out across the tundra. Sarnai looked back, again, wondering if she would see the stinging lilies, but she saw only the low, round mounds of the last of the core settlements fading fast behind them, their glowing house markers sprinkled across the tundra like tough little diamonds.

They traveled like that for two days until they came to the end of the core settlements and reached the truly wild tundra. Sarnai already longed for a shower and cursed her greasy hair. Living inside of a suit for as long as she intended to was going to get itchy and uncomfortable. What a fool she'd been to come out here. She could have survived tumbledown if it hit the core settlements. What did she care about the people on the edges? They had been dumb like her parents, to live out there all alone. But did their children deserve to die for it? That's what kept her up at night. That's what she dreamed about under the brilliant stars. She dreamed of her dead parents, and her brother screaming that he had seen a man with a dog's face while he tried to cut off his own hand.

The third day, they packed up the sled and Sarnai must have nodded off, because when the sled jerked to a halt, it woke her. The dogs were squawking and barking. Sarnai leaned over and saw the whole front end of the sled tangled in creeping black tendrils. As she hauled herself up out of the sled she saw Khulan forty paces away on the other side, taking great swings at the creepers with a machete.

Sarnai grabbed a flame pistol from the gear box in the back and sprayed at the black creepers. The creepers hissed at her, untangling their little hooked claws and swarming toward her. She jerked the pistol again, spraying more fire. This time the tendrils retreated.

Khulan yelled. Sarnai turned just in time to see him fall down, clutching at his arm.

Sarnai went around the sled, picking her way over to him as quickly as she could. Khulan lay in the snow. He convulsed. Sarnai tried to bend over. She didn't want to sit because she was afraid she wouldn't be able to get back up. Her braces were already getting clotted with ice here outside the sled.

"Khulan!" she said. "Khulan!"

He was motionless.

She gave in and shifted her weight, signaling to her braces that she wanted to kneel. They complied, plopping her onto the snowy ground beside Khulan. Sarnai ripped off her glove and checked for a pulse. Nothing. She removed his respirator and put her ear to his mouth. No breath. Not a sound. She knew this. She had seen this before, in older people in the settlement. Their hearts gave out, especially in the winter season when they picked up a shovel or a carcass as if they were fifteen again.

"Khulan!" she yelled again. Sarnai knew basic first aid, but it had been years since she had cause to use it. She checked to make sure his airway was clear and kept her respirator clear so she could breathe into his mouth. He was warm but so, so still, and with both their suits unsealed, that heat would not last long. Sarnai pumped his chest, counting off out loud as the dogs yowled behind her. Her fingers went numb, and she had to put her glove back on. Soon she was light-headed, winded. It was full dark now, and as she worked she took little breaks to shoot her fire pistol at the tangled creepers and seal herself and Khulan back into their suits. The temperature was dropping now, tumbling from forty to fifty below, and she knew there were bits of frozen mercury that had flitted into her suit. They couldn't go on like this much longer.

How long she kept breathing and pumping, she didn't know. But Khulan's body was cooling, and she was breathless. Finally, Sarnai let herself fall beside him. Tears stung her eyes but froze before they could fall. She put on her respirator and resealed her suit. She listened to the rustling of the creepers. Her lips tasted of whisky; the last tipple Khulan had taken. Sarnai gritted her teeth. She took up the fire pistol again and used the ski pole to help herself up. She waded through the snow, spraying long lines of fire at the creepers until they retreated back into their burrows.

Sarnai pulled out a blanket from the gear box and rolled Khulan over it, then wrapped him up and secured him using chemical tape. She grabbed his body and pulled and pulled until sweat rolled down her face and her arms ached, but she managed to get him to the sled.

"I have to go back," she said to Khulan's body. "We are both going to die for nothing. The plague will come here and rip through all of them. And what do I care? I'll live! I'm immune!" She yelled and swore until her voice was hoarse, then collapsed against the side of the sled.

She heaved in a breath. One breath, another, as she had done with Khulan. She let out a long, deep sob and pressed her gloved hands to her face. She could turn around. She was only three days out. She could go back. Sarnai stared long at Khulan's body. If she went back, then Khulan had died out here for nothing. Khulan, who had been born on the ships and first set down his feet here when he was five years old, the last link they had to some other time, some other place. He believed in their survival here.

Did she? Sarnai struggled to her feet again. She rolled Khulan off to the side of the sled and tucked him into a snowbank. He wasn't going to go anywhere, though a predator might take him—that was a possibility. She took a shovel out of the gear box and covered him as best she could, then planted a long red pole into the snow beside him, one of the emergency markers they kept. If any patrols ran out here, and they were few, they might find him. She left a recorded note on his pop-up display explaining who he was and where she was and where she was headed, then clunked her way into the sled.

Sarnai whistled to the dogs, and off they went, clucking and snarling toward the north, ever north.

"We are the chosen people," Sarnai's mother had told her while they huddled in the warmth of the blue globe that was the center of their home. "No other people have a world like ours, one so rich in resources. When the air is cleared we will trade with others, and we will sleep on piles of soft furs, and we will never be cold."

But her fathers had told her a different story. They were both lean men, but what she remembered most was the rumble of their voices and the roughness of their hands. "We will survive here because we care for each other," her older father had said, the one with the thick white beard. She had called him Baba, and the other, with the soft black beard, Papa. "We are all here for each other."

Her Baba patted her head and squeezed her arm, and it was now, in this memory, this dream, that Sarnai realized why she had not minded Khulan patting her arm. "No matter how terrible," her Baba said, and he smelled of lavender soap and sunshine in that moment, "we have one another. This world is harsh, but we have each other. You understand?"

She didn't, then.

Sarnai woke with a start. She felt cold and stiff. She lay in the bed of the sled, tucked neatly in its comforting embrace. A little sunlight peeked through the seams of the door to the tube, which she had closed the night before. She opened it, releasing six inches of snow into her lap. The world outside was brilliant white, and she closed her eyes and pressed her hand to her face, reflexively. Her head throbbed. She sucked in a deep breath and started to work her arms and shift her braces. She chanced another look out across the creamy white expanse, and there, over the heaped forms of the dogs curled up together, she saw a dark shape moving at the base of a sea of mountains in the distance.

She crawled out of the sled and fed the dogs the protein pellets from the gear box, all the while keeping her eyes on the figure. It wasn't human, and it was lumbering out in the far distance, but still looked huge. That meant it was likely one of the massive predators that stalked the settlements between the core and the rim.

Sarnai secured the fire pistol on her right leg brace and slipped back into the sled. She called to the dogs and off they went. In some ways, this journey was easier with one. There was no one to haggle with. No one to say when to stop or go. She and the dogs kept the pace. But it also meant that every hundred kilometers, she was the only one who could stop and feed the dogs and clean their feet—

twelve dogs, forty-eight feet—all by herself. She was exhausted at the end of every day. The days began to blur and shift together. The migraines hit her hard on the sunny days, and she could barely raise her head to call to the dogs during those hours. She was exhausted, and she stank, and after six days on her own, she became convinced that she was lost.

Worse, she was lost and something was following her.

Sarnai fed the dogs and sighted her route using her spotty GPS. There were still a few satellites aloft that had been released by the first settlers, but there was often weather-related interference. She snarled up at the sky and tucked the GPS back into the gear box. How terrible must that other world have been, for her people to travel across the yawning maw of space to land here? Sarnai settled back into the sled and yelled at the dogs to embark. The sled lurched forward, then jerked to a halt. She yelled again, but the dogs were yipping and cawing.

She struggled up in her seat and saw what they had caught a whiff of—the big, hulking thing that she had seen days before, on the horizon. It was a five-ton bear, and the long line of spikes along its spine were rippling. It snarled at the dogs from its perch twenty feet up on a low rise.

Sarnai yelled, "Go on! Get!" like it was some domestic animal. Instead, it trundled forward, toward the dogs. She had a terrible memory of Erdene arriving in the hub of settlements with just half her dogs and one arm missing, and it invigorated her. Sarnai called for the dogs to race forward, and they did, despite the bear. Sarnai raised her fire pistol at the bear as it plowed toward them, and pulled the trigger.

The bear's coat caught fire. It was so close she could smell the scent of burning hair and the stink of rotten meat that clung to its matted fur. The bear roared and broke off.

Sarnai called to the dogs, spurring them onward, ever onward, and they obeyed, kicking snow and dust behind them at the fastest pace she had seen them make on the wintry white terrain that made up the world between the core settlements and people on the edge, people like her.

How many kilometers had she crossed, now, since Khulan's death? Five hundred? No, much more. A thousand, easily. Sarnai hooted up at the sky as the lazy yellow sun crested the horizon. Whisky in a glass. A yellow-brown smear. She went to sleep that night exhausted and euphoric. She emptied out her waste and screamed at the sky because there were only her and the dogs to hear.

She had made it a thousand kilometers, easily. More than Khulan. More than many would have, she knew. And when the stink of the bear wafted in, she snorted and spat in its direction and waved her gun in the air, firing off plumes of flames.

"You can't hurt me!" she yelled. "You can't have me!"

It came for her at dawn.

Sarnai was sleeping fitfully. She dreamed of running. Running and running from something terrible. When she would look back, in her dream, it was only her Baba and Papa, but in that moment they were terrible beasts, frightening. She had never felt so terrified.

She woke violently to the stink of rotten meat. The bear's face was just inches from hers, and it bawled when she opened her eyes, and she screamed and gripped the pistol and let off a snarl of flame into its face. The flames singed its fur and feathers, sending a heady stink into the air.

The dogs were barking and squawking, and she didn't know how she had not heard them sooner, but the bear had crept upon her from the north, and the wind was coming from the south. The dogs had not noticed it. In that moment, she wanted to shoot them too, until the bear roared and snapped up one of the dogs into its great jaws. The bear was a massive thing, matted and shaggy, with a gory hooked beak and feet as big as Sarnai's head.

The dogs let up a great howl and cry. Sarnai shot her pistol again, singeing the bloody dog's hide instead of the bear's. The bear swiped a paw at her and caught her on the arm, slicing clean through her environmental suit and carving into her skin. Sarnai shot again, and again until the bear retreated.

She screamed at it and called the dogs, but they were not lined up. She had to scrabble out of the sled and get their tack in order. Once she was back in the sled, she watched the bear standing on the next rise as it snacked on its doggy treat, its great beaked face smeared with blood and offal.

"Fuck you!" Sarnai screamed, and then, to the dogs, "Go, get!" and then the sled was moving again, following the sled track on and on again, farther and farther from the bloody snow and the promise of death.

The halfway point between the core settlements and Batbayer came upon Sarnai suddenly. She had completely lost track of time, and she wasn't sure what she was seeing, even with the aid of the glitchy GPS.

The halfway house was little more than a humped shack in the snow, some old thing printed back when the first ships landed, and not upgraded since.

Sarnai was barely conscious when they arrived. She was aware of an old woman standing over her, tapping at her leg braces.

"When was the last time you emptied your bowels, girl?" the old woman said, and she put her gnarly hand to Sarnai's forehead and sighed. "You've got an infection, girl. Come now. Let's put your dogs to rest and get you tended."

Sarnai bumbled out of the sled and into the hut, only half-aware of where she was and what was happening. The woman was much stronger than she looked; she helped haul Sarnai inside, and it must have been the old woman who tended the dogs, because when Sarnai next became aware of her surroundings, she was in a warm bed, and the old woman was prodding at her belly. "You've got a urinary infection," the woman said. She had a face like a rotten apple, all puffy and pockmarked. Sarnai recognized a ruddiness to her complexion that indicated mercury poisoning.

"Not a big deal," Sarnai slurred, and she wondered if the woman had given her something for the pain, not realizing Sarnai couldn't feel anything.

"You could die from it," the old woman said. "It's serious enough. Hate to say this to a woman like you, all buff and beat up, but simple things kill."

"A bear got one of the dogs," Sarnai said.

"I thought so," the old woman said. "I can smell the fear on the dogs. That bear is tracking you. You won't shake it. You'll have to kill it."

"I have to make it to Batbayer. They are dying. Tumbledown."

The woman tapped her leg braces. "You had it, the plague. Tumbledown."

"A long time ago."

"You know why they called it tumbledown?"

"For the village," Sarnai said. "The first village it killed. Called Tumbledown."

"No," the old woman said, and as she took a cup into her hands, Sarnai saw a rash that spread up both her arms, turning her skin flaky. "It was a dark joke, from those who came to rescue them. They said they all fell down. Tumbled down."

"That's a bad joke."

"We are not all good people," the old woman said, proffering a cup. "But girls like you, they want to save everyone. They don't want to just fall down, eh? They want to get up."

"I can't make it the rest of the way."

"Of course you can. Batbayer is only sixteen hundred or so kilometers from here. Your dog team is nearly intact. It's possible. The only thing that could get in your way is you."

"And the bear," Sarnai said. "You said, the bear."

"The bear is just a bear," the old woman said. "You're a woman."

"That's worse."

"Exactly," the old woman said.

Sarnai blanked out then, from exhaustion or infection, she didn't know. When she came to, she was able to sit up. The old woman had taken off her leg braces, and when she saw that Sarnai was up, she brought her a bowl of soup.

"You'll need to cross the mercury sea, seven days out from here," the old woman said, raising a spoonful of broth to Sarnai's lips. Sarnai could feed herself, but she accepted the help because the world still felt so hazy. "That will be the worst of it, I think. That and the lonesomeness of it all. It is the lonesomeness that kills quickly. You have to beat your own head. That's what will kill the bear and the despair."

Sarnai crawled out of bed the next day. She dragged herself across the icy floor to where the old woman had placed her environmental suit. She pulled on the suit and then tackled the leg braces. She painstakingly snapped them onto her disproportionately skinny legs. The old woman was lounging on a low couch near the warm blue glow of the heat source. She raised herself up on one elbow.

"You're going on?" the old woman said.

"No choice," Sarnai said.

"There is always a choice," the old woman said. "I chose to stay out here." She pointed to a long scar on her head where the hair no longer grew. "See that? A bear once attacked me out there by the frozen lake. Wanted my fish. I said, fuck him. I tried to fight, but you know how that goes. I had to go still, very still, and it lost interest, but it did a good job fucking me up. I crawled in here and I sewed up my own head." She tapped her scalp. "We are stronger than we can imagine, you know that?"

Sarnai grimaced. "I have lived in the core settlements most of my life."

"Not all, though," the old woman said. "And what does it matter? I was raised there. We all came from the sky. We all make our lives. Our own futures. Who will you be, when you die? I will be the woman who sewed up her own head." She cackled.

Sarnai managed to walk out to the dogs and the sled. The old woman had unharnessed the dogs, and she did not come out to help Sarnai hook them back up. Sarnai brought them all back to the sled and laced them up. Her braces were moving more slowly. Her gait was herky-jerky, like a marionette on a string. But she didn't want to take the time to rub the braces down and clean them, not when she was so close.

She clunked into the sled and called the dogs, and off they raced. It was not until she looked back that she realized one of the dogs must be injured. She saw little spots of purple blood in their wake.

The bear was going to come snuffling for them. The bear, the bear, the bear . . . When she gazed back next, she thought she saw its hulking outline on the horizon, following the trail of blood. Faster, faster, they needed to ride faster.

The dogs raced up through low foothills and into a sparkling forest of jade and black stone. The dogs barely paid any mind to it, but Sarnai gaped. She had never seen such a thing. They raced and raced. She rode them hard, so hard that she lost one of the dogs, and she stared at its body the way she had stared at Khulan's, but she could not weep because she was out of tears. When they bedded down that night, she swore she heard the bear chomping on its prize, sated for a day, just a day.

Sarnai arrived at the mercury sea in just six days, not seven, the bear always just over the last rise. She did not hesitate in ordering the dogs across the sea, though they balked. Their hesitation lost them their lead, and now when she gazed behind her, she could see, clearly, the hulking shadow of the bear. She yelled at the dogs to "Get, get!" and they did.

The sled slipped across the sea, the dogs barking and yapping as they went. She consulted her GPS, pleased to see that despite her delay, she was making excellent time. She was only five days from Batbayer, maybe six. Her supplies would last that long, and most of the dogs would, too. Sarnai called again to the dogs. The mercury sea was vast. They had been out on it for an hour. She squinted, and her head throbbed. Her headache was coming, soon. She slumped back into the sled.

That's when the lead dog yelped.

The lead dog, Khulan's dog, the dog whose name was, appropriately, "Oh shit." Or perhaps just "Shit."

The dog yelped, then squawked. The others tried to bolt, and in their panic, they were able to haul the lead dog out of the mercurial lake. But as Sarnai sat in the sled she felt the ground beneath her slip, then crack. She managed to get herself half out of the sled before the ice snapped and the sled began to sink.

"Fuck!" Sarnai breathed, clawing the side of the sled. She huffed herself onto the mercury ice, but her legs dragged her down. Her leg braces. Goddamn, those braces. Sarnai began unbuckling the braces from her legs as she scrambled for purchase on the ice behind her. The braces slipped free of her legs and plunged into the metallic sea, sinking faster than the sled. Sarnai clawed her way up the ice, making little hiccupping sounds of distress until she was well clear of the hole.

When she raised her head, she found herself gazing directly into the face of the bear, a dozen paces distant. It inhaled deeply and then started toward her. She grimaced. "Life," she murmured, "is cruel and gross and awful."

The bear did not hear, did not care. She reached for the fire pistol, but it had been attached to her leg braces, which were now likely floating beneath the surface of the sea. She sucked in a long, slow breath. The bear advanced.

Sarnai cast about for a weapon. The sled was half submerged in the slushy mercury sea. It was then that she saw the machete that

Khulan had been using to cut at the creepers. She had stashed it back in the sled, and it glimmered at her now in the smeared yellowish light of the rising sun. Sarnai scrambled for the machete just as the bear broke into a run.

She grabbed the machete by the hilt and swung it full force into the face of the bear as it bore down upon her. Her swing caught the bear's massive beak. It reared back, yanking her arms with it, but she hung on and pulled the machete free. The bear's bulk had yanked her out of the sled and up onto the ice.

The bear came at her again. She held the machete close to her chest. The bear impaled itself on the blade, but with such force that it knocked the air from Sarnai's lungs. She rolled to the side, trying to pull the machete with her, but it was lodged in the rolling fat of the bear's chest. The bear stank of death; its own or hers?

Sarnai screamed at it and lunged for the hilt of the machete. She yanked hard, using all the strength in her upper body that she had honed for years while others used their legs, and she pulled the machete free. She swung again, more powerfully this time, and the blade sank again into the bear's flesh. The bear roared and grabbed her by the shoulder. It shook her, hard, and the machete tore free once again. She slammed the machete into its shoulder, again and again, screaming as she did it. The bear broke away from her and trundled away, snuffling as it did.

She tried to catch her breath. How was she going to make it another five or six days across the tundra without the sled? Behind her, the sled remained half-submerged in the sea. The dogs were barking and yelping while half of their number paddled in the mercury sea, rolling along its surface, spinning and turning as they floated along. Was this what had happened to Erdene and her dogs? Was Sarnai going to die out here the way they had?

Sarnai lay in the snow, watching the angry bear snuffle and snort. She empathized with it, but out here it was her or the bear, and she knew which she chose. She gripped the machete. Her legs were soaked in freezing mercury. How much longer until her suit gave out? But what did that matter? Whole settlements were dying. Human life on this planet might die out altogether. What did it matter how many limbs she had left? They were only for show, anyway. It was time she became what she was, instead of what made people comfortable.

Sarnai snarled at the bear.

It raised its head and roared at her.

She raised her machete.

Batbayer was a coastal city clinging to the edge of the sea. From four or five kilometers distant, it looked like a dead place, its longhouses layered in snow, its fires snuffed out.

But as the silvery sled came barreling down the low rise, there seemed to be signs of life, still. A long curl of smoke to the north. Snowy paths that had been clomped flat and dirtied by the patter of many footsteps.

Sarnai reined in the bear she had hitched to the front of her sled. "Ho now! Ho!" she called, and the bear responded, if not to her command then to the bit in its mangled beak.

Behind the sled, the six dogs that remained of her team took up the rear, squawking and barking as they caught the scent of Batbayer. Sarnai urged the bear forward, and together they careened down into the village, so fast and furiously that she had to throw out the sled's jagged anchor because she feared the bear would not come to a halt.

The bear reared up at the stony gate, roaring and snarling. Sarnai sat in the belly of her sled, soaking in her own urine. She had not dared stop to cath. Now she found herself without her leg braces, stuck here at the gates of the city she had come to save.

Sarnai pulled herself out of the sled. She rolled out onto the icy ground and crawled on her elbows to the gate. The bear snorted at her. She waved her machete at him, urging him back. Then she raised her fist to the gate and knocked.

Slowly, ever so slowly, the gate opened. Sarnai set her gaze on those who greeted her. They were just children, not much older than she had been when the plague claimed her family.

The oldest, a girl, started when she saw Sarnai and said, "Oh no! Do you need help? The plague is here. You're in danger here."

And Sarnai laughed. "I don't need help," she said, and she laughed again, so hard and long that she could not catch her breath. "I don't need help. I'm here to help *you*."

As Sarnai had predicted, the serum was ruined by the time she reached Batbayer.

But she was not.

There were still some elders alive, and they knew how to synthesize her antibodies at the little medical bay they had set up with the expansive view of the frozen sea. Sarnai spent longer there than she intended, but it was worth it. She got to watch the spring roll in and soften the seas. The little heads of spring flowers pushed their way up through the snow. While there would never be a true thaw on Narantu, there was a spring, and it was beautiful. The light was warmer, brighter, and those who remained in Batbayer came alive with the light and the green growing things.

While they could not print leg braces for her, they were able to give Sarnai a rolling chair and a new environmental suit, and she cried when she got them, though she could not articulate why. She rolled herself out in the chair along the heated and treaded paths, which made her way easier, though not easy. She wheeled herself up onto a concrete slab that overlooked the sea, and she could not help but think of all those creatures that would no longer thrive in the spring. They were the foxes and bears, so well-suited for the worst this world could offer. But in their place, other creatures were uncurling from their long slumbers. Creatures better suited to this softer weather.

Sarnai inhaled deeply and wheeled herself back down the path, toward the infirmary. On the way, she passed the cemetery, where the ashes of those who had perished were spread or buried, and their grave markers left for future generations. Who was to say, who must go and who must stay? The world decided. There was a bitter anger in that, that something as pitiless and uncaring as the world decided one's fate. But it was not for the core settlements to decide, or the village elders, or anyone else. Just the world. Only the world.

She used the handrail next to the path up to the infirmary to help herself up the shallow rise. The world might decide her life or death, but the settlements still played their part in making her feel welcome or not.

Once inside the airlock, she removed her respirator and pulled back her hood. She wheeled herself over to the bed on the other side of the infirmary, where the last of those who had contracted tumbledown lay in recovery. The little girl was just eight years old. She sat up and gazed out the window, hands in her lap. Her expression was familiar to Sarnai.

"You look like you are in need of hope," Sarnai said.

The girl turned her gaze to Sarnai, and her lips trembled, and Sarnai noted that the girl's left arm was still in her lap. The girl would not be able to move that arm any more than her own legs in the months and years to come. Sarnai wondered if she should tell her about the sex, or the cath, or the bag, and she decided not to. Those were already things the girl was learning to live with. The rest would come in time. For now, it was enough to live.

Sarnai wheeled herself up to the girl's bedside.

"Atasha," Sarnai said. "Would you like to hear a story?"

"Yes," Atasha said. The lip trembled again, and Sarnai reached out her hand and took the girl's right one, and squeezed it hard, the way that Khulan would have.

"Good, then," Sarnai said. "Let's tell a story about the world we'll make together."

WARPED PASSAGES

MY MOTHER LEFT ME for the anomaly when I was too young to see over the railing into the tangled gardens at the center of the ship, but not yet old enough to climb up onto it and jump into the lake at the gardens' heart. The people of the Legion had stopped counting time back in my mother's day, when the anomaly ripped through the fleet and halted us on our two-generation journey to a world that our prophets said would lead to our salvation. Now we were a static fleet, stuck in darkness, drifting nowhere, with uncertainty as to when and how our resources would run out. Would we starve in a generation? Two? Or would we asphyxiate first?

No one was quite certain. It had driven some people mad.

But for those of us who knew nothing else, it just made life that much more worth living. Living is a gift, when you're sure it could end at any minute. And life ended often, in the Legion. Accidents, plague, bad air, support system failures, insurrection, collisions . . . one by one the ships of the Legion would go dark, and those of us left would cannibalize whatever remained of them.

I suppose that would drive my mother's generation more mad

than it did me, because I had no expectations, not like she did. In school, aboard ship, they were told they would arrive in some brave new world God had chosen for them, and the prophets of New Morokov had charted. They were God's chosen people, with a real purpose, a plan. I was just a kid with an uncertain future, drifting through the detritus of the dying.

Everything had gone wrong just halfway into the trip.

The anomaly appeared and passed through the whole fleet, like a great, many-tentacled wave of glutinous energy. It split our ship in two, cutting right through the center of the lake, slicing open the hull in every direction. That should have been the end of us and every ship in the Legion, which were all halted in the same way. We should have been jettisoned into deep space. But though the anomaly breached the hull, the anomaly itself acted as a sort of sealant. There was no breach. But the engines could no longer power us forward. We were stuck in place, rooted to whatever these waves of foreign matter were.

From outside the ship, when I take the long trading walks between our home and those ships aligned with ours, the anomalies look like massive, irregular shimmering discs splitting through all five hundred ships of the Legion. They reflect light, and the ships, and each other, and our tools and clothing, but not our faces. You stare into the flat plane of an anomaly and it's like watching a ghost wearing your clothes. It's like they're eating our souls, my mother used to say, which made her choice to throw herself into one that much stranger. Why would you feed your soul to some alien thing?

My sister Malati says the anomaly is a great manifestation of our own consciousness. Everyone has theories about what they are. All we know is that they don't see our reflections, and that whatever steps into them never comes back out again. The scientists don't think the anomalies are alive, and prophets agree, but the way they act, sometimes, the way they ripple when you talk to them, makes me think otherwise. I spent my childhood throwing junk into those things until my mother caught me and slapped me for being wasteful.

"We need every piece of this ship to survive," she had said. "You don't recycle something, and it's lost forever. Do you understand? You risk your children's lives. You risk our future. Waste is a terrible crime."

I started crying when she yelled at me, because I didn't want to be wasteful. Losing or breaking something was the worst thing anyone could do, out here. It meant you would have to trade with another ship, or go on a dangerous scavenging mission to one of the derelicts at the edge of the Legion's gravity well.

When I was old enough to stand up on the rail and jump into the lake with my friends, during the very darkest of the ship's sleeping cycle, I was fascinated by the number of things captured in the shimmering face of the anomaly that bisected the lake. Ropes and chains and plastic tethers that had held instruments and small animals that my grandmother's generation had cast into the thing lay scattered on the banks of the far side of the lake, or tied off to metal balustrades, a record of two generations who had tried and failed to understand the anomaly. It was why jumping into the lake was considered so dangerous. It was easy to float into the anomaly if you weren't careful. And once you threw something in, you couldn't pull it back out. Not the tethers, or anything attached to them. No people, either.

There were many theories about the anomaly. Some said it was an inter-dimensional body, perhaps one that lived in five or six dimensions, and the half-circles of nothingness that split through our ships were simply the manifestation of it that we could perceive in our dimensions. Others thought it was a sentient thing, an unknown being. Some said it was the tears of God, who had wept when we left our home planet, and now punished our arrogance by keeping us here, bound by Her tears.

Me, I had grown up with the anomaly. It was just a part of life. It didn't scare me until my generation hit puberty, and some of us started giving birth to strange things.

But I'm getting ahead of myself.

I don't know whose idea it was, first, to sever a ship from the anomaly and retrofit it to fly again. It was an old plan, something from my mother's generation, before people gave up hope. Half a dozen ships tried it, cobbling together parts, selecting crews, but they failed every time. I learned about some of those attempts in school, and maybe that's when I came up with my own plan. Maybe that's when I realized what the problem was.

All of these people, they were trying to repair a ship and take other people with them. It was at least another generation more to the planet. Even if they got there and could mount a rescue, it would be another generation back to get us. That's two generations more we'd have to survive out here, and the reality is, we probably weren't going to make it that long. They'd return to a dead husk of ships, all spinning black around the great artificial sun and gravity well that held us together.

It was never the engineers who failed, in retrofitting ships to break free of the anomaly, or at least I didn't think so then. It was the people they involved. People fought about who was going to go, who was going to come back, and the ships were sabotaged long before they could break free. The one to reach as far as the edge of the Legion, the one that got as far as the outer rim of ships, was piloted by a woman named Pavitra Narn and carried just a dozen people. They had kept the whole thing secret right up until the time they opened the fuel tanks to feed the engine.

But Pavitra and her crew were still sabotaged. Probably by one of their own crewmates, or by a lover or a family member left behind.

The remains of that ship still circle the outer rim of the Legion, along with the escape pods.

It was after Pavitra's failure that people started using the escape pods. They thought they could escape the gravity well, I guess, though where they thought they'd go after that, I don't know. Maybe they just hoped to cling to a few more cycles of life, to gain themselves more time for a rescue. Maybe the clutch of years they could survive in a pod was more than they expected to live inside the ships.

When my mother had me, after her mother died, there was still some hope in her generation. But that's been gone a long time, now. Most old people sit in their quarters waiting for the end.

I knew, reading about Pavitra, that I was going to learn how to fix ships, and I was going to figure out how to get one out of the Legion. But I was going to do it right. I wouldn't tell anyone but my sister Malati, because though I was becoming a good engineer by then, she was a lot older than me, and already an ace pilot. She was allowed to drive our ship's only functioning transport on ship-to-ship runs and salvage missions, one of just a dozen people qualified for it.

Malati and I could do it. If I involved more people than that, it would never work. Someone would get angry. Someone would try and stop us.

Maybe even the anomaly itself.

So I stopped staying up late jumping into the lake. I didn't go out huffing chemicals with the other kids. I didn't screw around very much, which was a shame, looking back. Maybe I missed out on some things.

But I intended to build something better.

It was out on my third spacewalk, helping a team to gather salvage around a nearby ship now only half-populated, that I saw the ship that I would retrofit.

Pavitra's wreck had collided with another derelict floating at the edge of the Legion. If I told people I was studying systems on the derelict, I could easily get access to Pavitra's old ship and work to retrofit it.

From the derelict I'd also have a long view into the center of the Legion, and the two dozen ships already in the process of being devoured.

We didn't know for sure what had happened on those ships. Rumor had it that the people of our generation were giving birth to strange growing things, like tumors, and they were spreading fast, engulfing ship after ship. But none of those ships it happened to were allied with us, so we had only rumors. We did no trade with them, and many were openly hostile. We offered no aid. The ships that carried the people of the new prophets were only a fraction of the people who made up the Legion. Many followed other gods, or no god at all.

We simply sat in our sector of the Legion, staring at those transforming ships, as I did from the rim of the derelict, wondering when whatever fate had befallen them would reach us.

The engines that powered the ships were all closed organic systems, meant to exist in symbiosis with the rest of the ship. It was a concept that worked well as long as nothing happened to any other part of the ship, and maybe that was part of what was wrong with the ships being eaten. That's the theory I had, back then. The closed system made the ships harder to retrofit, but I knew Pavitra had already started that process. Though there was little enough left of her ship, getting out there to work on it every day would be easy. I could cover what I was doing by saying I was just studying it and applying what I learned somewhere else, on some other ship—ours.

It was a tricky, two-faced balance. I didn't know if I could pull it off.

I pitched the idea to my engineering instructor not long after puberty, and though much of the class scoffed at the idea of studying another derelict, the professor did not. I spent long cycles in meetings with engineers and scientists and then I was given permission to go out on my spacewalk. But I wasn't to do it alone, they said. They wanted me to take another student. I convinced them Malati was the best person to accompany me.

And so it started—my attempt to free us all from the death of the Legion.

The various systems of the ship were never meant to work independently, as I said, which was what made it so miraculous that the anomaly hadn't stopped the core life support functions of the ships. Their influence kept us rooted in space—no matter how much fuel we gave the engines, the ships of the Legions never moved. It was another bit of evidence in support of the inter-dimensional idea—if the bulk of the anomaly existed in some other dimension, then that was what rooted us here. It was as if some giant beast had thrown out its fingers or tentacles wide, snarled us in them, and fallen back to sleep while we writhed in its grasp.

The stuff that fueled the engines was a complex brew of engineered organisms that excreted a combustible compound. It was pumped into yet another engineered organism at the center of the ship, an organ we simply called the "engine," though it did not at all resemble anything like the early machines that bore that name in my History of Engineering classes. The engine powered all of the ship's systems, not just propulsion; it pumped vital heating and cooling fluid to various parts of the ship, and kept the complex algae bath that provided our oxygen at the correct temperature. Ours was not a fully sentient ship, but a hybrid of living and dead tissue. When I was younger, I had asked if the ships were alive, but the elders all said the ships were no more alive than an organ grown in a vat, like the time my aunt's heart was replaced by one grown in the medical bay.

"Is your liver a sentient thing?" my teacher asked when I protested. But when you worked on the ships you couldn't help but think of it like a living thing; a tethered animal.

I spent many cycles working to retrofit Pavitra's ship. Malati thought I was odd, at first. She laughed when I told her my idea.

But as the artificial sun went up and down and progress on the engine took shape, she stopped laughing, and started helping on our long forays across the tethers that we'd set up between our ship and the derelict.

Finally the day came when I had the last bit of retrofitted printed parts I needed to fire up Pavitra's old ship.

I sweated heavily in the suit I wore as I went hand over hand out on the tether to the derelict. Malati was already far ahead of me. We'd argued about something petty back on the ship, and she was ignoring me. She seemed much more graceful outside the ship than in it, but I was the opposite. The blackness beyond terrified me. I did every walk like this far too fast, to the point that my instructors often chided me about the need for caution over speed.

So I don't know why I hesitated, that day. You get used to junk flying around the Legion. Our gravity well was still active; it was all that held us together, and we thanked God for that afterward, but it also meant it was difficult for anything to escape the core. Things could be cast out, but never truly discarded.

I saw the piece of junk catch the light from the heart of the Legion before it struck. A sharp glint, nothing more. It zipped by so fast I barely had time to register it. You forget how fast things are moving around you when you're making the slow, arduous crawl between ships.

The aged piece of dead tech hurdled past me. It snapped the tether. The frayed end of the tether hit me in the face. I let go, grabbing at my face, fearful of a suit breach. I didn't realize I'd slid off the tether until I pulled my hands away, and by then I was already a hundred yards away from Malati, pinwheeling away from her at a constant speed. She had wrapped her hands around the broken tether. I could not see the expression on her face so far away.

I flailed, trying to see where I was headed. A knife of fear cut through my heart. I realized I wasn't spinning toward the Legion, but away from it. Reason told me I hadn't been thrown with enough force to escape the Legion's gravity, but reason did not quell my quaking fear as I tumbled between two great ships, signing for help as I careened past them.

They might not get to me in time, but Malati could send a shuttle out after me. If my air didn't run out, if I didn't career into one of the ships, if . . .

And that's when I realized that there was no safe passage between those ships.

Both ships were cut through by the anomaly. It was a broad, disc-shaped plane here, like a bladed saw that split both ships—and I was headed toward the center of it.

I cried out. I came closer and closer, powerless to stop myself. I saw the distorted reflection of my suit in the anomaly's shimmering face. A ghost suit without a body in it. To the anomaly, I was already dead.

Where did we go when we went through the anomaly? Where had my mother gone? Where had all the instruments gone? Where would I go?

"Please help me," I said aloud, and I must have been saying it to God, or maybe the anomaly itself, or maybe both, if they were indeed one and the same. "Please," I said.

I kicked and waved my arms, instinctive, knowing it wasn't going to help, knowing movement meant little in a vacuum.

I collided with the anomaly.

Bright white light burst across my vision.

I screamed. I remember screaming.

I wondered if my mother had screamed.

I woke in a warm, pale blue room.

Our medical officer, Jandai, stared down at me from within a heavy medical-grade suit.

"Do you know where you are?" she asked.

". . . Jagvani Station?" I said.

"And who are you?" she asked.

"I'm Kariz Bhavaja," I said.

She nodded ever so slightly, lips pressed firm. I tried to figure out what that meant.

"What happened to me?" I said.

"To hear the witnesses on the *Goravna* and *Arashakti* tell it, you passed through the anomaly," she said.

"I'm not . . . this isn't the other side?"

She raised her brows. "It's not the afterlife, if that's what you're asking. But you'll see that soon enough when you're pissing through your catheter," she said.

"But . . . no one comes out the other side of the anomaly alive," I said.

"Some do," she said. "But they . . . bring things with them."

"Is there something wrong with me?"

The pursing of the lips again. Then, "You're under medical watch for a few days."

"Quarantine?"

She nodded.

Quarantine lasted for ten sleep cycles. I asked about Malati, and Jandai said she was shaken, but fine. Malati came to visit me early in the quarantine, and we spoke softly through the protective film around my quarters.

"I think we should stop," she said.

"You want to die here, in the Legion?" I said.

She could not answer that.

So I counted my days in quarantine, which nobody in my generation likes to do, but sometimes you can't help it.

On the tenth one, I already knew something was wrong long before Jandai came back. At night, I had felt something stirring in my chest. And on the tenth morning, when I woke, I had a lump in my chest where one had not been before.

"We've detected something," Jandai said, and I did not let her finish.

"Get it out," I said.

"It's a living thing," she said. "Protocol is not to remove it until we understand what it is."

"Are you insane?" I said. "You *know* what it is! It's one of those things, it's—"

"We can't confirm it's what's been reported on the other ships," Jandai said.

"It's a parasite! It will kill me!"

"We have no evidence of that," she said. "The science council has recommended that we wait and see. We have a very strict policy about how we handle alien life."

"This is insane," I said again, as if by saying it I could make her understand it. But she was resistant.

"You can't legally keep me in quarantine any longer than ten cycles," I said. "You have to get rid of it or release me. I'll call an advocate."

"I've been given instructions to release you," she said, "but you'll be monitored."

This shocked me. I couldn't understand how they could permit me to leave the medical bay with some alien thing in me, but then I started laughing, because of course the alien things were already here, they were all around us, they had cut into our ships a generation ago, and now my mother's generation was just using me as some test tube to see what happened next.

They sent me home with painkillers and anti-inflammatories, and I lay in bed with my hands over my chest. I swore I could feel the thing growing inside of me. I must have dozed, but when I woke I had terrible heartburn, and spent half an hour vomiting bile.

I stumbled out onto the balcony overlooking the great gardens at the center of the ship and stared down into the lake, and then up at the shimmering anomaly that bisected it, and our ship. I understood my mother's compulsion to jump into it, then. I wanted to tear open my chest and get the thing out, but no one wanted to help me.

Was that why she had really jumped into the anomaly? Had it done this to her, too? And if it had, where had she come out again? Had they hidden her from me because she was contaminated afterward, like I was? I closed my eyes and imagined those other ships, the half-eaten ruin of them. Rumor had it the first few had removed these organisms, but they clung to the ship instead, and ate everything around them, devouring it like some fungus. If it stayed inside of me, it would eat me, too, and then the ship. The prophets had to know this. Why were they permitting me to walk around?

It wasn't going to last, I knew. So I went out to finish what I'd started. I found Malati in our quarters. She had the parts we had carried with us.

"We go again," I said. "We make it work this time. We aren't coming back."

"Are you mad?" she said.

"I know why it won't let us leave," I said, rubbing the thing on my chest. "The engines are alive. It thinks they are, anyway. I think the anomaly sees them as kin of some kind. It thinks we've enslaved them."

"That's a strange stretch," Malati said.

I knew I shouldn't have said it aloud to her. "I don't think it was always us who were sabotaging the ships that tried to get away. I think the anomaly made us do it, the same way it convinced the prophets to let me go from quarantine."

"If all we're doing is what they want, then we have no free will," Malati said. "I don't believe that."

"Some of us do," I said. "I just don't know which."

"Is that why we're going?"

"They'll stop us soon," I said. "This isn't going to last."

We took the shuttle this time, because Malati had access. I would deal with whatever the consequences were. But not Malati. Malati was going to be safe, far away from here.

It took two more sleep cycles to get Pavitra's wreck up and running.

"Why haven't they come for the shuttle?" Malati asked as I powered up the great monster of an engine.

"You should get settled in the back," I said. "I'll deal with them."

"What do you mean?"

"I'm not going with you," I said. "If I go, and that planet's already inhabited by someone who came after us . . . I'll have brought this thing there. I can't let this thing leave the Legion."

"I'm not spending all that time alone! I'll be an old woman when I get there. Don't you dare. I'm not doing it. We didn't go through all this just for you to stay."

"They want me to go," I said.

"What?"

"The prophets. That's why they didn't take it out," I said. "I don't think we have a will of our own anymore, Malati. Not all of us. I think the anomaly is affecting their judgment. It wants me to leave the Legion with this thing."

"That's mad."

"A lot of things are mad," I said. "But you won't have to be alone. I've fitted the rear with escape pods. They'll keep you in stasis for most of the journey. I'll show you how to use them. Switch out once, when the first reaches the end of its cycle, and you'll be there before you know it."

"I can't do this alone," Malati said. "First mother, then you—"

"You won't be alone," I said. "The fate of the whole Legion goes with you."

She firmed her mouth, then, though unshed tears made her eyes glassy.

I powered up the ship, and I put Malati in deep stasis in one of the escape pods I had hauled off the derelict and fitted into Pavitra's ship. The second waited nearby. I didn't know if she could last the cycles of rest she would have to be awake, in between, but if she didn't, then everything that remained of us would die out here. Or maybe, I thought, gazing out the port window at the growing tangles of fibrous matter eating the ships at the core—we would be transformed.

I kicked on the engines and set them on autopilot with a long timer. When I popped free of the ship and into the transport, the growing lump in my chest throbbed. My head ached. I piloted the transport away, quickly, and sat back to watch.

I half expected the ship to explode. I watched it power up and jump forward. It heaved toward the edge of the Legion like a shot. I held my breath as it cleared the gravity well.

Then the blue burn of the cruising thrusters, the intricate combination of organic fuels that burned so hot it powered the ship at near-light speed, blazed brightly. I'd only ever seen those thrusters chemically burn in vain, shown to us in recordings of the first few attempts they had made to free the Jagvani, so we'd know what it would look like if it ever worked again. But ours never got us anywhere. We were tethered in place.

Pavitra's ship broke away from the Legion.

I watched it for a long, long time. Long after it was even a speck in my field of vision. Behind me, the artificial sun at the core of the Legion came up, and bathed us all in orange light.

When I cycled back into the air lock of the Jagvani, Jandai was waiting for me.

"Come," she said, and I didn't ask what for, not even when she brought me to the medical bay and sedated me.

When I woke, the ever-present lump on my chest was gone.

Jandai sat beside me, and behind her, in a large glass cylinder, was a pulsing orb of tissue. It was covered in little tentacles, like cilia, all waving against its glass prison.

"Why won't you kill it?" I said.

"It's been attempted, on other ships," Jandai said. "It . . . fights back. But that's of no concern to us, of course. We have strict protocols about preserving life of any kind, I told you. It goes against everything we believe."

"Why now?" I said. "Because the ship is gone? Because they know I can't get them out?"

"It will serve a different purpose," Jandai said.

"How long have you all known what the anomaly was, and what these things are?" I asked. "How long did my mother know?"

"We agreed not to tell the third generation," she said. "It was bad enough for us, living with it. Better for you to believe escape was possible. Better for you to believe you had free will, and were not caught in the maw of some monster."

"Is the anomaly God?" I asked.

"It is a sentient being that is beyond our understanding. I suppose that yes, in a way, it is *a* god, if not *our* God."

I stared at the pulsing thing in the cylinder. "Will it eat the ship, like the others?"

She nodded. "In time. But by devouring the ship it will save us, in a way. We'll be transformed."

"It's turning the ships into living things," I said. "Real living things."

"We think it was drawn to them from some . . . other place. It saw them, perhaps, as a species that must be uplifted."

"Then what were we?"

She grimaced. "Parasites."

"Why let us think we had no future? Better to know the truth, so we can fight it."

"Fight a god? No. Your future . . . our future, will be in service to these things, as whatever they make us into. People will still live on the ships, but they, too, will become part of it, like any other system on the ship. They can't leave it without the whole system collapsing. We tried it, with some of the early ships. If you remove any of the components it grew around and incorporated when it was birthed, it dies, and so does everyone and everything else aboard. We wanted you to get away while you still could."

I tried to sit up, but the drugs from the surgery were wearing off, and my chest throbbed. "Why not take it out, then? I could have gone—"

"No," she said. "Not once you're infected. You're a part of it now."

"Why didn't you tell me all this?"

"Because you were our hope," she said. "If you and the others thought you had no future, you would fight to build one instead of accepting this one. We raised you your whole lives to accept God. How would you have reacted if you thought this was one?"

"Only Malati got away."

"I know. I guess it doesn't matter. It feels like we're the only human beings in the universe out here, but of course there are many others under many stars. She may arrive to a fully populated world."

"They'll rescue us," I said.

She laughed. "What will they rescue, if we are even still here, once we become like those other sentient ships and putter off to whatever destination they have in store for us? We're linked to these ships, haven't you been listening? We'll become part of these machines, birthing its parts, its organs, like insects. It's best they don't come. I don't want them to see us." She stood. "You should go now."

"Why did you finally tell me about all of this?" I asked.

"Your mother didn't throw herself into the anomaly," she said. "She was pushed on order of the prophets, because she was going to tell you and your sister that the anomaly was God's will, and we should not fight it. She was going to ruin the grand experiment. So instead, she became a part of it."

"You kept her from me," I said. "You made her a prisoner. Made her birth one of these things and told me she was dead."

"In the end, the process killed her," Jandai said. "What grew in her did not survive. I'm sorry. But the experiment is over now."

"These things aren't the monsters," I said. "*You* are. All of you."

"Maybe so," she said, and she stood and left the medical bay.

I lay alone in the room with the pulsing alien thing in the jar, the alien that would turn this whole ship into some kind of integrated machine, and I tried to come to grips with the scale of this betrayal. History was a lie. My studies were a lie. My whole life's purpose, all this work, my mother's suicide, all a lie. For what? For science. A grand experiment. A last attempt to save us. Our parents' generation could not live with the truth, so they just never spoke about it.

It had worked, absolutely. Malati was free. But should she be? I didn't know. If we all died here, was it so terrible, in the grand scheme of things? What happens next, when you realize everything is a lie, and life has no purpose?

When I was recovered, I went down to the lake and peered into the anomaly. My mother's generation knew what I did, now, and they had chosen secrecy, and despondency, and suicide. But they had forgotten that we were the same people who had left a blighted, overcrowded planet three generations ago to take a risk on a new life among the stars. We were made from stronger stuff than they imagined.

It would take my whole life, I knew, but I would figure out a way to control what we were becoming. If I could not stop it, I could figure out how to influence it. I was an engineer of massive organic systems. I had done what the best of us, Pavitra, had not managed: I had powered a ship away from the Legion. There was nothing I wasn't capable of.

"You cannot break us," I said. "No god ever has."

And I climbed back upstairs to the medical bay, and got to work.

OUR FACES, RADIANT SISTERS, OUR FACES FULL OF LIGHT!*

She was warned. She was given an explanation.
Nevertheless, she persisted.

. . . **WAS AN EPIGRAPH** engraved at the bases of statues around the city, meant to dissuade women from fighting monsters. But to Moira, the epigraph inspired. We all fight monsters, she knew. There was no shame in losing.

So despite or because of that epigraph, Moira intended to carry on in the work that had led to her own grandmother's death, and her mother before her, back and back, to the beginning of this world, and into the next. Someone had to hold back the monsters.

Moira left the confines of the gated city. She moved into the hills. She carried only a crystal staff. The city sent up the golems after her, as she knew they would. Many didn't understand that someone had to fight the monsters. Someone had to persist, or the city would be overwhelmed. She fought the golems, twisting their guts and gouging out their ticking hearts. Snakes and bears and other beasts bred to keep her behind the walls slithered and snapped and snuffled in her path. Moira wrestled them too, and emerged bloody and bitten, but triumphant.

She limped her way to the base of the great mountain that all her female kin had talked of for time immemorial. She climbed and climbed, until her shoes were shredded and her fingers bled, and her arms shook so badly she thought they would fail her. When she pulled herself up onto the great ledge at the top, she saw what remained of her sisters: wizened, mummified visages, scattered bones, discarded shoes, two broken crystal staves. She limped through the detritus of her kin and into the cave where the monsters lay.

The monsters rose from their beds, already armored and bristling for another attack on the city below. They came to extinguish light, and hope. She was here to remind them they wouldn't do it unchallenged.

Moira raised her staff in her hands and shouted. The monsters yowled and overtook her. She bludgeoned them, snapping and biting like the creatures in the valley, poking at their hearts with her staff until it hit home, ramming through the eye of one of the great giants. They fell together, she and the monster, gazing into one another's ruined faces.

One less monster to take the city, one less woman to defend it.

"Oh, our faces, radiant sisters," Moira said, gazing out over the monster's body at the scattered bones as the monsters snarled in the darkness, readying to tear her to pieces, as they had her kin. "Our faces, so full of light."

When Moira failed to return, and the monsters crept down from the mountains—one fewer this year, one fewer each year, one fewer, always one fewer, but never none, never enough—a statue of Moira's likeness was raised beside her grandmother's.

Each day, young women visited her statue. They ran their fingers over the inscription at its base. They did so generation after generation, as more statues rose and fell, more monsters came and went, and time moved on, the eternal struggle of light and dark.

The women pressed their hands to the words there until the only script that remained visible of the epigraph on Moira's statue was a single word:

"*persist.*"

see. Sheldon, Racoona. "Your Faces, O My Sisters! Your Faces Full of Light."

ENYO-ENYO

ENYO MEDITATED AT MEALTIMES within the internode, huffing liquor vapors from a dead comrade's shattered skull. This deep within the satellite, ostensibly safe beneath the puckered skein of the peridium, she went over the lists of the dead.

She recited her own name first.

Enyo's memory was a severed ocular scelera; leaking aqueous humor, slowing losing shape as the satellite she commanded spun back to the beginning. The cargo she carried was unknown to her, a vital piece of knowledge that had escaped the punctured flesh of her memory.

She had named the ship after herself—*Enyo-Enyo*—without any hint of irony. The idea that Enyo had any irony left was a riotous laugh even without knowing the satellite's moniker, and her Second, Reeb, amused himself often at her shattering attempt at humor.

After the purging of every crew, Reeb came into Enyo's pulpy green quarters, his long face set in a black, graven expression she had come to call winter, for it came as often as she remembered that season in her childhood.

"Why don't we finish out this turn alone?" he would say. "We can manage the internode ourselves. Besides, they don't make engineers the way they did eight turns ago."

"There's the matter of the prisoner," she would say.

And he would throw up his dark, scarred hands and sigh and say, "Yes, there's the prisoner."

It was Enyo's duty, her vocation, her obsession, to tread down the tongue of the spiraling umbilicus from the internode to the holding pod rotation of the satellite, to tend to the prisoner.

Each time, she greeted the semblance of a body suspended in viscous green fluid with the same incurious moue she had seen Justice wear in propaganda posters during the war. Some part of her wondered if the body would recognize it. If they could talk of those times. But who knew how many turns old it was? Who knew how many other wars it had seen? On a large enough scale, her war was nothing. A few million dead. A system destroyed.

The body's eyes were always closed, its sex indeterminate, its face a morass of dark, thread-like tentacles and fleshy growths. Most sessions, she merely came down and unlocked the feed cabinet, filled a clean syringe with dark fluid, and inserted it into the black fungal sucker fused to the transparent cell. Sometimes, when the body absorbed the fluid, it would writhe and twist, lost in the ecstasy of fulfillment.

Enyo usually went straight back to the internode to recite her lists of dead, after. But she had been known to linger, to sit at the flat, gurgling drive that kept her charge in permanent stasis.

She had stopped wondering where the body had come from, or who it had been. Her interest was in pondering what it would become when they reached its destination. She lost track of time in these intimate reveries, often. After half a rotation of contemplation, Reeb would do a sweep of the satellite. He would find her alive and intact, and perhaps he would go back to playing screes or fucking one of the engineers or concocting a vile hallucinogen the gelatinous consistency of aloe. They were a pair of two, a crew of three, picking up rim trash and mutilated memories in the seams between the stars during the long night of their orbit around the galactic core.

When they neared the scrap belt called Stile, Enyo was mildly surprised to see the collection of spinning habited asteroids virtually unchanged from the turn before.

"It's time," she told Reeb. "Without more fuel, we won't make it the full turn." And she would not be able to drop off the prisoner.

He gave her his winter look. She had left the last of his engineers on a paltry rock the color of foam some time before. He did not know why they needed the crew now; he did not have her sense of things, of the way time moved here. But he would be lonely. It was why he always agreed to take on another crew, even knowing their fate.

"How many more?" he said.

"This is the last turn," she said. "Then we are finished."

She let Reeb pick the new crew. He launched a self-propelled spore from the outernode well ahead of their arrival on the outskirts of Stile. The dusty ring of settlements within the asteroid belt circled a bloated, dying star. Had it been dying the last time they passed? Enyo could not remember.

Reeb's sister worked among the debris, digging through old spores and satellites, piecing together their innards, selling them as pirated vessels imbued with the spirit of cheap colonial grit.

Enyo had not seen Reeb's sister in many turns, when speaking of the war, of genocide—in terms outside the propagandic—was still new and unsettling and got them thrown out of establishments. Broodbreeders and creep cleaners called them void people, diseased, marked for a dry asphyxiation aboard a viral satellite, drifting ever aimless across limitless space. They were not far wrong. Sometimes Enyo wondered if they really knew who she was.

She heard Reeb's sister slide up the umbilicus into the internode.

Heard her hesitate on the threshold, the lubrication of the umbilicus slick on her skin.

"This your satellite?" Reeb's sister asked.

Enyo had expected to feel nothing at her voice, but like the body in the tank, she was sometimes surprised at what was fed to her. Something in her flared, and darkened, and died. It was this snapshot of Reeb's sister that she always hoped was the true one. The real one. But she knew better.

She swiveled. Reeb's sister did not take up the tubal port as Reeb did, but inhabited it in the loose way the woman inhabited all spaces, wrapping it around herself like a shroud, blurring the edges of her surrounds—or perhaps Enyo's eyes were simply going bad again. The satellite changed them out every quarter turn. The woman had once had the body of a dancer, but like all of them, she had atrophied, and though she was naturally thin, it was a thinness borne of hunger and muscle loss. Her eyes were black as Reeb's, but their color was the only feature they shared. She was violet black to Reeb's tawny brown, slight in the hips and shoulders, delicate in the wrists and ankles, light enough, perhaps, to fly.

"Reeb says you need a sentient spore specialist," the woman said.

"Yes, we have one last pickup. I need you to aid in monitoring our spore for the drop. I'm afraid if you do not, the prisoner may escape."

"The prisoner?"

Enyo had forgotten. This woman had not met them yet. She did not know. Something inside of Enyo stirred, something dark and willfully forgotten, like a bad sexual encounter.

"Where are the others?" Enyo asked.

"Aren't you going to ask my name?"

"I already know it," Enyo said.

The day Reeb's sister was born, Enyo had named her Dysnomia. She had cursed all three of them that day, and perhaps the universe, too. One could never be quite certain.

Nothing had ever been the same after that.

Because she could not go back. Only around.

The sound of the machines was deafening. Enyo stood ankle-deep in peridium salve and organic sludge. Ahead of her, Reeb was screaming. High pitched, squealing, like some broodmeat. But she could not see him.

Then the siren started. A deep-seated, body-thumping wail that cut deep into her belly. Now we turn, she thought. This is a very old snapshot.

Ahead of her, a few paces down the dripping corridor, Dax battered her small body against the ancient orbital entryway. Her tears mixed with sweat and grease and something far more dangerous, deceptive. Grew florets spiraled up the bare skin of her arms from wrist to elbow.

Enyo raised the fist of her weapon and called the girl back, "Don't go down there! Not there! The colonists are this way."

"I'm not leaving them!" Dax sobbed. Her white teeth looked brilliant in the darkness. What animal had she harvested them from? "I know what you did! I know you started this. You set this all in motion."

Enyo admitted that she had not expected it would be Dax who went back. Her memories were not always trustworthy.

The satellite took a snapshot.

Reeb's tastes were predictable in their disparity. He brought up his new crew to meet with Enyo in the internode. The first: a pale, freckled girl of a pilot whose yellow hair was startling in the ambient green glow of the dermal tissue of the room. Enyo could not remember the last time she'd seen yellow hair. The war, maybe. The girl carried no weapons, but her hands were lean and supple, and reminded Enyo of Reeb's hands when he was in his sixties: strong, deft, capable. Not what he was now, no, but what he would *become*.

The other crewmember was a mercenary: a tall, long-limbed woman as dark as the girl was light. Her head was shaved bald. She wore a silver circlet above her ears, and half of her left ear was missing. She carried a charged weapon at either hip, and a converted organic slaying stick across her back. She smelled of blood and metal.

"Do they have names?" Enyo asked Reeb.

"Dax Alhamin," the little pilot said, holding out her hand. It was a rude affectation picked up by many of the young, to touch when first meeting. They did not remember how the war had started, with a nit-infected warmonger who murdered superpod after superpod of colonists with a single kiss. Or perhaps they had simply forgotten. Enyo was never sure what side of the curtain she was on. The satellite distorted the universe at its leisure, often at her expense.

The other one, the mercenary, laughed at the open hand the girl proffered and said, "I'm Arso Tohl. I heard you have cargo that needs . . . liberating."

Dax pulled her hand back in. She was smiling broadly. Her teeth were too white to be real. Even if she was the twenty years she looked, no real person had teeth like that—not even a rim world god. Not even a warmonger.

"It's necessary," Enyo said. "We need to get back to the beginning."

"The beginning?" Dax said. "Where did you come from?"

"It doesn't matter where we came from," Reeb said. "Nor where we're going. That's not how a satellite like this works."

"I think I've heard of this satellite," Arso said. "Some prototype from the Sol system, isn't it? You're a long way from home. You were already old news when I was growing up."

Enyo closed her eyes. She ran through her litany of dead. At the end, she added two new names:

Arso Tohl and *Dax Alhamin.*

She opened her eyes. "Let's tell them how it works, Reeb," she said.

"*Enyo-Enyo* makes her own fate," Reeb said. "Her fate is ours, too. We can alter that fate, but only if we act quickly. Enyo guides that fate. Now you're part of it."

Arso snorted. "If that's so, you better hope this woman makes good decisions, then, huh?"

Reeb shrugged. "I gave up on hoping that many cycles ago."

"All that we are is sacrifice," Enyo's first squad captain told her. "Sacrifice to our countries. To our children. To ourselves. Our futures. We cannot hope to aspire to be more than that."

"But what if I am more than that?" Enyo said. Even then, she was arrogant. Too arrogant to let a slight go uncommented upon.

Her squad captain smiled; a bitter rictus, shiny metal teeth embedded in a slick green jaw grown just for her. The skin grafting hadn't taken. Enyo suspected it was because the captain forgot the daily applications of salve. People would take her more seriously, with a jaw like that.

"I know what you did, Enyo," her squad captain said. "I know who you are. This is how we mete out justice on the Venta Vera arm, to war criminals."

The captain shot her. It was the first time Enyo died.

As Enyo gazed up from the cold, slimy floor of the carrier, her blood steaming in the alien air, her captain leaned over her. The metal teeth clicked. Close enough to kiss.

The squad commander said, "That is how much a body is worth.

One makes no more difference than any other. Even the body of the woman who started the war."

As her life bled out, Enyo's heart stopped. But not before Enyo reached up and ate half her captain's spongy artificial jaw.

Enyo secured her comrade's skull in the jellied dampener beside her. All around her, the spore trembled and surged against its restraints. Reeb had created it just an hour before and clocked in the elliptical path it must take to get them to the rocky little exoplanet where the cargo waited. The spore was ravenous and anxious. Dysmonia already lay immersed at the far end of the spore. She looked terribly peaceful.

Dax eased herself back into her own jellied dampener. Torso submerged, she remained sitting up a moment longer, cool eyes wide and finally, for the first time, fearful.

"Whose skull is that?" Dax asked.

Enyo patted the dampener. "Yours," she said.

Dax snorted. "You're so mad."

"Yes," Enyo said.

Arso pushed through the still-slimy exterior of the spore and into the core where they sat. She spit a glob of the exterior mush onto the floor, which absorbed it hungrily.

"You sure there's no one on that rock?" Arso said.

"Just the abandoned colonists," Reeb murmured from the internode. The vibrations tickled Enyo's ears. The tiny, threadlike strands tucked in their ear canals were linked for as long as the living tissue could survive on their blood.

"It was simply bad timing on their part," Reeb said. "The forming project that would have made Tuatara habitable was suspended when they were just a few rotations away. They were abandoned. No one to welcome them."

"No one but us," Enyo said, and patted the skull beside her. For a long moment, she thought to eat it. But there would be time for that later.

"Filthy business," Arso said.

Enyo unloaded the green fist of her weapon from the gilled compartment above her. It molded itself neatly to her arm, a glittering green sheath of death.

"You have no idea," Enyo said.

Enyo screamed and screamed, but the baby would not come. The rimwarder "midwife" she'd hired was young, prone to madness. The girl burst from the closet Enyo called home three hours into the birthing. Now Enyo lay in a bed soaked with her own perspiration and filth. The air was hot, humid. Above her screams, she heard the distant sound of people working in the ventilation tube.

So it was Enyo who took her own hand. Who calmed her own nerves, who coached her own belabored breath. Enyo. Just Enyo. Why was it always the same, every turn? Why was she always alone, in this moment, but never the others?

She pushed. She screamed herself hoarse. Her body seemed to tear in two. Somewhere far away, in some other life, in some other snapshot, she was dimly aware of this moment, as if it were happening to some character in an opera.

The death dealers banged on the door and then melted it open. They saw she was simply birthing a child alone . . . so they left her. Sealed the room behind her. Like most rim filth, they hoped she would die there in child bed and spare them the trouble. They could come back and collect her dead flesh for resale later.

Enyo gritted her teeth and pushed.

The baby came. One moment, just Enyo. The next . . . a squalling,

writing mass no more sentient in that moment than a program-
mable replicator, but hers nonetheless. A tawny brown child with
her own black eyes.

"Reeb," she said.

She reached toward him. Her whole body trembled.

The second child was smaller, too thin. This was the one she
would give away. The one who would pay her way to the stars.

This one she called Dysmonia.

Enyo voided the body for delivery. Capped all the tubes. A full turn
about the galaxy in transit for a single delivery. A single body. Back
to the beginning. How many times she had done this, she wasn't
certain. The satellite, *Enyo-Enyo*, revealed nothing. Only told her
when it was hungry. And when it was time to station itself, once
again, on its place of origin.

She pushed the body's pod over and it floated beside her, light as
a moth's wing. She placed her fingers on top of the pod and guided
it down into the cargo bay. The body stirred gently.

The interior of *Enyo-Enyo* was mostly dark. Motionless. Not a
sound. They were the last of the living on *Enyo-Enyo*, this turn.
They usually were. The satellite was hungry. Always so hungry.
Like the war.

At the airlock, she stopped to bundle up. Stiff boots, gloves,
parka, respirator. The air here was breathable, *Enyo-Enyo* told her,
but thin and toxic if exposed for long periods. She queued up the
first phase of the release and waited for pressurization.

The vibrating door became transparent; blistering white light
pushed away the darkness of the interior.

Ahead of her: a snow-swept platform. In the distance, a cav-
ernous ruin of a mountain pockmarked with old munitions scars.
A sea of frozen fog stretched from the platform to the mountain.

As she watched, a thin, webbed bridge materialized between the mountain and the platform.

She waited. She had waited a full turn around the galaxy to come back here, to Eris. She could wait a couple terrestrial turns more.

The moisture of her breath began to freeze on the outer edges of her respirator. It reminded her of the first time she had come here to Eris.

Bodies littered the field, and Enyo moved among them, cloaked in clouds of blood-rain. The nits she had infected herself with collected the blood spilled around her and created a shimmering vortex of effluvia that, in turn, devoured all it touched.

"You must not fight her," the field commander shrieked, and Enyo knew some of the fear came from the waves of methane melting all around them as the frozen surface of Eris convulsed. "You must not stop her. She is small now. You must leave her alone, and she will stay small. If you fight her she will swell in size and grow large. She will be unstoppable."

But they fought her. They always fought her.

When she took the field, she flayed them of their fleshy spray-on suits and left them to freeze solid before they could asphyxiate, flailing in sublime methane.

There had to be sacrifices.

As she stood over the field commander, making long rents in her suit, the commander said, "If it's a war your people want, it's a war they'll get."

When it was over, Enyo gazed up at the thorny silhouette of the colonial superpod that the squad had tried to protect. Most of the Sol colonists started from here, on Eris. She would need the superpod, later, or she could never be here, now. Sometimes one had to start a war just to survive to the next turn.

Enyo crawled up into the sickening tissue of the superpod. She found the cortex without much trouble. The complicated bits of genetic code that went into programming the superpod should have been beyond her, but she had ingested coordinates from her squad commander's jaw, during some long-distant snapshot of her life that the satellite had created. Now the coordinates were a part of her, like her fingernails or eyelashes.

She kissed the cortex, and programmed the ship's destination.

Tuatara.

Reeb worked on one of the harvester ships that circled the Rim every four cycles. Enyo was twenty, and he was eighty-two, he said. He said he had met her before. She said she didn't remember, but that was a lie. What she wanted to say was, "I remember giving birth to you," but that, too, was a lie. The difference between memory and premonition depended largely on where one was standing. At twenty, on the Mushta Mura arm, her "memories" were merely ghosts, visions, brain effluvia.

When she fucked Reeb in her twenty-year-old skin, it was with the urgency of a woman who understood time. Understood that there was never enough of it. Understood that this moment, now, was all of it. The end and the beginning. Distorted.

She said his name when she came. Said his name and wept for some nameless reason; some premonition, some memory. Wept for what it all had been and would become.

"The satellite is a prototype," the recruiter said. The emblem on her uniform looked familiar. A double red circle shot through with a blue dart.

They walked along a broad, transparent corridor that gave them a sweeping view of the marbled surface of Eris. Centuries of sculpting had done little to improve its features, though the burning brand in the sky that had once been its moon, Dysmonia, made the surface a bearable −20 degrees Celsius during what passed for summer, and unaided breathing was often possible, if not always recommended. The methane seas had long since been tapped, leaving behind a stark, mottled surface of rocky protuberances shot through with the heads of methane wells. Beyond the domed spokes of the research hub's many arms, the only living thing out there was the hulking mop of the satellite. Enyo thought it looked like a spiky, pulsing crustacean.

"A prototype of what, exactly?" she asked. Her debriefing on Io had been remarkably . . . brief.

"There's much to know about it," the recruiter said. "We won't send you out until you've bonded with it, of course. That's our worry. That it won't take. But . . . there is an indication that you and the satellite are genetically and temperamentally matched. It's quite fortunate."

Enyo wasn't sure she believed in fortune or coincidence, but the job paid well, and it was only a matter of time before people found out who she was. The satellite offered escape. Redemption. "Sure, but what *is* it?"

"A self-repairing—and self-replicating, if need be—vehicle for exploring the galactic rim. It will take snapshots—exact replicas—of specified quadrants as you pass, and store them aboard for future generations to act out. Most of that is automated, but it will need a . . . companion. We have had some unfortunate incidents of madness, when constructs like these are cast off alone. It's been grown from . . . well, from some of the most interesting organic specimens we've found in our exploration of the near-systems."

"It's alien, then?"

"Partially. Some of it's terrestrial. Just enough of it."

"It's illegal to go mixing alien stuff with ours, isn't it?"

The recruiter smiled. "Not on Eris."

"Why Eris? Why not Sedna, or a neighboring system?"

"The concentrated methane that will give you much of your initial inertia comes from Eris. The edge of the Sol system is close enough for us to gain access to local system resources at a low cost, but far enough away to . . . well, it's far enough away to keep the rest of the system safe."

"Safe from what?"

"There's a danger, Enyo. A danger of what you could . . . bring back. Or perhaps . . . what you could become."

Enyo regarded the spiky satellite. "You should have hired some techhead, then." She was not afraid of the alien thing, not then, but the recruiter made her anxious. There was something very familiar about her teeth.

"You came highly recommended," the recruiter said.

"You mean I'm highly expendable."

They came to the end of the long spoke, and stepped into the transparent bubble of the airlock that sat outside the pulsing satellite.

"The war is over," the recruiter said, "but there were many casualties. We make do with what we have."

"It's breathing, isn't it?" Enyo said.

"Methane, mostly," the recruiter said.

"And out there?"

"It goes into hibernation. It will need less. But our initial probes along the galactic rim have indicated that methane is as abundant there as here. We'll go into more detail on the mechanics of its care and feeding."

"Feeding?" Enyo said.

"Oh yes," the recruiter said. She pressed her dark hand to the transparent screen. Her eyes were big, the pupils too large, like all the techs who had grown up on Eris. "You'll need to feed it. At least a few hundred kilos of organic matter a turn."

Enyo gazed up at the hulk of the thing. "And where exactly am I going to get organic matter as we orbit the far arms of the galaxy?"

"I'm sure you'll think of something," the recruiter said. She withdrew her hand, and flashed her teeth again. "We chose you because we knew you could make those kinds of decisions without regret. The way you did during the war. And long before it."

Enyo sliced open the slick surface of the superpod with her weapon. There was no rush of Tuataran atmosphere, no crumpling or wrinkling about the wound. No, the peridium had already been breached somewhere else. Arso and Dax hung back, bickering over some slight. Enyo wondered if they had known one another before Reeb picked them up. They had, hadn't they? The way she had known Arso. The snapshot of Arso. Some other life. Some other decision.

Inside, the superpod's bioluminescent tubal corridors still glowed a faint blue-green, just enough light for Enyo to avoid stepping on the wizened body of some unfortunate maintenance officer.

"Don't you need direction?" Reeb tickled her ear. But she already knew where the colonists were. She knew because she had placed them there herself, turns and turns ago.

Enyo crawled up through the sticky corridors, cutting through pressurized areas of the superpod, going around others. Finally, she reached the coded spiral of the safe room that held the colonists. She gestured to Arso.

"Open it," she said.

Arso snorted. "It's a coded door."

"Yes. It's coded for you. Open it."

"I don't understand."

"It's why you're here. Open it."

"I—"

Enyo lifted her weapon. "Should Enyo make you?"

Arso held up her hands. "Fine. No harm. Fucking dizzy core you've got, woman."

Arso placed her hand against the slimy doorway. The coating on the door fused with her spray-on suit. Pressurized. Enyo heard the soft intake of Arso's breath as the outer seal of the safe room tasted her blood.

The door went transparent.

Arso yanked away her hand.

Enyo walked through the transparent film and into the pressurized safe room. Ring after ring of personal pods lined the room, suffused in a blue glow. Hundreds? Thousands.

She glanced back at Dax. Both she and Arso were surveying the cargo. Dax's little mouth was open. Enyo realized who she reminded her of, then. The recruiter. The one with the teeth.

Enyo shot them both. They died quickly, without comment.

Then she walked to the first pod she saw. She tore away the head of her own suit and tossed it to the floor. She peered into the colonist's puckered face, and she thought of the prisoner.

Enyo bit the umbilicus that linked the pod to the main life system, the same core system responsible for renewing and replenishing the fluids that sustained these hibernating bodies.

The virus in her saliva infected the umbilicus. In a few hours, everything in here would be liquid jelly. Easily digestible for a satellite seeking to make its last turn.

As Reeb cursed in her ear, she walked the long line of pods, back and back and back, until she found two familiar names. Arso Tohl. Dax Alhamin. Their pods were side by side. Their faces perfectly pinched. Dax looked younger, and perhaps she was, in this snapshot. Arso was still formidable. Enyo pressed her fingers to the transparent face of the pod. She wanted to kiss them. But they would be dead of her kiss soon enough.

Dead for a second time. Or perhaps a fifth, a fiftieth, a five hundredth. She didn't know. She didn't want to know.

It was why she piloted *Enyo-Enyo*.

The woman waiting on the other side of the icy bridge was not one Enyo recognized, which did not happen often. As she guided the prisoner's pod to the woman's feet, she wondered how long it had been, this turn. How long since the last?

"What do you have for us?" the woman asked.

"Eris is very different," Enyo said.

The woman turned her soft brown face to the sky and frowned. "I suppose it must seem that way to you. It's been like this for centuries."

"No more methane?"

"Those wells went dry five hundred years ago." The woman knit her brows. "You were around this way long before that happened. You must remember Eris like this."

"Was I? I must have forgotten."

"So what is it this time?" the woman said. "We're siphoning off the satellite's snapshots now."

"I brought you the prisoner," Enyo said.

"What prisoner?"

"*The* prisoner," Enyo said, because as she patted the prisoner's pod something in her memory ruptured. There was something important she knew. "The prisoner who started the war."

"What war?" the woman said.

"*The* war," Enyo said.

The woman wiped away the snow on the face of the pod, and frowned. "Is this some kind of joke?" she said.

"I brought her back," Enyo said.

The woman jabbed Enyo in the chest. "Get back in the fucking satellite," she said. "And do your fucking job."

Back to the beginning. Around and around.

Enyo wasn't sure how it happened, the first time. She was standing outside the escape pod, a bulbous, nasty little thing that made up the core of the internode. It seemed an odd place for it. Why put the escape pod at the center of the satellite? But that was where the thing decided to grow it. And so that's where it was.

She stood there as the satellite took its first snapshot of the quadrant they moved through. And something . . . shifted. Some core part of her. That was when the memories started. The memories of the other pieces. The snapshots.

That was when she realized what *Enyo-Enyo* really was.

Enyo stepped up into the escape pod. She sealed it shut. Her breathing was heavy. She closed her eyes. She had to go home, now, before it broke her into more pieces. Before it reminded her of what she was. War criminal. Flesh dealer. Monster.

As she sealed the escape pod and began drowning in life-sustaining fluid, she realized it was not meant for her escape. *Enyo-Enyo* had placed it there for another purpose.

The satellite took a snapshot.

And there, on the other side of the fluid-filled pod, she saw her own face.

The squalling children were imperfect, like Enyo. She had already sold Reeb to some infertile young diplomatic aide's broker in the flesh pits for a paltry sum. It was not enough to get her off the shit asteroid at the ass end of the Mushta Mura arm. She would die out here of some green plague, some white dust contagion. The death dealers would string her up and sell her parts. She'd be nothing. All this pain and anguish, for nothing.

Later, she could not recall how she found the place. Whispered rumors. A mangled transmission. She found herself walking into a chemically scrubbed medical office, like someplace you'd go to have an industrial part grafted on for growing. The logo on the spiral of the door, and the coats of the staff, was a double circle shot through with a blue dart.

"I heard you're not looking for eggs or embryos," she said, and set Dysmonia's swaddled little body on the counter.

The receptionist smiled. White, white teeth. He blinked, and a woman came up from the back. She was a tall, brown-skinned woman with large hands and a grim face.

"I'm Arso Tohl," the woman said. "Let's have a look."

They paid Enyo enough to leave not just the asteroid, but the Mushta Mura arm entirely. She fled with a hot bundle of currency instead of a squalling, temperamental child. When she entered the armed forces outside the Sol system, she did so because it was the farthest arm of the galaxy from her own. When a neighboring system paid her to start a war, she did so gladly.

She did not expect to see or hear from the butchers again.

Not until she saw the logo on the satellite recruiter's uniform.

Enyo ate her fill of the jellified colonists and slogged back to the satellite to feed it, to feed *Enyo-Enyo*. Reeb's annoying voice had grown silent. He always stopped protesting after the first dozen.

She found him sitting in the internode with the prisoner, his hands pressed against the base of the pod. His head was lowered.

"It was enough to make the next turn," Enyo said.

"It always is," he said.

"There will be other crews," she said.

"I know."

"Then why are you melancholy?" If she could see his face, it would be winter.

He raised his head. Stared at the semblance of a body floating in the viscous fluid. "I'm not really here, am I?"

"This turn? I don't know. Sometimes you are. Sometimes you aren't. It depends on how many snapshots *Enyo-Enyo* has taken this turn. And how she wants it all to turn out this time."

"When did you put yourself in here?" He patted the prisoner's pod.

"When things got too complicated to bear," she said. "When I realized who *Enyo-Enyo* was." She went to the slick feeding console. She vomited the condensed protein stew of the colonists into the receptacle. When it was over, she fell back, exhausted.

"Let's play screes," she said. "Before the next snapshot. We might be different people, then."

"We can only hope," Reeb said, and pulled his hands away from the prisoner.

THE CORPSE ARCHIVES

THE BODIES YOU SPEAK OF, those that existed before the world was silenced and unmade, the bodies of my first memory, are those that danced naked on the hard, black earth around the fires our keepers allowed us. Our fires threw coals into the thick, hot air; coals that flared and darkened and died and drifted down upon us, coating our hands, our faces, our brown bodies, in black soot that made us darker than the earth.

Whenever I tried to join the dancers, the woman who called herself my mother would clutch me to her with her claws.

"Keep here, keep here, Anish," she would say. The lids never closed over her bulging eyes. Her mouth was cut wide, so wide that her face was all mouth and lips and teeth. I dream about her still, about her devouring me whole.

She was so beautiful.

"Don't you join that, don't dance that," she would say. "You dance that and you'll be like the rest of us. A mistake, a burned thing. Not made, not used, just nothing."

When the stack of synthetic logs burned down to a fine black dust, the woman who called herself my mother released me. I ran across the earth to join the dancers outside the covered sleeping pens. Here, they told me the stories of their bodies.

When I think of my first conception of a written record of the past, I think of a body called Senna who had a burn-scarred face with burned-shut eyes. It was this body that showed us how the sky burned when the keepers came; the rivers ran red as the ripple of welts that ran down across the body's throat, over the breasts, ending in a pool of scarred flesh that was once the navel. Senna went mad before the keepers finished writing on her. She screamed and cried and begged to be taken to the pens, to live out her life among the other partially perfected texts that the keepers could not bear to throw away.

I was the most hideous of these texts. I knew it even then, when the woman who called herself my mother could still carry me in her arms. The other texts had traces of unwritten flesh—smooth, incomplete, ugly—but I, I was completely untouched. The whole of my body remained as it had been birthed. I was grotesque, obscene. They were merely incomplete.

These incomplete texts told me I was placed there because the woman who birthed me was a violent body, a mad thing that marked her own history upon her body. She cut open the contents of her self and spilled them onto the cold metal floor of the birthing center . . . including me. She died in her own blood and entrails and my afterbirth.

I was the living text of my mother's existence, the other bodies said. That was why the keepers saved me . . . But knowing that did not make me any more beautiful.

The other body-memories of my life are later, much later, and these bodies, yes, these are the bodies that led me to Chiva, Chiva . . . the one you asked me about.

I think of them often, these bodies. Their hideously smooth skins, their ugly, round faces, the thick, dark hair of their heads and arms and legs. When I see these empty bodies, I remember the burning of the partial texts.

I remember the burning of my kin.

These obscene texts arrived through the circular gate of the compound under the heat of a summer sun that looked flat and orange against the blue, blue sky. They told me the keepers had sent for me. They loaded me into their vehicle and locked me inside.

The others they herded together at the center of our dusty compound. Hundreds of partial texts.

The bodies clung to one another. Clawed hands tipped in crescent-moon nails, twisted torsos wrapped in triangular blue welts, flattened palms fused to splayed hips, gaping mouths without teeth. These precious, beautiful bodies gripped their neighbors so tightly they rent flesh, drew blood.

I pressed my palms to the transparent window of the vehicle and called out to them. I screamed. And screamed.

But the vehicle was a closed box. I heard nothing but my own screaming.

The empty texts sprayed the bodies of my kin with a thin, reddish liquid that coated their faces, torsos, limbs. One of the empty texts ignited a flare. The red fire hurt my eyes.

Fire crawled across my kin like a living thing. Bodies bubbled and melted and charred.

I saw the terrified open mouths of my kin, but heard nothing. Those bodies that pressed against me at night, those bodies that probed my flesh with curious delight and hunger; bodies I had touched, caressed, held; bodies I had so envied and admired. Bodies perfected as mine would never be. Bodies I loved.

Before the sun touched the horizon, all the fire left of my kin was a fine grayish ash.

The empty texts strode back to the vehicle and put their flammable fluid into the back where I sat.

"You are called Anish?" one of them asked.

I nodded.

"Are you a dumb body, Anish?"

"Better hope you are," the other said. "If you're lucky they'll breed you and write on you. But if you're smart they'll make you an archivist. Better hope they don't, Anish. Better hope they just feed you so you fuck."

I did not know then what an archivist was. But I knew my mother had been chosen to breed, and had committed the most horrific of acts. Now only I remained to record the history of her existence.

I am most comfortable speaking of the archives, of written history. Here is truth that I touched and altered as necessary. Understand the archives, and you will understand the text of my unmaking. You will understand Chiva.

I passed the tests that said I was not a dumb body, the tests all empty texts must take in the compounds by the sea. The older empty bodies moved me and the other students to the archives. There, they kept us in separate rooms just big enough to lie down in. The keepers designated bodies that acted as our overseers, all of them smooth and empty texts like me and the other students. These overseers locked us in our rooms at night.

The night terrified me. I heard nothing through the thick walls. No bodies lay next to me. No flesh. I wanted skin pressed against mine, arms wrapped around me. I missed sighs and snores and the sound of mumbled conversations. I missed the feel of another's breath on my skin. I ached to be near the beautiful bodies of my youth.

When the overseers opened my cell each morning I eagerly followed the other students to the archives. A little group of seven of us stood in observance of a text, listening to the body tell the story of those events written upon its body. The archivists said this was not called storytelling—storytelling could be untrue, could be lies. Bodies narrated. Bodies told only truth.

The only bodies the overseers allowed us to touch were the texts. I remember the first real text I touched, the exquisitely complete form that I did not recognize as a body. I learned in that moment just how partial the texts at the compounds had been; how plain, how lacking.

Our little cluster of students stood in the text's allotted area of residence, a niche in one long wall in the Era of Exile corridor. Tubes embedded in the skin, connected to the floor, regulated the body's excretions. It received its food in a similar manner, twice a day, administered by the archivists.

The body existed solely as an organic text capable of narration. It bore no discernible face, only a slit for a mouth, and across the rest of the flat flesh where a face should have been rose fist-sized circular growths. Its hands were soldered to its knees. The skin stretched off the arms in one smooth flap, like wings. A length of silver wire wound around the throat, and the flesh had begun to grow over it.

I stood transfixed. The body spun my favorite tale of past truth in a pleasant, articulate voice that flowed smoothly from the slit of its mouth: the story of the keepers' voyage in exile.

I fell in love with its body.

I heard thousands of other texts in my years at the archives. I heard how the keepers found our world, a lonely planet seeded long ago by human beings who had forgotten what they were. The keepers' sailing ship burned down from the sky, and our kind went to them. The keepers freed themselves of their casings. They selected those bodies that they would communicate with and fitted them with inorganic devices that allowed the keepers to direct them.

"You were simply our curiosities in the beginning," my own keeper later told me at one of our dictation sessions, one of the last it held with me. "We took such delight with you and your kind. You had bodies that we did not, and we used you to enact that which we could not. Ah, Anish, our preoccupation with your kind was so much more delightful then. So base it was, our delight and your perversion."

Often I lay awake at night and closed my eyes, remembering those bodies that once surrounded mine. I ran my hands along my own flesh, across my throat, down my smooth chest, flat stomach, the insides of my thighs. I thought of another's body pressed against mine, so close I felt their breath. I often pushed myself up against the cold wall and lay there with my arms wrapped around myself, longing for the morning. I did not weep anymore. I found warmth and closeness with my own body, my mother's text.

And during the day, I had the archives.

I frequented the niches I knew the others had no interest in. I stood in front of those texts illustrating the unmaking of the bodies who ruled the world before the keepers came. No one wanted to view these texts; these twisted, angry figures that wept blood and cried out for a freedom their flesh still remembered. Many of the archivists wanted to burn them. I knew that as more keepers began to die, more texts would be purged, and these would be the first destroyed. So I spent my days with them. I wanted to remember them.

One day I found the body text of the keepers' emergence from their sailing ship, and their linking with the first bodies. I stepped up into the niche containing the text.

"Don't narrate," I told it. "I just want to touch you." But the body could not be silent. None of them could. It existed to narrate.

As the open scream of its mouth moved to form words, I ran my gaze across its form. The body lay flat on the floor, both arms raised up as if to shield itself from harm. From the torso downward, the body seemed to liquefy and spill across the floor. A section of the scalp and skull were missing on one side so you could see the shiny little chip embedded into the soft tissue. The eyes were always open.

My hands trembled. I knelt beside the body and traced the jagged, blue tattoos on its flesh with my fingers.

I wondered if it could feel pleasure, or anything at all. Anger? Loneliness? Or did the keepers order the archivists to deaden that too, as they deadened the body's flesh?

"So sad," I said. I moved my fingers down the torso, to the mass of featureless flesh. I stared at the wide, glassy eyes, brown as dust.

A gorgeous text.

I pulled my hands off the body and fumbled at the knot on my robe. I struggled out of the robe. I wanted to join my flesh to the body's, to become one text, the altered and the empty.

Only the mouth was open to me, wide and wet and full of teeth. My body shook with fear and anticipation. I wanted to silence the text.

Could I stop the words? Stop history?

The words stopped. History stopped.

I stared at the text and then back out into the hallway, afraid. What would the keepers think of a student that tried to silence their history? I tied my robe closed and ran from the niche, back to the main archives. My whole body trembled. I expected one of the overseers to find me, to say the keepers had seen what I'd done and would purge me.

Yet no one came for me. The other students continued to ignore me. The overseers still let me explore the archives alone.

So I went back to the texts. And I became addicted.

At the end of each class I went back to the far corners of the archives. I buried myself in texts. I silenced them. Silence the texts, silence the keepers, silence the world. I was an ugly empty text, but I had power over all of them, and their words, their truth.

I do not know how many texts I took pleasure in this way. Always I returned to my favorite, and told it to tell me its story in a different way, but it could not tell a story that was not true. It made me angry, so I did what I could to it. I tried to unmake it. There was no one to stop me.

Until.

I licked the mouth of the text, and heard:

"What are you doing?"

The voice was not the text's.

I fell back onto my robe and kicked away from the text.

One of the other students stood in the corridor, staring at me with large, dark eyes.

"I'm . . ." I said, putting my arms through the sleeves of my robe with limbs that felt clumsy, "I'm touching the texts."

"You're defiling them," she said. "You're silencing them. That's obscene."

"No," I said, and knotted my robe closed. I managed to stand on wobbly legs. "I was just—"

"I watched you," she said. "You're that strange body, that violent body, the one they brought in from the compounds. Anish."

She was older than I was, nearly an archivist already. I had seen her before, assisting in the cleaning of texts.

"Yes," I said.

"Why are you touching the body texts?"

"Because all of *you* are so ugly."

She laughed. When she laughed she threw back her head, and a snarl of dark black hair came loose from her twisted braid of hair. It curled down along the side of her face, touched the empty, appalling smoothness of her cheek.

"One doesn't touch the body of another," she said. "One only touches texts. Haven't you been taught that?" She knitted her dark brows so they formed one line above her eyes. "Do you think you understand them better, because you've silenced them?"

"I don't know," I said.

"They why do you do it?" she said. She stepped up into the niche. She approached the flat, featureless end of the text.

"I don't know," I said. "You've never done it?"

She shook her head.

"Then you won't understand," I said.

"Show me how you touch them," she said. I recognized a desire there, in her eyes, her voice, as if she held up a mirror to my own. No other empty text had ever approached and spoken to me.

I reached for her hand.

"Don't touch me," she said. "Just them."

We knelt over the body of the text.

"Here," I said, and moved my fingers up to the wire around the head. "Feel how cold the wire is. Imagine the way it feels, to have your flesh try to grow around it."

She touched the wires. I saw that her hands trembled. Did she have the same desire I had? The same fear and anticipation?

I moved my palms down across the jagged welts, traced them with my fingers. "They won't hurt you," I said.

She, too, ran her fingers along the tattoos, down across the throat, the shoulders, the chest. "I'm not afraid," she said.

But she *was* afraid of them. I already knew it, even then.

"Do they feel anything?" she said.

"I don't know," I said. "We're not allowed to ask, and I don't like them to talk."

I traced a line of tattoos that brought my fingertips to hers. She looked at our hands there, joined atop the text.

She withdrew her fingers from mine. "I told you not to touch me," she said. She stood up to walk away.

"Wait!" I said. "What are you called?"

"I don't tell dumb bodies such things," she said. She jumped from the niche and into the hallway.

I did not see her for many days afterward. The overseers had deemed my independent study complete, and they lumped me back into a student group watching the dictation sessions. The art of dictation was the most difficult an archivist had to learn. I had already accompanied the archivists on feeding and cleaning sessions, but it was the dictation that most interested me. Here I could perfect bodies with my own hands.

Sometimes I snuck away from a dictation session early and wandered the lonely corridors, passed row upon row of texts. Sometimes I came to corridors that had been barred with a thick, steel gate. These were the libraries that had already been purged. I had watched the archivists unhook the bodies from the tubing that bound them to the floors of their niches. The archivists carted the bodies out on long, wheeled trolleys. Piles of bodies. When I asked why they had to get rid of them I was always given the same answer:

"The keepers are dying. We must conserve only the most important truth."

But who decided what the most important truth was?

So I walked down the long halls, passing those texts the keepers still retained, and I searched for the student I'd touched over the text. I often dreamed of her. In those days my dreams of her were pleasant ones—our bodies entwined, my mouth on her skin. The dreams sickened me at first. She was ugly, incomplete. What kind of a body had I become?

Yet my desire for her was so great that I did not eat or sleep or visit the texts for three days while I looked for her. When I found her she was just outside one of the barred corridors, following a train of archivists carting out obsolete texts.

"Anish," she said.

"What are you called?" I said.

We stared at one another.

I wanted her name, as if knowing that, I could own her and begin to fill her emptiness.

"Help me with the cleaning of the texts," she said.

"Yes," I said.

She told my overseer that she wished to work with me, and my overseer agreed without hesitation.

She strode quickly back down to the archival corridors, so fast on her long legs that I had to struggle to keep up. She did not go down the long individual history corridor where most of the other students clustered. Instead, she took me back to the Unmaking Hall, where those exquisite texts of the end of human freedom were still held.

She stepped into one of the empty niches. She gazed around at the clean floor, the bare walls. "We took this one out today," she said.

I climbed up beside her. "Did you burn it?" I asked.

She nodded.

"They aren't going to recopy it?" I said.

"No. This corridor must be cleaned out by the end of the year. The keeper who oversaw its maintenance is dead."

"Dead? What about its own history?"

"It's already written on one of the bodies in the individual history corridor. It will survive in that, at least." She gazed into the hall, and I saw her look turn inward. "I want you to touch me, Anish, here, where the text would be."

I shivered.

She untied the knot of her robe, let the gray material fall open. "I want you to touch me the way you touch the texts."

She stepped directly in front of me. She reached out and unknotted my robe. She was so close I felt the heat of her body; her breath on my skin. I gazed at the flesh of her, the smooth, brown, hideously unmarred flesh. She was uglier than I was.

She placed her palm on my chest. I was trembling.

"I won't hurt you," she said.

"I know that," I said.

She pushed off her robe, and it piled around her ankles.

I wrapped my arms around her. She pulled our bodies together. For the first time since my arrival in the archives, I found myself pressed against a body that not only responded to mine, but wanted me there against it. This was all I had dreamed of doing during the terrible loneliness of those nights when I wrapped my empty arms around myself, trying to fill them.

We ended up on the floor that had until that day been housed by a body text, rubbing our bodies together against the same floor it had been displayed upon.

I tried to fuck every part of her, to join with her as I had the texts, but she pushed me away from her mouth and thighs and forced me down onto my chest, against the hard, slick floor. She pressed her whole body down onto mine, wrapped her strong hands around my throat.

"I own all the bodies here, Anish. Even you," she said. She laughed at me, released me.

I struggled up and tried to grab her the way I'd often been grabbed in the compounds. But she cried out in pain when I gripped her. She pushed me away with a strength I did not expect.

"You hurt me!" she said.

"I'm sorry," I said, and wondered how I had hurt her. This was what we had done in the compounds, all of us. The pain and fear and pleasure all went together.

"Don't ever hurt me again," she said. "If you hurt me again I'll burn you, Anish, just like the texts."

"I won't hurt you," I said. I would have promised her anything to be able to touch her.

She hit me then, across the mouth. I gasped at the shock of it, but I desired her as I desired the beautiful bodies of my youth. She brought pain and pleasure and fear.

"Touch me, but never hurt me," she said. "Understand that, dumb body?"

"What are you called?"

She turned away from me, jumped out of the niche, and gazed back up at me with her big, dark eyes.

"I am Chiva," she said, "and I am to be the librarian. Your body, all of these bodies, are mine, to do with as I please. You understand that, dumb body?"

Chiva wanted only unaltered bodies, ugly texts like me. She liked me best, she said, because I desired the texts, and she found that

so revolting that I became desirable to her. We spent our days entwined among texts, and I reveled in the feel of her body against
mine. For me, it was enough. My loneliness had ended, and the
archives were no longer so cold and empty to me. Chiva told the
overseers she was instructing me, and most of the time they did
not argue with her. I learned that there were not enough overseers
to look after us anymore, and the few that remained were happy
to pass my training on to Chiva, even though she had no direct
link to a keeper. She was as free as an empty text could be.

Sometimes she and I simply sat in observance of texts and listened to them narrate their histories. We lay in one another's arms
as the bodies told us a truth that would no longer exist by the year's
end. Chiva often wanted me to help her when the archivists purged
another text, but I refused.

"We just have to unhook them and put them on the cart," she
said, but I left her to it and ran off down the winding corridors to
find a quiet space. I did not like to watch them take the texts away.

I remember once when we lay across the body she had first seen
me with. We both curled up next to it, told it to narrate, but did not
listen. Instead, we spoke together in our soft lover's voices, heads
bent forward, bodies touching, rubbing against one another.

"We burn them down until they're just ash," she said, "when we
remove them from here."

"Why do you have to talk of it?" I said. Sometimes I thought she
took delight in the burning of the texts.

"You know what we used to do with the ash, when we burned
it all down? We gathered it up in big containers, and they shipped
it down to the synthetics factories along the coast, and you know
what they did with it?"

"Threw it into the sea?" I said.

She laughed. "No. They condensed it all down, mixed it with
chemicals and wood char and made synthetic logs for the living
compounds around the factories."

"Synthetic logs?" I said.

"Yes. I heard stories, not truth, of course, just stories, that the workers out there, the keepers would let them set the logs on fire, and they would dance around them. These naked, empty texts. They would just dance!"

I remembered the dancers. The orange flames leaping high in the air. I remembered how proud we all were of watching that flame, that one bit of making we were able to perform while the keepers owned our bodies. The smell of the black dust, the way it coated our bodies.

"Don't talk about burning things anymore," I said.

Our days were not to last, of course. Contentment never does, does it? But then, would we remember it as contentment if it was not bracketed with darkness?

"I watched you always, Anish," my keeper told me the day it died. "I watched you and wanted to be you, and when I could not be you, I wanted to unmake you. What we cannot have, we must destroy. But then, you already know that, don't you?"

My overseer approached me one morning after Chiva and I had fought. Chiva said that my silencing of the texts was a form of rebellion, of subversion. She said my body was not mine but hers, to direct as she pleased. I was nothing, she said, just a dumb body, an empty text.

My overseer waited outside my door.

"Come with me, Anish," he said.

I did not ask where we were going. Perhaps a part of me already expected this.

The overseer brought me to the center of the labyrinthine archives. I knew I would not be able to find my way back unaided. He palmed open a door and stepped into a domed room. At the center of the room stood a large, hexagonal structure. The air was much cooler and drier than in the archives. The overseer walked up to the structure, pressed his hand against it, and a section of the wall opened to admit us.

We stood inside a perfect hexagon. Lining the walls were row upon row of square, gray panels, each no bigger than my palm. All of them had one small light on the lower left-hand side. There must have been thousands of them, all up and down the walls, all around me. They stretched upward some twenty feet above me. Soft light illuminated the room from panels on the ceiling, panels much like the ones in the archives; only the light these emitted was less white, more orange. On these thousands and thousands of squares, all of the small lights were dark; all but the ones on one solid bank of squares on my right, a collection of perhaps a dozen yellow lights. I walked over to them.

"Are these the only ones left alive?" I said.

My overseer nodded. He went up to the wall, selected a square situated at the far left corner of the roughly circular pattern of lights, and pressed the panel. It clicked open.

I stared inside.

And was disappointed. All I saw was a long tube of wire connected to the shiny, black shell of the interior. The overseer unwound the wire and asked me to come closer.

"What are you doing?" I said.

"Adjusting you," he said. "Your communication hardware was fitted in the birthing centers, but never activated. This keeper wants to be linked to you. I have to attune your hardware to its settings. Be still. It will not hurt."

It hurt.

I tried to pull away from my overseer, but he held me tight. The tubing in my ear sent a wave of pain shooting through my ear canal and behind my eyes, and I heard a terrible hissing that filled my head.

When my overseer released me, I fell onto the floor. I held my head in my hands and gasped.

"So this is Anish."

My overseer had not spoken. I looked up at him, at the tubing he held, and glanced up at the casing of the keeper's square.

"Yes, that's mine," the voice said. Did the voice have a gender? I do not know. It simply existed. I call my keeper he because the pronoun my overseer used was male. When I think of my keeper I think of the body of the overseer—his ugly, unmarked body, the broad shoulders, flat face, narrow nose.

"What do you want with me?" I asked.

Laughter. The laughter of keepers is not a laughter you ever want to hear. It echoes in your head like stones down a very deep cavern, over and again, until it feels that your head has been broken.

"You are so silly, Anish. Such a lovely body, but full of silliness! Don't you know, haven't you guessed? Why would I bring an archivist here?"

"You're dying. You want me to write your history."

"You see? I knew all along you were not a dumb body. I would not have chosen you otherwise."

"But I'm not an archivist yet. I haven't been trained to write your history on bodies, or to teach them to narrate for you."

"More intelligence. Perception. Such quickness. Why aren't all bodies so? I have been watching you, Anish. I've seen the way you touch the texts. You have a reverence for our truth, don't you?"

Did I? I wondered if the keeper could read my thoughts, or if I had to say them out loud. I kept saying them out loud. The overseer remained in the room, but paid me little attention. "It will be good to record your—"

"Do you want to know the body I've chosen for you to dictate upon?" the keeper said.

I thought of Chiva. Her ugly, unblemished skin.

"I prefer the more educated bodies," my keeper said. "Best find one that comprehends truth and history, one that appears dull and animalian because it is concealing its thoughts from me, not blank and dull because it is empty. I experience too much emptiness in my own kind now. Too much death. You see us dying, do you not, Anish? But that will not save you from me. The absence of the future does not negate the past."

"Please," I said. "Choose another text. She's a good archivist, and she'll be a better librarian, when she's finished learning." If I unmade Chiva she would never be able to touch me again. They would lock her away into some hall where the only words she spoke were truth.

The keeper started laughing again.

"Chiva?" he said. "You are such a silly body, Anish! You thought I wanted Chiva? Oh no, oh no." Laughter, laughter, my head throbbing. "Haven't you guessed, Anish? I want you to unmake *yourself.*"

The world the keepers created had been falling apart throughout my life, but I had not noticed it. I did not think forward, only back. That was the nature of my existence. Now, though, none of my days were spent in causal, silent observance, sprawling lazily in the present while listening to the truth of the past. Now I was told stories, stories I knew could not be truth, stories I could not silence.

The stories my keeper told me did not match what all the texts narrated and illustrated. The stories it told confused and angered me, because if the texts were not truth, what was?

"Exiled us?" my keeper said. "Oh, pity no, that's the old religious pull, you understand? The persecuted few? Your people consumed it well the first few centuries, and that's why we've set that story down here in the archives. But that's not true, of course. We went out on our own, thought we were wonderfully special, thought we could leave our dead bodies behind and live in the synthetic ones forever. Ha! All fools. The last of the synthetic bodies gave out half a millennium after we crashed here. All gone. No more bodies. At least we had enough time to indoctrinate and implant you."

The voice in my head made me nervous. I could not halt his stream of stories. I could not ask him to be quiet, so I stole back to my little room and lay down. I avoided Chiva. My head always hurt.

"When will the sessions begin?" I asked.

"Oh, soon enough, little Anish," he said. A long pause. Then, "Let us see Chiva."

"I don't want to."

"I could make you."

"I thought you were here to unmake me."

"Ah! I thought we'd bred the cleverness out of you. Perhaps another day, then."

But in the morning my overseer waited for me again.

"It's time for the sessions to begin," he said.

I tried to protest, but my keeper grumbled, "Oh, it's not me, Anish. It's those ancient fools back there, spouting off about mortality. They're so old they've forgotten what it's like to have a body that's yours. Well then, since it's already scheduled . . ."

My overseer let me into the dictation room. He shut the door. I gazed at the apparatuses on the walls—the needles, the skin grafting equipment, the row upon row of shiny surgical tools, glass containers of narcotics.

"I can't do this alone," I said.

"Oh, I think you can," my keeper said. "I'll not ruin you so terribly as the others. I'd like you to function as I would, if I had such a delightful young body. Now sit on that stool and listen. You're not just here to tell *my* stories. The truth, as you call it, the stories I liked best, were the ones I had when I owned my own body. You've never seen mountains, have you? Lakes? River stones?"

I had never heard the terms before.

"I'm going to have your body illustrate the real truth about our kind," my keeper said. "I want you to be a literal text. Not one of those useless globs. I want you to be able to walk and spit and fuck.

After all, what is the purpose of a body but to exert one's power over another?"

I wondered if he spoke of my power or his own.

I spent our first three sessions learning to draw symbols. My keeper was able to direct me through the motions; he had a limited power over my body—enough so he could assist when I misplaced a stroke of the stylus.

Each night, he asked after Chiva.

"Don't you miss her terribly?" he said.

"Yes," I said, and thought, but you do enough talking for all of us.

The fourth session, I began to write. I can think of no other body but mine when I remember this session, this memory of writing. The way the precise tool inscribed my already numbed flesh in a long series of puckered marks that reddened or blackened as I pressed the button that allowed the ink to flow into the wounds.

Afterward, I always closed my eyes. When I closed my eyes I heard the words of the woman who called herself my mother. I felt her clutch at me with her claws. "You are already our history, yes?"

No, I thought. I am nothing. I am an empty canvas being filled. I won't be ugly anymore.

By the fifth session the markings covered my throat and shoulders. This will not be so terrible, I thought, watching the curious, red tattooed welts forming on my flesh.

I do not remember how long my keeper and I spent in the dictation room.

One morning I awoke in my own room and my door remained locked until well past midmorning. Another overseer arrived to unlock the door; I had never seen her before.

"What's happened?" I asked.

"The other overseer's keeper died," the overseer said. And nothing more.

With the death of that keeper came yet another purging of

the texts. Piles of bodies were carted out through the corridors. I watched them with a dizzy sense of horror.

After that, I slept in the dictation room.

Finally, the day came when I stepped out of our dictation session, the one that I know now was our last, and Chiva stood in wait for me. When she saw me, her eyes widened.

"It's true," she said.

"It must be," I said.

"You don't look like you," she said.

The markings now covered my torso all the way down my right leg and up to the thigh on my left, but I had only seen the black and red marks section by section, reflected back at me from a small, round magnification mirror that let me apply the tattoos with accuracy.

"It isn't so terrible," I said, but as I watched her eyes move over me I felt a stab of fear. "I'm still the same," I said. "I'm not going to be in one of those niches. I'm not—"

"You're just another used text," Chiva said. "You've lost your history and given it to a keeper. You're just another dead keeper's writing."

"You're wrong," I said. "You don't know anything about it. I'm beautiful."

"You're so stupid, Anish. Have you looked at yourself? You said you were your mother's text, our text. You're just another one of theirs now. Go look at yourself," she said. She turned and walked away from me, trailing after a trolley piled up with bodies.

I heard my keeper's laughter.

"What did you do?" I said. I walked back into the dictation room, pushed the small mirror back into the wall, opened up the panel where the full-length mirror was. I had been too afraid to look, before.

The body that stared back at me was never mine. I had always known it was not mine. I belonged to the keepers from birth, but it was my mother's body I spilled from, my mother's history I had always been. But no longer.

"What did you make me write?" I said. "What do these symbols mean?" Another question I had not asked during dictation, a question I feared the answer to. They were unlike any marks on the other texts.

"Words," my keeper said. "Not pictures of things, but symbols representing the sounds of the actual spoken words, words so old I thought I'd forgotten how to form them."

"What do they say?"

My keeper was silent.

"What do they *say*?"

"They negate all truth," he said.

"What?"

"I wrote words that told an untrue history. One different from all those others."

"You can't do that."

"Why not? Are you a fool? There is no truth, Anish. Only stories. Only things we wished had happened. Words unmade the skin that formed so smooth and perfect in your mother's body. And now we will finish negating the existence of the texts and the existence of all your bodies. We will finish unmaking history. We will unmake the world we crafted from lies."

"You can't tell lies on a body," I said. "You can't—"

"And what does Chiva's empty body attest to, Anish? What truth does she tell? She is empty and free and when the last of us dies she'll burn you, along with the rest of them, to be free of you."

"Shut up!" I said, and I slammed the mirror panel shut and ran out of the dictation room. I saw again the vision of my burning kin. "You can't negate their bodies!" I said, and I ran down through the corridors, my keeper's laughter ringing in my head.

Other students and archivists stared at me as I passed. I ran and ran, looking for the Hall of Unmaking. I knew the route so well, that place where Chiva and I had touched truth. Down this corridor, left, another left, and—

A steel gate blocked my path. I stopped. I stared at it.

"She likes to kill them, you know," my keeper said. "She likes to kill them because she's afraid of them."

"No," I said.

"You think that word saves you? It changes nothing. You think I can say no and go back to being an organic body? You think I can say *no* and cease to be a swimming mass of synthetic fluid and artificial synapses?" my keeper said. "That word cannot unmake what I became. You want truth, Anish? We envy your bodies. Your beautiful, smooth bodies. We covet them. We have built not an archive but a shrine, not a world of absolute truth but a world that records the stories we wish were ours by destroying you. We use flesh to fantasize about that which we can never be. You bodies are so stupid. You lie about this place talking of how ugly you are, running around in this artificial labyrinth of our making, your unmaking. You have not seen the sun in years now, Anish. You laze about here and squander your lives, and when we're dead you'll still lie about here as your bodies waste away. You'll exist only to preserve the history of our death, wishing always that you were something other than what you are."

"You're lying," I said. I pressed my palms to the cold steel of the gate. "These are just stories."

"But now I've had you write them on your body, little Anish. Now they're truth, aren't they?"

I turned away from the gate and began to run again through the halls. How long had we spent in dictation? How much had things changed? I saw more gates. Corridors ended abruptly. Those corridors still open had empty niches. What had happened to all the texts?

"How many keepers are left?" I said. My legs hurt. My throat was raw. "How many have died?"

"There are five of us left. We die in groups, you know. Just as we were made," my keeper said.

I stopped and stood still in the hall, breathing deep, gazing at the monstrous construction that enclosed us all. When the keepers died, would we be trapped in here? Trapped inside this hollow casing to die as the keepers died?

No. Where did Chiva take the texts to be burned? Not inside. There had to be a way out. I remembered the way it felt to dance in the dust. I remembered sun on my skin. How had I forgotten it?

I found Chiva with three archivists and another trolley heaped with bodies. When she saw me she looked away, but I grabbed her by the shoulder. The other archivists stared at us. I did not care.

"When you burn them, where do you take them?"

"What?"

"Where do you burn them?"

"Outside, of course," she said. "What's the matter with you? You never wanted to talk about it before. You ignored—"

"Show me," I said.

"We're going there now."

We ascended through a long, narrow hall, entered a cylindrical lift, and stepped onto ground covered in grayish ash.

I saw a blue sky striated in white clouds. The sun was so bright it hurt my eyes, and for a moment I was blinded. The yard was a broad, circular pit surrounded by a wall fifty feet high.

I collapsed into the grayish dust.

The archivists piled up the bodies, wet them with reddish fluid, and opened a bin of flares. The texts burned without making a sound. I watched the bodies flame, bubble, melt, and char.

The archivists did not even wait for this batch of bodies to finish burning before they took the trolley back to the lift.

"Chiva?" they called, but Chiva stood in front of me. The bodies belched smoke behind her.

The lift closed.

"What's wrong, Anish?" Chiva said.

I pressed my hands against my face, covering my eyes. "I'm unmade," I said. "There is no truth."

She knelt beside me. "Don't you know?" she said. "There never was any truth. We're just like these burned things."

I reached out to her, tried to hold her body against mine. I had missed her so much. Having her close meant I was not alone, trapped within these walls with a dying keeper.

I held her by the wrist. My grip was firm.

She stared at me. She stared down at my hand on her wrist. "Anish?"

I struck her, drawing blood. I saw the surprise in her face, the betrayal, because I had dared to try and write violence upon her body. She hit me back, so hard my nose burst.

Someone was laughing in my head.

I wanted her to tell me truth. I wanted to unmake her as I had been unmade, to write on her as I had been written upon. I could not tell my keeper no when he told me to write his lies. I would not allow her to be empty anymore, empty and free as I once was.

But she struck me again, smashing my nose a second time. Blackness smeared my vision. I fell to my knees.

I thought of the dancers, of our fire, the texts the keepers burned while I did nothing. I did nothing but watch, nothing but witness a truth no one would ever record. I wanted to silence Chiva as I had been silenced. But Chiva was not like me. She would never be unmade.

Chiva kneed me in the groin. She balled her fists and struck my face, pummeled my head. I curled into a ball in the dust and tried to shield myself against her. Then the beating stopped. I heard her walk away from me.

I raised my head and saw her walking to the bin of flares. She took one out and stumbled back toward me.

Now she would burn me.

I lay huddled in the dust, watching her approach.

She stood over me, the flare in her hand. She had only to ignite it.

"You love them, don't you?" she said.

I did not know what she meant. "Chiva, I—"

"You think you can control the world by hurting me? They un-made you. They ruined you, but you can't hurt them, can you? So you tried to hurt me. You think you can unmake me? You don't know anything about unmaking. I'll show you how to unmake the world."

She collected more flares.

"What's she doing?" my keeper asked, very softly.

I had almost forgotten him, this thing I could not silence.

Chiva walked to the lift with a heap of flares in her arms. The lift closed.

And I knew what she was going to do.

I ran to the lift. I descended into the archives.

I could already smell the burning bodies. A part of me hoped it was just the lingering smell of burning flesh from the yard. But then I saw the smoke. I heard the archivists screaming. I ran. I passed niches where the bodies inside were already aflame. I watched the history of Chiva's destruction of the past.

And then I saw her, heading back toward me, smoke billowing in her wake, her arms empty.

"I need more flares," she said, and she strode past me on her long legs, and her eyes were dark, her face grim.

"Chiva, please . . ." I did not dare touch her.

She walked away from me. The archivists ran madly through the corridors. I saw some of them huddled in the niches, weeping.

"Do something," I told my keeper.

"What? This is your creation, Anish, not mine."

I could do nothing. The keepers were dying. The past was burning.

I could do nothing but help Chiva with its destruction.

I went back out to the burning yard. Chiva was there, piling flares into her robe. She tossed me a flare. I made the choice. I took it, three more, and a container of flammable fluid.

We descended together.

We burned the world.

My mother was dead. Her history undone. The bodies were lies. My body was a lie. The world was a lie. I had hurt the one thing I knew to be real, to be true.

We parted in the individual history corridor. I stayed there while she continued to burn. I needed to find my keeper.

"Why are you looking for us?" my keeper said.

"Because it was always you and your kind I wanted to silence. Just as you silenced my kin."

"We'll die soon enough. Let us die."

"You didn't let *us* die," I said. "You used us. Destroyed us. Unmade us."

"No, Anish. You did that yourself."

I found the door. How I found it, I do not know, not to this day. I had walked so long and so far that I could no longer smell the smoke or hear the screaming. I pressed my hand against the door, tried to open it. It did not open.

"Let me in," I said.

"Just let me die," my keeper said.

"No," I said.

The door opened. I approached the large structure of the hexagon. The sliding door of the central storage chamber was already open.

I walked into the keepers' room. I stared at the last of the little glowing lights. Three. Just three little lights. Three dying keepers left to rule the world.

"I thought you said no," I said.

"I didn't let you in," my keeper said. "They did. You've burned the texts in the corridors they oversaw. Their overseers have run off. What do you expect them to do but die?"

I pressed open the panel of one of the squares. I ripped out the tubing and gazed at the shiny, black casing inside. I found a little groove on the underside of the casing and pulled it out. The whole black case came out smoothly, easily, as if it had been placed inside the square just a moment ago. It was rectangular, about as long as my arm, as wide around as my palm. I could not see inside.

I brought the case to the doorway and smashed it against the wall until the casing came loose. I sat on the floor and pulled at the casing until I succeeded in tearing it off. The rectangle inside was transparent. I saw the red fluid inside, long rows of metal chips, spidery wires and tiny hair-like filaments. I set the keeper in the center of the room and unpacked the second keeper. I set it next to the first, then pulled out the last case.

My keeper.

When I sat staring into my keeper's translucent body resting there in my lap, I said, "How long have you been watching me?"

"Forever," he said.

"You saw my mother?"

"The recordings used to be stored," my keeper said, "when there were enough of us to oversee them. She was an exceptionally violent body. I watched you birthed out of her death. I was linked to the overseer that pulled you out."

"You know everything about me."

"Our observation of your compound deteriorated just after I placed you there," my keeper said. "I sent the empty texts after you. They were going to burn everything, you know. But I knew you were still there. I had their keepers tell them to bring you back. I saved you, Anish."

"Why?" I said. "Why didn't you just let me burn with the others?" My tears fell onto the casing. I did not wipe them away.

"I watched you always, Anish. What we cannot have we must destroy. But then, you already know that, don't you?"

I closed my eyes. Thought of Chiva.

I set my keeper's casing on top of the other two. I carefully placed three of the flares under the stack of keepers. I poured the whole container of flammable fluid over the keepers. I held the last flare, and walked back into the doorway, away from the pool of reddish liquid. I lit the flare. It glowed white in my hand. The heat was so intense that I had to hold it away from my body for fear of setting myself on fire.

"What will you do now?" my keeper said.

"Tell stories," I said.

I tossed the flare. The room exploded in a wave of brilliant light. The flame roared up and out. The heat knocked me out of the doorway. I felt the sensation of flight. My body smashed against the far wall. The flame whirled above my head, curled back into the room.

It was very beautiful.

I did not see Chiva again. Most of the students and archivists had escaped to the burning yard, and I found them there. We climbed atop one another's bodies to scale the wall. From the top of the wall, I saw the maze of the archives, the great hexagons-within-hexagons that wound outward for as far as I could see.

The archivists told me Chiva was dead. They told me she choked on the smoke of the bodies and became lost in the maze, entombed forever. But I knew Chiva would never become lost in the archives. She knew them far better than I did.

We walked as far from the archives as we could. Most of us. Some collapsed and wept under the heat of the sun, frightened by the chill of the wind, the uncertainty of living outside of the archives. The day it rained we reached a small settlement like none I had ever known. No gates. No fences.

The bodies there were all empty, and they welcomed us. They smiled. They gave us food and drink, and they asked us to tell them stories. The others with me did not know what to say. It had been years and years, the new bodies said, since they had heard anything of the keepers, those strange beings said to have once ruled the world.

"We've never seen them," the bodies told us.

"I have seen them," I said, and they looked upon me: the tattooed partial text with burn scars on his face, his arms. I had no eyebrows, and most of my hair was gone. They called me an ugly body, but they wanted my stories.

And I told them all I knew, as I am telling you now.

No one ever asked about Chiva. Few of those from the archives remember her name. I thought the burning of the texts would erase all of our sadness, all that darkness. I thought we would forget. But now you come here to this little village, telling me there are free cities in the wilderness, and ask to dance around my fire and hear the stories of a past I thought no longer existed. If it does not exist, how can I tell it? There must be some truth, still, something to be remembered, if I can still speak.

No, no. I am tired. Too old for dancing. But you are free to stay, free to dance as empty bodies devoid of history or truth, unburdened by the knowledge of a world built long before you were born. Dance, yes, and I'll dream again the dream of Chiva, and the story of our unmaking.

THE WAR OF HEROES

THE HEROES LEFT THE MAN dying on the field, one of the thousands they pitched overboard from their silvery ships at the end of each battle with Yousra's people. Yousra brought him home and had him castrated, to ensure he spread no contagion, and put him to work in the village. The Heroes' men tended to eat little and work hard, and with so few people left in the village, his labor was welcome.

Plague had killed most of the village men when the Heroes first came. In those early days, Yousra's people had welcomed the cast-off men the Heroes dropped at the edge of every battlefield as some kind of tribute delivered from the sky. Now they recognized them for what they were: plague-ridden bags of pollution, another weapon of war, their seed meant to sour wombs and turn babies into monsters. But her people still needed the labor, so they castrated them and hauled them home regardless.

It was Yousra's task to kill the children resulting from such rotten unions; the plague ran deep now, rewriting the map of each child, so even now, three generations after they understood the threat, their children were still rotten. The children Yousra killed were already rotten and gangrenous in the womb. Killing such monsters did not frighten her.

The Heroes did.

The Heroes' man had big, bloodshot eyes set deep in a broad, flat face. Black blood clotted his cropped genitals. His wrists were rubbed raw. She saw bruises on his face and thighs, put there by his own people, no doubt, or perhaps some of hers, before she decided she wanted him. When she looked at him she was reminded of her own dying men on the hill of battle, the ones who tried to fight the Heroes when their big ships came overhead. Those men, she could not save. She settled for this one. They were not so different, the Heroes' men and hers. The Heroes might have come from some other star, but Yousra's people, too, had been born from the sky.

She took the man inside her house. He flinched under her hands. No one had ever seen the Heroes without their big suits of armor, only their men, so she supposed it was possible that the Heroes, too, looked much like Yousra. But she had always suspected they resembled insects, like the hard shells of their suits. It had taken eight of Yousra's people with machetes to overtake a Hero, once, but even when they did, the Heroes' reinforcements beat them away from the body before they could peel away the scaly layers of their suits. Why they left their men behind now, when all knew they were diseased, was uncertain. Perhaps they simply wanted to get rid of them, and could not bear to kill them any more than Yousra could.

"You're a wreck," she told the man. He whimpered. She pushed open his eyelids to examine his eyes. Gray eyes, unremarkable. Like her people, he had a clear, vestigial eyelid on the inner corner of his eye. Useful for the relentless sandstorms that wracked this part of the world . . . useful for the day when their crops were finally blown away and her people were cast back into the desert from which they came.

Prophetic times. End times. She did not expect to be alive by the time the desert reclaimed them.

She fed him milk of poppy mixed with afterdrake for the pain, then cleaned him up as he drifted in and out of consciousness. It was a wonder he had not bled out. Most did. She had to pinch and dig to find his urethra. She inserted a hollow bamboo tube to keep it open while the wound healed.

He did not recover quickly, or well. Yousra bathed him each day with water and diluted tea tree oil. She kept his wounds packed in precious honey to combat infection and ward off fever. At night, she woke to his cries, and soothed him like a child. As she held him, it reminded her of her own childhood, when she would hush her brothers' cries so they would not draw the scavengers. The man babbled in some unknown language. It sounded mushy, as if he were chewing a gob of sap, sticky and sweet. Every time they thought they understood the Heroes' language, they sent them men who spoke differently.

A few weeks later, when the village priest and his brother entered into an agreement with the potter woman on the edge of the village to form a marriage, Yousra was called to organize and bless the wedding, and the bride, and her most-likely rotten womb. Why her people married anymore, she did not know. She would bless this girl now and kill her monsters in a few months. Round and round, as their numbers dwindled, and the Heroes came through, building shining cities of glass and amber where once there were sprawling towns.

The bride dressed in the white of a martyr. Yousra had the Heroes' man bring her tools into the bridal tent. When Yousra was a child, weddings took months or years to plan. Now the time of engagement was a matter of weeks.

She called the Heroes' man simply "Boy," and he answered to it. He could walk, after a fashion, and that was good, because she had no use for a broken man. She bore some affection for the boy—how could one not bear affection for one you nursed and comforted? But she had borne affection for monsters, too, the ones that went bad days or weeks after birth.

And she had killed them just the same.

The bride, Chalifa, was lovely. Her mother was one of the first births Yousra had tended after her predecessor, the village head-woman and priest, had died in childbed.

Yousra had always hoped to be headwoman herself by the time Chalifa married, so the girl's wedding night would belong to her. Instead, Yousra merely outfitted the bride and gave her blessing.

"Will it hurt?" Chalifa asked as Yousra placed a circle of holly above her brow.

"It's a ritual unblocking," Yousra said. "It will make your first coupling much easier."

Chalifa took a deep breath. "I didn't mean the unblocking of the womb. I meant . . . the birthing."

"That's some time away," Yousra said carefully.

"If it's . . . If it's gone bad . . . I don't have to see it, do I?"

"No," Yousra said.

"You'll kill it?"

"Yes."

"Good."

Yousra opened her mouth to tell Chalifa what a fine choice she had made, what fine children she would have—the same speech she had given a hundred doomed women—but as she did, a dull, vibrating hum stilled her speech. The holly leaves on Chalifa's head trembled.

Yousra looked to the entrance to the bridal tent. The Heroes' man had paused also, water bulb in hand. The fine hairs on his arms and neck stood on end.

The hum grew to a tinny whine. It was like nothing Yousra had ever heard. She felt the air tremble. Heard a heavy *whump-whump,* far off.

Yousra gazed outside the bridal tent. Something silver streaked across the lavender sky, like a giant thrush. The other villagers had come out of their tents. They, too, looked up—rapt, open faces gazing skyward.

"What is it?" Chalifa asked.

The world went dark.

Smoke. Heat.

Yousra flailed in the darkness, pinned by the cloying weight of what must have been the bridal tent. She clawed for daylight. The air was bad. She gasped. Then screamed. Screamed and screamed and clawed at the tent, ripping and tearing at the hemp cloth. It wasn't until the hilt of her machete knocked her hip that she realized she still carried it.

She pulled out the machete and sliced open the shroud of the bridal tent. Smoky air rushed in.

Yousra stumbled out. A low fog of blue smoke obscured her view. She heard muted screams. One ended abruptly. Loose clods of dirt blanketed the far side of the bridal tent. The remains of another tent poked up from a heap of shattered earth.

The rest of the village . . . she saw only hazy snapshots amid the smoke-fog . . . curls of flame. Dark, bulbous shapes. Clumps of dirty meat. Smears of clotted blood and offal.

She stepped away from the ruins of the tent and lost her feet. She tumbled to the bottom of a deep crater. It stank of wet earth and copper and something else . . . sulfur? She clawed her way up the side of the crater.

A low rumble sounded overhead. Something blotted out the suns. She looked up and saw a slow-moving, silvery ship. Even in her terror, she gaped. She had never seen one of the Heroes' ships up close. She saw her own reflection, distorted, gaping back at her from the impossibly shiny craft.

Yousra ran back toward the bridal tent. She called, softly, for Chalifa. She hacked at the tent, but found nothing. Half the tent was buried in the soil thrown up from the crater.

Voices sounded, close. Then other sounds, unfamiliar. Clicking. A soft buzz. Footsteps across the earth. Not sandaled feet, no, but boots. Metal. The crisp creak, whine, and hum of something Other.

Yousra hid in the crater, and peered above its edge.

Shapes appeared from the smoke—blocky, gargantuan. She had never seen a Hero, not like this. These were massive, twice as tall as the tallest man she knew, as wide as she was tall, encased in blackish-green material with the glossy sheen of a damp leaf. The pieces of their armor came together at the seams, moved like scales. The heads were mounted with a single horn from which protruded a long mane of hair. In her mother's time, they'd thought the Heroes were shelled creatures, bestial. It was a decade before they knew that the hard shells protected a soft interior.

As Yousra watched them approach, she had a sudden, intense desire to cut each of them open, to discover—for herself—the truth of that soft inner core and how it had polluted her people.

Someone cried out behind her. She froze.

A figure broke away from the smoke near the ruined bridal tent and ran toward the Heroes. It took Yousra a moment to recognize the castrated Heroes' man. Had they come for him? Why? Curse me for a fool, she thought.

The boy babbled something at the Heroes in his mushy language. He prostrated himself and sobbed. Great, heaving sobs.

A strange sound came from one of the Heroes in turn. A *chuck-chuck-guffaw* sound that Yousra realized was laughter. The Hero struck the boy across the face with such force that it propelled him across the dirt and into the smoking heap of another tent.

The Heroes continued their *chuck-chucking* and walked on.

Yousra slid farther below the lip of the crater. Squeezed her eyes shut. She heard the Heroes, not a dozen feet distant, crunching across the ruined earth. They spoke in tinny, garbled voices. She listened as they walked past her . . . and away.

She stayed huddled in the dirt until long after she saw their silvery ship shoot back across the sky over the village.

By then, dusk had settled across the world, and the massive glowing orb of the trade moon had begun to fill the sky, like a chalky skull writ large. As it rose, its pale glow chased away the dusk, blanketing the world in a harsh moonlight that was strong enough to hunt by.

Slowly, carefully, Yousra crawled from her hiding place and crept across the dirt. A little ways distant, she saw the still form of the Heroes' man, crumpled in the dirt. She hesitated.

"Boy?" she called softly.

He did not move.

"Boy? Heroes' boy?"

He lifted his head. His eyes were watery, bloodshot. The entire right side of his face was a black bruise.

"Come with me," she said. "We aren't safe here."

He pressed his face back into the dirt.

Yousra gazed out beyond him to where the thorn fence had been. It was broken now. Bloody, tattered strips of it lay in wrecked clumps and tangles for a hundred yards in either direction. The fence would let in the contagion all around them. Even if she could bring herself to stay in the village, the horror of the contaminated world outside would overtake her. She was dead already.

Yousra watched the great God's Wheel rise in the sky, the incredible patina of stars—gold, silver, blue, green—that lent pinpricks of jewel-like color to the moon's white glow during the dry season. It was full dark, and the God's Wheel had risen above the tops of the walking trees.

The sky was oblivious to her troubles. The sky moved on. She should too. She went back toward the heart of the village. Something cried out behind her. She gripped her machete. Her fingers were slick. She dared look in the direction of the sound. Saw the familiar outline of the Heroes' man. He struggled toward her, clutching at his side. As he neared, she saw that though he was injured, he was not bleeding.

"Are you pleased with what your Heroes did?" she said. A hot surge of anger filled her. She raised the machete.

He cowered.

She stared long at his bruises.

"You," she said softly, and lowered the machete. She pointed out past the thorn fence, in the direction the Heroes' craft had gone. "You know where they are, don't you?" His expression did not change. She jabbed her finger at him. "There was a river that used to flow through our village to another, many years ago."

Her village hadn't heard from anyone outside the thorn fence in decades.

"Heroes," she said, and pointed again.

His eyes widened. That word, he knew.

"Take me to the Heroes," she said.

He seemed to weigh his options in the chill glow of the tiny moon. His stare met the hilt of her machete. Then, a small nod. Barely perceptible. He began walking out past the ruined fence, toward a twisted tree.

"Wait!" she called. "Wait!"

She pillaged the remains of the village and found water bulbs, red flour, rain clothes, and a torn knapsack.

Yousra shouldered the pack and started off after the Heroes' man. How long until she succumbed to some contagion out here? Until some insect or blight or fungus ate her from the inside? But how many Heroes could she take with her, before the end?

She raised her head and saw that the Heroes' man had paused at the base of the twisted tree that once marked her family's farm. Her heart ached. Not for him, or the lost farm, or her dead people, but for the hope of some uncertain future, something that wasn't already written.

Yousra stepped forward, like hurling herself into some nameless void, and started across the contaminated world to meet him . . . and his Heroes.

"There is nothing out here but desert," Yousra said, but the Heroes' man kept walking. He ate and drank less than she did, and that was a boon, because as the long days stretched out, Yousra found that she needed more and more of both.

Their first night in the desert, she had come down with some contagion. It bloomed amber-white in her mouth like a fungus. She thought herself dead right then, but the Heroes' man breathed into her mouth—she was too weak to argue—and the next morning the pain was less and the moldy fuzz in her mouth was gone.

Still, the man walked, and he said nothing. He had already tried and failed to go back to his people, so what did he expect to find way out here that would help him? All of her people's settlements out this way were gone.

The world spun into light and darkness another dozen times before Yousra finally smelled something salty and full of death, a scent she had heard of but never seen. They followed a long-abandoned track through the desert, passing the ruins of what must have once been cities, but cities the likes of which Yousra had heard of only in mythic tales. Staggering juggernauts stair-stepped into the sky, or spiraled up from the sand in great, corroded circles. Bits of shattered glass and rotten metal lay scattered across the way. She could make out the softer valleys of the roads, and elevated walkways with crumbling arches.

And there, at the far end of the broken city, was a flat, shimmering plain of water, dark as a stormy sky. She had never seen a body of water so great. It stretched across the whole of the horizon. She could not see the other shore. It made a great, roaring noise.

The Heroes' man picked up his pace when he saw it, and she had to slog to catch up. By the time she reached him he was already at the shoreline, his toes sunk into a battered beach made up of tiny fragments. Yousra scooped up a handful of the stuff and saw that it was made of shells, rocks, knobs of metal, and other, stranger kinds of materials, like ivory or obsidian, but softer. Many of the shapes were knotted and irregular. Far off, she saw great iron spires jutting out of the water; waves crashed against stone and metal structures, and something else—massive shimmering fins, like the hulking back of some great monster. She gazed across the water and saw more and more structures breaking the waves around them.

"Did the Heroes do this?" Yousra asked. "Did they sink this city? Is this our city or theirs?"

He did not answer. Instead, he waded into the water and went kicking out into it like he was made for the water.

Yousra walked up onto a weathered pillar and watched him swim out toward one of the great fins. Was this his plan all along? Some death rite where he drowned himself?

She looked behind her, into the wretched city, and back in the direction of her own ruined settlement. Her feet were beginning to itch already, probably with some terrible contagion. If she stayed here alone she was likely to die here as surely as she would have died in the settlement.

Better to die in the water, then.

Yousra jumped off the pillar and swam out into the sea after the Heroes' man. The water was so clear she could see the ruins below her. They were not buildings, she saw now, but vehicles. She was not a good swimmer, but the day was clear and the current was not too strong. When she needed to rest she clung to the big fin of some wreck and caught her breath. The wrecks below her were ships very much like those the Heroes piloted to every battlefield, only they were not silvery pods, but black, tentacled things with great soaring fins and rotten, fleshy-looking hulls.

When she reached the Heroes' man, he was standing on top of the largest vehicle. The water washed over his feet, coming as high as his ankles. He got onto his hands and knees and pressed his palms to the surface of the ship.

Yousra dragged herself up next to him just as the skin around his hands puckered and pushed outward. He stepped back, bumping into her, and she caught him against her so he didn't fall over. He was warm and trembling, and did not pull away as the flesh of the outer hull pushed outward and opened up above the surface of the water.

He finally left her arms and descended into the ship. Its surface changed, conforming to his feet and hands, making perfect holds for him.

Yousra followed, fearful it would only respond to him, but it conformed to her body, too, and as her head sank below the lip of the wound, it sealed behind her. For a heart-pounding moment she feared she had been eaten, left to suffocate in the darkness. But as the Heroes' man walked ahead of her, the corridors lit up with green, bioluminescent flora. She marveled at the walls, and ran her hands along them. The man led her into the belly of the thing, a great round room. It was featureless save for a bulbous dais at the center of it.

"You know how to work this ship?" Yousra asked.

The man said nothing. He walked slowly around the room.

Yousra said, "Can you power it? We could fight them. We could destroy them, with this. Are these theirs? Can you use them? I know you understand more than you can speak."

The Heroes' man did not look at her. His shoulders tensed, though. She gently stroked his arm. "They did this to you," she said. "They polluted you, then threw you away to your fate. You are as much their victim as we are. Help us beat them back and reclaim the world."

He said something in his Heroes' language. Stopped. Tried again, in hers. "World is large."

"It is," Yousra said. She thought of all the grotesque, mangled babies she had killed, the women gone to rot, the men gone to madness. "But if you can pilot these ships, we can teach others. We can make our own army, large enough to take back the world."

Yousra didn't know if that was true. She didn't know the extent of the Heroes' armies. They came from the sky, and the world was large. There could be thousands, hundreds of thousands, of them. More than that? She could not imagine numbers so large. But whatever the number, she would fight them. She would kill them as she killed the rotting, monstrous children they infected her people with.

He made a little whimpering sound. She opened her arms to him, and he pressed himself against her like a child. And perhaps he was; they all were, fearful children stunted by this mad war that neither understood. What did the Heroes want? She found, more and more, that she didn't care so much about answers as revenge. She closed her eyes and thought of her smoking village, the scattered body parts, the huffing laughter of the Heroes.

"Come with me," Yousra murmured in his ear.

He raised his face to her. His eyes were wet. She kissed him, softly, as she would kiss a sister or a child. Yet when he pressed back, his need was evident. His body was hot against hers, and she responded in kind, surprised at her own desire. She pinned him to the floor of the ship and nipped at his neck, and straddled his wiry thigh. When her leg rubbed between his, where his sex had been, he cried out, and pushed her away.

Yousra tumbled off him, sat hard on her rump, and came back into the world. Desire was a drug, a potent one, and it muddled all sense. It had been so long since it had carried her away that she felt drunk and disoriented now; it was like drinking a pot of liquor after a year of nothing but brackish water. Warm, delirious.

The man sat up beside her. He was breathing heavily. He did not look at her, but stared straight ahead, hands wrapped around his knees.

"What do they want, your Heroes?" Yousra asked. She reached for him, gently, and stroked his jaw. He flinched, but did not pull away. The skin there was fuzzy. He was too young for a proper beard, or perhaps his kind did not grow them as well as hers. Perhaps all their men were this hairless. She wondered, for the first time, if the Heroes' men left on the field were lost children, like the monsters she murdered out by the thorn fence.

He took her wrist, not ungently. "No knowledge," he said.

"They tell you nothing?"

His lips firmed. Not a frown, not quite. He touched his temple. "No knowledge," he said.

"You must remember something," she said. "You yelled at those Heroes. In the village. What did you tell them?"

He stood and walked over to the dais at the center of the room. He placed his hands in the middle of it, and the room became translucent.

Yousra gasped and scrambled up. The ocean surrounded them, full of derelicts and grimy whorls of rusty filth. It was only now, with a clear view of the ocean, that she realized there was nothing living here in the sea, either. It was as dead as the rest of the world.

The Heroes' man stepped up onto the dais. He pointed at Yousra, said, "Yours," and then a fine mist of fleshy webbing descended from the ceiling and enveloped him.

Yousra shrieked and fell back against the transparent wall. She had a moment of vertigo, her mind fearing she would be cast out to sea, but the wall held. The webbing fully enveloped the Heroes' man, rooting him into place like another fixture of the ship. But as it did, the ship itself came alive around her. The translucent walls flickered with blue and yellow lights. The ship shuddered; great gouts of the disturbed sea bottom clouded the water all around them.

Yousra climbed toward the dais. She touched the outline of the man's foot, now covered by the ship's flesh. The ship lurched again, and she stumbled back. The ship rose from the bottom of the sea, up and up and up. As it did, the motion of it stabilized, and Yousra walked closer to the transparent wall and gaped as the ship parted the waves and came up over the sea of dead.

She gazed back at the Heroes' man, and the great dead village behind them. Why had the Heroes abandoned the ships here, if they could pilot them as easily as this man? Surely he was piloting it in some way. It seemed a terrible waste to leave all of this here.

The walls shimmered, then went opaque. The darkness was abrupt. Yousra feared they would fall out of the sky. Then, blinding white light. She raised her hands to her face. When the light dimmed, she pulled her hands away, and saw that the city below them had been transformed. Now it was a bustling metropolis with great tangled buildings grasping toward the sky. Massive floating bridges moved over the ocean. Ships like the one she rode in traversed the air all around them. She thought herself mad until she noted the position of the God's Wheel in the sky. It was in the wrong position. She was not looking at a current vision, but a past one. Somehow the ship had captured it; perhaps the ship was a living thing, and had remembered. Was the Heroes' man tapping into that memory?

As she watched, a great rain of fire came down from the sky and destroyed the peaceful city. The bridges exploded. The ships turned and fought while the city burned. And then came the Heroes' ships, the familiar shiny silver arrows.

The Heroes decimated the people. The ships that were being attacked fled to the water, seeking reprieve. Most were destroyed.

Then blackness. When light returned, the walls were again translucent, and the city was old and dead again, and the God's Wheel was in its proper place.

Yousra felt a terrible fist of dread in her stomach. She turned back to the Heroes' man, suspended now, merged with the ship.

"You're not one of the Heroes," she said. "You're one of these people. Some other people they destroyed, like us." Of course the Heroes had not piloted these ships; only people from this city could pilot them, the way the Heroes' man was doing now. What a fearful, sick game the Heroes played, sending their own captives to Yousra's people. What did they expect to happen? They knew Yousra's people would torture them, murder them. She felt foolish, then. Why would the Heroes infect their own men and condemn them to such a fate? No wonder the man looked so much like her people. They were not so different, just separated by time.

What baffled her was that the city below had very clearly been dead for centuries. And though Yousra's people had been known to live for a century and a half, this man was clearly very young. Where had he come from? What had the Heroes done, to keep him so young? And why throw him out now?

Yousra pressed her hand to his form again. "If there are more of your people, we can find them," she said. "They can pilot the ships. We can seek revenge, together."

The ship was hovering above the ocean now, motionless. The suns were lowering on the horizon. Yousra waited. What did she have to offer him? He had a ship, and a world that had been dead for longer than he had been alive. What must he have thought, awaking to find himself dumped in her village and castrated?

But she firmed her resolve. "I'm not your enemy," she said. "The Heroes did this to us both. They pitted us against one another. They will not expect us to work together."

Yousra considered the flesh of the ship. Clearly these were organic things, and she knew how to heal, and birth, and kill, if necessary. "If these ships are alive," she said, "they could be changed.

Transformed. Perhaps we don't need to find your people to pilot each one. Perhaps there is a way to link them, and feed them."

The ship began to move.

Yousra turned to watch as it sailed over the ocean, back toward the city. It settled down in a great, dead patch of ground opposite the road, close enough to the sea that the waves lapped at its sides.

"Are you with me, or do you want me to get out?" she said.

The walls lit up again, and replayed the death of the city.

"All right," she said. "This may take some time."

And so began Yousra's life at the edge of the sea. She had spent so long engaged in the act of death that she had almost forgotten what it was like to birth something. It did not take long to realize that the key to unlocking the ships was the blood of the Heroes' man. Now that she knew he was not one of them, though, she tried to think up another name for him. Boy, Ship, Man, Child . . . Easy names. The names of things. But she could not get them to stick in her mind.

She bled him in the morning, cutting through the webbing the ship had wound about him and carrying it in one of the old water bulbs. Then she would swim down to another of the derelict ships, and pour the blood onto the dais at the center of each, and watch the webbing come down and devour it. The ships woke; lights rippled across their surfaces. Their skins shone. But she could not figure out how to link them. Could the Heroes' man pilot them all, now that they were away? Could she connect them together, through some kind of umbilical system?

The ships themselves were very much like children. Abused, neglected children buried at the bottom of the sea. She began to learn their fits and starts, their needs and wants. It was why she could not bear to sleep inside the ship where the Heroes' man stood trapped, because it was clear he had become the ship. Each day she bled him, there was less blood. The outline of his form in the webbing grew smaller and more twisted and disfigured each day.

The ship was eating him, devouring him. She hoped some part of his consciousness would go on, but she feared that the ship would simply require more bodies, more death, to power itself.

"I will give you death," she whispered to her ship one night while the God's Wheel whirled in the sky. The skin of the ship seemed to murmur beneath her fingers. She took comfort in that. "Will you help me, in exchange for bodies?" she asked. Another ripple. The skin of the ship warmed beneath her fingers.

She slept well that night.

It was months into her life on the beach, bleeding and waking hundreds of ships, that she found the sepulchre. She was scavenging for food in the city, hunting rodents and beetles. Much of her diet was fried grasshoppers and withered tubers. Her gums bled now, and the vision in her right eye was not the best. Two lumps had formed on her ankle, and another on her wrist. She had lacerated the one on her wrist, and it had oozed thick, gummy fluid. Not cancer, then. Perhaps. But it would come for her, out here in the toxic world beyond her village.

She found a rodent's burrow, and dug into the rubble around it to try and ferret it out. Her stick hit a spongy spot, and poked right through it without resistance. She cleared away the debris and found that the metal over the spongy surface had rotted away. Beneath the metal was a scabby substance, clotted. She dug through it and peered into a great black space. When she pushed her head through, the space lit up with green, bioluminescent organisms. It was a vast space, far larger than she had anticipated. It went on and on.

Yousra slipped down into the cavern. All along the walls, on both sides, ran coffin-like indentations in the fleshy corridors. Inside were bodies, row after row of bodies, their faces serene, their flesh—

Yousra touched one of them. Its flesh was cool, but still pliable.

Bodies. Like a gift from the gods.

Yousra did not think about why they were there, or how to wake them, or how long they had hidden here while their city was destroyed. No, she focused on her goal. She made a sledge and hauled them—one after another—across the dead city and into the sea and into the ships that littered the ocean bottom.

She went to bed smelling of the sea. Tasting it on her lips. Sometimes she thought about the lives the bodies must have had before she had found them, but mostly she thought of her village, and the babies.

The twenty-eighth body she pulled through the ocean and deposited on the dais of a ship woke up.

Yousra saw the eyelids flicker. He began to cough. His skin warmed. She patted the dais and yelled at the ship, willing the webbing to come down faster.

As the webbing crept up over the man's feet, he began screaming and screaming, babbling at her in some language. She recognized it. The same one the Heroes' man had used. She did not look away, but met his gaze until the ship wrapped him in its fleshy embrace.

Then she patted the cocooned man and murmured, "You belong to me now, ship. Follow me, and I will keep you fed."

When she ran out of bodies, she went back to her own ship, and found that the dais that had once contained the Heroes' man had grown upward to touch the ceiling. His body was gone, absorbed, but the ship had built something in its place. When Yousra pressed the pillar now, the ship shuddered under her touch.

"Let's find some Heroes," she said, and the ship rose from the beach.

Yousra stood in front of the pillar, back pressed against it, and pointed to the horizon. "They come from the sky," she said, "this way," and the ship moved the way she pointed.

The ship moved across the sea, so fast that they reached the other side in just a few breaths. It slowed as they reached land. Yousra saw a glimmer of silver below, and just as she thought to tell the ship to get closer to it, the ship sank toward the glinting metal.

The metal was not a large ship, not like the ones that had moved over Yousra's village and destroyed it. It was much smaller, with room for perhaps just a handful of people. Two Heroes stood just to the left of the vehicle, inspecting a tall mound scattered with the detritus of living that a family would leave behind when they fled quickly.

"Destroy their ship," Yousra said.

The ship around her hummed. Yellow lightning crackled across the surface outside. Then a brilliant flash.

When Yousra could see again there was a great crater where the Heroes' ship had been. She told her ship to land, and it did, and she walked out to see what she had done.

The air outside smelled like stone after a hard rain. The fine hairs stood up on the back of her neck. The Heroes' ship had been liquefied, its parts melted down and splattered across the crater. The bodies of the Heroes lay thirty paces away. Their bodies had collided with large trees, and shattered their trunks to pieces.

Yousra made her way to the bodies, her bare feet making prints in the loose soil, and stood over them. One had been run through with a great tree branch with such force that it severed through the suit. The other had lost its head; bits of ship debris had blown clear of the crater and cut the head neatly from the body.

Yousra found the great helmet and picked it up. A head rolled out and settled at her feet. She crouched beside it and turned it over so she could see its face. Blood and bruising mottled the features, but it was not some alien, chitinous thing as she had suspected. Yousra sat beside the body and pulled the gory head into her lap. She rubbed the brow and fingered the braided hair and wondered how a people so like hers could do what these Heroes had done. She had thought them monsters from some other star, but the face in her lap was not so different from the man who had sacrificed himself to power the ship, not so different from hers.

She gazed up into the sky at the God's Wheel, still faint now in the daylight. She imagined a whole people who had gone up there and come back here to see what had become of their ancestors, only to destroy them for being too weak, too tied to the soil, and the seasons. What they wanted did not concern her, but she mourned the fact that they were able to do what she was about to do, and that what she was about to do was only what she had learned from them.

Yousra set the head beside her and picked up the helmet. It fit her head easily. Instead of tunneling her vision, it gave her a full, enhanced view of her surroundings. Like the ship she rode in, it was transparent here inside of it, so every way she turned, she could see the world, only augmented with symbols and shapes and mists that appeared otherwise invisible. Perhaps these suits detected heat or gases, and gave them form. She did not know, but she could learn, the same way she had learned the ships.

Yousra had her suit. She had her army. She was ready.

It took a long time to burn down the world.

Yousra would not have thought it would take so long, with so much of it destroyed already, but there was far more of the world than she was prepared for. The Heroes inhabited great swaths of it. Her living army of ships was two hundred strong, and they rose from the sea at her command and destroyed at her word. There might have been a large armada of Heroes' ships when they first came to Yousra's lands, and the lands of the man whose people had made the cities. But there was no longer an armada of ships that strong here. What the Heroes had left to mop up what remained of the people here was small in comparison to what Yousra had seen in the vision the ship showed her.

Her army of ships blew their silver vehicles out of the sky, rained molten metal and torn, suited bodies across the world. She traveled over great barren spaces, inhabited by nothing but rocks and dead, rolling weeds. The remnants of thorn fences made for abstract art pieces, scattered and broken across the lands at the edge of the worst of the blight. She found a large fleet of silver ships—thirty, in total—camped at the base of a craggy mountain range, and rained lightning-fire down upon them until the bases of the mountains were coated in molten silver.

As she watched smoke rise up from the dead forests surrounding the camp, she wondered why the Heroes had not destroyed them as she was doing. Perhaps, after decimating the man's people, hers were not considered a threat. And why would they be? They had no ships, no cities. Just death and disease. No, the Heroes had done something more terrible to them. They had toyed with them, as if they were nothing but insects or rodents. Murdering Yousra's people would have been too easy. The game was in watching them slowly suffer and die.

Her murdering went on for some time, until she dreamed of steaming craters and molten silver, and woke to see the same. Her ships were taken down one by one, a battle at a time. It did not alarm her, though, because this was the end she expected. This was a war of attrition.

She had just three ships left when she approached the last of the Heroes' settlements. She had to assume it was the last because she had traveled across the world for days and days and seen nothing but death and ruin and rot. The cancer in her left leg had gotten worse; her ankle had swelled up so big that she walked with a painful limp. A lump in her neck was the size of her fist now, and it pressed against her windpipe as she breathed. She was not long for this world; she was poisoned. This was likely her last camp.

She commanded the ships to fire, but as they did, four silvery Heroes' ships emerged from the muddy lake bottom. They fired at her ships, downing two. Her ship screamed into defensive maneuvers and fired at them, speeding in and out of range on its own, powered by the will of the man it had eaten. The Heroes' ships exploded, but the wreckage cloud was so vast that it clipped her ship, and suddenly she was hurtling down, and down, and she hoped this would be her death, a fitting death, ground into the mud with her ship.

Smoke. Heat.

Yousra crawled up through the suffocating flesh of the ship, tearing her way out, sucking for air. Her skin ached and burned and she feared the ship was eating her to save itself.

She popped free of the ship and slid down its surface and into the long poppies in the field. She wore her Heroes' suit, but not the helmet; it had been wrenched free in the accident.

Yousra pulled off her gloves, as well, because she felt too hot. Behind her, the ship that had led her glorious army burned hot and white. She shielded her eyes and limped away, sucking heated air and smoke.

When she reached the tree line, she pulled off the rest of the suit and cast it into the poppies. It was strange to see something alive, out here, but she had reached the very end of the world, the end of everything. She leaned over and tried to smell the poppies, but her nose didn't register any scent. She rubbed her smoke-stung eyes. Something moved at her left.

When she turned she saw it was a Hero, her own armor battered and smashed as Yousra's. The Hero, too, had removed her helmet and gloves. She was a young woman, half Yousra's age, hair braided back from a lean face that reminded Yousra of Chalifa, the bride from her own village.

Yousra cast about for a weapon, but saw nothing. The Hero had none either that she could see, but would be trained in war, and the only war Yousra knew was fought from inside a ship.

"You deserved all of this," Yousra said.

She didn't expect a response, but the Hero said, "It was necessary."

"Necessary to who?" Yousra said. The Hero spoke with an accent, but not a thick one. They knew her language, at least. Probably that man's, too, though. It meant nothing. They would kill anything. Knowing her language made them better killers, in fact. "You murdered my people. You murdered the world. What do you have to say to that?"

"We were civilizing you," the Hero said.

"This?" Yousra said, gesturing to the steaming craters, the dead ships, the dying poppies. "This is civilization?"

"There can be no civilization without war," the Hero said.

"You are a twisted, corrupt people," Yousra said. "You have no idea what living is."

"We had to break your villages," the Hero said. "Wreck your world. Or you would not walk into the light. You would never explore the stars. You would never come after us."

"You're mad," Yousra said.

"This is what happened to us," the Hero said. "A people from another star rained fire on us, and lifted us up. We had to lift up another."

Yousra thought she should feel something. Like the Hero had torn some piece of her. But as Yousra stood before her, barefoot, bloodied, her hair a matted tangle and what was left of her robe a tattered ruin, she realized they had nothing else left to break. It had all been done.

"You wish to break me?" the Hero asked softly. "As you have been broken? I am sorry, dear one, but you are not the first we have civilized. Nor will you be the last. Soon we will rise again, and take another star. An alliance of Heroes the like of which the universe has never known."

"Heroes . . ." Yousra said.

"Yes, Heroes. It's fitting, isn't it? What your kind call us."

"You don't know what the word means," Yousra said.

"It translates very well into our language," the Hero said. "A Hero is one who not only slays monsters, but creates monsters to slay. That is what we have done here. It's what you have become. A Hero. Now you, in turn, will make Heroes of others."

"What if I kill you here?" Yousra said.

The Hero shrugged. "All the better." She dropped to her knees. "Do it. Complete our mission here. Continue the cycle. Raise up another. Colonize the stars."

"No," Yousra said.

"Then we will find another," the Hero said. "Do you understand yet? You sacrificed a boy to your cause. Murdered babies born wrong. Left men to die outside your fence. And my people, yes, we are people, though we are ruthless, you destroyed us with as much care as if we were insects. This is who you must be, to rule the universe."

Yousra sat across from the Hero. "I don't want to rule the universe," she said. "I want two husbands, eight children, and a village full of friends. You took that from me."

The Hero leaned toward her. "Take it back."

"That's what you don't understand," Yousra said. "I am too old to believe it can be returned to me. There is no substitute for my life. You are young, you don't know that yet. But you will. You should have chosen a younger woman."

Yousra got painfully to her feet. Her ankle throbbed. She began to walk toward the lake.

"Wait!" the Hero said. "We can cure you. Give you resources. We can give you a whole army. As many husbands as you desire. Have children, surround yourself with a new family. Your people have passed the test of personhood. You are civilized! You can be uplifted now! You are true people, and as true people, we invite you to join our federation of worlds."

But Yousra was already at the end of the lake. She kept walking.

The water brushed her ankles, cool and calming after all that heat and death. She gazed up at the God's Wheel in the sky, brighter now as the light withdrew from the heavens.

The Hero was right, in that there was nothing she had not sacrificed to get here. But now, at the edge of the lake, under the eye of the God's Wheel, she found that after all this time, she did not like what she had become. The choice of what to do now that she could not go back was still hers, and it was a welcome choice, easier than anything she had done so far.

Yousra walked into the lake. It was so clear she could see the ruins in the bottom; the derelict boats and scattered stone animal pens and circular foundations of old houses.

The Hero was shouting at her, but there were no more silvery ships in the sky. No one to save either of them. They were left to their own choices.

Yousra closed her eyes as the water lapped up above her head, and she remembered all those dead babies. The castrated men they thought belonged to the Heroes, the broken cities, and the ships she had melted away.

She could reward herself for becoming this woman, and take the spoils granted. But the spoils were not hers. They were rewards taken from the bodies of others. Rewards built on death and lies and revenge. If that was the universe these people wanted to build, she wanted none of it.

The water was very cold. She swam down and down and looped her belt through a hole in a derelict boat, and when she could stand it no longer, she took a breath, and inhaled cold, clear water, and screamed and screamed into the darkness.

"Run it again," the girl said.

"It's just a simulation," her mother said. The barren waste of the world being terraformed behind them came briefly back into their vision as the headwoman's watery grave faded from the viewing lens.

"Again," the girl said. "I want to know if she makes a different choice."

"She doesn't," her mother said. "It's why there was still a world here at all, when we came back up from the banks underground after our long sleep. If she had chosen differently, we all would have died, or become part of her terrible army. We would have been different people."

"Again," the girl said.

Her mother frowned. "Would you have chosen differently?"

The girl said nothing.

Her mother played it again, and again the Heroes left their men on the dying fields, and again, Yousra made her choice.

THE LIGHT BRIGADE

THE WAR HAS TURNED US INTO LIGHT.

Transforming us into light is the fastest way to travel from one front to another, and there are many fronts, now. I always wanted to be a hero. I always wanted to be on the side of light. It's funny how things work out.

But I've been doing this long enough now to know what I really am.

I didn't believe we could turn people into light when I signed up for service after the San Paulo Blink. When you saw what the aliens did to that city without even sending an army there, you knew you had to do something, even if it was dangerous. What happened to all those people doesn't compare to what I have to do. I guess the Blink gave me an idea of the tech involved in what we were expected to do, as corporate soldiers. But it's hard to understand a thing when all you know about it is what people say about it. It's like having sex, or getting into a fight. You don't understand it until you do it.

We jumped first during our six-week orientation, which the CO still calls basic training, even though there hasn't been a public army in almost a century. They inject you with a lot of stuff in training. They don't even wait to see if you wash out, because even if you wash out, they still need you. You don't opt out of this war anymore, not like you could in the early days. If you want to eat at the corporate store, you support the war.

Anyway, you don't even know what any of this shit is they're pumping you full of. They say it makes you faster, smarter, tougher, and who wouldn't want that? You can't say no. Not that you'd want to. Not if you're a real soldier.

And I am. I'm a real soldier.

A real fucking hero.

I'm made of light.

They say the first drop is the toughest, but it's not. It's the one after that, because you know what's coming. You know how bad it is, and what the odds are that you'll come back wrong.

Who are we fighting? The bad guys. They're always the bad guys, right? We gave these alien people half the northern hemisphere to rehabilitate, because it was such a fucking wreck after the Seed Wars that nobody cared who settled it. Nothing would grow there until they came. The aliens had this technology that they developed when they split from us on Earth and built their colonies on Mars. We cut ourselves off from them when they left, so it was a real surprise when some of them asked to come back. I guess they thought they were saving us, but we don't need saving. The tech, whatever it was, got rid of all the radiation and restored the soil, probably the same way it did on Mars after the Water Riots. And stuff grew. We trusted them, but they betrayed us. That's what the networks say, and that's what my CO says, but I'm here because they betrayed San Paulo.

That one I could see. That one I could believe.

Anyway. The drop. The first drop.

You burst apart like . . . Well, first your whole body shakes. Then every muscle gets taut as a wire. My CO says it's like a contraction when you're having a kid, and if that's true, if just one is like that, then I don't know how everybody who has a kid isn't dead already, because that's bullshit.

Then you vibrate, you really vibrate, because every atom in your body is being ripped apart. It's breaking you up like in those old sci-fi shows, but it's not quick, it's not painless and you're aware of every minute of it. You don't have a body anymore, but you're aware, you're locked in, you're a beam of fucking light.

You're a Paladin. A hero of the fucking light.

My first drop, we came in on our beams of light and burned down the woods the alien insurgents were in before our feet had even corporealized. We burned up at least a dozen of the enemy right there. But the worst one was the second drop, like I said, when we came down to protect a convoy under fire in the aliens' territory in Canuck. We came down right there in their farms and traded fire. It's confusing when you come down in the middle of something already going on, OK? Sometimes the energy weapons go right through you, because there's not enough of you stuck together yet. But sometimes you've come together just enough, and they hit you, and either you're meat enough for it to kill you, or all your atoms break apart, and you're nothing. You ghost out.

I've seen a lot of people ghost out.

I came together and started firing. It's what they train us to do, so it wasn't my fault. I hit an alien girl—some civilian at the farm. She wasn't even fifteen. I could hear her and her mother screaming. Their whole family, screaming, because I'd hit her and her legs were gone.

When the fight was over, our medic went to help them, but it didn't matter. She wasn't going to walk unless somebody regrew her legs and only executives have those corporate benefits. I only fired once. One shot. But one is all it takes. You just have to deal with it, when bad things happen to you, especially if you're an alien, because nobody wants to help you.

I deal with it when bad things happen. So should she.

I still hear her and her mom screaming sometimes.

They're aliens, sure.

But.

But it wasn't so long ago that they lived here, before they all ran off to Mars and made some big colony. We welcomed them back like they weren't aliens, but they are. They are aliens. They aren't like us. They are really different. They have a whole other language. Different clothes. They have these socialist ideas that mean shitting on you if you're an individual at all. They're just drones, really, doing whatever their collective tells them. They're aliens. They're the enemy.

I can hear her screaming.

You still don't get it.

I'm not stupid. I don't believe everything they pump us full of. I don't believe all the networks. I've been on too many grassy alien fields for that. Seen too many people dead—ours and theirs—and the faces all look the same. I ask about the San Paulo Blink a lot now, and nobody has good answers for me. Like, why did they pick San Paulo? And, why did these aliens come down from Mars but the others didn't? And, if what they did in San Paulo was so bad, why are we using the same tech to fight them?

They don't like us to ask questions. They try to train it out of you, not just if you're a corporate soldier, but for workers, too. The corporation knows best, right?

I dated this girl once, this really smart girl. She was getting a Ph.D. in one of those social sciences. She said there's this thing called escalation of commitment. That once people have invested a certain amount of time in a project, they won't quit, even if it's no longer a good deal. Even if they're losing. War is like that. No one wants to admit they're losing. They've already lost so much.

You know what you are. What you're becoming. And you can't stop it. You're committed. It doesn't matter how much people scream or how many you kill whose faces look like yours. This is your job. This is what you're trained for. It's who you are. You can't separate them.

Do you get it?

When I signed up after San Paulo, me and my friends were shocked that the recruiting center wasn't packed. Where were all the patriots? Didn't they know what the aliens had done? Didn't they know we had to defend ourselves? I thought all those people who didn't sign up were cowards. While you were all upgrading your fucking social tech and masturbating to some new game, we were fighting the real threat. We were real adults, and you were cowardly little shits.

I joined up because the aliens were ruining the world. I joined up because I thought I was the good guy.

We're the good guys.

We're made of light.

I wish I was as stupid as I used to be.

I see things, when I become the light. You're not supposed to.

I want to tell you there's a humming sound, when you start to break apart, but the shrink says that's impossible. Light doesn't hear things. They tell us that we can't see or feel anything either, but that's a lie, and anyone who's been through it and tells you they don't see or hear anything is lying because they don't want to spend the rest of their lives in a freak house. We all see things in transit. It doesn't mean you're bad or crazy. It doesn't mean you're a bad soldier.

I'm not a bad soldier.

The first time I saw something I remembered was on my third drop. I saw a white rose on a black table. That's it. Just a single image, a flash, fast as the moment it took me to make the transit. The shrink says it's just my brain making things up. Faulty electrical charges, a side effect of the process that breaks up our atoms.

But I saw that image again a couple weeks later, in real life, inside my own meat. I went out to dinner with my squad, and we sat at these dark tables and this lady came around, this old bag lady, and I'm not sure who let her in, but she came around with roses and she was selling them to people.

One of the girls bought a white rose from the lady and laughed and put it on the table. A white rose on a black table. It was placed on the table just the way it was when I saw it in transit during the drop. I stared at it a long time, so long the bag lady tapped my shoulder and asked if I wanted a rose. I shrugged her off, but she squeezed my bare arm and said, "You will go back to the city. You will know why it's full of light." And then she left us.

I drank and laughed and tried to forget it, but it was creepy. And the visions kept happening. I kept seeing things twice—once in transit, and once in real life.

I told the shrink about it and she said it was just déjà vu, when you think you've seen something you've seen before. It happens a lot and it's not weird, she said. No one is sure why it happens more to members of the Light Brigade than other people. (We call ourselves the Light Brigade. The CO hates it). She said we get it even more than people with epileptic seizures. It's the folks with seizures that make them think it has something to do with electrical discharges in the brain that cause faults in the way you store memories. It's not that you've really seen what you're seeing before, she tells me. It's that your brain already wrote the memory, but the conscious part of you doesn't register that it was written just a blink ago. You *feel* like it was a long time ago, but it wasn't. It's a false feeling. Or maybe, she says, it's just that there are some familiar things in some setting you're in, and so you feel it happened before.

It was when she gave me that "Or maybe" part that I realized they have no idea what they're talking about, just like with everything.

And once I started seeing things . . . I started trying to prolong them, those visions. I started corporealizing a half second after everyone else, then a second, then a few seconds, then a full minute, and lingering in those visions just a little longer.

If I was making it all up, if it was déjà vu, how could I do that?

But because I'm not stupid, I go along with it. I tell her yeah, sure, that makes sense. It's just a faulty memory. It's just being part of the Light Brigade.

You see things other people aren't supposed to see.

When did it change, for me?

Not orientation. Not the first drop. Not that girl I hurt. Not the déjà vu.

It changed when we cornered them in their biggest city, a year into my service. Virgin target, the CO said; totally untouched by drones and viral bursts and our Light Brigade. They wanted to see how some new weapon would perform against a target nobody had touched.

I should have guessed what the weapon would be.

I was part of the squad that volunteered to deliver the weapon. They didn't just inject us with shit for this one; they put us under. I don't know what they did. When I woke up, the world was a little green around the edges, and it was tough to figure out how to make words for a couple hours. My tongue was numb. I couldn't feel my toes. But after that I felt pretty normal. Or, what I'd consider normal by then; waking up with night sweats, puking after anxiety attacks. Normal.

Then they sent us out. Busted us down into light.

I broke apart fast, faster than ever, and in the agonizing few seconds it took us to reach this new front at the speed of light, I saw a glowing green field full of bodies heaped up like hay bales. They weren't alien bodies. They were *us*. Our suits. Our faces. And they spread out all around me, as far as I could see. There was a big city in the distance, a city I didn't know, its shining spires reflecting a massive sea that was so still it might have been a lake.

Something had gone very wrong here. We had done something very wrong, and we had paid for it. I stretched the moment out, tried to hold it. I didn't just get a few seconds this time, but a couple minutes. And I could . . . sort of sense myself there, like I was visiting myself. But how was I there, over that city, and over this one, at the same time?

I had this moment of dissonance as I was coming together over the drop zone, like I saw that city and this one lying right on top of each other.

Blink.

My vision blurred, and I was over the real city, the *now* city, the alien city again, the virgin target we were there to destroy. The city I'd come to obliterate.

We started corporealizing over the enemy's biggest port city, the shining pearl of that empire they carved out in Canuck. It unfurled from the flat black desert they had turned into a golden prairie, the way I imagined Oz appeared to Dorothy at the end of the yellow brick road.

It was beautiful. The pinnacle of some great civilization. So clean and light and . . . new. New like nothing on the rest of Earth was new, all of us building on top of the dead civilizations that came before us, the ruined landscapes. Seeing their untouched city, even our best made us look like what we actually were—vagrants living on the bones of something greater that had come before.

We landed and scattered inside the spiraling towers. I arrived a good two minutes after everyone else, and I heard the screams of those who had corporealized inside buildings or walls or those who'd gotten stuck in the pavers. One woman waved her arms at me as I passed, stuck halfway into the ground. Others I passed were already dead, their bodies put back together in a steaming mess of broken flesh and meat.

This was the stuff they glossed over when they pumped you full of drugs. This was the bad part about becoming light. Sometimes it fucked you up.

Sometimes you couldn't put yourself back together again.

I once asked the shrink if maybe it's not déjà vu and maybe we really do go somewhere else when we become light.

"Like where?" she said.

"I don't know," I said. "Maybe I'm visiting myself in other places, other times." I tried to be nonchalant, only half-serious. "I jump ahead in time, maybe."

She swiped something onto the cloudy data projection in front of her and grounded me for six weeks of psych evaluations.

I didn't bring that up again.

But I was figuring things out. Things they didn't want us to understand.

Overhead, waves of our drones came in behind us to draw fire from the shining city. They swept across the neatly tilled fields and buzzed over us. I expected to hear the enemy's defensive guns, or see the wheeling kites of their own organic weaponry flooding the sky in response to the onslaught. But the air was silent save for the soft whirring of the drones and the chuffing of our boots on the paving stones.

I always expect the alien cities to be red, like Mars, but not even

Mars is red anymore, they say. The people that went to Mars did the opposite of what we did back here. They took something red and dusty and turned it into a sea of light. I hear there are giant wispy trees and shallow lakes and a big freshwater ocean there. Here, except for what the aliens did in far Canuck, it's gray and mostly lifeless; a paved-over world where we're scrabbling for fewer and fewer resources.

They were going to save us, they said.

But they betrayed us.

Liars.

Aliens.

I saw movement in one of the buildings and shot off a few bursts from my weapon. The façade cracked and wept brown sap. Everything was alive in their cities, even the buildings. Everything bled. But I didn't see any aliens, just us in our boots.

We crawled over that place, looking for the enemy. But the city was deserted. Maybe they'd abandoned it, or they'd found out we were coming and hid in bunkers. I don't know.

But we couldn't just come all this way for nothing. We had to do what we came for. We had to be weapons.

We assembled around the heart of the city's square the way we planned in training. We raised our energy weapons and set them on the new setting, the one engineered specifically for this mission. We pointed our weapons across the broad square at one another. Set them at a high charge. Waited for the signal.

I started to vibrate. We started to come apart.

The trick was to wait, to be patient. But no one had actually tried to use the light like this before, no living person. It was something they'd done with simulators and robots that fired at each other. It's easy for a robot, to fire at another robot. Harder for a soldier to fire at the person next to them. The one you'd take a hit for. I'd fire into my own face first, I thought, when they told me what we had to do.

But we're the Light Brigade. We do what they tell us to do.

The vibrating got worse. Then the cramping. My body seized up. I gasped. Somebody shot their weapon; too soon. A scream. A body down. Another shot. Too soon.

Goddammit, hold it together.

The contraction stopped.

The world snapped.

I didn't look at the mirrored helmet of the soldier across from me. I looked at the purple patch on their suit, the one that said they were one of us, the Light Brigade. I pulled the trigger.

Everything burst apart.

We were full of light.

"I'm tired of taking care of living things," my CO told me once outside the mess hall, right before that operation. "There's so goddamn many of you. I can't even go home and take care of my dog at night without getting angry at it. Too much fucking responsibility."

"Sorry," I said.

"For what? It's not your fault. The war's not your fault. Not my fault either." But she said the last part differently, like she didn't quite believe it.

And I wondered if she was right to doubt it, because it *was* our fault, wasn't it? We fought this war willingly. We gave our bodies to it, even if we're only here because of the lies the corporations told us. What if there was a war and nobody came? What if the corporations voted for a war and nobody fought it? You can only let so many people starve. You can only throw so many people in jail. You can only have so many executions for insubordination to the latest CEO or Board of Directors.

We are the weapon.

We fired on one another as we broke apart, and created an explosion so massive it obliterated half the northern hemisphere.

Everything the aliens made grow again, we turned back into dust.

We were the weapon. We were the light.

That was when it changed, for me. It's like, you think you're brave, so you carry out your orders. You do it even if you know what the outcome is going to be. You do it because you always wanted to be a hero—you wanted to be on the side of the light. It's not until you destroy everything good in the world that you realize you're not a hero . . . you're just another villain for the empire.

There weren't many of us left to see what we did, and maybe it was better that way. It was all over the networks, the destruction of half a continent. They didn't say how we did it. They didn't say we shot each other up to do it, or say how many of our people died in the explosion, their essential elements broken apart. And right beside these pictures of this barren, smoking wasteland were pictures of our own people cheering in our dingy little cities built on the bones of our ancestors. We had scorched the fucking earth, but everyone cheered because we'd gotten back at those aliens, those liars, those betrayers.

I saw those images and I knew what I had to do. Because I still wanted to be a hero. I still had a chance. But it meant giving up everything I believed in. Betraying everyone I cared about. Being everything I'm supposed to hate.

I know what I need to do because I've seen it.

A white rose on a black table.

Heaps of bodies lying on the field like hay.

I know where I need to go. I know what's next.

The CO gave us leave, those of us who were left. I spent mine look-ing up the city from my vision, the one I saw in transit. There are a lot of cities by water, but none of ours have brilliant green fields like that. All of our shining cities are surrounded by gritty labor camps.

I didn't realize how much they lied to us on the networks until I saw the alien cities. Until I killed the aliens myself. They had made a beautiful world from our shit, and we hated them for it, because they were free. No one owned them.

Betrayers, they said, on the networks. Liars.

They had made the land grow things again, but that was *all* they were supposed to do. They weren't supposed to be free be-cause no one is free, and they weren't supposed to be able to defend themselves because no one can. When we found out they could fight back, when we found out about the organic kites that could take out a drone with a single shattering note, or the EMPs that disabled our networks the first time one of our armies rolled by to see what they were doing, the corporate media started building the narrative—the aliens were liars standing in the way of corporate freedom of commerce.

And then San Paulo.

In San Paulo, the aliens had retaliated. They had turned every-one into light.

A whole city had disappeared.

What nobody said is that San Paulo was where the corpora-tions kept a lot of their most profitable labor camps. My cousin was there, so far in debt to the corps that she couldn't get out. I joined the Light Brigade so that wouldn't be my fate, too. The corps take care of you, as long as you give them everything.

Maybe the aliens did those people a favor. Now that I'd been light, I started thinking that maybe they didn't die after all. Maybe they just went somewhere else. Maybe the aliens found out what we were, too, and tried to save us from ourselves, the way I was now trying to save them.

The San Paulo Blink showed the corporations what was possible. And they used the tech to fight back.

The aliens gave us the light.

Eight million corporate slaves, gone in a blink.

And our response: half a continent scorched of all life.

Maybe the light was our downfall. Or maybe we'd been falling the whole time.

After a couple days' leave, after I located the coordinates of where the city in my vision used to be, I asked to go out on the next offensive. The city I'd seen in my vision had been one of the first we destroyed in the early days of the war, after we tried to invade and they retaliated. In the archives, I saw the city the same way I had in my vision: heaps of our bodies on the green grass fields all around the city.

In the here-and-now, we were still looking for rogue aliens, trying to find out what had happened to all of them, but I already knew. I wasn't there to help them clean up. I was there because I wanted to jump with them.

I could blink forward. And now I knew I could blink back.

My CO gave me a look when I made the request, like she was trying to figure out if I was crazy. She told me that if I could pass the psych eval, she'd approve my next drop. I asked her if she ever gave her dog away, because it was too much responsibility.

"My dog's dead," she said.

"That makes it easier," I said.

"No," she said. "It doesn't. But I guess you can't save everything."

No, I thought, you have to choose.

I almost turned back, then, but I was too committed. Escalation of commitment.

The shrink asked me a lot of questions, but I knew the ones that mattered.

"So do you still think you can travel in time, when you become light?" she asked.

I laughed. "I haven't had any of that déjà vu since the last drop. Those aliens are dead. It's over."

I passed my evaluation.

I prepared for the drop. Closed my eyes. Held on to my sense of self while everyone else broke up around me. I pictured the city in my head, the place I wanted to go back to.

We broke apart.

And I saw it—I saw the alien city of my vision, again surrounded by brilliant green fields. The shining spires. The inland sea. It wasn't the city we had scorched when we became the weapons—though it was just as surely obliterated in the here-and-now as that city was. This was the capital. The center of everything. Those spires were their ships, grounded forever at the foot of the gleaming sea. I had arrived before our first offensive on this city, before the fields were full of the bodies of our people. Before we knew the aliens could fight back.

I came down into my own body, trying to yank myself together, but it was like trying to put together a bucket full of puzzle pieces as somebody poured it out around you.

There were no bodies yet. I had time.

I skimmed into the city, past crowds of startled onlookers. I still wasn't fully corporeal, but I was getting there. I needed a few more minutes. I needed to tell them. Just as I was able to draw air into my lungs, I felt my body vibrating again. It wanted so badly to come back apart and go where the people in charge had sent it.

I held it together.

I yelled, "They're sending us. We're weapons. We're going to scorch the whole continent."

They all stared blankly at me, like I was some dumb beast, and I wondered if they understood Spanish. I tried again in English, but that was as many languages as I knew.

When I didn't say anything else, the crowds dispersed and the people went on their way.

But one of them came up behind me, and I recognized her. It was the bag lady from the restaurant. She put her hand on my arm and squeezed, but it went right through me. I was coming apart again.

"It's you who brings the light," she said. "We won't be here when it comes. You can do what you need to do now without fear for us."

I broke apart.

Saw nothing. A wall of blackness.

Then, another city.

But not the one my CO had sent me to. Someplace else. I was skipping out of control. I was losing it.

I knew this city because I had grown up here, before it became a work camp. I was eight years old now, staring into the lights of San Paulo. The ocean wasn't as close as it is now, but I could smell the sea on the wind.

I knew this place, and this day.

My cousin was with me, young and alive, laughing at some joke.

I wanted her to be safe forever. I wanted us all to be safe.

I stared up at the sky. Mars was up there, full of socialists.

But they hadn't lied to us after all, had they?

It was my lie. My betrayal.

I held out my hand to my cousin. "Have you ever wanted to become the light? Go anywhere you want? Be anyone you want?"

"It's impossible to be anyone you want," she said, and I was sad, then, for how soon the corporations took away our dreams.

"Hold my hand tight," I said. "There's going to be a war soon. There's going to be a war, but no one will come."

That's why the aliens weren't in the city when we arrived with our weapons.

It was because of me. My betrayal.

And so was this.

I blinked.

I was high above the city now, still in San Paulo, but the sea was higher, the sprawl was even greater, and I could see the work camps circling the city one after another after another.

Eight million people.

What if there was a war and nobody came?

I broke apart over San Paulo.

I was a massive wave of energy, disrupting the bodies around me, transforming everything my altered atoms touched.

We became eight million points of light.

I broke them all apart, and brought them with me.

You can't save them all. But I could save San Paulo. I could take us all . . . someplace else, to some other time, where there was no war, and the corporations answered to us, and freedom wasn't just a sound bite from a press release.

This is not the end. There are other worlds. Other stars. Maybe we'll do better out there. Maybe when they have a war here again, no one will come.

Maybe they will be full of light.

THE IMPROBABLE WAR

THE WALL WAS MADE from the faces of the dead.

If First Officer Khiv turned from it quickly, she could glimpse her probable future: her face on the wall. The wall had started as a war memorial. With the advent of technology that captured the soul, it had become something else. Now it was a massive probability engine, the souls of the dead merging into one sentient consciousness. Seeing the promise of her future reflected here told Khiv time was short.

Four million soldiers in gleaming obsidian suits stood on the wall. Khiv climbed after them, pressing her boots into the worn moues of writhing faces, and took her place beside them while the engine that was the wall heaved beneath her.

"How will we fight?" the generals had asked when their old enemies had risen up from the north. "We have given up hierarchies, and hate, and war. Going to war will destroy all we've built on the ashes of the corporations that once drove our governments. We will again become slaves to war."

It was Khiv who told them, after she trained her country's first army in a century.

"We will fight them with the love of our dead."

Now the enemy swelled before them on the other side of the wall, their soldiers enhanced with spidery metal suits, commanding nanotech swarms that made the air sharp and hot as her people's memory of war.

As the enemy prepared to strike, Khiv gave the order. Four million soldiers threw themselves from the wall.

"Love drives the engine," Khiv had told the generals. "The love the dead have for us."

The wall heaved, its sentient engine whirring, calculating. The souls within did what they had to preserve the peace they had died for.

The bodies of both armies exploded like stars.

Not a likely eventuality. But within the realm of probability.

Scholars would argue which side the wall took when it obliterated the armies. Some said it chose neither. It chose the future where those its gibbering souls loved would survive.

And in that future, there were no soldiers.

ABOUT THE AUTHOR

KAMERON HURLEY is an award-winning author and copywriter. She has a bachelor's degree in historical studies from the University of Alaska and a master's in history from the University of Kwa-Zulu-Natal, specializing in the history of South African resistance movements. She is also a graduate of Clarion West.

Hurley is the author of *The Light Brigade*, *The Stars Are Legion*, and the Worldbreaker Saga, which is comprised of the novels *The Mirror Empire*, *Empire Ascendant*, and *The Broken Heavens*. Her first series, The God's War Trilogy—which includes the books *God's War*, *Infidel*, and *Rapture*—earned her the Sydney J. Bounds Award for Best Newcomer and the Golden Tentacle Kitschy Award for Best Debut Novel. It was followed by a collection of stories, *Apocalypse Nyx*. Hurley is the author of the essay collection *The Geek Feminist Revolution*, which contains her essay on the history of women in conflict "We Have Always Fought," which was the first article ever to win a Hugo Award.

Hurley's short fiction has appeared in magazines such as *Popular Science*, *Lightspeed*, *Vice Magazine's Terraform*, and *Amazing Stories* as well as anthologies such as *The Lowest Heaven*, and *Year's*

Best SF. She has won two Hugo Awards, a British Science Fiction Award, and a Locus Award, and has been a finalist for the Arthur C. Clarke and the Nebula Awards. Her work has also been included on the Tiptree Award Honor List and been nominated for the Gemmell Morningstar Award.

In addition to her writing, Hurley has been a Stollee guest lecturer at Buena Vista University, a LITA President's Program speaker, and taught copywriting at the School of Advertising Art. Hurley currently lives in Ohio, where she's cultivating an urban homestead.